Margaret Skea was born in Belfast, growing up there through the 'Troubles' but now lives with her husband in the Scottish Borders. An Hawthornden fellow and award-winning short story writer – credits include Neil Gunn, Winchester, Mslexia and Fish – her first novel, *Turn of the Tide*, set in 16th century Scotland, won both the Beryl Bainbridge Award for Best First Time Novelist 2014 and the historical fiction section in the Harper Collins / Alan Titchmarsh People's Novelist Competition. The sequel, *A House Divided*, was long-listed for the Historical Novel Society New Novel Award 2016.

For more information about Margaret Skea, or to contact her, please visit her website
www.margaretskea.com

sanderling

Also by Margaret Skea

Munro Series
Book 1 *Turn of the Tide*
Book 2 *A House Divided*

Katharina Series

Book 1 *Katharina: Deliverance*
Book 2 *Katharina: Fortitude* (Due early 2019)

Short Story Collection

Dust Blowing and Other Stories

BY SWORD
AND STORM

Margaret Skea

sanderling

First published by Sanderling Books 2018
© Margaret Skea 2018

The moral right of Margaret Skea to be identified as the author of the work has been asserted in accordance with the Copyright, Designs and Patents Act 1988

Printed and bound by CPI Group (UK) Ltd, Croydon, CR0 4YY
Cover Design by www.hayesdesign.co.uk
Sword Photo: the Johnnie Armstrong Gallery, Teviothead
A CIP record of this book is available from the British Library

ISBN: 978-0-9933331-8-7
Sanderling Books
28 Riverside Drive
Kelso
TD5 7RH

Contents

Character List 8

Part One 11

Part Two 156

Part Three 280

Historical Note 522

Glossary 524

ENGLAND

London

English Channel

r. seine

Caen

FRANC

Angers

Nantes

r. loire

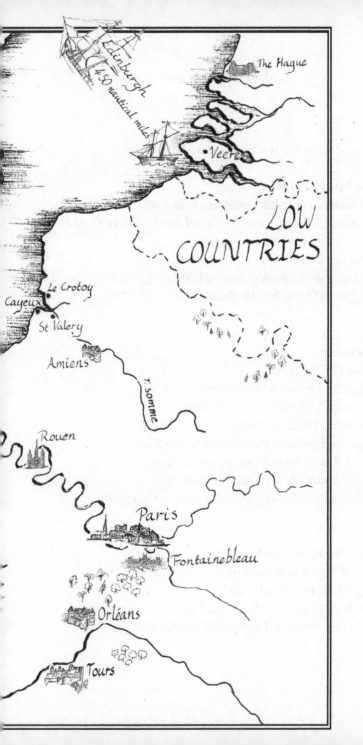

Edinburgh
450 nautical miles

The Hague

Veere

LOW
COUNTRIES

Le Crotoy
Cayeux
St Valery
Amiens

r. SOMME

Rouen

Paris

Fontainebleau

Orléans

Tours

Main Characters

All characters are real unless noted otherwise.

The Munro family
(All members of this family are fictional.)
Sir Adam Munro, now a colonel in the Scots Gardes,
  serving Henri IV of France
Kate: his wife
Robbie, a sergeant in the Scots Gardes
Maggie and Ellie: his daughters

In France
Henri IV of France
Gabrielle d'Estrées: his mistress
César and Catherine: their children
Mercoeur: Duke of Brittany
Rosny and Sully: close advisors to the King.
André Ruiz: a Spanish merchant in Nantes
Angus Muir: a Scots Garde (fictional)
Madame Picarde: seigneur of a farm at Cayeux (fictional)

The Montgomerie Faction
Earl of Eglintoun: head of the Montgomerie clan
Hugh: Laird of Braidstane
Elizabeth (formerly Shaw): his wife
Catherine, Mary and Sybilla (Sybie): his children

George: Hugh's second brother, a cleric at the court of
    Queen Elizabeth I of England
John: Hugh's third brother, a physician
Alexander Montgomerie: King James VI's 'Master Poet'
Robert Montgomerie: a cousin, serving Maurice of
    Nassau in the Low Countries
Andrew (Dand) and Annie Baxter: a cottager's children
    (fictional)

The Cunninghame Faction

Earl of Glencairn: head of the Cunninghame clan
Lady Glencairn: his wife
John: his brother
William: his eldest son and heir. Master of Glencairn
Patrick Maxwell of Newark: a Cunninghame cousin
Hamilton and Fullerton: friends of the Master of
    Glencairn

Others

John Shaw: a merchant, Elizabeth Montgomerie's brother
Sigurd Ivarsen: a Norwegian merchant (fictional)
Grizel (formerly Montgomerie): his wife
Ivar, Isabella and Gerda: his children (fictional)
Griet: Daughter of the marshall provost at The Hague
    (an historical character, original name unknown)

James VI of Scotland and others of the court

Part One

April – October 1598

The best wisdom that I can
Ys to doe well and drede no man.

Proverbs of Good Counsel 1450

Chapter 1

At first it was no more than a whisper, carried on the breeze. *The King is coming.* A priest crossing the cathedral close heard it and, shaking his head, boxed the ear of the urchin who dared give it voice – a malicious rumour, surely, Mercoeur's flag still fluttering above the chateau, but no less dangerous for all that. For a rumour once started could travel like flame through the city, trailing destruction in its wake. The boy, one hand clamped to the side of his head, retaliated with a well-aimed kick, before darting through the gate leading onto the Grand Rue to melt into the crowd that thronged there, his excitement undiminished.

It was not rumour, not a flame; rather water, a trickle become a stream, slipping through the dense alleyways, lapping at the doors of the narrow half-timbered warren of houses jostling each other as they stretched upwards to find a sliver of sky. It gathered momentum, flowing southwards to the Rue des Jacobins and La Fosse, to the hôtels of the merchants who grew fat on the spoils of commerce. It reached the Maison de Tourelles, and the ears of André Ruiz, who, so the story went, had once entertained an emir with capons and truffles, frangipane and apricot tartlets, custards and cheeses and succulent curls of artichoke, washed down with the finest of wines from the Loire. Ruiz regarded the messenger with narrowed eyes, his fingers raised to his lips and pressed tight together in contemplation. After a pause in which the messenger studied the floor, awaiting dismissal or the flare of rage of which the merchant was on occasion capable, Ruiz nodded twice and thrusting back his chair called for his cloak. If the tale should prove to have substance he would take care to ensure he was among those who greeted this king, for what use wealth if gain could not be made of it.

A second stream, become a river, rushed past the Chambres des Comptes, along the Rue des Carmes and through the Place de Changes, carrying with it the great and the good of Nantes until finally it disgorged them into the Place de Bouffay, where they clustered in groups, their conversation muted. The square was strangely lifeless: cleared of the market stalls, free of the claims and counterclaims of the traders as they cried their wares. Outside the ducal palace, which now served as the law courts, a bevy of servants from the chateau swept the square clean and soldiers dismantled the pillory and gallows. For who could tell what effect the sight of gallows might have on this king, who was coming to Nantes not as a guest, but as a general, to receive the surrender of Mercoeur and thus the submission of Brittany.

In the white heart of the city, in the limestone basilica of Saint-Pierre, the priest, turning his back as if it made him invisible, hitched up his cassock and rubbed at his shin, his other hand fumbling for the beads hanging around his waist. 'Hail Mary, mother of God, preserve us now and at the hour of our death. Hail Mary, mother of God…' The familiar repetition slowed his heartbeat and steadied the tremor of his hand, but the unease remained. Nantes was the last stronghold of the Catholic League, and professor of the true faith or not, there was no knowing how Henri of Navarre, for that was how he was still thought of in this city, would respond to the capitulation. It would perhaps be best to spend whatever time was left to him in imploring God for protection, lest human mercy was not forthcoming. He was still on his knees when he felt the draught from the sacristy door behind him, rapid footsteps traversing the nave. A hand on his shoulder shook him from his semi-slumber, the boy's whisper crystallising into a summons, just as the bell of the collegiate church of Notre-Dame began to toll.

Henri IV of France reached Nantes' Saint-Pierre gate as the final stroke died away. With him, a fraction to the rear, a contingent of Scots Gardes, foremost among them Adam Munro. Barely six months since he had been honoured with a position in Henri's personal bodyguard, seven since the Scottish King, James, had made him knight, Munro was thinking of the events of the last year: of his wife Kate's capture and trial, William Cunninghame's deserved disgrace, his own ennoblement. Grateful as he was, he would give it all up in a heartbeat if it meant he could be back at Broomelaw with his family and living at peace with their neighbours.

The King pulled to a halt. Munro, his attention brought sharply back to the present, signalled to the men behind him to do likewise. The response was instant, yet Munro, attuned to the slightest nuance, felt the tension rippling through them and understood there were some, not privy to Henri's private feelings, who wondered, along no doubt with the townsfolk of Nantes, what sanctions might be imposed on this most troublesome of cities. Facing them, mounted likewise, was Mercoeur, Duke of Brittany, whose formal submission to Henri at Angers was now to be confirmed. Mercoeur slid from his horse and, presenting his sword to the King, knelt on the hard-packed earth, though Munro noted a hint of arrogance remaining in his eyes. Accepting the sword, Henri indicated for him to rise and beckoned him close, bending down a fraction to speak to him, the words quiet, as if for his ears alone. Nevertheless, Munro, at Henri's shoulder, did hear, and understood the weariness they represented.

'And can I trust you now?'

Mercoeur raised his head to meet the King's gaze, then dipped it again in acquiescence. 'Sire.'

It was enough. Henri touched his shoulder with the reins and indicated the city gate and the press of people filling it. 'I have a wish to greet my people.'

Remounted, Mercoeur led the way into the city. Just inside the gate, Henri halted again, catching the duke unawares. Munro hid a smile. The pause was brief, yet long enough for those who had flooded to Saint-Pierre to get first sight of their king to raise an uncertain cheer, which Henri acknowledged with an upheld hand.

His words were simple, delivered in a manner that made all who listened feel he spoke directly to them. 'Good citizens of Nantes, I thank the God whose faith we share, that the gates of your city are this day opened to me...'

A further cheer, more prolonged, more confident, and as it died away Henri enfolded the crowd in his smile and nodded to Mercoeur, who moved off, the King and his bodyguard following, the duke's men bringing up the rear. The crowd parted to allow them through, then closed up behind them and surged with them through the city, past the cathedral chapter with its cluster of buildings housing the choir school and the bishop's palace, downwards towards the newly swept square, where the dignitaries of the municipality, both secular and ecclesiastical, waited to make their submission. The speeches began, slow and ponderous, the words like weights anchoring Nantes to the new order, to a king who had waited nine years for this moment. Munro, sufficiently alert to note even the smallest movement among the crowd, nevertheless allowed his thoughts to drift again, to Kate and her impending confinement, and to their own peace that should surely now be within reach, as first the bishop, then the governor, then the leaders of the mercantile guilds and the chief officer of the coinage, stepped forward to pledge allegiance to their King. It was hard not to reveal his boredom at the speeches, ill-prepared as they were, for this was no royal progress, months in the planning, but a trap sprung suddenly, in a manner and at a time of Henri's choosing. And that, Munro thought, was generally impeccable. They came to the final ceremony – the handing over of the key to the city. Even Munro was caught off guard by the silence that followed, the King allowing it to stretch well beyond expectation – he makes them pay, if not in blood, then in discomfort.

The silence was broken only by the jingle of harness and the soft snorting of the horses, until the King, inclining his head to each corner of the square in turn, made his reply. It was simple but effective, his voice carrying over the heads of the dignitaries, reaching to the back of the crowd. '...by the mercy of God I accept this key in the spirit in which it is given, but our earnest desire is that it be matched by the keys to the hearts of the good people of Nantes.'

Munro saw a flicker of annoyance in Mercoeur's eyes, quickly hidden, as the crowd erupted in a roar of cheering and clapping, which drained away as it became clear Henri wished to continue.

'Among the infinite benefits which it has pleased God to heap upon us, the most signal and precious is his granting us the strength and ability to withstand the fearful disorders and troubles which prevailed on our advent in this kingdom. Today, in this place, we have finally surmounted the waves and made our port of safety. Last night the sun set on war, tomorrow it will rise on peace. But first there must be freedoms set out and pledges given. I welcome you, my people, to return this afternoon to hear the proclamation that will usher in a golden age for Brittany, and for Navarre, and for all the cities and provinces of France.'

Munro was aware of the tension in Mercoeur, as if

he thought Henri's speech less a plea for unity than a pre-emptive strike, designed to win away the people's allegiance and thus diminish his own authority. As well it might be, and to judge by the crowd's reaction, successful, those at the front reaching up towards the King, as if simply to touch him would be a privilege.

In a transparent attempt to reassert control, Mercoeur stepped forward, gesturing to the people to give way. 'If it please you, Sire, your journey has been long and no doubt wearisome. There is accommodation prepared in the chateau, refreshments also.'

Henri gave a last wave of acknowledgement for the crowd, and was turning, when a man pushed his way through to bend on one knee before him. This time the look Munro caught in Mercoeur's eyes was speculative, but he leant towards Henri and gave no sign of any discomfort as he said, 'André Ruiz, Sire, one of our foremost merchants. Of Basque descent, but he has traded here for many years and is a valued member of our Chamber of Trade.'

Henri stretched out his hand and Ruiz touched his lips to it before rising to his feet, his expression bland, his voice smooth.

'When you are rested, Sire, I would be more than honoured if you and,' he glanced towards Mercoeur, 'our good duke would consent to dine at my house. It cannot rival the chateau, of course, but it is well appointed nevertheless and the skill of my cook legendary.'

'Indeed, Sire.' Mercoeur's face was expressionless, though Munro suspicioned inwardly he was less than pleased by the invitation. 'Many in Nantes can testify to that.'

'Well then,' Henri's smile encompassed them both, but his answer was for Ruiz alone, 'two o'clock?'

There was a quiet triumph in Ruiz as he bowed and retreated, matched by a carefully concealed irritation in Mercoeur as he once more indicated the way to the chateau. Built more than a hundred years since, as the principal residence of the Breton dukes, it covered an area nearly as wide as the square where the ceremonies had taken place and was entirely self-contained, with its own water gate onto the Loire, its protection provided both by the presence of the garrison billeted within its walls and the tall granite towers rising above it, dominating the south of the city. A dismal grey when wet, the massive walls glittered in the morning sunshine as if studded with silver.

If Mercoeur had expected Henri to remount to ride the short distance along the quayside, he underestimated him. The King, exhibiting the sure touch that had served him well when entering other cities, as one by one they had fallen to him, chose to walk the short distance along the Briand-Maillard. He stopped frequently to speak to those lining the route, to ruffle the hair of children clinging shyly to a mother's skirt, and to touch his fingers lightly to the heads of infants thrust at him for his blessing.

'In Nantes barely an hour and he has the townsfolk eating out of his hand.' The Garde beside Munro tossed a glance at Mercoeur's retreating back. 'The common folk at least.'

Munro grinned. 'It is a gift few men have, to appear at once so far above the rest of us to be almost a God, and yet so near they can be touched without fear of burning. As for Mercoeur, if he knows what's good for him and plays it right, he may yet walk away from here with further honours rather than censure. And lest you think it a weakness on Henri's part, it is a ploy that has served him well many times in the past.'

Chapter 2

Shadows lurked in every corner of the bedchamber given over to Henri, despite the candles blazing in wall sconces and in the elaborate candlestick gracing the table in the centre of the room. April or not, a fire had been lit, the flickering flames alternately flaring and fissling, the scent of resin sharp – unseasoned wood, Munro thought, as he hesitated in the doorway. The summons from the King was a surprise. In the months that had passed since his return to France and his accepting, when pressed, Patrick Montgomerie's former position in the Scots Gardes, he had often been present in the capacity of guard as Henri hammered out policies with his advisors. He had trained himself to remain impassive, whatever the topic, allowing the words to flow over him like water, but it was impossible not to listen, and little by little his opinion of Henri as a tactician had risen. A private audience, however, was something new, and not altogether welcome.

The King beckoned Munro towards the fire, indicating the chair opposite. 'Come, join me.'

Munro dipped his head as he balanced on the edge of the seat. 'Sire.'

'Sit down properly, man. I cannot converse with someone who perches like a rook about to take flight.'

Munro slid further onto the seat until he leant against

the chair-back, his gaze fixed on the King.

Henri continued, 'As you know, I am invited, with Mercoeur, to dine at the Maison de Tourelles.' A pause. 'I wish you to accompany me.'

'As your bodyguard, Sire?'

'In a manner of speaking, though I do not wish it to appear so. I intend to sign the Edict there.' There was a glint of humour in the look he shot at Munro, tempered by the sober note in his voice. 'There is a certain irony that it be witnessed by a citizen of the country which has caused us so much grief in the past, and may yet. What think you?'

Munro risked, 'You are sure of Ruiz' motive in issuing this invitation?'

'Oh, yes. I have Mercoeur's assurance Ruiz thinks only of establishing himself on the winning side. For the moment that will serve me well enough.' Another glimmer of humour. 'And I believe him that he is noted for the quality of his hospitality, both food and wine. It will no doubt be preferable to the fare served in the Gardes' quarters.' He glanced down at Munro's boots, still coated in dust. 'You will, I imagine, wish some little time to prepare. We shall leave on the three-quarter hour.'

Munro, his forehead puckered as he thought on the careful course Henri steered, the rapids that, official surrender or not, might yet trouble him, was glad to escape into the sunshine and make his way back to the room assigned to him, to set to polishing his boots.

It was little more than a few minutes' walk to the Maison de Tourelles, but Henri chose to ride, for a second time wrong-footing Mercoeur, who had failed to order horses to be brought. In consequence, it was ten minutes past the hour when they arrived at André Ruiz' house. It was one of a collection of imposing limestone hôtels crying wealth and privilege, the salon into which they were ushered light and elegant. The plaster on the walls was tinted a soft shade of peach, complemented by a frieze on which nymphs and shepherds cavorted under the benign gaze of white-winged cupids, bow in hand. Munro instinctively drifted towards the window to survey the street below and the waters of the Loire beyond. In each direction he saw wooden bridges spanning the river, linking the mainland and the islands that together comprised the city. Six in all, they rose wide and high, fringed with houses and shops along their length. Beneath them, small river craft passed back and forth between the eastern and western port areas, ferrying goods unloaded from the larger ships unable to pass through the city.

Ruiz came to stand beside him. 'It is a fine sight is it not? Nantes is proud of its bridges, and justly so, for the council derives much revenue from the tolls, far in excess of the costs of maintenance. Traversing the Loire is a privilege for which most are prepared to pay, and handsomely.'

Though what he said could be construed as a pleasantry, Munro had the sense it carried the warning: *Do not think I am unaware of the King's lack of trust, or why you have chosen to enjoy the view.* Satisfied he had a grip of the various points of access to the Maison, Munro turned, his smile disingenuous. 'I cannot help but admire, for we have none such in Ayrshire.'

'And in Edinburgh?'

Munro thought of the Water of Leith, of the wharves bounding it. 'Nothing to match this.' It seemed to satisfy Ruiz, who retreated to the centre of the room, where Henri and Mercoeur conversed with every appearance of ease.

At the far end of the salon a pair of double doors swung open, leading onto another room, equally light, though this time the walls were a pale lemon, the frieze, in keeping with the room's use, a succession of gilded cornucopia from which an abundance of fruits spilled in a riot of fecundity. Ruiz bowed, gestured for his guests to precede him. The King and Mercoeur led the way, Munro following, to take their places at a table set for four, the space between them yawning, a liveried servant standing behind each chair. Munro was hard put not to reveal his awe. In the sunshine flooding through the windows the table dazzled: silverware glittering, glass goblets refracting the light into a rainbow of colour shimmering on the highly polished wood and delicately patterned dishes. At each place was a finger bowl and a damask napkin folded into the shape of a swan. Beyond it, a cruet set: miniature bowls of salt with curved spoons and boat-shaped jugs for oil and vinegar. In the centre, a woven silver-gilt basket filled with rolls, some braided, others twisted into

25

ram's horns. A far cry from the table setting of a laird's house in Scotland, or even, Munro imagined, though he had never been privileged to see it, of the Scottish court.

The food came, course after course, each accompanied by a different wine; not hearty platefuls, which would have been Munro's preference, but exquisitely presented tastings: a clear soup, on which floated small cubes of bread, roasted to a crisp; quails' eggs nested on a bed of watercress; curls of smoked fish, no more than an inch in width, decorated with a trickle of a piquant sauce that lingered on Munro's tongue. There was a slight hiatus, then a dish of what looked to Munro like crushed ice was placed in front of him. Unsure how to tackle it, he hesitated.

The King was leaning forward. 'Señor Ruiz, if what is to follow matches what has gone before, your chef deserves to be legendary. Nor is it everyone,' he waved his spoon at his dish, flicked a glance at Munro, as if an answer to his unspoken question, 'who can produce such a palate-cleanser.'

Ruiz dipped his head but failed to conceal his smile of satisfaction. 'Sire.'

After a few moments, in which Munro allowed the last spoonfuls of the flavoured ice to slide over his tongue, Ruiz raised his hand. The dishes were removed, to be replaced by the meat courses: slivers of beef served with horseradish and chestnuts; thin slices of chicken with ribbons of purple carrot and shredded cabbage; tiny lamb cutlets decorated with sprigs of rosemary, accompanied by a mint jelly. In the pause, in which the finger bowls were whisked away and returned refreshed and the wine

26

glasses replaced for a third time, Munro thought of the lambs at Broomelaw: had they been slaughtered so young, there would have been insufficient meat to see them through the winter. Dessert was a multitude of bite-sized millefeuille pastries, filled with custards and claret-soaked fruits, dotted with cloves and sprinkled with cinnamon, which melted in the mouth in an instant. A veined cheese with oatcakes preceded the final triumph: a meringue confection in the shape of a galleon, with rigging and sails of spun sugar, which, when cut open, revealed a frozen cream glacé laced with ginger on the cusp of softening.

Munro hadn't expected to be filled when the first dishes had appeared, but as the parade of courses finally came to an end, he wished he could loosen his belt; but more worrying, when he stood up, was the slight fuzziness around the edge of his vision and the swirling sensation in his head. Dangerous, should it be obvious. He caught what he thought was a flash of amusement in Ruiz' eyes and so held himself upright as they made their way back to the salon, keeping his gaze fixed on the straight edge of the door, like a guiding light into harbour.

Henri came straight to the point. 'Grateful as I am for your hospitality, Señor Ruiz, I have some private business to conclude with Mercoeur. We could of course retire to the chateau, but…'

The merchant was quick to take the point. 'No need, Sire. If you will permit me,' he rose, 'I will ensure you are not disturbed.'

Henri nodded, waiting until the door shut behind him. Mercoeur glanced at Munro as if to suggest he should leave also, but the King shook his head. 'Sir Adam stays.

27

It is my thought to share with you the substance of the edict I intend to proclaim tonight. I would not wish you to be caught unawares. But nor,' he stretched his lips into a smile that failed to reach his eyes, 'will I brook any opposition.'

Munro watched the conflicting emotions Mercoeur tried, without success, to conceal, as Henri laid out the main provisions, point by point. He was clearly happy with the re-establishment of the primacy of the Catholic faith, and that all church properties seized during the years of war should be returned. Equally so, with the ruling on tithes and the restrictions to be placed on the exercise of the Reformed religion, both in Paris and at court. Clearly more contentious was the freedom of conscience for Protestants in all other parts of France, Nantes included, especially their right to schooling and admittance to university. His relief was obvious when Henri stressed the need for reconciliation and his desire that all the wrongs of the previous years be forgotten. His unease that Protestants should be allowed to exercise judicial authority, obvious also.

Henri, coming to an end, turned to the arrangements for the proclamation, his gaze fixed on Mercoeur. 'I am aware some of the provisions I have made will not meet with universal approval, so I depend on you for any necessary precautions that must be taken. I do not wish to appear aloof, however, so I expect them to be discreet.' He shifted his attention to Munro. 'I wish you to attend me to the ducal palace and afterwards go to the chateau. The edict you will deliver to me publicly and with some ceremony. The Gardes are noted for their ceremonial function. Let that be what is visible this afternoon.' A glimmer of a smile. 'Aside from their other uses.'

The Place du Bouffay was packed tight as Munro and his small contingent of Scots Gardes approached. People were crammed into doorways, leaning out of windows, filling every available space, apart from an area Mercoeur had marked off in front of the steps where the King had chosen to make his proclamation. Munro noted the soldiers positioned around the perimeter, ready to quell any trouble should it arise but, in keeping with Henri's instructions, standing at ease. There was a stir, a shrinking back, as the Gardes entered, sunlight glancing off their sword hilts. The horses' manes and tails were braided with gold cord, their tackle gleaming. Munro dismounted, passed his reins to the Garde nearest to him and mounted the steps. The remainder fanned out to form a guard of honour, lining both sides of the cleared space, keeping a firm hold on the horses. As befitted their training, they stood motionless, though one lifted his tail and deposited a steaming pile of ordure on the cobbles, causing those of the crowd nearest to step back. Munro caught the movement out of the corner of his eye and swung his head round, relaxing again as he noted the cause of the stir.

Mercoeur was standing in the doorway of the ducal palace, as if he was in charge of the performance to come. There was an audible drawing in of breath as the King appeared, no longer in the drab garb of a general, but glittering, his cloak catching the sunlight as he moved. Henri allowed the cheer that greeted him to roll around the square, then held up his hand for silence. Munro stepped forward, proffering the edict, and the King, accepting it, began to read.

'We have, by this perpetual and irrevocable edict, established and proclaimed and do establish and proclaim: one, that the recollection of everything done by one party or the other, during all the preceding period of troubles, be obliterated and forgotten as if no such things had ever happened...'

Munro, scanning the crowd, saw he carried them with him throughout the lengthy preambles on the relative positions of both religions. Henri's voice rose and fell, his timing perfect, his varied tones clarifying and emphasising the key points. '...three, we ordain that the Catholic Apostolic and Roman religion shall be restored ... without hindrance ... Six, in order to leave no occasion for troubles of differences between our subjects, we herewith permit those of the said religion called Reformed to live and abide without molestation...'

There was a ripple of unease when he came to the eighteenth clause. '...we forbid all our subjects ... from carrying off by force or persuasion, against the will of their parents, any children ... to cause them to be baptised in the Catholic Apostolic Church...' followed by a renewed settling as he continued, '...the same is forbidden to those called Reformed...'

The longer Henri spoke, the more Munro's admiration

increased. It was a thin line he was attempting to tread between the old religion and the new, at one moment placating the Catholic party, the next making concessions to the Huguenots. A high-wire act, at which Henri seemed to excel.

He was almost at an end, the majority of the troublesome points already covered. Munro exhaled, feeling the tension that had gripped him from Henri's first words begin to drain away.

A movement to his left, a momentary glint as if of sunshine on metal. Reacting instinctively, he flung himself sideways, knocking into the King, causing him to overbalance and fall onto the steps. Had Munro been facing straight onto the square, the single shot would have taken him in the heart, as it was it slammed into his shoulder, knocking him off his feet. Mercoeur scanned the crowd, who stood as if frozen by the enormity of what had so narrowly been averted, the fear of what might come. Someone at the front shouted 'Vive la Roi, vive la Roi', his cry taken up and echoed all around the square. Despite Mercoeur's efforts to dissuade him, Henri was back on his feet, facing the people, accepting their homage. As the sound faded, the man who had begun the homage dropped to his knees, removing his bonnet and bending his head to the ground, his action spreading like a wave until the square was a sea of bowed heads, the only movement the stirring of hair in the breeze. A second shot rang out, taking down the last man standing, who radiated defiance, his arquebus dropping from his hand as he fell. Mercoeur gestured for him to be taken away, but Henri halted the soldiers moving towards the space that opened around the man and addressed the crowd again.

'Lift up your heads, and look on this man and on your King, and know that we hold no other citizen of Nantes guilty of this crime. All we ask is that your submission this day marks the end of the conflicts that have so burdened our country as to come close to destroying it.' He stretched out both arms, as if in benediction, then, palms up, raised them slowly, the people rising in response, their renewed 'Vive la Roi, Vive la Roi,' building to a crescendo of cheering and stamping of feet, in which Munro, slumped against the door of the palace while a soldier made a makeshift bandage from the remains of his sleeve, recognised the mingling of relief.

Chapter 3

It was relief of a different sort Kate felt, as she drove the cart homewards from the main square in St Valery. They had been at the farm midway between Cayeux and St Valery eight months now, and although her understanding of the local patois, and more importantly her ability to converse in it, was improving, she still found market day a challenge, the temptation to bring Ellie, who chattered happily as if it was her native tongue, hard to resist. Resist she had, for it was imperative she became not just familiar with the dialect, but fluent, if she was to be of use as a healer — how easy it is for a child, how much more difficult for an adult. It was a relief also to be sitting down, to have the weight off her feet, though she could have wished the track was smoother, for the constant jolting made her back ache and set the babe within her kicking, as if it too protested the roughness of the ride. It had been a good day, as the empty baskets rattling in the back of the cart testified, and she looked forward to placing the proceeds in the wooden box residing under Madame Picarde's bed, and to sharing in her pleasure.

Which brought her to thoughts of Maggie, who, despite Kate's best efforts, couldn't yet be brought to derive any pleasure from being here. Like Kate, she had found it hard to get a grasp of the patois, but unlike

Kate she seemed determined to fail, choosing rather to isolate herself in her attic bedroom, coming out only when given a specific task to perform and at mealtimes, though sometimes not even then. Kate had been by turn sympathetic, irritated and finally angry with her, but to each Maggie's reaction was the same, which was no reaction at all. Munro's counsel, when he and Robbie had paid their first visit to the farm, had been to give her time, for she of them all had lost most by the move from Ayrshire to France, and no doubt she would come round. It was her quietness that continued most to worry Kate, all the bounce gone out of her, the independence of spirit and feistiness, which had been her hallmark, dissipated, perhaps never to return. Kate's fear, which she could not share, was that it was the memory of the horror at Saltcoats, when she had come on Kate slumped on the garrotting chair, almost dead, blood from her ears and nose blooming crimson against the alabaster-white of her face, which had taken root in Maggie's soul and haunted her yet. There was no way to be sure without questioning Maggie directly, and if she was wrong, the damage she might do by bringing to the surface an image Maggie had succeeded in burying was impossible to gauge. It was an argument she played out in her mind daily, a risk as yet she felt unable to take. The other option, distraction, had proved disappointingly unsuccessful.

As a result of Madame Picarde gossiping of her new family and, in particular, Kate's talents, it had taken only a month for Kate to receive the first tentative requests for help: for a persistent cough, a weeping eye, a boil that refused to settle. She had called for Maggie to accompany her, but each time Maggie refused, saying, 'You hardly need two of us for that,' before retreating once more to her room.

Hard on the heels of those first visits, Kate found she was pregnant, though, as a result of the trauma that had brought them to France, she was unable to calculate with any certainty a due date. She had consoled herself, and also Adam, when she wrote to tell him of it, that in the later stages it would become clear. Although she had felt perfectly well, it was an opportunity to involve Maggie, playing on her age and the discomfort of trekking about the countryside in the farm cart, which was their only means of transport. And perhaps Maggie might have stepped into her shoes, but the villagers, who had only just begun to accept Kate, weren't ready to trust one so young, and so, when news of Kate's condition spread, the calls hadn't come. Perhaps when the babe was born she could insist on Maggie's help and begin the process of building confidence in her. She was shutting the yard gate just as Ellie came hurtling out of the farmhouse door shouting.

'Maman, Maman.'

Kate fended her off with a smile. 'Whoa! I have no wish for the babe to be squeezed out before time.'

Ellie, with an 'Excusé' and an absent-minded pat for Kate's stomach, let loose a torrent of speech, half in the patois and half in Scots, in which Kate made out 'Isabella' and 'Aunt Elizabeth' and 'Mary'. She placed one hand gently against Ellie's lips. 'Slow down, and speak clearly, and in one tongue only if you please. I cannot follow that jumble. There is news from home?'

'Not news,' Ellie was hopping up and down, 'people!'

And then it was Kate, who, abandoning the pony and cart, turned Ellie round and flew with her across the yard and into the hubbub of the farmhouse kitchen. She skidded to a halt, drew breath, her heart lifting. And heedless of the babe and the discomfort, she was hugging and being hugged indiscriminately by Grizel and Elizabeth, Sigurd and John Montgomerie, while the cluster of children milled around the kitchen chattering non-stop, leaving the adults little chance of being heard above them. It was Madame Picarde who gathered them up and shepherded them across the yard with the promise of bantam chicks to be discovered in the barn and a motherless piglet needing feeding.

In the peace that descended, Kate, belatedly realising her legs were like jelly and her heartbeat too fast for comfort, sank down onto the settle by the hearth. 'I hadn't expected ... it is so good to see you all.' Then, almost afraid to ask, 'What of Agnes? I had thought she might have wished to come.'

Elizabeth made a face. 'I'm sorry, Kate. We did try to bring her, but she wouldn't be stirred. She maintained once had been more than enough for her. That her lack of French and dislike of foreigners was sufficient reason to remain rooted to Scotland, where she belonged.'

Kate sighed. 'When she first followed us here we thought it would be for good, so it was a bitter day when she decided to go home again.'

'She was torn, that I do know.' Elizabeth hesitated, then continued, 'And in truth when she returned to Braidstane I feared for her, for it was as if, without you, she was diminished beyond repair, all her spark gone. It was then John suggested taking her to Broomelaw. Of course, he didn't say that to her, having seen enough of her character to know an oblique approach was called for. Instead he came bewailing the difficulty of finding anyone at Renfrew whose pottage had a flavour worth talking about, and his inability to keep on top of even the most minimal housekeeping. When he concluded with the fear that his tenancy would leave Robbie's inheritance in worse condition than he found it, she rose to the bait and insisted on accompanying him to sort the house out. And I imagine him also.' She grinned. 'There are times when I suspect he almost regrets the impulse, for there is no doubt who is in control.'

Kate laughed aloud at the expression on John's face confirming Elizabeth's assessment. She placed a hand on his arm, smiled up at him. 'There is no shame in that. Adam was entirely under her thumb, though in company she could make a good play at being the servant. A fiction he was aye grateful for.'

There was a pause, as if Elizabeth weighed her next words carefully.

'She aged when you left and that cannot be reversed, but back at Broomelaw she is in her own place again, and I think, though she wouldn't admit to it, having only John to look to is a welcome respite, for her stamina is not what it was.'

Kate said, 'Is it wrong to have hoped we could have her here, with us?'

'Not wrong, but perhaps too much to ask.' John turned the question back on Kate. 'Did you find it easy?

To come here? To speak a different language? To live a different way? And you are little more than half her age and with twice the education. However much she loved you all, and that is not in doubt, for she talks of you often, it would have been doubly difficult for her.'

'I know, but it's hard not to think we deserted her.'

'Think rather that you left her as the custodian of Broomelaw, and in the fullness of time Robbie will be the gainer from her guardianship. For that is how she sees herself.'

Kate placed her hand on her stomach, her change of subject an acceptance of John's argument. 'How long can you stay?'

'Three weeks, perhaps four … if you'll have us … depending how long Sigurd's business holds him at Veere.'

Kate turned to Sigurd, who was standing behind Grizel, one hand resting on her shoulder. 'You must return to the Low Countries?'

Sigurd's regret was clear. 'I'm afraid so, but John can remain, and as the noise children make is a novelty for him, he will likely survive the ordeal. The crossing was enough for me.'

Grizel looked up at him, her tone mock severe. 'That wasn't what it looked like when you played the teacher, showing the bairns how to be sailors.'

Elizabeth chimed in. 'Or gave them turns at the helm, helping to steer.'

'It was the only way to keep them quiet for more than a minute at a time. Four bairns on board at once, forbye the infants, are a mite hard to handle.'

'True.' John was at the window, laughing, as Madame

Picarde attempted to stop Isabella chasing the piglet around the yard, with the clear intention of cuddling it. 'I think, Sigurd, we should leave these ladies to gossip in peace. Madame looks as if she could do with some help.'

Elizabeth asked, 'Where's Maggie?'

Kate sighed. 'In her room I expect. She … has not adjusted well … not at all really. It is my greatest worry.' She stood up. 'But where are Gerda and Sybilla?'

Grizel nodded towards the ceiling. 'Up the stair, though how they can sleep through all the racket the others make is beyond me.'

'I'll see if I can winkle Maggie out. We'll not disturb them by going to look?'

'They're both the best of sleepers, thank God, for all that they're only seven months old. And as alike as two peas in a pod. You'd think they were sisters instead of cousins. We can't get any of the children to say "Sybilla" though – they all insist on her being called Sybie – I imagine it'll stick. Had they been troublesome the crossing could have been an ordeal right enough. And to be truthful, though Sigurd spoke in jest, he is right, a small ship does magnify sound. At Braidstane, when the bairns are running around outside, it doesn't seem so bad, and if they do fight they can be banished to opposite ends of the tower, or the barmkin, but confined as they were on the crossing, it was important to keep them occupied.' Grizel fell silent.

Elizabeth said, 'John was so good with them. I wish he had a wife and bairns of his own, for I think he'd be a good husband and father. I had thought, when he first came home, there was perhaps a story to tell, a visitor he

39

might be preparing us to receive, but nothing was said and it's likely too long ago now.'

Kate halted at the foot of the stair, remembering John sitting in the bastle house talking of the Florentine girl, of her father's opposition she was prepared to ignore, before her mother's illness held her there against her inclination. And among her own prized possessions the da Vinci sketches intended as a bribe to encourage John to leave, which, though he was incapable of destroying them, the memory they evoked had rendered them too painful for him to keep – if John had not shared his story with his family, then neither could she. Her attention was caught by a shout of laughter and a squeal from outside, and she glanced towards the window in time to see John tossing Isabella into the air, swinging her round. 'So I see. Does he favour anyone at home, or at court?'

'Not that we've heard. Though there are plenty who'd be willing. And for all he eats more than is good for his waistline, he isn't a poor catch.'

'What poor catch?' John filled the doorway. 'I trust it isn't fish you're talking of Elizabeth, for I'm famished.'

It made them all laugh, and in the ensuing bustle as supper was laid, the topic was forgotten. Only Kate, with reason to understand, noted John's attention straying to Isabella's dark curls, a wistful expression in his eyes.

Chapter 4

The second summons from the King was not a surprise, for Henri was not a man to forget to give thanks when due, and Munro, as he crossed the courtyard to the entrance to the chateau, rehearsed what to say. It would be a week or two at least before he would be fit to resume his duties in the King's bodyguard, and in the circumstances he thought Henri likely to be sympathetic to a request for leave. To go home and be with Kate for the birth of their child would be ample compensation for the throbbing in his shoulder, which persisted despite the distillation of poppy seeds administered in the infirmary.

The guard who ushered him into the King's apartments winked at him. 'Land or a title, which are you hoping for?'

Munro grinned back. 'The title I have is sufficient. And the land. Leave will do me.'

'More fool you. It isn't every day you save a king's life. If I'd been so lucky I'd make the most of it.'

'You don't have a wife to see, a new bairn to welcome.'

'Another mouth to feed? All the more reason then to look for recompense.'

Above them they heard the click of a latch. Munro glanced up at the line of light slanting down the stairs. 'I'd better go.' He climbed swiftly and, halting in the doorway, bowed to the King, trying not to react to the sharp stab of pain that shot from his shoulder to his elbow.

Henri, clearly noticing his discomfort, asked, 'How fares your shoulder?'

'Well enough, though I doubt my usefulness for a week or two.'

'The proof you gave of your usefulness today far outweighs any loss of your services that may come as a result, though I have no wish, for your own sake, that you be incapacitated for any longer than need be.' Henri stared into the fire as if seeing in the flames a memory that troubled him. 'Patrick Montgomerie was your friend as well as your commanding officer. I am grateful you share not only his loyalty, but his quickness of mind and action also. Do not fear your willingness to sacrifice yourself in my cause will be forgotten.'

'It was my duty, as it was Patrick's. Any one of the Gardes would have done the same. I was closest to hand, that was all.'

'Nevertheless, I am conscious of the debt I owe and will repay it.' Henri was swivelling the ring on the third finger of his right hand. 'What of your wife? She is well?'

Though it provided the perfect opportunity to make the request for leave, the abrupt change of topic wasn't what Munro was expecting, so he hesitated. Henri had often proved himself interested in the personal concerns of his men, but generally in moments when affairs of state weighed light, not as now, when he had come to Nantes to set the seal on an agreement which should bring a peace to France not known for nigh on thirty years.

'A birth is expected, Sire.'

'It worries you?'

'My wife is not,' he hesitated again, 'in the first flush of youth, and though her other pregnancies were without difficulty, there is always the possibility of mischance.' Too late, he thought of Gabrielle d'Estrées in a similar condition and wished his words back.

'Indeed.' It was clear Henri was also thinking of his mistress. 'Let us pray God for good fortune to them both.' Once again he changed tack and Munro again found himself at a loss.

'Your seigneurie, who manages it?'

'The woman whose land it is. And there is a farm boy for the heavy work, for before her pregnancy Kate's hope had been…' He stared into the fire in his turn, wondering if he dared voice Kate's wish.

'Lady Munro's hope?' Henri prompted.

'In Scotland, she was a herbalist, and a midwife, and wished, Picardie not being overrun by any such, to carry on the work here also.'

'The lack of a priest to certify her is a problem? I shouldn't have expected a Protestant stronghold such as St Valery would have felt bound by such conventions.'

'It is not the town that is the problem. No one there has denounced her, indeed a few brave souls have sought her assistance, but it is in the surrounding countryside, closest to the farm, where most play safe. It has been frustrating for her.

'That is but one illustration of why the edict I proclaimed today is long overdue and will, I trust, go some way to solving problems such as these. The incident in the square another such.'

43

A log flared in the hearth, crumbled to ash – if I was of a superstitious bent, Munro thought, I might think it an ill omen. But foolish to look for trouble where there might be none. They had found no evidence the would-be assassin had any accomplices and there had been nothing to fault in Henri's handling of the event. If it were the last shot in a lengthy war, then perhaps it had been worth it. He stifled the thought as almost treasonous, and lifted his head, aware the King was still speaking, but with no idea of what he'd been saying. He was about to frame an apology, but Henri, clearly mistaking his intent, stopped him.

'Hear me out. You have a wife. I have one I would make my wife if I could. You will shortly have a child. So will the Duchesse de Beaufort. No doubt you would wish to spend more time with your wife and family, as I hope I may do.'

'Of course, but...'

'Well then, there is no reason to refuse my request.'

Munro was cursing his inattention and searching the conversation for a clue as to what Henri's request had been, when the King, again misinterpreting, said, 'You are a knight and your wife a lady. Why should she not be at court? If it is her status that concerns you, then there are other honours that could be conferred. I want people about me I can trust. And you have shown I can trust you. If your wife has a gift as a healer, that is a bonus, for I would place no bar to the practice of her skill at court. What say you?'

Knowing it was less a question than a formality, Munro took a deep breath. 'I am honoured, Sire, deeply so, as I know my wife will be, but I cannot answer for her in this regard. She is…' He was seeking a way to explain his reluctance to force Kate into any course of action when, unexpectedly, Henri laughed.

'They are alike then. All the more reason the Duchesse would benefit from your wife's company. By all means consult her, but when you do, stress the benefits of such an arrangement. Your son is already in Paris, you have daughters for whom much may be done, and another babe coming who would no doubt benefit from preferment when the time is right.'

Munro hesitated again. 'There is the matter of religion. The embargo of the Reformed worship in Paris and at the court. In that respect, as in others, the St Valery area suits our family well.'

Henri waved aside the argument. 'With discretion some arrangement can be made. The proclamation was necessary, and that particular concession a sop to those who favoured the League, but you should know what my own feelings are: those who follow their conscience are of my religion and I am of the religion of those who are brave and good. Your family fits on both counts.'

It was foolishness to continue to protest, and risk trying Henri's patience too far, but Munro felt an obligation to the woman who had provided a safe haven for his family when they needed it most. 'There is Madame Picarde to consider. She has been kind enough to name me as her heir and thought to have my family's company to see her through her latter years.'

A hint of steel entered Henri's voice. 'I'm sure she will not refuse her King.' And then, with a smile Munro thought designed to disarm, 'Speak to Rosny. I'm sure he can find some solution, that she does not remain alone.'

It was now or never. 'If it please you, Sire, as I am useless here at present, might I be permitted to go home and tell them myself what is your pleasure?'

'Of course. I do not expect you will wish your wife to travel to Paris before the birth, nor to undertake the journey without an escort, but when you speak to Rosny, make clear all is to be made ready for when the time is right. The Duchesse de Beaufort I know will look forward to meeting your children, as you have met hers.' Henri's smile was unforced. 'Once you have set things in motion for your return, you are free to go. Return to me when you have made ready and I will give you letters for Rosny, and among them my authorisation to smooth your travel.'

Chapter 5

Munro didn't know whether to be elated or dejected as he crossed the courtyard to the quarters assigned to the Gardes who had accompanied Henri. His mind was spinning – the majority of the regiment had been left in Paris to protect the Duchesse de Beaufort and the remainder of the court, Robbie among them. It would be good to be able to take word of him to Kate, and making by Paris, though slightly further than going direct to Cayeux, the roads would be of better quality and thus the speed at which he could travel increased. Decision made, he hurried the preparations and went to the King to take his leave.

Morning dawned crisp and clear, though still with a nip in the air. It had been de Biron's suggestion Munro make the first part of the journey by river, an idea that had grown on him while he slept. To have taken his own horse was impractical, and the quality of hired horses so variable, the less use he had to make of them the better. The deciding factor had been the pulsing pain in his shoulder depriving him of sleep, which awake continued to trouble him.

Standing at the landward side of a small vessel as she slipped her anchor and drifted out into the flood, his breath curled away from him, the breeze from the water lifting the hair that sprung at the back of his neck. It was another reminder of Kate, of the way she distracted him by tangling her fingers in his hair as he sought to manage the farm accounts. A boy ran along the quay, chasing the ship and waving at the crew as the sails filled and she began to pick up speed – would this new babe be a boy? He hoped so. It was odd to think he was now a man of property in both Scotland and France and with full rights to each. Broomelaw was waiting for Robbie should he wish to settle there, but there was also the seigneurie at Cayeux to consider, and a boy to inherit it would mark a new beginning for them all. He had repeatedly told Kate the gender of the child mattered not at all, but it wasn't true, or not entirely so. Much more important though was that she had remained well throughout the pregnancy, a blessing that didn't come to everyone, especially to an older mother. He smiled to himself, imagining her response if he let slip he thought her over-old to be carrying a bairn, but from the moment she'd confessed her condition he hadn't been able to avoid worrying: about her health, about the dangers of the birth, about the babe itself. He had a cousin whose wife had a late child, a girl who proved to be simple, and that a heartache he would not wish on either Kate or himself.

Carried on the incoming tide and aided by the westerly wind, they left the boy far behind, and with him the bustle of the city, though he could still hear odd snatches of fish merchants crying their wares on the wharves. The events of yesterday were likely today's gossip; tomorrow they might almost be forgotten. He turned from the rail and bumped into a sailor hurrying along the deck, setting his shoulder throbbing, a confirmation it was the right decision to cover two-thirds of his journey by ship. Whether it would prove faster than horseback remained to be seen.

At first they made good speed, even after they left the tidal waters and began to travel against the flow, the westerly more than compensating. As they slipped past villages and through vineyards that depended on the river for irrigation, Munro returned to the rail to watch the countryside go by. On his left the valley stretched wide and flat, row upon row of vines marching into the distance, the neat lines broken every now and then by a wine press or cluster of farm buildings set around a chateau built of honey-coloured stone. On his right the ground rose in a gentle swell of hills carrying the eye far into the distance towards the mountains beyond. Munro hoped they might reach Tours by nightfall, but when he voiced the thought, the captain of the ship laughed at him.

'Pigs might fly. Come to think about it, flying would be the only way to make that speed.'

'How far will we get then?

'It depends. If the wind drops we'll be reduced to oarsmen, who aren't any match for the wind on a good day. If we were a slave ship now … that would be a different story. As it is,' he considered the sky, 'thirty miles would be a fair estimate, with good fortune and a following wind as they say.'

'I have a wish to travel fast, perhaps unreasonably so.'

'Fugitive from justice, is it? And I thought you a fine upright gentleman, as befits a Garde.'

'My wife is in the later stages of pregnancy, and I wish to be there to see her through.'

'A first?'

'Fifth.'

'You should be bored by the whole process by now then. And happy to leave the womenfolk to get on with it. Children are a mite over-rated. Wives too, come to that. Troublesome creatures with less sense than a flea … A ship now, that's another thing altogether.' He was smoothing his hand along the top rail as if caressing it. 'This lady has done me proud over many years. You couldn't beat her.'

Munro grinned, unable to take offence, though he suspected Kate might have managed, and was about to respond when he felt the deck judder beneath him followed by a grinding sound as the ship halted abruptly. The ship canted and he began to slide. He grabbed for the rail to regain his balance, but missed, and catching his foot in a coiled rope landed on his back and skidded across the deck to fetch up against the coping around the hatch leading below. Above his head the canvas was flapping, the captain running up the deck bawling out orders as he went, sailors springing to his bidding. Munro hauled himself back to his feet and, ignoring the throbbing in his shoulder, made for the rail again and, hand over hand, followed the captain to the prow. Still keeping a firm grasp of the rail to counter the slope of the deck, he offered, 'Can I help?'

The captain was dismissive. 'The best help you can be is to stay out of our way. We have enough work to do without having to concern ourselves with a lubber who cannot stay upright without support. I suggest you go to your cabin and wait there.'

Munro, his shoulder feeling as if someone was hammering nails into it, was relieved, though he wouldn't have admitted it, and as he retreated to his cabin he thought of Kate and feared the thirty miles the captain had promised might very well shrink to twenty, or none at all if they were thoroughly grounded. He lay on his bunk, holding onto the edge so as not to slip onto the floor, listening to the running footsteps overhead, to the shouting, the rustle of canvas and the rattle of chain as the anchor was let loose. Another shudder, the ship settling further into the mud, then a knock at his cabin door.

The boy who poked his head round was no more than ten. 'Cap'n's compliments, sur, ah've to tell ye to content yerself for we'll likely make no more progress tonight. We've hit a sandbank and will need to unload the cargo before we can attempt to get free. If we can't manage after that we'll have to wait for a tow.'

The head disappeared and Munro lay back down, but he couldn't settle. The disdain in the captain's voice had rankled and, pain in his shoulder or not, he could at least help with the cargo. The captain nodded as he reappeared and waved towards the rope ladder snaking over the high side of the ship, his tone marginally more gracious than previously.

'I daresay you can help stack the casks on the bank.'

Munro's arm was aching before even half of the cargo had been hoisted from the hold and safely delivered ashore, but he continued as if it troubled him not at all – *Pride is a hard taskmaster*, Kate would say, and she'd be right. The captain thought him useless, and whatever the discomfort, he would prove him wrong. The sun was high in the sky when he set the last full cask down and straightened, rolling his shoulders to release the tension in his neck and arms. The sailors were swarming down the ladder and stretching out on the banking, the last on board lobbing down loaves before edging down the ladder with a cask balanced on one shoulder, wine trickling down his back.

'No point in waste, lads,' he said as he propped the cask, burst side up against the remainder. He reeked of claret, and one of the other sailors made a comment, which drew a burst of laughter. The accent was too thick for Munro to follow what was said, but he got the gist as the first sailor pulled his shirt over his head and, miming wringing it out, flung it at the commentator. 'Be my guest.'

The loaves were broken apart and passed from hand to hand, the boy sent scurrying back onto the ship to fetch a couple of wooden tankards, which, filled and refilled, did the rounds.

Munro found the captain beside him, risked, 'Are

sandbanks a common hazard?'

'In the summer, yes. When the water level is low, safe navigation requires constant vigilance, for they shift with the strength of the currents. In winter the issue is flooding. Spring and autumn are normally easiest, for it is possible to avoid both, but the Loire is capricious and cannot be depended upon, like most females.'

He stood up. 'Back to work, lads. With luck we may be able to prise ourselves free.' He looked down at Munro. 'You're not as useless as you look. We could maybe use another pair of hands.'

Watching from the bank, Munro was impressed with the ease with which the sailors moved about the ship, despite the heavy list. The captain was leaning over the side towards the prow, a single rope belayed around his waist. A sailor, tied to it, was working his way along, stopping every few feet to thrust a pole into the mud below. Munro heard the sucking sound each time he withdrew it, the sailor's voice muffled and indistinct. It was clear from the captain's expression it wasn't good news. At last the captain straightened, barked some orders, which sent all but three of the sailors back to the ladder leading to the bank, Munro following. The remainder disappeared below deck, to re-emerge carrying long poles, which they handed down to those onshore. The boy grabbed Munro's arm and indicated for him to take hold of the end of one of the poles, which a sailor was manoeuvring into the mud beneath the ship's hull. It was not what Munro, or his shoulder, needed, but he had no intention of refusing. He scanned the sky – plenty of light left yet; if they could get away they might yet make some headway. He grasped the pole, added his weight to that of the other sailor also bearing down on it.

The man who shared the pole, clearly seeing Munro's upward glance and guessing his thoughts, said, 'It isn't the light that will be the problem if we can cut loose, but rather the wind, or lack of it.'

Munro glanced over his shoulder at a line of trees marching away from the river, the rustling of leaves clearly audible. 'The breeze is steady.'

'Now it is, but oft-times it drops in the late afternoon.' The sailor winked. 'It is generally a welcome respite, supposing we are near enough a good berth, unlike here, if you take my drift.'

Twice they leant on the poles at the captain's bidding to no effect, but the third time there was a sucking sound and a fractional shift of the hull before it settled again. At the fourth attempt the shift was obvious, the list of the deck less, the distance from the banking more. The captain shouted encouragement and they bent to take the strain again. The boy at the tail end of the pole next to Munro was doing his best, though his best was having little effect. Munro suppressed a smile, silently commending the boy for his dogged persistence.

The ship lurched, shifting sideways, the captain shouting, 'One more heave, lads,' exultation in his voice.

The sailor next to Munro bared his teeth. 'I think you

must be a praying man, sur, for ye may yet get yer wish.'

Munro was grinning as the prow rose, the captain hoisted aloft, his grip on the rail sure, as the ship swung and dropped towards the water, the splash as it met the surface raising a cheer. There was a crack as a pole snapped, but, muted by the cheer, Munro was the only person to catch the sound, and as he turned his head he saw the boy catapulted into the air and deposited in the river. His arms were flailing, his cry cut off as his head disappeared under the water, and for a moment Munro was back at the sands by Rough Island as the sea claimed Archie and Sybilla. He resurfaced and Munro wrenched his own pole free and, flinging himself flat on the bank, stretched it out towards the boy and screamed at him to grasp it. He lunged and caught it but his fingers slipped, his face disappearing once more under the water. Munro lifted the pole clear and inched closer to the edge of the bank, waiting for the boy to bob up again. This time he managed to grip the pole with both hands and to cling on as two others helped Munro to draw it back. A third knelt at the edge of the banking, and, reaching down, grabbed the boy by the shoulders and lifting him turned him onto his side and thumped his back, his efforts rewarded when he coughed, spewing river water and weed onto the grass.

Munro rolled over onto his back, his breath coming in gasps. As he reached for the hand outstretched to pull him to his feet, he felt a stab of pain, as if his arm was trapped in a vice from which he couldn't break free, the sky rotating.

When he came to, the captain was looking down at him, leached of colour. He felt a dampness seeping into his shirt, fingers probing the wound. He fainted a second time. There was water on his face, in his mouth, choking him, and he fought to rise to the surface, to escape the waves, to breathe air again. Voices around him, disjointed. 'He's coming round.' 'Leave him be.' 'Time enough for a drink when he's upright and fully awake.' And then he was, the captain's face swimming into full focus against the clear blue of the sky. His hand searched the ground around him, found it firm.

'Lie still. That wound needs looked at. I'll be as gentle as I can.' Then, 'What happened to you?'

'I was shot.'

There was a new respect in the captain's eyes. 'It was you saved the King?'

'I but did my duty.'

'Now we are also in your debt.'

'The boy?'

'Is fine.' There was a hint of a smile on the captain's face. 'In better shape than you as it happens.'

Chapter 6

It was Ellie who brought the word. She'd taken the Ivarsen and the Montgomerie children to introduce them to her friends, Kate telling Grizel and Elizabeth not to expect to see them for several hours at least. 'Maybe not even for luncheon, for Ellie has made herself popular and there are plenty of houses where she is regularly fed. Though five extra mouths might be a step too far.'

They were in the garden, comparing life in Scotland with that in France and Norway, Kate translating for Madame Picarde. She had insisted Maggie join them, hoping that something said might raise a spark, even if it was to contradict, for anything would be preferable to her habitual silence, which even their visitors had failed to breach.

On the previous evening John Montgomerie had done his best to rouse her, regaling them all with tales of some of his patients at court, their ills mostly self-inflicted or imaginary, but she had refused to be drawn into even the semblance of conversation. When she left the table to help with the clearance of the dishes, Kate had apologised, but he waved her words away.

'She is young and won't be able to nurse her grievances forever. I have more interesting tales I can tell, that aren't for everyone's ears. When we are settled again I'll make another attempt to stir her.' And so he did, when the younger bairns had been shooed off to the attic bedroom they all shared, the sound of their chatter floating down the stairs.

Kate thought of going to reprimand them, to insist on sleep, but Elizabeth said, 'They have but a short time together, and who knows when it may happen again. Let them enjoy it while they can.'

John, with a glance at Maggie's bent head, and a moue of apology for Elizabeth and Grizel, had settled by the hearth and proceeded to present more lurid details of his work: the stitching of a man's stomach who had been gored by a bull, his intestines spilling from the wound like a jumble of wool; the amputation of a leg gone gangrenous, the smell of the discarded limb enough to make the man who had been pressed into service to hold the patient still double over, so that John feared he might vomit onto the raw stump. He moved on to describe the dissections carried out by Peter Lowe at Glasgow. 'It was a privilege to be invited to observe, and the jars of specimens that form the core of his collection will no doubt have pride of place in the new college for surgeons James has in mind to establish in Glasgow. His intention is to rival Padua or Florence...'

For the first time Maggie lifted her head, and Kate, feeling a flicker of hope, was keen to continue the conversation but had been thwarted by Madam Picarde, who rose, making the excuse of checking on the children, her face white. Grizel rose also, shaking her head at John, and followed.

Kate, seeing sadness settle on his face, thought his

pause less a courtesy to Madam Picarde than the result of a memory stirred. She thought on the girl in Italy from whom he had been separated, felt a flash of anger – God should not divide us so. And hard on that thought a vision of the kirk in Renfrew, the voice of the minister as he hunkered down beside a young Maggie, with a gentleness quite other than his thunder in the pulpit. 'It isn't God who divides, child, but man who is mistaken.'

Now Maggie sat, once again expressionless, the conversation flowing around her. Kate fought her irritation and forced herself to concentrate, for it wasn't so easy to translate, though no doubt good for her. There was word of a storm coming, Madame Picarde worried it might blast the fresh shoots of grain just showing in the Low Field. Elizabeth picked up the thread, talking of the food scarcities of the previous winter, when Scotland's harvest had also been poor, the cost of wheat rising so that the burghs had been forced to set a maximum price for bread.

'Not that it stopped the profiteering. There are aye folk willing to forestall and to hoard food to other's detriment...'

She broke off and Kate turned to see what had distracted her. The children were at the turn of the lane, and even at a distance she could see they were white-faced and subdued. Instinctively she counted – all there, all standing. Thank God. She rose to meet them, but Elizabeth was ahead of her.

'Let me, you know what bairns are like. It may be nothing more than that a favourite kitten has died.' She reached the gate just as the children did, but Ellie, ignoring her, broke into a run, flinging herself at Kate, tears beginning to spill down her cheeks.

Kate caught her. 'What is it, poppet?'

'Tomas.' Ellie was still wailing.

Kate gave her a gentle shake. 'What of Tomas? You must tell me.' She was gripped by apprehension. It was a mite early in the season for the pest, but the fear of it was ever present. 'Is he ill ... has there been an accident?'

'He fell. Onto a pitchfork. His leg is...' Ellie buried her face in Kate's chest, her body quivering.

Above her head Kate met Elizabeth's gaze. Without a word Elizabeth prised Ellie free of Kate and hugged her close. Grizel was heading to the barn, calling for John, who, taking one look at the children's faces, set off at a run to the paddock. Kate grabbed Maggie and, without allowing her any chance to protest, made for the stillroom. By the time they re-emerged, Maggie carrying the basket, the pony and cart were waiting at the gate, the seat padded with a blanket, others piled in the back.

Madame Picarde touched Kate's arm and gestured towards the farmhouse. Kate nodded. 'If we need to bring him here, we will.'

The cottage was less than half a mile away, at the edge of a copse, John handing Kate down while Maggie leapt out the other side. The boy was lying on a palliasse in the corner of the cottage's only room, a rough blanket laid across him, one leg exposed, blood oozing through the rags with which it was bound. His mother was at his side, dabbing at his face, and Kate saw he was conscious, but barely so, the only sound his low moaning. She knelt down beside him, touched the mother's arm. 'May I?'

She nodded and shuffled back a fraction to give Kate space, her hands clasped so tight the knuckles showed white. Kate spoke softly to the boy, glad of the effort she had made to get some grasp of the patois, hoping it would be enough to reassure him. 'I'm going to unwrap the wound and take a look. This may be painful.' She looked up for Maggie and found her already twisting a clean rag to make a gag, dripping a tincture of poppy-seed onto it. 'Bite on this, it should help.' He opened his mouth and obediently clenched his teeth on the rag.

Maggie squatted beside him, slid her hand into his. Her speech was halting, reinforced by gesture. 'Sometimes it helps to have something to hold.'

His grip tightened as Kate began to undo the makeshift bandage. The last layers were soaked in blood, the ragged breeches beneath, likewise. Kate touched the mother's arm again. 'I need water, boiled and set to cool.' Without a word she got up and ducked out of the doorway. Around the back of the cottage Kate heard the clank of a bucket, water sloshing into a pan, the whoosh of bellows as the fire was encouraged into a blaze. John was by her side, cutting away the rough linen, exposing the full extent of the wound as Kate reached into the basket for a tightly stoppered jar containing wine.

With her free hand Maggie stroked the boy's forehead, smoothing down his hair, and whispered encouragement

61

to him as Kate washed out the puncture wounds with the wine. His face was drawn and he clutched Maggie's hand. She glanced at Kate and when she nodded an affirmation dripped more sedative onto the twist of rag in his mouth so that the grip on her hand loosened and his eyelids fluttered shut.

Kate drew in a deep breath. 'We need that water if we are to have this stitched before he wakes.'

Maggie rocked back onto her heels. 'I'll go.'

While they waited, Kate stretched upwards to relieve the ache in her back and pressed her hand against her ribcage. 'This would be a mite easier without this little fellow.'

'Do you wish me to do it? I hesitated to offer because…'

'Thank you, John, but no. If I am to make a reputation here it must be on my own merits, not as someone's assistant. But I'll let Maggie do the binding once the wound is stitched and perhaps send her to change the dressings also.' She touched her stomach again. 'I may be otherwise engaged in any case.'

John glanced towards the doorway. 'Sorry as I am for the lad, this may be what Maggie needs.'

'I know, but it is a guilty thought, that we may profit by his pain.'

John looked at the wound, clear of dirt, fresh blood seeping from it. 'He will recover, and by your skill. You have no need to feel guilt.'

62

Kate knotted the last stitch and turned with a smile for the boy's mother. 'He will do bravely now, though he will need the dressings checked and changed daily. Maggie will do that for you.' She was putting her hand on John's shoulder to lever herself to her feet when the door was flung back against the wall. The man framed in the opening was swaying from side to side, his eyes bloodshot. One moment Kate was rising from her knees, the next she was knocked backwards to fall heavily against a barrel, the metal binding cutting into her side. John moved to help her, but the man who had pushed her down swung round, his fist smashing into John's jaw, felling him also. Kate was pulled to her feet and dragged outside.

The boy's mother was hanging onto the man's arm. 'Pierre, please. Madame Munro was helping!'

He shook his wife off as if she had no more weight than a rag doll and hustled Kate towards the track. 'We don't need the help of the likes o' her. She's a heretic and likely wi' the evil eye.' He lifted Kate bodily and flung her face down in the back of the cart, and she felt the first sharp shaft of pain – dear God, please not here, not now.

His wife flew at him again. 'For pity's sake, Pierre, think of her child.'

'An' that's another reason why I don't wan' her here. It's ill-luck, a woman in her state.'

John emerged from the cottage, Maggie half supporting him. The man spat at John's feet. 'Get out. This is a Christian house and I want no truck wi' the devil or his brood.'

Maggie darted back to the cottage to retrieve the basket, whispering in passing to the woman who leant against the doorframe, her face white, 'I've left the dressings and an ointment, in case I cannot come myself.'

The woman, casting a scared glance at her husband, mouthed, 'Evening-time.'

John was helping Kate down from the cart as the second pain struck. Elizabeth, who had opened the door at the sound of their arrival, saw Kate stiffen, her hand going to her stomach, and jerking her head towards the barn, she said to John, 'Take the bairns to feed the piglets, we have other work to do.' And then, as if to forestall a protest, 'This is her fourth confinement, John, the other three coming without incident. If we need you, we will call.'

He gathered the children around him. 'Who wants a piggyback?'

There was a chorus of 'Me, me,' from all of them except Ellie, who stood in the background, her eyes still red and puffy. He fended them off. 'All right, all right, I shall be a donkey and you can take turns.' He hunkered down beside Ellie and tilted her face upwards. 'Tomas is going to be all right, though he'll not be running around with you for a week or two yet.'

She smiled, sunlight sailing from behind a cloud, then, 'Can I have a piggyback too?'

Kate had barely reached the top of the stair before she was seized by another contraction, and then another, pain on pain, each one stronger than the last. She was leaning on Elizabeth, crossing the landing to reach the privacy of her bedchamber, pausing with each spasm to breathe deeply, in an attempt to ride it out.

Maggie took charge. 'This is too fast. We need to gain her some respite else she won't have the strength at the end to push.' Her brow was knotted in concentration. 'There is a remedy...'

Kate gasped out, 'In the stillroom, on the top shelf. The small sachet at the right-hand side. Mix it with three parts wine, for it's gey bitter, I...' She grasped the iron bedframe, hung on for dear life, as water and blood gushed out of her.

Semi-conscious, she allowed herself to be helped out of her gown, into her shift, onto a chair. Maggie was at her elbow, holding a wooden tankard to her lips, and she drank, then spewed half of it up again as she fought to counter the vice gripping her stomach. Someone was boring a red-hot poker into her back, twisting it towards her pelvis, and from far away someone screamed. She was falling, the chair disappearing beneath her, all around darkness, the screams fading into the distance.

Twice more she came to, hearing a constant keening, like the wind in the trees below Broomelaw when storms blew from the north, but was unable to pinpoint the source. She was trying to claw her way up the slope, to reach the safety of the barmkin, arrows raining down on her, piercing her stomach, her abdomen, her groin. She could see Munro at the barmkin gate and wondered why he didn't come to help her. She felt her head raised, liquid she didn't want trickling into the corner of her mouth. In a lucid moment she recognised the symptoms, tried to control her breathing, to bear down on the pain, to work with it; but this was beyond her experience, a monster she was powerless to resist gnawing at her insides. Someone was shouting. Faces closed in on her. Elizabeth and Grizel, John Montgomerie, Maggie. A voice, dull and defeated, said, 'We're losing her.' And then another voice, high-pitched, determined. 'We can't, I won't let her go.' They were blocking the light and she fought to get past them, to reach the brightness beyond, where sun shone on a meadow dotted with bluebells and clumps of celandine. She could hear the sound of water, see a stream trickling over moss-covered rocks, its banks smothered in wild garlic, and Anna, her arms full of wild flowers, her hair lifting in the breeze, beckoning. She tried to call out, to rise, to reach her, but was held back, hot tears gouging her cheeks as the light began to fade, and Anna with it.

When Kate next surfaced it was to shadows, to a single candle flickering on the mantleshelf and Maggie kneeling on the floor beside the bed, her head on the coverlet, fast asleep. Kate tried to pull herself up, felt the hollowness within, began to cry.

Maggie was awake in an instant, crying and laughing all at once, hugging her. 'All is well.'

Joy flooded Kate. 'The child?'

'A boy.' Maggie was triumphant. 'And demanding. Elizabeth has gone to feed him sugared water, for fear he would wake you with his girning. I think he will be as greedy as Robbie.'

Outside the door, muffled whispers, the swish of a skirt, a faint hiccup and a sigh and they were all there: Elizabeth placing the babe in her arms and Ellie clambering onto the bed.

'I fed him, Maman, I fed him.'

John Montgomerie radiated pleasure and relief, and all the children, Ivarsens and Montgomeries both, in their nightclothes, clustered at the end of the bed, unexpectedly shy. In the background Madame Picarde, beaming, as if she were the grandmother of them all.

Kate's eyelids began to droop, her head to nod, and Elizabeth, indicating to Maggie to stay, for this was her moment, shooed everyone else from the chamber. Maggie perched on the side of the bed and stroked the babe's palm, smiling as the fingers curved around hers, clutching it tight. She drew a deep breath. 'I'm sorry,' she began, 'I've been…'

Kate stretched up and touched her lips, halting her. 'This past year has been a difficult journey for all of us.' She looked down at the babe nestled in the crook of her arm, and back to Maggie. 'I'm proud of what you did today, for Tomas, for the babe, and for me. I think for a moment I almost left you…'

'Don't…'

Kate smiled at her. 'I won't. But if I had, understand
I could die content, knowing Ellie and the babe would be
in safe hands.'

Chapter 7

Munro also was in safe hands, the rest of the journey without incident, the helmsman keeping to the centre of the shipping channel even when it would have been polite to edge sideways to allow another vessel to pass with ease. He saw little of the first night, unaware of when they dropped anchor by the village of Ancenis, the sailors, as regular customers, piling ashore to enjoy the comforts of a tavern by the waterside. The following two days passed without him stirring, knocked out with some concoction of the captain's own that kept him motionless in his bunk, not even the storm which battered the rigging, so that it creaked and groaned as if it could come crashing down at any moment, rousing him. The captain ordered the lowering of the sails and set every available oar. By dusk on the third night they had Orleans in their sights, halting, when the sun slipped below the horizon, at a village just short of the town, pinpricks of light like glow-worms illuminating the shoreline.

Munro woke to see the boy sitting cross-legged on the floor of the cabin, wedged into the space between the bunk and the wall, stitching at a sail he set aside as soon as he saw Munro stir. He disappeared without a word, and Munro heard his running footsteps on the deck overhead.

The captain ducked his head through the low doorway, haloed in the sunlight spilling through the opening to the deck. 'Feeling better?'

Munro swung his legs over the edge of the bunk, raised his left arm, cautiously. 'Yes … *what* was in the drink you gave me? I went out like a light, and judging by the sun have slept well past my usual rising.' And then, aware of the lack of motion, 'We've stopped. There is another problem?'

'No.' The captain grinned. 'We have reached Orleans, where I believe you wish to leave us.'

'Already? But I thought it was to take two days?'

'So it did, and you have slept through, storm and all.'

Munro looked around for his cloak.

'Rest easy, it's early yet, and though I understand your wish for haste, you won't be leaving us without eating something to set you on your way. The Forest of Orleans is a drear place with little opportunity for sustenance. I have ordered breakfast to be laid in my cabin, if you will care to join me there.'

While they ate the captain stretched back in his chair, said, 'We are in your debt, but I have little to offer but thanks.'

Munro was shaking his head. 'No need, I couldn't watch the lad drown and I the nearest to him.'

'Your own place, where is it?'

'Between Cayeux and St Valery, in Picardie.'

'Ah, I have a cousin with a ship at Le Crotoy, if you should ever be in need.' He stood up and rummaged in the cupboard above his bunk, emerging with a copper coin stamped with the impression of a head with short

70

curly hair topped by a laurel wreath, the inscription around the edge in Latin.

'Roman?'

'Indeed. We found a cache of them as a boy, and though most were sold, my cousin and I kept one apiece as a novelty. Present it to Pierre Du Bois, and tell him you came from me and he will be at your service.'

Munro left the ship, the thanks of both the boy and the captain ringing in his ears, a flask of the best claret and a fresh loaf in his saddlebag, along with a roundel of hard cheese with a bite to it as sharp as a stoat's teeth. Munro, curious, questioned the sailor who carried his saddlebag down the ladder. 'Is your captain as solicitous of all the crew? He seemed overly affected by the boy's rescue.'

'Didn't you know?' The sailor flung back his head in a guffaw. 'They are father and son.'

'But the lad is so fair.'

'The mother also, in character as well as colouring. And for all his bluster the captain dotes on them both.'

Munro headed north through the forest, making straight for Paris on a horse that, though it was the best to be had, was somewhat lacking in the speed stakes, which, had he been travelling over open ground, would have been frustrating.

'Steady, but sure,' the ostler had said when he handed

71

Munro up. 'And with stamina to match the best of them.'

That, Munro thought grimly, as the horse plodded along, his head drooping, will be nothing short of a miracle. On Sweet Briar, or indeed any of the horses it had been his good fortune to ride in the Gardes, he would have been confident of covering the distance to Paris by moonrise; as it was, he wasn't sure of arriving at all, unless it was on foot. But in this at least the ostler had spoken the truth, the horse, though looking as if at any moment it might sink down underneath him and expire, continuing to plod without the need of a spur. Only once, as they passed through the village of Artenay, did it lift its head, to snort as if giving a good day to a mare tied up at the lychgate of the churchyard, who whinnied at them as they went. When Munro stopped to draw water from a free-flowing stream, he left the horse un-hobbled, confident it wouldn't stray far, or not at any rate so fast he couldn't catch it if it did.

He sat on a carpet of dead leaves, propped against the trunk of a plane tree, enjoying the dappled shade, drinking the wine and eating the bread and cheese, and thinking on the birth, wondering if he would miss it. He had been there or thereabouts for the births of all his children, greeting them within hours of their arrival, and each time he had found himself surprised afresh that such a little scrap of humanity, resembling nothing so much as a stewed plum, had the power to move him. Surprised also by the strength of the grasp of the tiny fingers as they closed around his forefinger, and by the volume of the crying issuing from such small lungs. He sent up a prayer for mother and babe that it all might pass safely, and another for himself, and this perhaps a selfish thought, that the birth might be delayed until his return. It was a prayer unlikely to be answered, for Kate, and she more deserving of an answer than he, would likely pray for the opposite, that the bairn might come early and save her a week or two of discomfort.

Remounting, he pressed on into the forest, the canopy overhead dense, the track he followed scarcely visible. The only sounds, bar his own passing, the scuffling of small creatures in the undergrowth and the occasional grunting of a wild boar. Once or twice he saw the white scut of a deer as it melted into the trees, and heard the tap, tap, tap of a woodpecker as it searched for grubs in the bark of a tree. Here, in the darkest part of the forest, where even the whisper of wind-stirred leaves seemed sinister, there was no sign of any habitation, so that he prayed he might be free of the woods by nightfall. When rain came, dripping through the branches, he searched about for shelter, but found none – it would be a fine thing to catch a chill on the road home and be forbidden to see Kate or the child lest, God forbid, he bring ill to them. In the late afternoon the rain stopped, the forest thinning, allowing the sun to trickle through the canopy. The temperature began to increase, steam rising all around, as if from a tin tub on washday.

The light was beginning to fail when he reached the perimeter of the forest and saw Paris, at this distance no more than a pall of smoke rising from a thousand chimneys, punctured by church steeples pointing heavenwards. In less than an hour the city gates would be shut, and, not wishing to be trapped outside, he muttered an apology for the presumption and dug his heels into the horse's flanks for the first time. Startled, it tossed its head, straining against the bit, but, perhaps recognising Munro's determination, it began to trot, and as he continued to press, broke into an ungainly canter.

They made it, but not by much, the guards dousing the brazier smouldering by the gateway as Munro approached. They were beginning to pull the heavy gates together when he called out to them, 'Wait, in the King's name.'

'Cutting it fine, in't you?' The soldier who held the gate was scowling. 'In the name of the King, you say? Prove it.'

Munro proffered the authorisation, thankful now for the commission he'd been given by the King and the papers that accompanied it. The guard returned them to him with obvious reluctance, as if he resented that he had no excuse to arrest Munro for the temerity of delaying him. When he presented himself at the Louvre, Munro was ushered straight into Rosny's presence. He had hoped to be able to deliver the letters, speak briefly of his own affairs and the King's wishes in respect of them and then head to the Gardes' quarters to find Robbie. Rosny clearly had other ideas. He welcomed Munro, offered refreshment in a manner that indicated it would be impolitic to refuse, and settled down to quiz Munro on all the details of the entry to Nantes and the events thereafter. He had been leaning back on his chair, but shot upright as Munro told him of the attempt on the King's life.

'This is the fourth time we have come near to losing him, and each time a closer call than the last.' He broke the seal and read the King's letter. 'It seems the King and all of France is in *your* debt. I trust you will not find the repayment more of an ordeal than a recompense.'

It was a comment uncomfortably close to the mark.

'Rest assured all will be made ready, but do not feel you must ask your wife to travel until she is ready. The Duchesse de Beaufort will understand her need for delay, even if the King does not.'

Chapter 8

The bells were chiming midnight by the time Munro reached the courtyard of the Gardes' quarters. Despite the late hour, candles flickered in many of the upper windows and raucous singing rolled from open casements – easy to see the majority of the Gardes were on stand-down, and making the most of it. It had been some months since Munro was last in Paris, and he looked forward to seeing Robbie, if only briefly. A new thought – perhaps he could take him home to the farm for a day or two; it would please Kate to have the whole family around her, especially with the babe to come. He would speak to Rosny again in the morning.

The quarters Robbie shared with half a dozen others were under the eaves at the top of a narrow stair. Munro was taking the steps two at a time when above him the door opened, spilling light onto the staircase. A Garde reeled out and began to stagger downwards, holding onto the rail as if his life depended on it. Halfway down he paused, and looking upwards directed a stream of obscenities in Dutch at the still open door. Not wishing to be drawn into anything, or even to have his rank noted, for he was on leave and intended it to stay that way, Munro pressed himself against the wall as the soldier lurched past, stumbling on the bottom few steps before making it to the courtyard.

Robbie's face was flushed, his forehead damp. Munro noted the wariness in his eyes and the tremor in the hand holding his cards. Most of the men at the table with him were Gardes and known to Munro, though one, lounging against his chair-back, was a stranger, something in his glance as he looked up sending a chill down Munro's spine.

'Father!' Robbie made to stand up, but the unknown man reached out and grasped Robbie's arm.

'The game is not quite finished.' Another glance at Munro, a contemptuous curl of his lip. 'No doubt your father can wait. He would not wish you to run out on your obligations, I'm sure.'

'No, indeed. I can wait.' He leant against the wall with every appearance of ease, and crossing one leg over the other he stood his foot upright, resting on the toe of his boot. His thumbs were hooked over his belt, but his right hand remained close to his sword hilt. He watched through narrowed eyes as the game played out, sure the stranger cheated, but unable to see how it was done. Robbie's playing, however, was erratic, careless, and Munro's lips tightened – the boy was a fool. If this was how he played all evening it was no wonder he was losing. The shake in Robbie's hand grew more pronounced each time he lifted his tankard to his lips, and twice Munro thought of stepping in and ending it, twice restrained himself. It was unfair to judge Robbie on this game alone, and something in the confidence with which the stranger picked up his cards reinforced Munro's suspicion: he knew he couldn't lose, whatever Robbie drew.

77

When the end came, Robbie gripped his drink, asked, 'Will you accept an IOU?'

The stranger leant back, his voice pleasant, ice in his eyes. 'I think perhaps not. I have not always found the word of a Garde...'

Munro's tone was also pleasant, his expression likewise cold. 'I will sign it. Do you doubt *my* word?' His hand dropped to his sword, the implication clear.

The stranger inclined his head, presented the billet. Munro read the terms, inwardly furious, but signed without any appearance of hesitation.

'Sirs.' The man rose to his feet, scooped up the billet and departed, his steps on the stairs sure.

There was a moment's silence, Robbie closing his eyes, then he burst out, 'He cheated. I know he did. No one could have all the luck he had.'

The other Gardes weighed in in agreement, the resulting hubbub causing Munro to slam his hand down on the table.

'Enough!' His gaze swept over the men, his mouth tight. 'Enough,' he repeated, more quietly. He gripped Robbie's shoulder. 'We have much to talk of. It might be best if you share my quarters tonight.' It was not a suggestion.

Munro flung himself onto the only chair. 'Who is he?'

'Monsieur Droit. Though he is anything but, I'm sure of it.'

'How did he come to be among the Gardes?'

'By introduction, a month ago.'

'And you have been losing ever since?'

'No. At the first we all of us won some, lost some, Droit included. There was nothing to indicate anything other than the turn of the cards. Until a few days ago. He suggested we play prime. Duncan lost heavily, then Angus, then Wilhelm. He left the game early tonight and it wasn't the most amicable of leavings.'

'Tall, stocky, and with a mouth on him he didn't learn at his mother's knee? I saw him as I was coming up.'

Robbie nodded. 'He was in deep last night and hoped to be able to extricate himself tonight. Once he saw it was impossible, he bailed out. I doubt his only recourse will be Del Sega, for Droit has refused to wait until payday.'

'Del Sega?'

'A moneylender ... among other things. He is generally more obliging.'

'And his terms?' Munro flicked his hand at the billet lying on the table. 'Are they an improvement on Droit?'

Colour spread from Robbie's neck into his cheeks. 'They say he doesn't seek to bleed us dry.'

'No doubt. Why kill the goose that lays the golden egg?'

Robbie's face was still slicked with sweat, his hair curling damp on his neck. Munro took pity on him, scrabbled in a chest in the corner of the room and flung him a towel. 'This Monsieur Droit. Knowing he cheats is not enough. It's proof we need.' He produced a set of cards. 'Sit down, and play out the game, or as much of it as you can remember.'

79

A cockerel in the garden of a nearby hôtel crowed. Munro was still sitting at the table, shuffling and reshuffling the cards, but looked up as if surprised to see the line of light squeezing around the edge of the shutters, touching the pallet on which Robbie lay, still sound asleep. He stood up and threw the shutters open to reveal a clear blue sky without a hint of cloud – it would have been a fine day for travelling. Behind him, Robbie stirred and struggled to his feet.

Munro said, without turning, 'I had intended to leave for home this morning, and seek permission to take you with me. Now I think perhaps we must remain for one more night.'

Robbie came to the window and leaned on the sill as if requiring the support, but there was a new note of hope in his voice. 'You know how he did it?'

'I have at any rate a suspicion, and we have no alternative but to try.' He was spinning the ace of spades in his hand. 'Droit's terms are outrageous. If I were to lose to him we would scarcely be worse off. If I can prove he cheats, much the better.'

'You?'

'You don't think I'd risk you playing again?'

Robbie was silent for a moment, then, 'If you play, he will not cheat. But if I was to seek to recoup my losses, that would tempt him. If you are watching you will surely be better placed to find him out.'

Munro thought of Kate, of what she would think of the plan, but there was sense in it. Forbye it was the only chance of extricating Robbie. 'Fetch food, enough to keep us going for the day. You have a bit of learning to do. Enough to ensure Monsieur Droit is unlikely to win by fair means. If we can push him into a corner, where to cheat is his best option, we may have him.'

A game was already in progress. If M Droit was surprised to see Robbie, he hid it well, rising and pulling up another chair. His tone was good-humoured. 'Here to see if you can recoup some of your losses?'

Robbie had been well schooled. 'If the game is fair.'

Droit's face darkened, then cleared. 'As always, as always.'

It began as before, first Robbie, then other of the Gardes winning a trick or two before Droit began to raise the stakes. The other players began to drop out, and Droit, with every appearance of sincerity, suggested Robbie, whose losses had been up to this point modest, might also wish to call it a day. Robbie, who had contrived to look as if he drank much more than he had, shook his head. He nodded to the Garde who stood at his shoulder. 'Deal.'

The game began in earnest, going first one way, then the other, but each time Robbie the loser at the finish. He began to look flustered, to take more frequent slugs from his tankard. Munro, who had slipped into the room unnoticed, stood in the shadows behind M Droit, watching. It would have been tempting to smile at the job Robbie made of leading his opponent on, had it not been for the memory of the previous evening when it had been all too real; that alone was sufficient to ensure his total concentration. The candle at the centre of the table had burned down almost to nothing and begun to smoke when Munro pounced, grasping M Droit's wrist and twisting it so that the edge of an ace was visible in his sleeve. Droit tried to rise to his feet, to bluster his way out, but found himself surrounded, four sword tips pointing at his throat. 'Your hands on the table if you please.' Munro plucked a second card from his other sleeve, flung it down. He grasped M Droit's unbuttoned doublet and opened it wide, exposing the lining. There were pouches along each side, the tip of a card protruding from each one.

'Well, well.' Munro looked at the other Gardes. 'What should we do with him, lads?'

M Droit shifted, as if about to try and make a break for the door, one of the Gardes turning his sword and driving it into the table top between Droit's forefinger and thumb.

'Not so fast. You have, I believe, some papers we would wish to recover. After that ... we'll consider. Cheats are not well thought of hereabouts.'

There was a nip in the air when Munro and Robbie emerged from the stairwell to cross the courtyard towards Munro's quarters.

'That'll teach him.' There was satisfaction in Robbie's voice. 'I don't think Monsieur Droit will trouble the Gardes again.'

'More to the point, has it taught you? Sort one cheat out and ten more line up to take his place. I have no wish to have need to bail you out again.'

'You won't.'

Munro sensed Robbie's fractional hesitation. His voice sharpened. 'Is there anything else you're not telling me? Any other debts, gambling or otherwise, you have accrued?'

Again a slight pause, followed by a too-hearty, 'No!'

'See that there isn't. One mistake I can forgive, a second I could not.' They had reached the brazier in the centre of the yard, and pausing, Munro opened his palm and tossed the crumpled billet into the smouldering embers. There was a curl of smoke and a flare of light, flames licking the edges of the paper, turning it brown, then black, before flaking into the ash. 'I will speak to Rosny in the morning, ask permission for you to attend me home.'

'But...'

'No buts. Your mother would wish it and it will do no harm for you to be absent for a day or two. Remove you from temptation's way.'

'When will we leave?'

'Tomorrow, I hope. This debauchle has held me up long enough.'

Chapter 9

The sun was breaking through the early morning mist when Munro presented himself at the entrance to the Louvre, flexing his arm to relieve the stiffness in his shoulder. The young Garde nodded him through. 'Ye'll find all is hubbub inside. The Duchesse has been safely delivered of a son, and to see the way the King struts you would think he delivered it himself...' He broke off, a flush spreading across his cheeks. 'I did not mean any dis...'

Munro favoured him with a glare. 'I will ignore your comment ... this time. Take care you do not repeat the folly.' Then, 'The King is here?'

'Aye, arrived in the nick of time. And has promised the wine will flow tonight. But I wouldn't think he'll be wanting to talk of anything other than his son.'

'It's not the King I wish to speak to, but Rosny.'

'Him an' all, strutting about as if it was all his own doing. Though I daresay if it's a favour you're after, today might be the day to ask.'

Munro was walking through the gallery en route to search out Rosny, when he heard his name bellowed behind him. He turned to find Henri approaching. 'Sir Adam! I thought you'd be safely at Cayeux by now.'

Munro bowed. 'So did I, Sire. But several things

prevented me. I was just on my way to find Rosny to request if I might take my son with me for a day or two. It would please his mother.'

'If it is to please your wife I will be happy to give my permission.' He placed his arm around Munro's shoulder. 'But first, the Duchesse has presented me with another son, and as it will be part of your role to guard him, I wish you to meet him.' He drew Munro towards the royal apartments. 'Wrinkled plum as he is just now, he has a pair of lungs on him that bodes ill for those who might wish to cross him when he is full-grown.'

The Duchesse was sitting up on the bed, a shawl shot through with threads of silver around her shoulders. Munro thought of Kate, wondered if she too was by now safely delivered, and how different her clothing would be. If she was to come to court it might be an expensive business.

'Duchesse.' He bent over her hand, soft and smelling of almond, and had to force himself not to pull back – was he never to be free of reminders of Annock?

The King drew Munro to the cradle, pulled back the blanket. 'Look, he is a fine fellow, is he not?'

Munro, peering in, saw a tightly swaddled hump and a tiny head with a shock of dark hair, one up-flung arm poking out the top. He was indeed a plum colour, but would no doubt fade to pink in time. Henri stroked the babe's cheek, clearly delighted when he turned his head and attempted to suck on Henri's finger.

'A lusty lad, indeed, Sire, who will no doubt make you proud one day.'

'And you,' Henri said. 'For it is my wish you will not

only guard him, but also, when the time comes, have a part in his training.'

Munro dipped his head and said with a sincerity he didn't feel, 'I will be honoured, Sire.'

The bed creaked as the King sat down, trailing his arm across the Duchesse's shoulder. 'We have called him Alexandre, a fine name for a fine boy.' The babe's head was shifting from side to side, his mouth moving as if searching, and finding nothing his face crumpled and he began to wail. The wet nurse was there in an instant to lift him, as Henri nodded a dismissal to Munro.

'Away home to your wife, and I trust you have as much joy as we in your new addition. Ask Rosny for another letter, saying you are on the King's business, no doubt it will suit you to ride post-haste. But do not remain too long. We look forward to repaying our debt.'

Munro and Robbie wasted no time, and leaving the reek of Paris behind them, they headed north. For Munro it was a journey full of memories, replicating as it did much of the route to Amiens. It hardly seemed only a year ago, yet so much had changed. It had been from Beauvais that Henri had sent the main force to Amiens under de Biron, while he and some of his personal guard had set off on a round of the barracks to muster more troops. And Patrick with him. This time, without the artillery and the baggage wagons to slow them down, they covered the ground at more than three times the speed, reaching Beauvais by dusk. Though, by the time they arrived, his shoulder was aching and when he removed his jacket his shirt was stained with fresh blood. He eased his arm out and pulled away the bandage, then ripped a strip off his shirt tail. 'Make it tighter, for I'd rather not have to slow our pace for the sake of a wound that should be half healed by now.' The straw on the taproom floor of the inn seemed as if it hadn't been changed since last they had passed, and reeked of stale wine and spilt ale, Munro sweeping mouse-droppings off the table top while they waited for the maid to bring their supper. He didn't expect much of the food, and so wasn't disappointed, the meat mostly gristle, the gravy thin, the bread likely two days old. He thought back to their field camp, to the grumbling of some of the men – a taste of this would fairly have silenced their complaints. He pushed the food around his plate, determined to find somewhere better to break their journey when he brought Kate to court.

Robbie was subdued, and Munro, mistakenly thinking it was all as a result of the narrowly averted disaster with Monsieur Droit, tried to make conversation as if the events of the past two days hadn't happened. Finally he said, 'If it is your mother worries you, I have no intention of sharing anything of what transpired with Monsieur Droit. While she would applaud the end result, I'm not so sure how she would view my part in it all. You at least have the excuse of youth.' It was meant as reassurance, to draw a smile, but Robbie didn't respond, and pleading tiredness, he took himself to bed.

Munro, despite that he had lost a full night's sleep, took

himself out. He headed for the perimeter of the village, to where the French force had encamped, enjoying the quiet, the fresher air, the chance to think – something was bothering Robbie, and if it wasn't M Droit, perhaps Kate could wheedle it out of him. Thought of Kate brought him back to the bairn, to the fear he had tried and failed to subdue these six months past: the sense that the deaths of Anna and Archie and Sybilla, the loss of Broomelaw, their exile, had not been punishment enough for his part in the massacre at Annock. That God would yet exact some further retribution: *an eye for an eye, a tooth for a tooth.* How many had died that day? He could no longer remember, though some of the faces swam before him: Eglinton, Braidstane, the boy. Around Robbie's age. He found himself praying, the words dropping into the silence like stones. 'Lay not this sin to his charge, nor to Kate's.' Prayed also that God was listening. Kate would say God was aye listening, which was not necessarily an easy thought, but for once he found it a comfort. He returned to the inn to be lulled into sleep by the scratchings and scuttling of mice in the walls and in the ceiling above his head, and Robbie's rhythmic snoring by his side.

Once past Breteuil, Munro's spirits lifted. Whether it was the sunshine, or the fresher air or as a result of his praying, he wasn't sure. Only that the feeling which had weighed on him the previous evening was gone, to be replaced by a sense of well-being. With most of France at peace, and the negotiations for a treaty with Spain also close to conclusion, the future he planned for his family seemed within reach, and if for a time it was to be at court, rather than the quieter life of a seigneur at Cayeux, no doubt they could learn to live with that.

He quickened his pace, Robbie matching him, glad of the horses Rosny, following the King's instructions, had made available to them. And so it was that he was smiling as they entered St Valery through the Nevers gate that gave access to the medieval city. They passed the church of St Martin's with its chequerboard walls of flint and stone and came to the Calvair des Marins, a higgledy-piggledy jumble of half-timbered houses overhanging each other as they leant towards the sea. With every yard his spirits rose. They were nearly home. Opposite them Le Crotoy, where the King had stayed two years past, and which as a result had been exempted from taxes – a farm there would be the thing and perhaps, if he kept in the King's good graces, achievable. He chuckled, Robbie looking at him quizzically,

'What?'

'No matter. We have been fortunate to find one farm to our liking and shouldn't be greedy for more.'

Robbie, indicating insight that took Munro by surprise, said, 'Surely with the war all but over, Henri's need for money will be less and taxes may decrease.'

'Taxes never decrease, only increase less at some times than others. We may hope both the harvest is plentiful and the coming year is one of those times.' The Guillaume Towers reared in front of them, the gate and drawbridge thronging with people. The town gave every impression of prosperity, which was a good sign. Munro and Robbie headed towards the coast. In the distance, a cart, the creaking of the axles as it bumped over ruts in the track reminding him of the trip he had taken from Cayeux to St Valery with Madame Picarde, Ellie bouncing up and down beside him. There was something familiar about the set of the head of the driver. They urged their horses on, catching up as the cart passed the last of the straggle of houses on the fringe of the town. The carter turned his head as Munro drew level, then pulled the horses to an abrupt halt, Munro likewise.

'John Montgomerie, by all that's wonderful, how do you come to be here?'

'Elizabeth and Grizel plagued Sigurd to bring them for a visit and I was press-ganged into accompanying them.' John affected reluctance, but his broad grin suggested otherwise. 'It is a merry household you will find, for eight bairns makes for a lot of noise, forbye Maggie, who can hardly be considered a bairn, and the latest arrival as rowdy as the rest.' He held out a hand to Munro in congratulation, began, 'You have a son…' He was talking to thin air, Munro already racing ahead of him, a cloud of dust from the track billowing up and drifting backwards, hiding him from view.

Munro was stretched out, his back resting against the

carved bed frame, his fingers teasing at a curl of Kate's hair as she sat propped up against deep pillows, the only sound Patrick's vigorous suckling.

'I have called him Patrick John,' she'd said, as he burst into their chamber, startling them both. Patrick, lying on her lap, had jerked, both arms flying upwards, his mouth puckering as if he was about to cry. As he settled again, she asked, 'You don't mind, do you, Adam? That he isn't named for you.'

For a moment Munro thought of the months of worry, now past. 'You could have called him Methuselah and I wouldn't care. Just to see both of you alive and hale is all that matters.'

Laughter rippled through Kate. She stared down at the babe. 'Methuselah would seem rather a weighty name for one so small.'

'Patrick John it is then.' Munro laid his hand against the smooth curve of her cheek. 'Seriously though, the Montgomeries have been good to us. To call him after them is a fine thing, though I might have expected you to choose Hugh to follow Patrick.'

Kate flushed a becoming pink. 'It isn't John Montgomerie he is called for, though so I have allowed them to think. It is for John Cunninghame I named him, for we owe him perhaps more than anyone.'

He nodded. 'It is a worthy thought. A pity he may never know it.' His tone sobered. 'Would that John had been Cunninghame's heir and not William, for then there would have been no debt to pay. Have you heard any word of how he fares?'

'Nothing. According to John Montgomerie, William

hasn't yet been allowed back to court, and rumours from Kilmaurs no longer stretch to Broomelaw, or so he says.'

Grizel ducked her head around the door. 'Are you able for coming down to supper, Kate?'

'Oh yes. I'll be but a few minutes more.'

Munro tilted her face so that she looked straight into his eyes. 'Why wouldn't you come down to supper? What aren't you telling me?'

'It's nothing. And I haven't had a chance to tell you anything yet.' She hugged Patrick closer to her. 'A man in the village took against me coming to tend his son while pregnant, that is all. He pushed me and I fell, and that was when the labour started. It was a somewhat ... different experience from the others, but as you say, I'm hale, we both are, and that's what matters.'

It was a merry supper, the children allowed to wait up well past their normal bedtime, the talk flowing backwards and forwards between news of Scotland for Munro and Robbie's benefit, and news of France and the court, and of life in the Gardes, for the visitors.

Munro, without thought of where the conversation might lead, began to speak of Henri and the latest addition to his family. 'Alexandre was born on the same day as Patrick,' he began, 'and who knows what might come of that coincidence.'

Ellie said, 'Who's Alexandre?'

'The King's son.' Too late, Munro saw Kate's shake of the head.

Ellie's brow was knotted. 'But he hasn't a queen. Has he?'

Munro, with a look of apology for Kate, ruffled Ellie's hair. 'It is different for kings. One day you will understand.'

'It isn't different for our king,' Catherine Montgomerie said. 'Uncle John treats our queen…'

'And neither should it be for Henri.' The note of censure in Kate's voice was clear. Munro tried to recover the situation. 'Alexandre's mother is Henri's wife in all but name, and once the King has his way, will be truly so.'

'Then will she be queen?' Ellie asked.

'So Henri hopes.'

'Why not now?'

Maggie was dismissive. 'Because she is only the King's mistress.'

'Like Moder,' Isabella said.

There was a moment of silence before Isabella, clearly aware of something wrong in what she said, fled to Grizel and cooried in, looking up at her, lip quivering. 'Far calls you Mistress Ivarsen.'

Grizel hugged her tight. 'So he does, poppet, and so I am, but that's a different kind of mistress. A good kind.'

Elizabeth stood up, gathered the children. 'Time for bed.'

'But…' Ellie began.

'No buts.' Elizabeth was firm. 'Time enough tomorrow for your questions.'

'Bairns,' John said. 'Aye getting the wrong end of the

93

stick.'

'Husbands, more like,' Kate said. 'Their mouths aye running ahead of their brains.'

Munro was contrite. 'I didn't think. In Paris it is hard to consider Gabrielle d'Estrées as any other than queen, for so Henri treats her.'

'And Marguerite de Valois? What of her?'

'The marriage foundered almost before it began, for neither of them took any pleasure in it.'

'Nevertheless it *is* a marriage.'

'One Henri will have annulled as soon as it is possible to do so.'

'How convenient,' Kate said. 'How much will it cost him?'

'Enough, I imagine. But he will consider it worth every ducat. I do believe he truly loves Gabrielle and she him.'

Madame Picarde was matter of fact. 'He should hurry up and marry her then, legitimise those poor children.'

John snorted. 'Hardly poor. Petted rather, I imagine, as bastards that a king recognises usually are.'

Munro said, 'Recognised yes, petted no. The Duchesse has more sense in that regard than many mothers.'

Kate was caustic. 'Not enough sense to stay out of the King's bed, at least until she had a ring on her finger.'

'Politics are difficult. I'm convinced that when our peace is secure, marriage to the Duchesse de Beaufort will be the King's first priority.'

'If she is as important to him as you say, it should have been his priority long since. Or do politics trump morality?'

Munro, recognising the dangers in the serious turn of

94

the conversation for the news he had come to bring, and bitterly regretting the careless comment that had been the start of it all, sought to repair the damage. 'Of course not. But…' He had been going to say it was easy for folk in their own station for whom dynastic considerations did not apply, but Kate was too quick for him.

'There should be no buts, whatever the station.' She glanced across at the sand clock on the dresser, closed the conversation. 'Time for bed for us all, if we are to be fit for looking to the children in the morning. They may have been late tonight, but it doesn't mean they will lie long.'

Chapter 10

As predicted, the children were up and about at first light, their childish squeals the first sound Munro heard. He had shared a small chamber with Robbie, his excuse, that he wished for Kate to have as much rest as possible between feeds, passing without comment. Now he stood by her bed as she also stirred and thanked God once again for her safe delivery.

She cocked her head to one side, listening, then smiled up at him.

'It isn't only the children who are squealing. You'd best go and rescue the poor piglet that Isabella is intent on mothering, or it may not survive to feed us next winter.'

He leant down and kissed Kate's forehead. 'Forgiven?'

'Almost.' Her tone was mock-stern. 'And maybe altogether if, in future, you can think before you speak.' Her eyes darkened as she glanced at his arm. 'What happened to your shoulder?'

He looked down at his shirt, at where the cloth was stained brown. 'A flesh wound, of little consequence, and one I have reason to be glad of, for it is how we are here now.'

She pulled herself further up in the bed. 'Tell me.'

'Someone took a shot at the King. I deflected it, that is all.'

'All?'

'Yes. I saw the man raise the gun and I pushed the King out of the way...'

'And in so doing took the ball yourself.'

'It was a scrape only. And is my duty. Any one of the Gardes would have done the same. It happened to be me.'

'I hope Henri knows how fortunate he is to have loyal men around him.'

'Oh, he knows, and is generous in his appreciation.' This is the moment, he thought, I should tell her now. He opened his mouth but was interrupted by renewed squealing from the yard.

Kate smiled at him. 'Go on, make another rescue, and when you are done I will see to your wound, while you confess the whole story.'

The piglet rescued and the children released again, with clear instructions not to torment the stock, the adults settled at the table, Kate drawing Adam aside. 'Your wound.'

'It'll keep. I'd rather not make a fuss before everyone.'

'Promise me you'll let me look at it later?'

'I promise.'

John Montgomerie began talking of his call to Fife.

'Why Fife?' Kate asked.

'To treat Queen Anne's brother who had taken a chill

97

at the butts. She fusses over him as if he were a bairn.'

Elizabeth frowned. 'He may only be the Duke of Holstein, but he makes a progress as if he were the monarch himself, half of Fife vying with each other to provide the best entertainment and the finest food. The whole of the kingdom may be bankrupt by the time his tour is ended, for the rumour is he stays another two months or more.'

'You're not enamoured of him then?'

'I'm not enamoured of anyone who thinks as much of himself as he does.'

'And the King? What does he think?'

'It pleases the Queen, and James is disposed to like anything that makes her happy the now.' John smiled at Kate. 'Nor has he forgotten the part you played in her happiness. A bairn safely delivered is worth a king's ransom to James.'

'I bailed out before the end. I daresay he hasn't forgotten that either.'

'The King is your friend, and who knows when that may be useful.'

Elizabeth, in a transparent attempt to include Robbie, asked, 'How do you find life in the Gardes? Is your father troublesome? A hard taskmaster?'

Robbie managed a laugh, but his face flamed.

Munro rescued him. 'I scarcely see Robbie, for while he remains with the main body of the Gardes, I must act as nursemaid to Henri.'

'We hear of him though.' Robbie had recovered enough to deflect the attention away from himself and back to Munro. He addressed Kate. 'Hasn't he told you?

Father is a hero, the King's friendship for him likely stronger than James' for you. He saved the King's life and was injured in the process.'

They were all speaking at once, demanding to know the details.

Kate's hand strayed into Munro's. 'He told me it was nothing.'

'Enough that we have all been offered…'

Kate cut in, her voice sharp. 'Offered what?'

'I shouldn't have said…'

'No, you shouldn't.' Munro tried to laugh it off. 'I should have, would have, except I haven't yet had a chance.'

He took a calculated risk – to mention the King's offer now, publicly, might lessen the odds of Kate dismissing it out of hand.

'The King has invited us to court.'

Kate stiffened, looked as if she was about to protest, and Munro hurried on. 'All of us. That he may meet my family. It is over-generous in the circumstances, but intended as a kindness.'

'And the farm?' Kate placed a hand on Madame Picarde's arm, as if in reassurance.

It was an idea which had only just occurred to Munro and he blurted it out without taking time to consider. 'Madame Picarde also, if she wishes. Rosny is to see to finding reliable men to look to the farm on her behalf while you are absent.'

Madame Picarde was patting Kate's hand, the tremor in her own more obvious than usual. 'I don't think…'

'This isn't something to be decided on a whim. We

will take time to consider.' Kate turned to Munro. 'We do have time?'

'Yes, the King does not expect you to travel until you are fully recovered from the birth.' Honesty forced him to add, 'Though he hopes you may not be too long delayed.'

John, as if he recognised the need for a change of subject, said, 'Tell us more of Nantes. Will the edict hold?'

It was safer ground. 'I hope so. It was a lengthy stand as Henri read it out. I'd hate to think we'd stood through it all for nothing.' That brought laughter, in which Munro detected a general relief. 'There are over one hundred and fifty separate provisions, some public, some secret, forbye the letters patent. The King walks a tightrope, but if it can be ratified in all the parlements, it should bring peace and safety to France at last.'

'And religious freedom also?' That was Kate.

'For the most part. There are a few minor concessions he was forced to make to the Catholic party, but the Huguenots will rest easier in their beds once the terms of it are known.' He saw the speculation in Kate's eyes, knew he would be quizzed thereafter, but sought to change the direction of the conversation by talking of André Ruiz. 'The agreement was signed in a merchant's house in Nantes, and this will amuse you, the owner is a Spaniard. It appealed to Henri's sense of irony.'

Grizel asked, 'How was a Spanish merchant so honoured?'

'He had the temerity to be the first to invite Henri to dine and the King took the opportunity presented to him. I don't think it was altogether to Mercoeur's pleasing, but he was powerless to protest lest his new-found allegiance be cast in doubt. You ladies would have enjoyed seeing his house. Even a philistine like myself could appreciate the fineness of the decoration and the furnishings.'

'Describe them then,' Elizabeth was leaning forward. 'I had thought to begin a programme of improvement at Braidstane. Perhaps you can give me some ideas.'

Munro took a swallow of wine and launched into a description of the pale pastels of the walls, the contrasting vibrancy of the friezes, the ornate woodwork, the polished floors, the gleaming tableware. There was amusement and perhaps a tinge of contempt in his voice as he talked of the appearance of Ruiz' servants, the opulence of their livery, but his grudging admiration for the food, as he rehearsed each course, was clear. 'To be truthful, there is nothing in Ruiz' house that would be out of place in the Louvre. He has done well for himself, and seeks to continue to do so, hence his courting of the King.'

'From what you've said before, I wouldn't have thought Henri susceptible to such things.' Kate's brow was furrowed.

'Neither he is, and though Ruiz thinks he plays the King to achieve his own ends, the truth is the King played him. Now one who was a potential enemy, and with considerable power, is forced into friendship. I think at long last the crown is secure.'

Munro noted Kate had gone quiet, as if something else troubled her, and to redirect the conversation he said, 'Speaking of secure, what of the English crown?'

John pursed his lips. 'Elizabeth hangs on, though the rumour is she isn't as strong as she seeks to appear. They

101

say John Dee is a frequent visitor.'

Kate's interest was piqued. 'If she has turned to a quack like him she must be ailing.'

'So you would think,' John continued. 'And reading between the lines of George's letters, there are many at court who suspect her on the way out. Indeed, the talk is that Cecil is in communication with James and they have devised an elaborate code in which to write.'

The children had drifted back into the house and were playing a game of hide and seek. Ellie was hiding in the pantry and stuck her head out. 'What's a code?'

Munro said, 'A secret way of writing so that only those sending and receiving the letters know what is said.'

Her squeal drew the others and they clustered around Munro, Ellie hanging on his arm. 'Show us, show us.'

'Now you've done it.' Robbie was laughing. 'They won't be content until they've seen a sample.'

'We'll have to satisfy them then.' John winked at Ellie. 'Where's your slate. Robbie will show you how to make a code.'

Munro ducked his head to hide his smile, and beside him he felt Kate shake, though her voice was steady. 'What a good idea. You were aye inventive, Robbie.'

'That,' said Munro, as they watched Robbie heading for the salon, the children flitting around him like so many sparrows, 'was below the belt.'

'I know,' said Kate. She hesitated. 'Has he settled in the Gardes? I noted his flush when Elizabeth quizzed him.'

'There are a hundred reasons why he might flush and likely none of them significant. He is both popular and competent, that I do know.'

102

The children's voices were fading, Robbie's deeper tones lost among the high piping squeals of the girls.

Kate was smiling. 'He'll enjoy to teach them and it won't need to be an elaborate code to satisfy.'

'I suspicion,' Munro said, 'we shall find them writing messages to each other in code for days to come.'

'Some welcome peace and quiet, then.' Elizabeth's tone was dry. 'I, for one, won't object to that.'

In the privacy of their chamber, Kate asked, 'What exactly happened with the King? I know you didn't wish to speak of it before everyone, and perhaps it was just as well, but you cannot keep the details from me. And don't say just a scrape. I saw the way you favoured the other arm when Ellie tried to swing on you.'

He was looking down, removing his boots. 'It was nothing.'

'Really?'

'There have been several attempts on his life and all of them thwarted. This was, we hope, the last, and least likely to succeed.'

'Show me.'

He undid his shirt, eased it off his shoulder, unable to hide a wince as he did so. The bandage underneath was stiff with dried blood and it was clear that at some stage in the last twenty-four hours the wound had reopened. She ordered him to the window seat. 'Sit here. I'll get some warm water and a fresh dressing. It's as well you slept next door last night, my sheets were freshly laundered.' As she dribbled water onto the bandage and began to ease the layers of muslin back, she said, 'What is it ails Robbie? He has made a reasonable play of things since you arrived, but something's not right.'

Munro weighed up the honesty he and Kate had promised each other against his word to Robbie, decided there was little point in concerning Kate with his brush with Monsieur Droit, for that was a mistake unlikely to be repeated. 'I don't know. He was subdued for most of the journey home, and though I gave him ample opportunity to share whatever troubles him, he was as close as a clam. I thought perhaps he might be more open with you.' He winced again as the last layer of the dressing came away and with it a dark scab. The flesh underneath was still raw, beaded with tiny spots marking the end of blood vessels.

Kate gave a half-smile. 'It's clean enough, which is the most important thing, but not fit to be left open to the air yet awhile.' She pressed the flesh around the wound, nodded again. 'No sign of inflammation or any hardening. It seems it won't trouble you for long.' She turned him around and examined the shoulder from the other side, the exit wound similarly clean. 'Just as well the ball went right through.' Her fingers were cool on his shoulder, her actions deft as she re-dressed the wound.

He felt the need to reassure her. 'I know now why Patrick chafed at his role in the Gardes. For the most part it is a tedious chore requiring only the ability to stand still for long stretches at a time without betraying so much as a flicker of a reaction to any conversations taking place.'

She slit the muslin, tied off the bandage, her words a sigh. 'Thank God for that.'

Munro felt a stab of guilt for what he did not admit, that he had no relish for the weeks of inaction likely to come.

A movement in the cradle, the beginning of a whimper. Kate moved to unhook it and began to swing it gently. 'It doesn't end, does it, this worry for your children? You think that as they grow it will be easier, but sometimes it's the reverse.'

'Maggie?' he queried.

'If it hadn't been for Tomas' accident and his father's reaction, you would have found her with hardly a word to say. Even John couldn't arouse an interest, despite the stories he told.' Her mouth curved, the dimple appearing in her cheek. 'Though he had Madam Picarde near to fainting several times. These last two days, it seems Maggie may have come alive again, and I cannot but be glad, however guilty it makes me feel.'

He came to stand behind her, slid his arms around her waist. 'By all accounts you did what you could for the boy, and with success. Think instead on that.'

Chapter 11

Munro had been home for two days and it was clear to him that Kate, though cheerful, and enjoying this latest child, hadn't the stamina that had followed her previous births. His fears renewed, he sought out John. 'She has not said what happened at the birth, and I haven't wanted to press her, but…'

'Let's walk.'

They followed a path through the woods, moving in and out of the dappled shade, new leaves unfurling all around them, underfoot a carpet of fresh green shoots of wild garlic competing with spreading primroses coming into bud, above them birdsong, and the whisper of branches stirring in the breeze. They reached a clearing where a fallen tree trunk lay, smothered in ivy, the root ball teetering on the edge of a stream. John sat down, motioned Munro to do the same.

'You should know we almost lost her. Indeed, there was a point when she seemed to want to go. The labour was almost done, but she was barely conscious, not responding to instructions, and I began to fear that if we were to save the babe I'd have to cut. Then, of a sudden, her eyes were open and she looked up and smiled, but not at us. It was when she said "Anna" that Maggie became hysterical, crying and shaking her and calling her name over and over. I would have put her from the room but Elizabeth stopped me. It was then the turn came. Kate sighed and said "Anna" again, but this time with a sadness in her voice. She stopped fighting but had not the strength to push. The marks on the side of Patrick's head, they are from the forceps I used to grip him. She tore, but there was no alternative.' John took a deep breath. 'She hasn't talked of this at all?'

'Only to say she had a fall and that the labour was different from those that went before.'

'I cannot be sure, but my suspicion is that the difference came not because of the fall, but because she was attacked and thrown bodily into the cart. It brought on the birth, and likely the speed of the labour, but there is other damage, which is why she takes longer to heal. She will be bravely again, that I promise you, but I think it unlikely she will have another child. Indeed, it might be safest if she does not. '

Sigurd blew in on a westerly wind that drove the tide far into the channel between St Valery and Le Crotoy, fighting the strength of the river flowing towards the sea. And with him, a letter from Hugh. The gossip from England was entertaining enough: the paste on the old Queen's face so thick it might as well have been applied with a trowel, the effect, though it would amount to treason to voice it, grotesque. Mention was made of the lords who favoured

James' right of succession, those that were less sure. Of the other candidates for the crown, Arabella Stuart gained in popularity what she lost in terms of experience and suitability. *'There are aye folk who think much of the opportunity to better themselves by the means of manipulating a puppet monarch and position themselves accordingly.'* Kate could almost hear the confidence in Hugh's voice as Elizabeth read: *'James is unconcerned, and rightly so, for there is little fear her party will prevail. They may band together the now, but when the time comes they will be snapping at each other's heels, unable to agree as to who should have the pre-eminence. As to the situation at home, James has it well in hand.'*

Elizabeth fell silent and held the letter out to John, pointing at Hugh's scrawl with her finger. 'Is it possible?'

'What?' Kate's instinctive stab of fear was quashed as Elizabeth turned, hope shining in her eyes.

John scanned the paper, whistled. 'There are plenty who'll find it hard to stomach, but it's not before time.'

'What?' Kate said again, barely resisting the urge to grab the letter and read for herself. Munro came to sit beside her and put his arm around her shoulder as John read: *'The King has flexed his muscle, and blood feud is outlawed. The penalties sufficiently severe that even the most belligerent, of whom we could name at least one, will think twice of disobedience.'*

Elizabeth's relief was heartfelt. 'If it can be maintained we will all sleep easier in our beds…'

Kate saw, with a pang, that the events of the previous year continued to cast a shadow over Braidstane, one the Montgomeries had been at pains to conceal from her. She reached out a hand to Elizabeth. 'Pray God it will mean the end of trouble, for you as well as us.'

Elizabeth's answering grip was tight. 'Amen to that.'

John was continuing to read aloud, the other news both more disturbing and intriguing. Hugh had written, *'There is mention of a 'project' by which James will march on the Borders and demand his right of succession be recognised.'*

Kate was bewildered. 'Why should that be necessary? Surely it is the English court that matters, not the Debatable Lands.'

'Yes ... and no. The north of England has aye been a law unto itself, as the south of Scotland is ... or was. James is perhaps wise to seek approval outside of London. Though I doubt the old Queen would think it any other than presumptuous.' John's eyebrows disappeared into his hairline.

'What?' Once more apprehension tightened like a knot in Kate's stomach.

Elizabeth, looking over his shoulder, read out: *'The Earl of Tyrone has promised James assistance, Mountjoy also.'*

Munro said, 'Calling on Ireland. Is that not an even more dangerous game?'

'Indeed.' John bit his lip.

Munro squeezed Kate's shoulder as if in apology for asking, 'What else is there?'

'A piece of gossip which in the wrong hands would be considered truly treason, in English eyes at least.' John paused. 'Nor, I think, would James be pleased to know it was being bandied about. Hugh should have more sense than to commit it to paper.

'John,' Kate tried, but failed to hide her exasperation, 'just tell us. Better the devil you know, as they say.'

They say Essex gets above himself, the Queen's favour more

109

capricious than before, so he too is courting James.'

Kate relaxed a fraction. 'All this talk of the English court. Dangerous or not, we have received it safely and can consign it to the fire. Once burnt it can do no further damage.' She glanced at Elizabeth. 'No doubt you would have preferred news of Hugh himself, and of Braidstane.'

Elizabeth had also relaxed. 'You know Hugh, personal news comes very far down his priority list. He might tell us he had contracted the ague, but only if he was at death's door and wished us home for a fond farewell. And even then he might fail to mention it. I have grown used to accepting if he writes at all it is evidence he is hale.'

Grizel laughed. 'We all do.' She slipped her arm through Sigurd's. 'You're surely back sooner than you thought. Can you bide a while?'

He appeared to think.

Isabella, who had attached herself to him like a limpet from the moment of his arrival, was clinging onto his arm, saying, 'Oh pleeease,' her vowels stretched.

He swung her up, settled her on his arm. 'Perhaps I could delay our departure by … a week or more, if,' he looked at Kate, 'we will not outstay our welcome?'

Grizel was shepherding the children up to bed, the menfolk clustered around the hearth, the talk again of politics, but this time it was Sigurd quizzing Munro about the French court, the likelihood of peace with Spain, whether there was as much jostling for position among the French lords as was endemic in Grizel's description of Scotland. Kate caught snippets of the conversation and once or twice saw Munro glance in her direction, as if there was something he had not yet shared with her. Which brought her thoughts back to the reading of Hugh's letter and the feeling Elizabeth too had hidden something. She was standing by the window, staring out, turning the letter over and over in her hands, as if, Kate thought, just to touch it brought Hugh closer.

She joined her. 'Are you homesick, Elizabeth?'

'No, no. It is lovely to be here, to see you settled and content. This is the first time I have travelled further from Braidstane than Greenock since the Queen's entry in ninety-one. When Hugh is away, sometimes I have envied him his freedom to go where and when he likes. And now I have a taste of that freedom.' Her voice was light, but she continued to rotate the letter.

Kate touched her hand, stilled her movement. 'What is it you're not telling me? Does it concern us?'

'Not directly. Not at all really, as you are here and safe.'

'What then?'

'Hugh makes mention of Hamilton. It is he James uses to negotiate with the nobility in Ireland. Indeed, he has given him the task of writing a treatise on James' claim to the English throne. Hugh is not best pleased with his restoration to favour.'

Kate in her turn was staring out into the dark, her fingers plucking at the folds of her gown.

'I knew it would upset you. That's why I didn't want you to know. He cannot touch you here. Nor, I imagine,

111

would he. He would be a fool if that lesson was not well learnt, and whatever else we may say of Hamilton, he is no fool.' Elizabeth had begun to swivel the letter again. 'But I worry for Hugh. He thinks of taking a land grant in Ireland when the time comes, and now it seems Hamilton has similar ambitions. Hugh already mislikes him. If they are to be rivals in this also … what use blood feud outlawed in Scotland if Hugh will carry his antagonisms over the water to Ulster?'

Kate was looking down at her skirt, picking at a burr clinging to it. 'I cannot help but feel the problem between them can be laid at my door.'

'The blame doesn't lie with you. They are chalk and cheese. James Hamilton is a scholar, that alone damning him as a weakling in Hugh's eyes. And Hamilton has no respect for soldiery, and, courtier or not, Hugh is at heart a soldier. ' Pink colour stole into her cheeks. 'Don't you remember my mother's funeral, the aggravation between them then? By getting at you, William thought to hurt us. And it was to that end he was able to draw Hamilton in. He would have had nothing against you were it not for our connection.' She crossed her arms over her chest. 'We can none of us forgive him for what he did at your trial, but for Hugh to challenge one riding high in the King's favour is not wise.' A pause, as if she considered whether to speak or not, then, with a sigh, 'If I'm honest, there are times I envy you all this. The chance to start afresh, to be free of history, of obligation.'

It was a new and surprising perspective, Kate's reply determinedly encouraging. 'Perhaps Ireland will be your answer, and if what they say of the old Queen is right, maybe sooner than you think. Hamilton is in Dublin, is he not, while Hugh looks to the north? That is surely space enough to keep them apart?'

Kate was sitting on the window seat, a shawl around her shoulders, Munro stretched out at her feet. A single candle burned low and began to gutter, globules of wax dripping onto the candlestick. Waving away the spiral of smoke, she tackled Munro. 'We once promised there would be honesty between us. It is our most valued possession.' She captured his hand, traced the scar on his palm. 'But since you returned there is some secret you haven't shared.'

'And you have told *me* all?'

She bit her lip. 'That's different, Adam. Birthing is women's business. In a week or two I shall be recovered and the difficulties forgotten.'

'And then?'

She coloured, accused, 'You've been talking to John.'

'Wouldn't you, if I had been ill and not making the progress you expected?'

She recognised the justice in it. 'It is not an easy thing to confess, to be unable to bear another child. It seems like a failure. I was waiting for the right moment.'

He stood up, put both arms around her, pulled her against his chest. 'You have never been a failure. Nor ever will. Not to me.' He was resting his chin on her hair. 'But as for my "secret", as you call it, I too was waiting for the right time.'

'Tell me now.'

He led her to the bed and they lay side by side, the top of her head level with his throat. 'The invitation to court, it is not the temporary thing I implied earlier.'

'Go on. If I do not know the truth, I will imagine, and that will be far worse.'

She listened, without comment, only once or twice betraying by an involuntary movement that what he said troubled her.

He concluded, 'I'm sorry, Kate, I did not wish for this.' A deep breath. 'If there was a way to refuse…'

'Henri has said he would welcome my skill at court?'

'Yes.'

'Well then, taken in the round it may not be so bad. The business in the village was an ugly thing, and I keep thinking … it could have been Maggie attacked.'

He sat up abruptly, but she pulled him down again.

'Not that. But it wasn't just my pregnancy the boy's father objected to, but a suggestion of the evil eye.' She pulled the shawl across her chest, an unconscious reaction to the memory of the interrogation she'd suffered at the hands of Cowper. 'I cannot go through that again.'

He drew her close, stroked her hair. 'Nor will you. I will do anything, anything, to spare you that.'

Her head was on his chest, her breathing returning to normal. After a moment's silence, she said, 'What of our religion? Will the King allow us freedom of worship?'

'So he has promised,' it was his turn to hesitate, 'though there is a general embargo on the Huguenot faith

114

within the boundaries of Paris and for five miles around. It is one of the concessions, wrung from him by those of the Catholic persuasion.'

She unpicked a ribbon in her shawl and threaded it back and forwards through her fingers. 'How then can he offer us an accommodation?'

'He is the King, and such things can be arranged, provided they are done discreetly.'

'Discretion?' She made a sound halfway between a snort and a sob and he tightened his arm around her.

'We have none of us managed well in that respect in the past, but I daresay we can learn.'

The candle flickered and went out. She settled against him, yawned. 'I daresay we can. And we can talk again tomorrow, when there is not a babe that may waken at any moment … It was not what we looked for, but if I have learned anything in the last year, it is that we must make the best of what we have.'

Chapter 12

The tenantry around St Valery was a-stir, preparations being made everywhere for the St Mark's Day's processions. Madame Picarde, as a good Catholic, thought it vital for the harvest to come and neither Munro nor Kate was disposed to object. Sigurd appeared to find their acquiescence amusing, but Grizel said, 'You needn't laugh. They owe her much, and if a saint's day or two will make her happy, who are we to quibble at it. It is but one way of praying for God's blessing on the crops, and who can say it will be any less effective than another? No doubt God can hear our heart and our intention whatever the trappings. And besides, take away the mummery and it is at bottom a festival the bairns may enjoy. If you wish to pray for anything, pray for fine weather, that it may proceed as planned.'

Ellie piped up. 'We've been praying, for days and days, on our knees and everything, so God must be listening.'

Sound came first. The rise and fall of voices, sonorous, musical. Initially a blend in which neither words nor individuals could be distinguished, but as the procession came closer it gained both in clarity and volume. It was recitation, not song, yet had the sense of a choir: the booming bass notes of the miller and the smith, and the tenant farmers whose land comprised the Picarde seigneurie, underpinning the strong tenor of the priest. The mellow tones of wives and daughters: altos and mezzo-sopranos masking the quaver of a grandmother whose voice had begun to crack. The piping of children, like a chittering of starlings, and soaring above them all, the choirboys from the church of St Martin.

It was an impressive sight, the priest at the front, holding aloft the silver cross set with a single ruby, the pride of St Valery. Behind him the altar, carried by the chosen men, an honour every youth, religious or not, coveted for the esteem it conveyed, and the chance that the girl of their choice would look with favour on them, for a night at least.

As they came round the edge of the home field, the foremost man stepped on a stone, which rolled under his foot, so that he stumbled, the altar swaying. Madam Picarde's hand flew to her mouth, her body tensing, and Kate, beside her, heard the desperation in her echoing of the litany, her heartfelt sigh of relief as the altar was steadied again and moved forward without mishap. When the procession reached the farmyard, they joined it, the children following Ellie, squeezing in by her particular friends, the adults closing up at the rear. Among the children was the boy whom Kate had treated, hobbling along on a home-made crutch. Kate caught the eye of his mother and was rewarded by a radiant smile, but the father who marched with her looked away and spat into

117

a furrow.

The procession wove through the fields in a continuous succession of prayers for the crops, clear or mumbled as each was able, many no doubt thinking of the feasting to come. Kate, watching the line of children hopping and skipping, thought, with a pain underneath her breastbone, how many of them might be missing from the Feast of the Nativity. Odd that it was children who were most at risk in the summer, carried off by malaria or sweatings or chronic diarrhoea, while the winter epidemics stole adults, the old an expected loss, the fit and hale harder to accept. She thought of Patrick John, of the months to come, and prayed God he would be spared to them. He was their new beginning, the seal on their new life, a joy that couldn't be suppressed.

The dinner, which Madame Picarde presided over as the seigneur, was in full swing, the farmyard cleared of animals and spread with fresh straw. Long planks resting on trestles stretched across the yard, spread for the occasion with bleached linen, dotted with bunches of bluebells. All along their length stone jugs brimmed with wine, baskets were piled high with crusty rolls and platters with salted pancakes. Overseeing each trestle was a chosen man, who carved the smoked hams and cut wedges from the wheels of hard cheese, and saw to the fair division of the pork ribs, the roasted chicken pieces and last year's jars of onions pickled in vinegar. At one side, the children, with a trestle to themselves, squabbled over chicken drumsticks and slices of spiced sausage, clashing their tankards of watered ale together in mimicry of their elders.

Munro and Kate were seated with Madam Picarde at the head of the table nearest the farmhouse door, along with the priest, the rest of the Munros and their guests spread along the trestles among the tenants of the seigneurie. Kate was watching Robbie, seated among the young men of the district, their trestle the noisiest of all. He seemed relaxed for the first time since his return with Adam, but she wasn't sure if whatever had troubled him had faded or if it was the wine that gave him ease. Whichever, it was good to see him laughing, the tension in his face dissipated – perhaps tonight, when the festivities were over, might be a good time to question him.

Madam Picarde leaned across. 'A pity Robbie can't stay. He seems to find the company of the Bachellerie agreeable. Perhaps he may be able to visit again for a patronal festival, when the young men come into their own.' Her eyes misted. 'My husband led the Bachellerie in his youth, and so when it was our marriage, the festivities they organised were somewhat…' she was searching for a word, 'boisterous.'

The priest, whose eyes were beginning to glaze, interrupted her. 'Monsieur Picarde was a good man. A popular man. A leader of the district, aware of the obligations of his position, a patron of the church.' He looked at Munro, then at Madam Picarde. 'Would he have willed the seigneurie to a heretic?'

119

She hissed at him. 'Better a heretic than a sot of a priest who is a disgrace to his profession.' She levered herself to her feet, the signal for the feast to end, and all around the yard benches scraped across the cobbles. Her hand was on Kate's arm, as if in apology. 'Don't mind him. He's long had his eye on our land, ever since the last of my sons was killed.' And then, as if she read Kate's thoughts, 'You needn't worry I've antagonised him for your sake. He won't remember the conversation by the morning. He never does.'

Chapter 13

The horse was in a lather, the rider leaning low over his neck as they galloped along the track. Munro was in a line of men stretched across the outfield, prising loose stones that every year worked their way towards the surface of the soil. In the four weeks he'd been at Cayeux he had found himself relaxing into the life of the farm, despite its unfamiliarity. At Broomelaw the rhythm of the year had been determined by the needs of the stock: the timely servicing of the cattle and sheep, a successful over-wintering, and the lambing and calving to follow. Here, the cycle of seedtime and harvest dominated. John Montgomerie was to his left, Sigurd and Robbie to his right; all pressed into service for fear the weather might break and the late sowing be delayed. Different problems, Munro thought, but the same satisfaction to be gained from a successful outcome. He straightened, flexing his back, and glanced back at the farmhand coming along with the horse and cart, the children scurrying around him gathering the piles of stones studding the ground – a tedious task, no doubt the lad was happy to have extra hands to share it. He was aware of an ache at the base of his spine, a counterpoint to the pain in his shoulder, which continued to trouble him, unwelcome signs he was neither as young nor as fit as he once had been, despite the new babe in the cradle.

The thrumming of the horse's hooves intruded into his thoughts, and he raised his hand to shade his eyes and saw Robbie also straighten, radiating tension – he is hiding something. Munro put aside his unease as he headed for the farm gate – there would be time to quiz Robbie later, and like it or not he would winkle the problem from him. In passing, he noted that Robbie relaxed as the rider's speed became apparent, for it was only a King's man, who had the right to ride on the road at such a speed – at least whatever troubled him was unlikely to be related to his role in the Gardes; another debt perhaps? Maybe there would be advantages in being to hand in Paris for a time, and with Kate there also; surely between them they could sort Robbie out?

He reached the yard gate in time to open it for the rider, who brought the horse to a quivering halt and slid from the saddle. Dust coated him from head to toe, muting the colours of the King's livery, and as he raised his gauntleted hand to wipe away the beads of sweat glistening on his forehead, he left a pale smear, which served only to emphasise the grime.

He bowed and, with a questioning glance at Munro's working attire, queried, 'Sir Adam Munro?'

Munro nodded, looking down at the mud clagging his boots, and smothered a smile – no wonder the messenger had doubts. 'You have a message from His Grace the King?'

He fished in his doublet for the letter. 'I am to wait for your reply.'

Munro recognised his weariness and gestured him

towards the house. 'A bite to eat, then, while you wait, and a chance to refresh yourself.'

'Thank you. I won't say no to either.'

He found Kate. It was not the way Adam had intended to reopen the matter of the King's request, hoping instead to allow time for her to get used to the principle of the thing before they discussed the practicalities, but it seemed the King had other ideas. He read the letter again, hearing Henri's voice in every syllable. There was little preamble and no subtlety, which, allied to the haste with which it had been dispatched, was disquieting – another attempt on the King's life perhaps, or the rumour of one?

It seems I have a greater need to surround myself with those I can trust than I had at first thought. Your wife is no doubt safely delivered of her child, and though I do not expect she will wish to take the arduous journey to Paris for a week or two yet, I wish you to return without delay. The messenger has been instructed to bring a reply. Let the reply be you.

Kate handed the letter back, took a deep breath. 'Of course I will come now, but I had thought we would have longer, that proper preparations could be made…'

'No.' Adam spoke more sharply than he had intended. 'The King does not expect it and nor do I.' He made an attempt to soften his tone. 'You must wait until you are stronger. When the time is right I will send a carriage, that you may travel in more comfort.' It was an open acknowledgement of the toll the pregnancy and birth had taken on Kate, and they came together, the kiss gentle, undemanding, their breath mingling, though there was a fierceness in the way Adam tangled his fingers in the hair at the nape of her neck, and in the tightening of his good arm around her waist.

She drew back a fraction to reach up and run her hand along the roughness of his chin. 'These last years, we were too much apart. Paris will not be so bad.'

Through the open shutters, Munro could see a patchwork of colour, the rich brown of the newly ploughed field, where the others still worked, contrasting with the soft green of fresh grass in the pasturelands beyond. On the breeze the scent of the sea mingled with wild garlic. The younger children, perhaps distracted by his departure, had returned to the farmyard, Ellie and Isabella sitting on the gate, their legs swinging. There was a high-pitched squeal, followed by a lower protest and then a babble of voices all shouting at once in a mix of Scots and French and Norwegian. Ellie stalked off towards the barn, head held high. He thought of the noise and the stench and the airlessness of the city, and, lest Kate should divine his thoughts, moved to the cradle and slipped his finger onto the sleeping baby's curved palm, felt it clutched tight. He knew it was but reflex action but nonetheless moving.

Her eyes were luminous, damp with unshed tears, but her voice was steady. 'I will be bravely soon, and once arrangements are in place for the running of the farm we will follow you.' She came to stand beside him, leant her head against his shoulder, the touch, though light, sending a spasm of pain down his arm, so that he had to steel himself not to flinch. She was speaking again, but quietly, as if to herself. 'I do not know if Madame Picarde can be persuaded, for her whole life has been here or hereabouts, but with or without her we will come. And perhaps it is as well for us to be absent for a while. The unpleasantness with Tomas' father ... I had thought it was just that I was a stranger which made folk wary, that in time they would accept me, but for all that St Valery is Huguenot, much of the countryside around Cayeux still favours the old religion, and it is a short step from that to superstition.'

Ignoring the discomfort, Munro placed both arms around her. 'Warring over religion has been a way of life here for so long it has crept into the bones, of some folk at least. In time it will be different, and if a while spent at court means you come back as one of the King's apothecars, for most that will be sufficient.'

He had the sense she wasn't really listening, his efforts at comfort wasted, confirmed as she said, 'If we are in Paris, I may be able to sniff out whatever troubles Robbie. And Maggie will, I think, relish the opportunities it may give her...'

She was looking down at the worn edge of her slippers. 'Will we be forced to bide at the Louvre?'

He rested his chin on her head, squeezed her arm. 'I have money saved. There will be ample to ensure you do not disgrace me.'

She burrowed deeper into his chest, changed tack. 'I fear for Ellie. She is so settled here.'

He had a vision of the court, of the hierarchy among

125

the children, of Ellie's gregarious character, and sought to be encouraging. 'She will make friends anywhere. It is her nature.'

Kate sighed. 'That's what I'm afraid of.'

It was not her only fear. Marching alongside it the continuing worry that Robbie was in some difficulty from which he couldn't extricate himself and her continuing concern for Maggie, though for her a move to Paris might be a positive thing. Threaded through it all, and emphasised by the stiff way Munro held his arm, the thought that, despite all his protestations, the role of King's bodyguard held its own dangers.

At the last, as Munro bent to kiss her, he attempted to dissipate her unspoken fears. 'The treaty with Spain is all but concluded. Once it is signed and sealed, the role of the Gardes will be little more than ceremonial. And likely boring with it. It will be a fine thing to have my wife to return to at night.'

She sensed a tension in him his heartiness failed to conceal, but responded as if she took him at his word, as if she didn't think this new peace perhaps a fragile thing, her husband and son still at risk. Echoing his words, 'It will be a fine thing to see my husband daily,' a hint of forced mischief as she tightened her arms around his waist, 'though maybes boring with it.' Their shared laughter the send-off she wished for him, whatever her own unease.

She watched from the gateway as he and Robbie disappeared over the brow of the hill to answer the King's summons, the content of Henri's letter, abrupt and enigmatic as it had been, imprinted on her mind.

'The worry is more when they are out of sight.' Elizabeth slipped an arm around her waist. 'At least, so I always find with Hugh. The ills you imagine are generally worse than those that are realised...' She broke off, and Kate knew by the tightening of her grip that she too thought of Irvine, of Kate's trial and the disaster so narrowly averted.

'All that is behind us now.' Kate sought to reassure herself as much as Elizabeth. 'And if we could only stay here, quiet and peaceable, I think I might begin to believe it. But with Adam and Robbie in the Gardes...'

Elizabeth waved a hand towards the outfield and the string of men working their way back towards the farmyard. 'Whether here or at court, this *is* what you have now, and a babe in the cradle whose inheritance it will be. It is a far cry from the bastle house at Braidstane and William's shadow hanging over you. Adam is right, once peace with Spain is confirmed there will be no reason for either of them to be in danger. The negotiations are well in hand, are they not?'

'In hand, yes, but as to well, or more to the point, *when* they will be concluded, that is a different matter altogether. The principle may be agreed, but the practicalities are more problematic.'

'If they have got this far, surely neither side will want to risk a return to war? The Gardes are likely already safe, and when you are in Paris, you will see that for yourself.'

'I wish I could have gone with Adam now.'

Elizabeth squeezed Kate's waist again, this time with a smile. 'I hesitate to commend his good sense twice in five minutes, but in this too I think he is right. You will be bravely soon enough, and besides, a little delay will give time for Ellie and Maggie to come to terms with the change. Forbye Madame Picarde and the arrangements to be made for the farm. Not to mention how hard we would have taken it to be thrown out, our visit truncated.'

Kate allowed her shoulders to relax. 'As regards Ellie, I dread telling her she must give up all the friends she has made here and start over. But Maggie may relish it, for Adam says there will be opportunities for her in Paris that would not have been dreamt of in Ayrshire, or here either, for that matter.'

'And you will all be together, think on that.'

Chapter 14

The sounds of children playing in the gardens floated up to where Kate sat in their apartment in the Louvre, her hands lying idle on the embroidery in her lap. An autumnal breeze drifted in through the partially open casement, a welcome reprieve from the oppressive heat of the four months since her arrival. Behind her, in the cradle, Patrick John snuffled and made small grunting sounds, mimicking those of the spaniel puppy the Duchesse de Beaufort had given to Ellie as it also lay fast asleep, curled in front of the fire. It seemed it hadn't been a mistake accepting the King's invitation to court, though there were things Kate still found hard to get used to. At the farm and to the surrounding villagers she had been plain Madame Munro, for it had been clear that if she was to gain acceptance in the region and an opportunity to work as a healer, it would not be by emphasising her status. Here, though it sometimes sat as uneasily on her as the name Grant had done at Braidstane, her title was essential to command respect. The servants whom Munro had been forced to employ kept their distance, their deference a stark contrast from Agnes' attitude. Kate missed her, her insight, her unquestioning loyalty and even her acerbity, but she kept the sense of loss to herself, for weighed against the undoubted advantages that had come of their move, the comfort of their new quarters, the daily companionship of Adam, and especially Maggie's renewed enthusiasm for life, it was as nothing. Madame Picarde had remained at the farmhouse, despite all of Kate's efforts to persuade her to the contrary, and she too was a miss.

Her refusal to accompany the Munros to court had been categoric. 'I have lived here forty years and am grown so far into the soil that to uproot me now would likely be the death of me, and I am not ready to die yet.'

It was an argument impossible to counter without seeming unfeeling, so Kate had given way with good grace, and with a promise that in subsequent years, when the heat grew oppressive in Paris and the court deserted the city, she too would escape and bring the children home for a visit. It still felt somewhat odd to think of Cayeux as 'home', but Broomelaw was a lifetime away, and though in trust for Robbie, she doubted if she would ever see it again. And to be honest, she wasn't at all sure she wanted to, not when it had been William who'd rebuilt it, and doubtless to *his* taste. Even Elizabeth's assurances, that it had been rebuilt to the original plan and that by the time she visited John Montgomerie had replaced all the furnishings, failing to convince her.

'There is no trace of William there, I promise you,' Elizabeth had said, as together they sorted the laundry, standing far apart to pull the sheets taut and straight before folding them over and over until, meeting in the middle, Elizabeth surrendered her end to Kate.

She had pressed the sheet against her chest, much as she had done with her fist when she pleaded with King

James not to insist she went back to Broomelaw. 'I will sense him on every step of the stair, imagine him lurking around every corner, and much as I appreciate James' ruling and indeed hope one day Robbie will bide there, for me it will be forever tainted.'

'Someday,' Elizabeth said, 'when Robbie is there, and with a family to his credit, you will feel differently. A house is the people in it, not the stones, and the reality will drive away the ghosts. Especially...' she'd cocked her ear at a sudden wail from the chamber overhead, 'when there are a ween of bairns running about. No self-respecting ghost would suffer more than five minutes of that.'

Although Kate laughed at the image Elizabeth conjured, it hadn't changed what she felt. 'Whatever has been done or not done, it won't be the same and I would aye be harking back. It's easier and better I put it out of my mind altogether and focus on making here our home.' She wasn't sure Elizabeth agreed with her, but she'd picked up the next sheet without comment and they'd returned to the folding, and in the time that remained before the visitors returned to Scotland, Broomelaw hadn't been mentioned again.

Now that Kate was ensconced in the Louvre, with its formal gardens and fountains, manicured lawns and avenues of trees standing tall and straight, like a regiment of soldiers on parade, there was little to remind her of the unruly hillside in Renfrewshire, rampant with gorse and bramble and pines that grew at an angle, canted by the prevailing winds. For which she was thankful. And though it was much the best not to look back, she sometimes found herself wondering what her mother would say could she see her now: Lady Katharine Munro, her husband a favourite of the French King, herself surprisingly close to his mistress, despite her strong feelings on the morals of the situation, which, though unvoiced to any but Adam, continued to trouble her.

The sky darkened, as if a shutter had been closed over the sun, and there was a rumble of thunder followed by a rattle of hail against the window. She could hear Ellie, her voice high and fluting, rising above the rest, and though Kate couldn't make out the words, it was clear she was shepherding the other children indoors. It still made her smile to hear the more formal cadences of court French, with which Ellie had, in a matter of weeks, replaced the patois of Picardie. She sounded as if she had been at court all her life, and Adam had been right, in this as in so many things: she'd made friends quickly, and equally quickly had become the leader of the pack. In particular, César de Bourbon followed her around like a faithful dog, which also amused Kate, though Adam was less happy.

'He is the King's son, and his betrothal to Mercoeur's daughter an important facet of the peace. I do not wish our daughter to be the means of rocking that boat.'

She'd hidden her amusement. 'They are but children. Let them play. He's four and Ellie nine. Any attachment he has is but the normal reaction of a young child towards an older one who offers him attention, that's all. Time enough when he is grown for him to be sacrificed to the needs of France.'

'As long as Ellie is not sacrificed also.'

She'd come to stand behind him, her hands resting on his shoulders, her thumbs massaging the back of his neck, drawing the tension out of him. 'Don't look for trouble where there is none, the attachments children form rarely last into adulthood.'

'Ours did.'

'You were not the King's son, nor we at court. And besides,' she'd tugged at his hair, 'when she is sixteen and full-grown, he will only be eleven and still a child in her eyes. And even if they were closer in age, I would see to it Ellie had more sense than to look to a King's son, bastard or not.'

She was jolted out of her reverie by running footsteps in the corridor, and with a quick glance at the cradle, she hoped the coming disturbance wouldn't wake Patrick John. The door burst open, a clutch of children spilling in, talking over each other, shaking the melting hail from their clothes.

César ran to her, burying his face in her lap, and though his voice was muffled, his fear was apparent. 'Did you hear him? The giant?'

She stroked his head. 'It was but thunder and nothing to be afraid of.'

His head came up and he stepped back. 'I am not afraid.'

'Of course not.' She bit her cheeks to avoid smiling at his hauteur. 'You are a brave boy, and had it been a giant, which it was not,' she added hastily, when she saw the renewed wobble of his lip, 'you would have protected all the other children.' There was a knock at the door. She set aside the now damp embroidery and stood up.

The young girl framed in the doorway was out of breath and flustered. 'My lady, I...'

133

'It's all right.' She shooed all but Ellie towards the door. 'They would outrun anyone. But they will need a change of clothes before le déjeuner, for we would not wish any to catch a chill.' She rested her hand on César's head. 'Especially this young man.' Behind her, Patrick John began to cry. 'And I have a babe to see to.'

Chapter 15

The hailstorm that drove the children indoors stopped as quickly as it had started, but not before it caught Robbie and the Garde with him as they made their way back to their quarters, the long-standing problem that had driven them into the heart of Paris' commercial quarter unresolved. They halted in the shelter of an overhang, to allow the worst of the storm to pass.

Angus Muir pulled his cloak across his chest in a vain effort to defeat the wind funnelling down the alleyway. 'Can't you speak to your father?'

'No!' Robbie was adamant. 'We, or rather you, got us into this mess and we shall have to get ourselves out of it.'

'But when Monsieur Droit was cheating us all, your father helped. Why not in this also?'

'In this you were not cheated. It was your folly to get in so deep, mine to agree to go guarantor on your behalf. A folly I should have confessed to when Father dealt with Monsieur Droit. His forbearance then might have sufficed for all.' He struck his fist against the wall. 'He asked if there was anything else he should know and I told him no, for it wasn't my debt to confess, and I never expected to be called on to honour it.'

'I never intended you would be either, but with our

pay so in arrears…'

'Oh, I don't blame *you*, Angus, or not entirely. But if I were to speak to Father now he would think only of the earlier deceit. I'd prefer he knew nothing of this.'

'What other option is there?' Angus turned his back towards the wind. 'I have no one I can tap, and if the bill is sold on, who knows where it might land up and at what interest.'

Robbie was sliding his boot back and forwards through a pile of hailstones driven into a corner of the wall, churning them to slush. He lifted his head, a decision made. 'The debts will not melt. You have only one option, and may pray he is less grasping, or at least that he gives you more time.'

'Del Sega?'

'Who else?'

'Six months' pay may not be enough to meet his terms, if I am to eat in the meantime.' Angus was grim.

Robbie bared his teeth in a rictus of a smile. 'Eating will be the least of our problems if we cannot settle this bill and speedily. Del Sega makes plenty from the Gardes and we may pray he will not wish to lose the trade by exorbitant demands.'

Angus tried twice more to convince Robbie to appeal to his father but Robbie was adamant in his refusal. So it was that two days later they found themselves on the threshold of Del Sega's rooms.

'This is a pretty pickle, is it not?' Del Sega did not rise from his chair when the servant ushered in the two Gardes, nor did he offer them a seat. He poured himself a glass of Madeira and rocked back in his chair, swirling the wine round and round in the glass.

Angus licked his lips. 'I will repay you.'

'I don't doubt it. The question is when. And on what terms.' Del Sega scratched with his quill on a scrap of parchment, the figures dancing in front of Robbie's eyes. After another silence he looked up, his voice deceptively mild. 'Did you have a time in mind?'

'I am due arrears in pay and could assign them to you.'

Del Sega raised one eyebrow. 'And you will have them when?'

Robbie shifted as if to speak, but Angus gave him no chance. 'They are promised within the two-month.'

'Indeed. I trust they are substantial. As substantial as your debt.' He dipped his quill in the inkpot. 'One hundred écus.' A pause. 'Each.'

'It is not my debt...' Robbie began.

'This is your name, is it not?' Del Sega's voice was controlled, deceptively pleasant.

'Yes, but...'

'You have guaranteed the debt, and therefore share the liability. I cannot take the bill on any other terms.'

It was outrageous, but Robbie, recognising the futility of any further protest, reached out his hand for the quill.

The paper signed, Del Sega rose and fetched two more glasses. 'You will take a drink with me?' It was less a question than a demonstration of authority, which they chose to obey.

They walked in silence through streets churned into mud by the melting hail, each of them buried in their own thoughts. As they turned into the archway leading to their quarters, Angus said, 'I'm sorry. If there had been any other way…'

'Like what? Bluster it out? Use the force of the Gardes to buy us time?'

'Perhaps we should have tried.'

'And risk losing our position altogether? I think not. It is a deep enough hole without making it deeper.'

'A speedy end might be better than slow starvation.'

'We will not starve.'

'You will not starve. You have family who will no doubt welcome you to their table as often as you like. Whereas I…'

'Robbie.' The voice behind them was cheerful. 'Caught in the storm, I see. It was a mite heavy.'

They turned together, straightened and stood to attention. Munro waved aside the formality. 'Where were you? I've been looking all over and no one seemed to know your whereabouts. Good job it wasn't the evening, or I might have thought you away racking up more gambling debts.'

Robbie laughed, he hoped convincingly. 'We were away looking at some horseflesh.'

'There is a problem with your horse? I can help you out if you have a need for more cash than you have to hand the now. Until the current arrears are through.'

'Not me, sir.' Robbie gestured at his companion. 'And not a necessity, but it sounded as if it would be worth a look.'

'And was it?' Munro looked at the other Garde. 'If you do not take it, perhaps I might consider it, for my mount has grown sluggish of late.'

Robbie improvised. 'Poor lungs,' he said. 'A wheeze on him that would do justice to a dying man, so not worth a sou, never mind the price that was sought. Certainly not worth getting a foundering for.' He dipped his head and shook it, scattering drops of water around his feet. 'Why did you need me?'

'Your mother had a notion of seeing you, before she'd forgotten altogether what you looked like.' There was a note of reproof in Munro's voice. 'So I contracted to bring you for supper.' He nodded at Robbie's companion. 'You're welcome to join us, if you wish, though with Ellie and Maggie and the babe it isn't always the most peaceful of meals.'

Robbie hoped very much he would *not* wish, for with two of them there was twice the risk something would slip out, and was therefore relieved when the offer was gracefully refused.

'Another time then.' Munro bowed and putting his arm around Robbie's shoulder led him away. 'For your mother it is the silver lining of leaving Scotland and now of coming to court, that we might all be together more often, and I am minded to make it so.'

'She would not wish to be back at Braidstane?'

'No...' He hesitated. It had been Kate's choice that Robbie had been spared the full details of the horrors of that August morning at Saltcoats, the execution attempt that had so nearly succeeded. 'Suffice it,' she had said,

139

'that he knows William Cunninghame brought charges against me, and that it was by the joint efforts of the King and John Cunninghame that my innocence was established. One day he may bide at Broomelaw, and if there is to be any chance he may do so in peace, the less he knows of what happened the better. Besides,' she had gripped his hand so tight it belied her valiant attempt at humour, 'I did not look my best, and as he was not there to see it, I'd prefer no one painted the picture for him.'

The fourteen months since had not dimmed the memory Munro carried always: of Kate, stretched out on the ground, dead as they thought, John bending over her, alternately thumping on her chest and dipping his head to touch his cheek against her mouth and nose to check for any sign of a breath. On her other side, Maggie, kneeling, ashen-faced, shaking uncontrollably. It was an image he had no wish to share, but perhaps Robbie deserved to know the truth. He opened his mouth, but Robbie beat him to it, jolting him back to the present.

'And William Cunninghame? Will he have forgotten us? Or forgiven the loss of Broomelaw?'

His answer was indirect. 'If the Earl of Glencairn has any sense, William will not be allowed to remember. Nor to harbour a grudge. They need James' patronage, and Glencairn will not wish anything to threaten that.'

Chapter 16

It was a view echoed at Kilmaurs, though in a more acrimonious atmosphere. Glencairn thumped his hand on the table, making the dishes jump. 'How many times must I say we must make the best of it we can. And if that means burying this obsession with Broomelaw, William, then bury it you must.'

'It is the Munros that should have been buried, every one.' William's reply was muttered into his drink, but clear enough for Glencairn's face to darken further.

'They are alive and nothing we can do will change that. Nor, if you have any sense, should you even think other.'

'There was a time when you would not have been so mealy-mouthed. Have you forgotten the loss we sustained?'

'I have forgotten nothing. Neither the loss I sustained in the repairing of Broomelaw,' the emphasis was clear, 'nor the ransom James required for your good behaviour. It was for our family's reputation only I paid up so promptly. Had we not been like to be the laughing stock of the county I would have left you to cool your heels a while longer at Ardrossan as a guest of the Montgomeries.' He thumped the table again. 'And perhaps I should have done. It might have taught you some humility. Your mother thought you changed for the better when you took on Broomelaw, but it seems it was but a cheap veneer, splitting at the first sign of heat. It is more than a year now and still you go about with a face as sour as curdled milk, and a temper to match.'

William turned his back, made for the door.

Glencairn roared at him. 'Do not turn your back on me, William. Try me too far and you may regret the consequences. You are not my only son.' It was an unfortunate choice of words, echoing as they did Munro's taunt on the shore by Rough, when he'd had the temerity to challenge William as if he were his equal, the trouble caused then the root of all the ills since.

William turned, took a step towards Glencairn, to enumerate Munro's faults, but the set expression on his father's face gave him pause.

Glencairn continued as if William had made no move at all. 'And while I'm handing out home truths, there is word going about that Hamilton has been reinstated at court, no doubt as a result of convincing James he recognises the error of his ways in that business with Mistress Munro. It might behove you to emulate him. A little toadying with James aye goes a long way.'

'Not far enough to bring back Broomelaw.' William's fists were clenched. 'John Montgomerie sits pretty there, and as for Munro, word is he is among the French King's personal bodyguard now, courtesy of James' generosity with his titles.'

'Forget Broomelaw, forget Munro. We have our own position to maintain. The old Queen cannot last forever, and when James succeeds her I intend for some of the rich pickings at the English court to fall into my lap. If

142

anything you do threatens that…' He swept out of the room, leaving the sentence hanging, the implication clear.

William growled at his retreating back. 'What can I do, stuck here?' It was a continuing grievance, for which he held his father responsible; he hadn't yet been given permission to stray beyond the bounds of the Cunninghame lands. Had Glencairn done a little toadying to James himself, no doubt the restriction would have been lifted long since. He mimicked Glencairn, '*Hamilton is reinstated, you should emulate him.*'

'Emulate who?' Lady Glencairn hesitated in the doorway.

'Hamilton. It seems he has re…' William corrected himself, 'is high in James' favour and set fair to get land in Ireland when the time comes. While I…'

Lady Glencairn sighed. 'Can you not *try* to be content? One day you will be earl. Is that not enough for you?'

He countered her question with one of his own. 'Do you not regret the loss of Broomelaw, the effort that was wasted?'

'The Munros' loss was greater. Six years in hiding and for what?' She was picking at a skelf on the window ledge. 'I never understood it. Why when they were attacked by reivers they did not turn to us for support.'

'They had come to favour the Montgomeries, and that a disloyalty hard to understand, or excuse.' He ground out a spark that arced from the fire onto the hearth at his feet. 'They forfeited all rights when they allowed themselves to be thought dead. We repaired the tower in good faith. Why should we have been forced to hand it back?'

'It was not ours to keep, William. Surely, you must see

143

that? I do not know the circumstances that caused them to assume a false identity, nor how your uncle found them out and sought the King's intervention on their behalf. Nor do I want to, for I suspect I was spared the details as a kindness. But this I do know...' she turned to face him, her chin lifting, 'once it was known they were alive, we could not in justice have retained Broomelaw ... And perhaps it was justice that we bore the expense of the repair.'

William shifted, thought: she does know, or at least suspects something. He prepared to bluster, but she continued.

'A small recompense for our failure at the time of the reivers' attack. Had we done our duty by them then, they might have not had to suffer as they did.'

'We didn't know what had happened. How could we?'

'We didn't ask, and that makes us at least part responsible.'

Glencairn was framed in the doorway. 'You are not still talking of Broomelaw?'

'Mother is.' William pretended a concern for her. 'There is no need to be troubled for people you've never met, nor to distress yourself by thinking on them.'

Lady Glencairn refused to be deflected. 'I cannot help but think on them. And wonder why they did not return home when the opportunity arose. I would have liked it fine that they could be back in their own place.'

Glencairn's voice was smooth. 'It is hardly surprising Mistress Munro wished to accompany her husband to France.' And then, as if to pre-empt another, more difficult, question. 'Nor that James would choose to ennoble them as a result of her service to the Queen. We should be glad for them, should we not?'

'Of course, but…' Lady Glencairn's brow was knotted. 'That is another thing hard to understand, if, as you say, Mistress Munro's service was of such value, why James would allow them to leave Scotland before the Queen was brought to bed.'

Glencairn waved his hand as if to signify the answer was obvious. 'Her Grace was in good health, and having passed the most critical stage, there was no reason to detain Mistress Munro, especially as John Montgomerie, Braidstane's physician brother, undertook to see her to full term. I imagine it was that favour that encouraged the Munros to make Broomelaw available to him. A temporary arrangement, I believe, until their son is of age, or they choose to return themselves, whichever is the sooner.' He turned to William, his eyes narrowed, as if he dared him to say anything. 'And however much you may regret the Montgomerie's continued rise, the King's wish is law and we do well to respect it.'

A clatter of hooves and the jingle of harness in the courtyard brought the conversation to an abrupt halt. Glencairn moved to the window and peered out. 'Maxwell of Newark! What's he doing here?' He half turned. 'I'll see to him, dissuade him from staying long.'

Lady Glencairn, her forehead puckered, said, 'Patrick Maxwell? That is a surprise. These past months he has become a stranger to us. I shall call for refreshments, for we must not be inhospitable.' She moved towards the door, but Glencairn halted her.

'He is not welcome here and I do not wish for you

145

to pretend he is. The cooler his reception, the sooner he will leave.'

'Why?' She looked at William. 'You were thick once. I did wonder if there had been a falling out, but bad blood between cousins does no one any favours. If he has come now with an olive branch, would it not be good to accept it?' When neither he nor Glencairn responded, she pressed. 'What did Maxwell do? What have I not been told?' Her gaze switched from William to Glencairn, and back again, her mouth tight. 'Were the Munros' troubles his doing?' She reached out for the table as if for support. 'Did you have part in it?'

The earl was dismissive. 'It was nothing that need concern you. A court matter only. But suffice to say I would prefer him to keep his distance. The connection is not a useful one.' The lie was fluent. 'Indeed, it was to avoid the contact that William has remained here or hereabouts of late. So that when he returns to court it will be plain to Maxwell, and to anyone else, their acquaintance is at an end.' There was the sound of voices at the foot of the stairwell. Glencairn moved to the door. 'Stay here. It seems avoidance has been insufficient. This time I shall make sure he gets the message.'

Chapter 17

The moon was riding high, the stars standing out like pinpricks in the clear October sky. Kate and Adam leant side by side on the balustrade of the terrace overlooking the knot garden. In his hand was an invitation from the Duchesse de Beaufort, requesting the presence of the family to a supper evening. The air was crisp and cold, frost sparkling on the flags beneath their feet. Kate puffed out, watching her breath curl away from them and disappear into the darkness. 'Adam...'

'Mmm?'

She gestured up at the stars. 'Do you remember the last time we stargazed? With Archie ... and Sybilla...'

He placed an arm around her shoulder. 'Perhaps it's best not to remember. We have a different life now.'

'I know, but ... it worries me that we are different too.'

'How can we not be? So much around us has changed, we cannot expect to have stayed the same.'

'Outside, perhaps. But inside, can we not at bottom be the people we always were?'

He turned her to face him, smoothing out the pucker on her forehead with his thumb. Smiled his lopsided smile. 'Lady or no, to me you will always be Kate. And tricky as ever.'

She wriggled free. 'I'm serious, Adam. This is serious.'

He placed both hands on her shoulders. 'Tell me then.'

She took a deep breath, tapped the card in his hand. 'Do we really belong here?'

'We are here at the King's command. Belong or not, we cannot alter that. And besides, my livelihood is here.'

'Could you not have been happy with a seigneurie in Picardie?'

'It's not so simple.'

'Why not? It was what you first thought when you told me of the farm.'

He was looking past her to the outline of the palace behind them, candles flickering in a myriad of windows. 'All those years I was in the Gardes and you were in Scotland and I had no idea whether you lived or died … all I wanted was to have you with me and safe, and if we couldn't be at Broomelaw, then the farmhouse in Cayeux seemed the next best thing. If I could have come home then, brought you back then, perhaps I could have settled for that.'

'What changed?'

'I changed. For three years I was a soldier in the service of the French King, with the normal loyalty that required. But when Patrick died, I saw in Henri something more than a monarch, and though I am not altogether comfortable in my new role, the loyalty I feel for him now is different, more personal. I cannot walk away.' He swallowed. 'But if you … I could speak to Henri. Ask that you be excused if it is what you want.'

'No. I'm sorry, I didn't intend…' She stretched up and cupped his face in her hands. 'Perhaps it is the moonlight made me maudlin. We are here and together and that is what matters most, only…'

'Only?'

'Only at Broomelaw, black was black and white was white, and to hold to truth and to morality seemed a simple thing. Here … I tell the children one thing and they see another and I don't know how to handle it.'

'Gabrielle d'Estrées?'

'Yes. As a person I like her, admire some of her qualities: her devotion to her children, her kindness, her lack of pride. But I wish to be a good Christian, and as such how can I condone the life she, they, lead. Henri has a wife. Should he not have tried to make his marriage work?'

'As I said before, it was a marriage neither wished and doomed from the start. What Henri wants more than anything is to make Gabrielle truly his wife, as she has been in all but name for long enough.'

'If it were just that she was Henri's mistress, perhaps I could find a way to explain it, as a common-law wife maybe, but it is the dalliances neither he nor she seem to consider of importance. Maggie I can no longer protect from such knowledge, but what if Ellie were to quiz me? She is too young to be faced with such issues.'

'Children are pragmatic. They accept what they see, and what she sees is Henri and Gabrielle as happy in their family as we are in ours. Of the rest she knows nothing. Best to leave her in her innocence for as long as you can. Why should she carry a burden of conscience because of the behaviour of others.' He tilted Kate's chin upwards, forced her to meet his eyes. 'Why should you?'

She tapped the card again. 'We will go then?'

'How can we not? Aside from any other considerations, Robbie and Maggie both may benefit from the Duchesse's interest.'

'I know, but that doesn't altogether sit easy with me either. I was not brought up to patronage, nor to the pursuit of it. Sometimes I wish...'

'Don't.' It was his turn to breathe deeply. 'Remember what you said at St Valery? *We must make the best of what we have.* It is as good a rule to live by as any. He hesitated as if reluctant to raise the shadows of the past, then continued, 'Broomelaw was not without difficulties, nor Braidstane, and even the farm was not the secure haven you hoped for. At least here our lives are not threatened.'

'And our souls?'

She had no idea where the verse came from, for it was not his normal practice to quote Scripture, but it gave her solace nonetheless when he said, *'It isn't what goes into a man that defiles. Only what comes out.'* And, perhaps fearing it wasn't enough, added, 'We stand and fall on our own merits, Kate, not those of others.'

Chapter 18

The salon was ablaze, a hundred candles flickering in sconces around the walls and in the chandeliers hanging at regular intervals down the centre of the room, the gold threads in the braided rope supporting them casting flashes of light across the ceiling. Gabrielle d'Estrées was seated at the far end, her head bent towards César who stood on tiptoe whispering something into her ear. She looked up as the Munros were announced, and waved them forward. As she swept a curtsey, Kate focused on the brilliance of the sapphire on the third finger of the Duchesse's right hand – there was news then, to warrant such a confident display.

'Sir Adam. Lady Munro.' Gabrielle tapped Adam's arm with her fan and nodded towards the window embrasure. 'The King wishes to have words with you.' Her eyes were alight as she turned to Kate and motioned her to sit down. Ellie had been dragged away by César, but Maggie and Robbie were standing at Kate's shoulder. She glanced up at them, indicating they should move back.

Gabrielle directed Robbie's attention to a small man with a disproportionately large head who was standing by the fireplace. 'Perhaps you would like to introduce your sister to Monsieur Daumont. He may not look much, but his intellect is impressive and, as his interests lie in the medical sphere, I'm sure she would relish the opportunity of a conversation. You may tell him I sent you.' He was looking across at them and the Duchesse tilted her head, receiving a bow in return. 'Go on,' she said. 'You will not be bored, I promise you, though once started on a topic close to his heart you may struggle to get a word in edgeways.' She settled more comfortably on the chaise longue, turned to Kate on the seat beside her, patted her stomach. 'I am to be blessed again, in the spring. Children are a blessing, are they not?'

Kate looked at César, who was dragging Ellie round and round the room, pausing each time they passed the table laden with pastries to pop one in his mouth, and found it impossible not to smile. He was dressed in blue satin, the lace on his collar and cuffs miniature replicas of his father's. An attractive child, with a mop of curls and wide eyes that seemed most suited to laughter, he would likely grow up to be a heartbreaker, regardless of his station. She felt a pang. As the King's son his future in that regard was already set, a dynastic arrangement for the good of France, with all that remained to be decided whether he and his younger brother could be formally legitimised or would carry the burden of bastardy all their lives. Though it was scarcely a burden in these circles, whatever it might have been in Renfrewshire. Dragging her thoughts back to the present and to the Duchesse, she said, 'Indeed they are, and to be cherished and enjoyed, for they will not...' she gestured at César and Ellie, 'stay children for long.'

Henri was marching Munro up and down, one arm about his shoulder, and Kate suspected by the broad smile on the King's face and the glance he shot at Gabrielle that he was sharing the same news.

Gabrielle arched her back and shifted on the chair, a momentary flicker of discomfort in her face. 'When my time comes, I trust I shall have you to aid me. I believe I can depend on you to do your best, for me and my child. It will be a service, not just for me, but for the King, and if things play out as we hope, for the whole of France.'

It was a statement, not a question, but one Kate felt deserved an answer. She had never yet refused a request for help, from wherever it came. The memory of the summons to minister to Queen Anne, and the trouble that had ensued, flashed through her mind, and she felt a flicker of relief – at least she need have no fear in that respect here. 'You have my word.'

There was a burst of laughter from the group of young men now clustered around M Daumont. Kate looked across in time to see Maggie toss her head, the colour blooming on her cheeks an indication that, whatever had been said, she was the butt of the merriment. She was drawing herself up as if to retort, Robbie placing his hand on her shoulder, his concern for her pleasing.

Gabrielle's amusement was obvious. 'She can look after herself, that one. I do not think she needs her brother's protection. As for those young men who think themselves so superior,' she made a dismissive gesture, 'I suspect they will find it was not the wisest of moves to make your daughter an object of mirth.'

There was one of those moments of silence that falls on a room, broken by M Daumont as he addressed the tallest of the young men surrounding him. '...on the contrary, Anton, I will be more than happy to have this demoiselle in my class, for she already exhibits a greater understanding of the study of anatomy than all the rest of you put together. As well as the humility to know there is much more to learn, and a willingness to be taught. An ideal pupil in fact.' He bowed to Maggie. 'I begin my classes at nine o'clock, sharp. If you can be there on the morrow, you will be welcome.'

This time the flush that spread across Maggie's face was one of pleasure as she sank in a curtsey, her dip of her head in acceptance of the invitation, suitably grateful. 'M'sieur.'

'You see?' The Duchesse was laughing. 'I did not send her to speak to Monsieur Daumont on a whim. I knew he would be impressed and would offer her a place. And don't worry about the other students. Give her a week and they will all be eating out of her hand. Or if they are not, they are even more foolish than they look.'

Her attention switched to Robbie. 'Your son shows a pleasing concern for his sister. I must think of what can be done for him also.'

'His father...' Kate began.

'Cannot be seen to favour him. Indeed, he will likely suffer under a more rigid regime than the rest of his fellows in the Gardes. Therefore an opportunity to rise must come from elsewhere.'

'You are too kind. Especially...'

'Do not think I am unaware that we disagree on some essentials, but we share a love of our children, do we not?' Gabrielle looked across to where the King and Munro had paused to catch Ellie and César before they caused any damage as they darted in and out of the furniture in some game of their own devising, little Catherine toddling along in their wake. 'As, I think, do our menfolk.'

Henri was lifting Catherine high in the air, the child squealing with delight, while Munro had one arm around Ellie's shoulder, smiling down at her, the other around César.

A sombre note crept into Gabrielle's voice. 'In other circumstances we four could have been fast friends. Why not here, now?'

Part Two

February – June 1599

Oh how this spring of love resembleth
The uncertain glory of an April Day
Which now shows all the beauty of the sun
And by and by a cloud takes all away.

Two Gentlemen of Verona Act 1 Scene 3

Chapter 1

'Whatever possessed you, Hugh?'

'A little sympathy wouldn't go amiss.' Hugh Montgomerie winced as John finished the binding of his ankle and rose to his feet, casting a glance towards the window, which stood open despite the season and through which the hubbub of Edinburgh's Canongate provided a constant background noise.

'For a sprain?' John's exasperation was clear. 'In other circumstances perhaps, but you may count yourself lucky that's all you have. Breaking the embargo on carrying arms on the High Street could have got you killed, or spending the next month cooling your heels in the Tolbooth. Not to mention what Elizabeth will say should she get to hear of it.'

'Never mind Elizabeth,' Alexander Montgomerie halted in his pacing up and down, 'if James should find out, then we all may suffer for it.' He glared at Hugh. 'And while you might warrant any penalty you receive, you have family who do not deserve to be brought down because of your lack of control.'

'I had reason…' Hugh began.

'Oh, no doubt.' Alexander made no attempt to conceal his irritation. 'You always have reason. How many times am I going to have to get you out of trouble? I begin to wish I hadn't favoured your cause with the King, for it seems you can do little other than lurch from crisis to crisis. It is barely eighteen months since the debauchle with the Cunninghames at Irvine, and while that wasn't your fault, it brought us all to the attention of the King, and he is apt to remember the attention and forget the cause.' He paused to draw breath, and John cut in.

'Where were you going anyway when you were apprehended?'

'To the McMorran's.'

'And that required you to carry a firearm in broad daylight?'

'Not that, no.'

'What possible excuse can you have?'

'Word was Hamilton has taken lodgings in the same tenement, and if I were to meet him...'

'You would nod civilly and pass on without conversation...' Alexander was caustic. 'If you had any wit, which I begin to doubt.'

'And if he would not pass *me* by?'

'You are in control of your own temper, not his. And besides, he is so newly restored to James' favour I do not think he would risk threatening that.'

'You know he has designs on Ireland, as I have. The rumour is we might be in competition.'

'Rumour is aye based on the flimsiest of evidence, and rarely accurate. Ireland is a sizeable territory and no doubt has plenty of space for you both. Besides, it is much more likely it will be to Dublin he looks, for it is there his other interests lie, while you look to the north.'

'How *did* you sprain your ankle?' John, having dealt

with the injury, was now professionally interested in its cause.

'It was an unfortunate error. I heard a commotion behind me and drew my pistol, thinking I was in danger, only to find it was a scuffle between traders. It was ill-luck two of the watch chose that moment to appear.'

'Consider it rather providence it was the watch and not the King's men.' Alexander had calmed down somewhat, but he wasn't ready to let Hugh off the hook just yet. 'You cannot depend on luck, Hugh, if you are to make anything of being here. It is sound judgement and discretion that is required around the King and a considerable dose of respect – if not for the man, at least for the title.' He subsided onto a chair. 'Have you heard from George?'

'We had a letter a week or two ago.'

'What is the word from England? The old Queen surely cannot last much longer?'

'That's what we all thought last year, and the one before that.' Hugh's grin for John was wicked. 'They say she suffers many ailments that none can alleviate. Now, if you were there, you could perhaps help her along … a little. It would be a kindness and a blessing for all concerned.'

'Don't joke, Hugh.' Alexander stood up again and moved to the window, checked it was secure. 'We are not in the privacy of Braidstane here. Such jesting is dangerous, should there be any listening ears.'

'We are not in London, either, and I daresay James himself might have such thoughts.'

'Whether he does or not, he would not be so foolish

as to share them, and in this, at least, you would do well to follow his example, for to treat the life of one monarch lightly is to threaten the whole fabric of the institution, and by implication James' position also.'

'What is the situation in London?' John asked. 'Is the court still there? I heard rumours of an epidemic of the sleeping sickness.'

'The court remains, for the time being at least, though George did mention some sickness, but it is confined to the poorer folk and therefore not thought to be a danger to those of higher rank.'

'Epidemics,' said John, 'tend not to ask of rank before they strike. If the sleeping sickness is rampant, no one is truly immune.'

Alexander's interest was piqued. 'But are some illnesses not more prevalent in the lower classes?'

'Of course, and some may be avoided altogether if diet and living conditions are good. The bent leg, for example, is rarely seen among the nobility, but afflicts many of those less fortunate. The cause is not yet clear, though suspicions have been voiced, and until we know for sure we cannot hope to address the issue. But infection, that is a different matter, and no respecter of persons – it can sweep through a community in days and decimate it.'

'And the sleeping sickness? What do you know of it?'

'Very little, other than when it strikes few survive, and the end comes quickly. There has been a suggestion it comes from the continent, but as to the truth of it I cannot say.'

Hugh was becoming restive. 'Can we think on

something more pleasant? Food, for example.' He swung his leg off the chair, but before he could set his foot to the ground, John stopped him.

'You need to stay put, for a day or two at the very least, to allow that ankle of yours time to recover.' He winked at Alexander. 'Perhaps we should be glad of it, for it will give us some respite from worry.'

'If we can be sure the watch had no idea of his identity and that they will not come knocking on our door with a warrant.'

'Rest easy, Alexander. They have no idea who I am and even less of where I hail from. When they challenged me I put on an accent so thick I'm certain they would swear to it I was from the far north. Indeed, that is the excuse I gave for not knowing of the new regulations.' He wobbled his foot. 'And if they had been less officious and minded to let me go on my way without attempting to confiscate the weapon, I wouldn't have had to leg it.' His pistol was lying on the table. 'I am not so well off I can stand the loss of a weapon, especially one that has served me well in the past.' He rubbed absent-mindedly at his shin, which was beginning to discolour. 'And if there had not been an idiot who pushed a cart into the thoroughfare without so much as a glance to see if anyone was coming, I would not have had to leap out of the way, twisting my ankle in the process.'

'If,' Alexander said, without a trace of the sympathy Hugh clearly desired, 'you had kept to the rules the King has laid down and hadn't carried a pistol in the first place, you wouldn't have been tempted to draw it, and none of this would have happened. Now, I'm off out for supper.'

He turned to John, the corner of his mouth lifting. 'Coming?'

Hugh made to get up again, and John, laughing openly, said, 'Have some sense, Hugh. We won't let you starve. But you might have to wait a while.' A wicked grin of his own. 'If it teaches you patience, I'm sure Elizabeth, for one, will not object.'

They stood in a queue at the pastry shop, their breath curling away from them as the lad who served counted out change for the goodwife at the front, one bawbee at a time. John's sigh was audible, his sideways comment to Alexander equally so. 'Some folk have ill-luck in their apprentices. An ability to count at more than a snail's pace wouldn't go amiss.'

'Trust me, the pies here are the best in Edinburgh and worth waiting for. We could get speedier service elsewhere, but I wouldn't recommend it.'

'And would you recommend leaving Hugh to his own devices for long?'

'He'll not be going anywhere fast for a day or two. Worry instead about whether James will call for him before he's ready to be up and about. And his injury needing to be accounted for.'

They shuffled forward, John picking up the threads of their earlier conversation. 'Is there any danger Hamilton will threaten Hugh's ambitions in Ulster?'

Alexander shrugged. 'I've no idea. Though I would expect him to look first for advancement in Dublin or thereabouts, for he has excuse enough with the college, but the English settlement there is well established, and whether newcomers would be welcome, or indeed if there is room for them at all, is debatable.'

'Did the Queen not try to plant the northern counties also?'

'She did, but with less success. Whether it was to do with the calibre of those she sent or the stubbornness of the native population, I'm not sure. There are pockets of English settlers, but they are scattered, and swathes of the country lie empty, of English and Irish alike, for where the Irish could not defend, it's said they burned all behind them as they fled.'

'Is it garrisoned?'

'I believe so, at Carrick, on the Antrim shore. But how strong a force it carries, or how reliable the troops are, is another matter. Outposts like this are apt to be rather lax on discipline and the soldiers often with little interest other than in the female half of the population. But there has been no serious trouble there for a while, so I do not think anyone on this side of the water much cares.'

'There will be pickings then, when the old Queen dies.'

'Yes. Which is why Hugh's lack of discipline is frustrating. There is a fine line to tread with James, and Hugh would do well not to stray from it. Little use ambition if it cannot be supported by sound sense.'

'Perhaps a day or two confined to quarters will help in that regard.'

'Something needs to.' Alexander paid for the pies,

his comment only partly in jest. 'Do you have many customers die of starvation while they wait?' The boy smiled and nodded as if it had been a compliment, so that John was still laughing as they turned onto the Canongate. A door to their left opened, spilling a group of courtiers onto the street in front of them, blocking their path. John stiffened. He had not crossed paths with Hamilton since the events at Saltcoats, but it seemed that despite the disgrace he suffered then, Hamilton had lost none of his swagger.

'Well, well. Who do we have here? The King's *preferred* physician? And his *Master* Poet?' Each of the references carried just enough emphasis to be insulting, and Alexander, even as he resisted the urge to respond in kind, felt a fleeting sympathy for Hugh, allied to a thankfulness for the minor injury that kept him indoors and out of trouble. Following his own advice, he bowed.

'Hamilton. And Fullerton.' He made to walk on, but Hamilton halted him.

'You will not refuse to take my hand? Or that of my good friend here? Courtesy costs little.'

Alexander bowed again, the touch of his fingers on the proffered hand judged to a nicety, with just enough contact to avoid the excuse for offence, while still managing to suggest a fear of contamination. His tone was bland, his smile fixed. 'We are in somewhat of a rush.' He held up the package. 'Pies, which we don't wish to become entirely cold before we reach our lodging.'

'For yourselves only? I heard Braidstane was with you.'

'So he is. And waiting for his supper. Another reason we won't detain you.'

'Ah.' Hamilton nodded, as if to indicate he had made a connection. 'He stays indoors to avoid the night air? Or is there another reason he fears to be abroad? It wouldn't by any chance have been him who had a run-in with the watch earlier? Gossip had it that it was someone from the north, but gossip can often be wrong.'

Alexander feigned mild interest. 'Someone had a run-in with the watch? News to me.' He glanced again at the package. 'A little gossip aye adds spice to food. I daresay these could be reheated. What was the bother about, do you know?'

'Carrying a firearm, I believe. And drawing it, to the fright of the good citizens of Edinburgh. Clearly someone of hot temper and little sense.'

Alexander laughed. 'Plenty of possibilities there then. The city is aye full of hotheads, with little between their ears but bones. Thank God for the watch, I say. I hope they make a good job of cleaning up the streets, for I favour James' ruling against the carrying of arms. It would be a fine thing if we could all go about our business, night or day, without having to keep a weather eye over our shoulder in case of trouble.' A bell began to toll the hour. He put his hand on John's shoulder. 'We really should get going. You supped late, but I did not and am a mite hungered now, and,' he gestured towards the sky, 'it will be dusk soon and not the best of times to be out.' He took a calculated risk. 'Besides, Braidstane, I believe, was busy at the palace most of the day, so unlikely to have had much opportunity for eating either.' He laughed again, including Hamilton and Fullerton in the joke. 'And as you'll maybe be aware, Hugh prizes his stomach and is aye keen to keep it happy.'

'Give our regards to Braidstane.' Hamilton's words were fine, if you disregarded the curl of his lip, which Alexander, increasing the pressure on John's arm, did, though John sensed he would dearly have liked to wipe the supercilious smile from Hamilton's face. His sympathy for Hugh resurfaced – he was dangerous. It would be as well to keep Hugh away from him even when his ankle was recovered, lest the obvious ill-will between them spill over into outright antagonism … or worse. Alexander bowed for a third time. 'Good day, Hamilton. Fullerton.'

Chapter 2

Dusk had turned to full dark as Robbie slipped through the gate from the Gardes' quarters and turned along the alleyway. He had waited for what seemed like hours after returning from a visit to his mother for the lights to be extinguished one by one, as the Gardes settled for the night. Silence filled the courtyard, broken only by the soft snorting of horses in the stables and the scufflings of the rodents who came out while the world slept, to steal what food they might.

It was six weeks since the interview with Del Sega, and though there was still two weeks to go before a settlement was due, Robbie had decided to seek out the moneylender on his own, to ask for an extension of the time, for the arrears of pay had not yet materialised, and he was fast losing confidence they would come in time. He had little doubt an extension would be possible, but dreaded the terms that might be exacted. The existing agreement was crippling enough, but Del Sega held all the cards, and whatever he demanded would have to be found. If he had not signed on Angus's behalf, if he had been more honest with his father when the opportunity arose, if ... He sighed. It had seemed so little risk. As indeed it would have been had the pay not been delayed. For Angus' original debt had begun small, the interest also, so that he had been lulled into a false confidence he would be able to meet it with ease. But as the interest increased, so the debt multiplied beyond belief. And hence the need to involve Del Sega. He would not make that mistake again. A crescent moon sailed from behind the clouds, driving him into the shadows. Those who walked the streets at night were seldom up to good, and he had no wish to attract attention, for should he fall foul of any such and the reputation of the Gardes be tarnished as a result, his father would not be best pleased. Nor to hear of his foolishness in standing over a debt that was not his when he had no money to cover it.

He was skirting a disused building, the windows planked, weeds growing through the cobbles surrounding it, when he heard the screech of an un-oiled hinge and saw a thin line of light slanting across the empty square – not entirely derelict then, but the use to which it was being put was clearly not something that could stand the scrutiny of daylight hours. Robbie pressed himself back against the rough stone, prayed for a cloud. It seemed his prayer was answered as the sky darkened, the moon all but extinguished, the shadows around him deepening. Or perhaps, he thought, it was not his prayers, but those of the four figures who slipped through the line of light and merged into the shadow of the wall no more than twenty feet from him. He edged away from them towards the corner, tensing to take flight should the need arise. His hand was outstretched, feeling for the outlines of stone, and as he inched his way, he lifted and placed his feet with care, lest he trip on the uneven cobbles and betray his presence. He reached the corner and expelled a silent breath of relief, just as a flicker of light, as if from a lantern uncloaked and as quickly covered again, flared a few feet to his left. He swung his head around in time to catch a glimpse of the figures, a bundle slung between them, striking out across the open space towards the alley he had come from – odd, if it *was* a body they carried, as seemed likely, why they would be heading for the outskirts of the city rather than the river, where a corpse could easily be disposed of, the pockets full of stones to ensure it didn't emerge to haunt anyone. None of his business, and he had his own problems to sort.

He was reversing his steps to resume his journey when a figure blundered into him. His instinctive reaction was to grasp the man by the throat and spin him round, pinning him against the wall, his other hand clamped over his mouth. He had a fraction of a second to register the slightness of figure, the smoothness of skin, before he felt the upward thrust of a knee in his groin and teeth sinking into his hand.

Ignoring the twin pains, he pressed his body against what he now realised was only a boy, a hand at his throat, and made his voice deliberately harsh. 'Stay still if you wish to live.' He could feel the flutter of a pulse under his fingers, its irregularity matched by a trembling in the boy's limbs. The breathing became ragged, the body sagging beneath him as if in a faint. Taken off guard, Robbie released his hold to grab the shoulders and slide the boy to the ground. With a wriggle and a twist the boy evaded his grip and took off. Cursing himself for falling for such a simple trick, Robbie leapt after him, all attempt at silence forgotten. His longer stride more than compensated for the boy's start, and he managed to catch him just as he turned to dodge into a concealed opening on the far side of the square. This time Robbie gave no quarter, diving for the boy's legs and flooring him, the crack as he went down as loud in the surrounding silence as a thunderclap. He pressed a knee on the boy's back – a pity to treat him so roughly, but if the other men who had preceded him were alerted, who knew what the outcome would be. He made his voice gruff, to lend conviction to the lie and to give himself time to work out what he would do with the boy. 'Make a sound and I *will* be forced to kill you.' The boy's yelp of pain was abruptly cut off, and mindful of his youth, Robbie said, 'But if you lie still until the coast is clear, I *may* allow you to live.'

He was holding his breath, his ear tuned to the slightest of sounds. From the alleyway ahead he heard a slithering as if of a boot skidding on excrement, followed by a thud and an exclamation, instantly stifled. There was a rustle of canvas and a series of grunts, and though he couldn't see anything, he guessed the men were redistributing the weight of their burden. He waited until he was sure they would be well clear of the alley, then lifted his knee and, standing up, pulled the boy to his feet. The moon sailed out from behind the clouds and Robbie saw from his face that, though he was lanky, he was indeed young, very young. The moment's pang he felt for the weight he had put on the child's back changed to a reluctant admiration as the boy sagged again. This time Robbie's grip was firm. He admired the spunk but had no intention of letting the boy escape before he ensured his silence. 'You'll not catch me out that way twice, so you needn't bother trying.' He kept his hands on the boy's shoulders. 'Stand up straight and let me look at you.'

The boy attempted to straighten, but when he placed his weight on his right foot, he crumpled again. Robbie saw the spasm of pain that flashed across his face, remembered the crack as he brought the boy down, and shifting his hands to the boy's armpits, supported his weight, his tone softening. 'Let's find you somewhere to sit and I'll look at that leg.'

'There's a horse trough, behind the chur—'

'Church?' Robbie asked. It was beginning to make sense. If it was indeed a church, its plain nature indicated it wasn't Catholic and therefore must be Huguenot, which explained both the boarding, and the secrecy with which the body was being moved. No doubt they were headed to carry out a burial by their own rites, a ceremony forbidden within five miles of the city. Not criminals then, at least not in his eyes, whatever the law said. With a second pang, he bent and scooped up the boy and recrossed the square. There was unlikely to be any danger here.

The boy gasped as Robbie set him down on the edge of the trough and bent to remove his boot. The leather was of good quality, the stitching fine. Robbie paid closer attention to the boy's clothes, which were, or had been, decent, though his jerkin now sported a tear across the neck and the waistband of his breeches was hanging by a thread. Another debt to be added to his score. He ran his hand over the boy's foot and ankle, probing gently with his thumbs as he had seen Kate do a hundred times. He rolled up the boy's breeches to continue his examination, pausing at the indrawn breath. Although the skin wasn't broken, he could feel a sharp edge of bone on the back of his leg. 'Where do you live, boy?'

The boy kept his mouth clamped shut.

'Your leg is broken. If you tell me where, I will take you home.'

He saw the boy's eyes slide to his uniform, recognised the root of his fear. Countered it. 'I am a Scots Garde, and Protestant, as I think you are. This night's secret is safe with me.'

The wariness remained in the boy's eyes and he stayed silent.

'You should not have been here?' Robbie queried.

A nod, and a strangled sound in his throat. 'Well, neither should I. But while I can get home by myself, you cannot. So I can either leave you here, to be found by the watch, should they do a round, or I can carry you home. Your choice, but I know what mine would be.' He paused. 'And I suspect your mother would agree with me.'

A single telltale tear tracked through the grime of the boy's face and he turned his head away, scrubbing at his cheek.

Robbie sat down on the trough beside him. 'It is your mother they take to burial?'

Again a nod, accompanied by a tremor.

'Who is at home then?'

It was no more than a whisper. 'My sisters, sir.'

'Well then, I'd best get you back to them. By now you may be missed, and you wouldn't wish to add that worry to their distress.' He bent to put one arm under the boy's legs, the other around his back, and as he did so the light from the moon fell across his hand, the teeth marks, where he had been bitten, still visible.

The boy looked down at them. 'My sister will be cross. I should not have bitten you.'

There was real regret in his voice and Robbie swallowed his amusement. 'I think perhaps I am the greater sinner, for I broke your leg.'

'But you did not mean it, while I…'

'Was defending yourself against an unknown assailant. I'm sure that will be excuse enough.'

The wariness disappeared from the boy's eyes, to be replaced by an impish light. 'It was a good escape.'

'It was indeed. One day you may tell your children you tricked an officer of the Scots Gardes.' He settled the boy against his shoulder, allowing the broken leg to dangle clear. 'Now, we need to get you home.'

The girl who opened the door to Robbie registered relief on her tear-streaked face. She reached out to take the boy from Robbie's arms, but he shook his head. 'Easy now, the leg is broken. Where's best to lay him down?'

She glanced at his uniform, hesitated, her lower lip caught between even, white teeth.

'I am a Scots Garde,' he said, 'and of your persuasion.' It was not strictly true, but near enough for the present circumstances.

Relief flickered across her face again and she stood

aside to allow him to enter. 'On the settle will be fine for now.'

'Do you have someone to look to his leg?'

'I can try, but I do not have expertise, and the man who could have helped…' she hesitated again, 'is away.'

'The burial party?'

She tensed, shot a frightened look at the boy. 'François?'

'He didn't tell. I saw for myself, but it's all right. No one will hear of it from me.'

She took a deep breath and, kneeling down, wiped the dirt from his cheeks. 'Don't worry, François, I'll sort your leg.'

'No,' said Robbie, 'best not. If you do not have the expertise, more harm might be done. My mother is skilled in such things.' He calculated. 'I can fetch her in less than an hour.'

'But it is the middle of the night. Will she mind?'

'She will not refuse a request.'

'Even for us?'

'Especially so, for she will recognise the difficulty in finding other help.' The boy's eyes were dark, the pupils enlarged, his cheeks the colour of skimmed milk. He shifted on the settle, his face twisting in pain. Robbie said, 'Have you brandy to hand?'

'Brandy, no. But we have willow and mandrake. Which might be of use.' For the first time since their arrival, she smiled, a dimple appearing in one cheek as, belatedly, she said, 'Thank you for bringing him home.'

He found himself hoping the boy would indeed sleep and thus have no time to talk of what had happened before he and Kate could return. Not that it mattered if he forfeited the girl's good opinion once all was known, for it was but a chance acquaintance, but if Kate could give the boy relief, his conscience could be salved. He bowed. 'I'll be as quick as I can.'

Chapter 3

Kate wasted no time, other than to ask for details of the injury, when Robbie reappeared at their apartment requesting help for the boy. He cast a covert glance towards the bedchamber and was rewarded by an answer to his unspoken question.

'Your father remains in quarters tonight.'

He tried to hide the relief he felt, and thought he had succeeded, until she said, 'So you needn't fear an inquisition, for the time being at least. Time enough to explain the circumstances when the child's injury is seen to.' She became brisk. 'Five minutes is all I need to get dressed, if you will wake Maggie.'

'Can't you come alone?'

'Whatever secrecy is required, you may be sure Maggie will not betray you.'

'It isn't my...' he began, but she cut off his protest.

'Get Maggie.'

The sky was lightening as they turned into the narrow street. The wind had risen, stirring the rubbish that gathered in corners, strewing it across their path. In the wind was a hint of snow, the first flakes drifting onto their shoulders as they reached the door of the house. Robbie hadn't noticed before, but it was sandwiched between what seemed to be two shopfronts, to go by the width of the shutters covering the windows. He stepped forward to knock, his heel sliding on the damp cobbles, and he lurched for the doorframe to stop himself falling. Above his head a well-polished boot swung from a chain, but the sign over the shop to his right groaned, its hooks rusty, the picture of a pile of books, cracked and peeling – not many customers then, or perhaps a deliberate ploy to keep unwanted noses out of the stock the shop held. As he rapped on the door he saw Kate glance upwards, her lips compressed, though whether for regret that books were not more highly prized, or concern that they had strayed into an area of the city where dangers lurked, he couldn't be sure.

The girl who opened the door to them was a mirror image of the one he'd met earlier, though smaller, her smile for them tentative. She called over her shoulder, 'Eugenie?'

'Let them in, Netta, quickly, before they're seen.'

The voice was as he remembered it, low and husky, and as they stooped to enter he found himself noticing details he hadn't had time to see before: a chipped eye tooth, the wayward curl protruding from the edge of her cap, cheeks the colour of sea-pinks.

Kate took charge, kneeling beside the settle where the boy lay, eyes shut, his chest rising and falling rhythmically. She nodded her satisfaction. 'Has he been asleep long?'

'Perhaps a half-hour? It took some time for him to go over, for we only had willow and mandrake.'

Kate smiled at her. 'It was a good thought in the circumstances.'

Robbie saw her quick glance around the room before

she began to ease the boy's breeches above his knee, clearly wishing to hurt neither the lad nor the family's finances.

She ran her hands over his leg. 'If the sedative has only recently taken effect it's all the better, for I will need to manipulate the bone back into position before splinting it.'

Eugenie's tongue flicked out, moistening her lips. 'Will it pain him a lot?'

'It will not be pain-free, but with help to hold him steady may be speedily done. And afterwards there should be a little discomfort, nothing more, until, that is, the bone begins to knit, which is often when the pain is felt most, but by then most folk can see the end in sight and bear it. What age is he?'

'Nine. But thinks himself fourteen, or so he tries to act. And indeed he is clever enough for fourteen, and brave. Or foolish, depending how you look at it.'

'Brave certainly,' Robbie said. 'And quick-witted. I can testify to that.'

He was watching Eugenie and was rewarded by a shy smile.

Kate nodded to Maggie. 'You feel. Tell me what you think.'

Maggie ran her hands over François' leg, said, 'It is a fracture of the fibula, but only marginally out of line, and once reset and bound in place, he should make a full recovery.'

'Well done.' Kate motioned to Robbie to hold the boy's other leg, and to Eugenie to hold his shoulders, while Maggie, without being told, grasped his ankle. Kate mouthed, 'One, two, three!' And as Maggie pulled the leg towards herself, Kate put pressure on the sliver of bone to nudge it sideways and back into place. The boy made an incoherent sound, part way between a gasp and a mutter, beads of sweat breaking out on his forehead before he settled again.

Behind them, Netta was sniffing, and Maggie, letting go of the boy's ankle, turned and put her arms around her. 'It's fine. He'll be fine.'

Kate looked to Eugenie. 'I need bandages, thin strips for preference, and two pieces of wood, flat if you have them.'

Eugenie was chewing her lip, her brow wrinkled, then she rose and disappeared through a door at the side, to return, not with wood, but with two pieces of thick leather. 'We don't have wood, though I could go to try and get some … there is a carpenter a few streets away, but … would these do?'

Kate tested their rigidity. 'Yes indeed. In fact, they may be better. Not so heavy, and if we can contrive a crutch for him, make it easier for him to get about.'

Robbie, now he was no longer needed to restrain the boy, stepped back into the shadow of the doorway, and leaning against the frame, he watched Eugenie as she dampened a cloth and wiped her brother's face. He could see a hint of the swell of her breasts at the neckline of her gown as she bent over him, a smattering of freckles peppering her nose. Her fingers were slim, the nails trimmed short, and he found himself wondering what it would be like to have her bend over him and wipe his brow.

'Robbie!'

179

He started.

'I'm aware you've been up most of the night,' Kate glanced towards the line of light visible around the edge of the door, 'but I'd prefer you not to fall asleep now. We do not wish to have to carry you home.' She turned to Eugenie. 'Now that François is sorted, I think we should introduce ourselves properly. We know your names, it is only right you should know ours.' Robbie was aware of her fractional hesitation, as if offering her name raised the ghosts of memories she would rather remain dormant, then realised his error, and her sensitivity, as, disregarding her current status, she said simply, 'I am Kate Munro, and my husband is in the Scots Gardes. As is Robbie. And this,' she indicated Maggie, 'is my elder daughter, with ambitions to be a physician. Something that may be achievable in Paris, though it would not in Scotland.'

François stirred, and muttered, 'I didn't mean it, Eugenie, I didn't.'

She stroked his forehead. 'Shush, shush.' When he settled again she looked up at Robbie, concern visible on her face. 'What didn't he mean?'

Robbie thought of the teeth marks still visible on his hand and shoved it behind his back lest they be seen. 'I think he feared bringing me here, that I might be minded to report what I stumbled into in the square by the church. At least until I told him I was a Scot and Protestant. But you needn't worry. We none of us think what was done tonight a crime, though I regret his broken leg.' His eyes were fixed on hers, willing her to smile – tiger's eyes, he thought, noting how the flecks of gold in the brown reflected the candlelight.

180

Kate said, 'The leg will mend, but he should not attempt to walk, even with a crutch, for a week or two, and after that it will be another month or more before he should dispense with the splints. You are happy to remove and replace them as necessary?'

Eugenie nodded, the corners of her mouth upturned. 'Which won't be often. Cleanliness isn't his first priority.'

Kate stood up with a laugh. 'Indeed. Well, he will be a captive to your ministrations for some time at least.' She hesitated. 'I would like to come back, if I may, to check on his progress.'

'Of course.'

'And if you should need me in the meantime, send word to Robbie or my husband. That is likely the easiest way.'

'Thank you,' Eugenie looked at Robbie, 'for bringing him home.' And to Kate, 'For coming out in the middle of the night, to people you didn't know. If...' a tear formed at the corner of her eye, 'if my mother...'

'It's fine.' Kate placed a hand on her arm. 'Indeed, it is more than fine, for I have missed the opportunity to treat folk, and it is a pleasure to be able to do so, especially when the outcome will be good. Now, we'd best be off, for my younger daughter may wake looking for breakfast, and if she finds none of us there, will not take it kindly that we have gone without her.' She raised one eyebrow at Robbie. 'And you should appear at your quarters before they think you a deserter.'

Eugenie flushed. 'You will not be in trouble on our account?'

'No.' Robbie dearly wanted to smooth away the

pucker on her brow. 'There is no fear of that. A night away is neither here nor there when we are in quarters...' He broke off and darted a glance at Kate, and then, his colour deepening, at Eugenie. 'Not that I make a habit of it.'

Maggie was laughing. 'I think you'd better stop, before you dig yourself a bigger hole. You needn't worry, Mother, no one would have him anyway.'

At the end of the alley Robbie looked back, to find Eugenie still standing in the doorway, Netta beside her. To distract himself from the memory of her tawny eyes, he dropped his hand onto Kate's shoulder. 'It was a kindness not to reveal your title. They would likely have been embarrassed.'

'It would have been a foolishness to do otherwise. Best that they think me simply a soldier's wife and you a Garde's son ... for all our sakes.' She reached up and touched his hand. 'Have a care, Robbie, a close connection here may not be wise.'

Chapter 4

Wise or not, Robbie did not wait for Kate to make a return visit to the Rue Colin Pochet. Instead, three days later, despite the storm which had been threatening all morning, he slipped away to check on François, or at least that's what he told himself, and also what he said to Eugenie when she expressed her surprise at seeing him again so soon.

At first she seemed distant, as if his appearance was an inconvenience she could have done without. 'You need not have concerned yourself. He is well looked after.'

He had no idea how to break through her reserve. 'I don't doubt it. It was rather to check he was obeying my mother's instructions I have come.' That drew a small smile, so he offered, 'And to add my support to *your* commands.'

Her smile died and he thought perhaps he had gone too far, his suspicion reinforced when she said, 'It isn't necessary. I wouldn't wish to trouble you further than we have already.'

She looked towards the inner chamber door as if to indicate she was capable of seeing to François' needs, the colour coming and going in her cheeks, her chest rising and falling as if she had been running. He risked, 'If you wish me to go…?'

She was twisting the cord holding the bundle of keys at her side. 'I'm sorry. That was discourteous ... and inappropriate in the circumstances. Will you take some refreshment? My father will wish to meet you, to add his thanks to mine.' She indicated the door in the far wall. 'He's in the shop, but Netta will tell him you're here. And in the meantime, you may come through to speak to François. I know he will also be happy to see you.' A hint of mischief. 'To see if your hand is on the way to recovery.'

Robbie thrust his hand behind his back. 'He told you?'

'Not intentionally. He was shouting out in his sleep the first night, saying over and over he didn't mean it...' Her expression was thoughtful. 'Did you know if you question someone in their sleep they will most likely answer, and truthfully?'

'I never heard such a thing.'

'Well you have now. And I can attest to the truth of it.' There was no doubting her smile this time, indicating that whatever he said, it could not have been so bad.

'What *did* he say?'

'That he shouldn't have bitten you. That it was not well done.'

She nodded towards his hand, hidden behind his back. 'You needn't try to hide it. I have seen already that he broke the skin.'

He held his hand out. 'But as you also see, there are only the smallest of scabs to show for it.'

There was a hint of a lilt in her voice. 'You will not be scarred then?'

'I don't know ... perhaps it may be easier to judge

184

when I next call, to set your mind at rest.'

'With your mother, I presume?'

He was almost sure she was laughing at him, but thought of what else François might have said in his sleep was still troubling. He had to ask. 'Did he ... say anything else of what happened?'

'How you came to break his leg, you mean? That, too, he divulged in his sleep, and though the details were hazy, I think I have the gist of it.'

He focused on the tawny flecks in her eyes, wished he could gauge from her tone whether or not she was annoyed at what had happened, if that was why she had been less than welcoming, and if there was anything he could say to make it better. 'I'm sorry. It was an accident. I wouldn't have wished to hurt him...'

She spoke so quietly he thought he might have misheard. 'Nor I to have him so, but I cannot altogether regret it, for if it had not happened you would not have had cause to come here.'

His heart was pounding in his chest so hard he thought it must be audible. 'Eugenie...'

She turned her head away. 'I shouldn't have spoken so. Especially with my mother ... it is not fitting.' And then, in a rush, 'She had been fading for so long, I hated to see her suffer, we all did, so that it was almost a relief when she went. But now, it is hard not to feel guilt at such thoughts, nor to think it wrong to smile when we should be grieving. My father tries to bury himself in his work, but inside I know he is bereft. He is with us in body, but not, I think, in spirit. Which is hard because...' She broke off and again a flush spread from her neck and up her throat. She had crossed her arms against her chest, and he longed to uncurl her fists, to offer her some comfort, to say, *I know what it is to lose someone.* For though it was not the same, were not all deaths in a way a waste? He settled for the mundane, safer ground, which he hoped would give her time to recover her poise.

'Your father is a cobbler?'

'By day, yes.'

He saw the tip of her tongue again caught between her lips, and recognised it as an habitual gesture she was likely unaware of, but which he found endearing. Afraid he might once again be straying onto dangerous ground, he nevertheless asked, 'And at night?'

She drew a deep breath, as if making a decision. 'At night he is a pastor, and much beloved, but in this I very much fear he may be suffering a crisis of faith.'

He had no idea how to answer, for though he wouldn't say he *didn't* believe, his faith, if it could be called such, had for many years been an abstract thing, which rarely impinged on real life. He thought of the deaths that had touched him personally: fellow soldiers, who had given their lives in service of the King; others who had died in less worthy circumstances, a knife in the guts in a drunken brawl, or through contracting the French pox. And in the forefront of his mind, as always when he was forced to think of death, the last image he had of Anna, as she was carried home in the factor's arms, limp as a rag doll, her head lolling, her hair brushing at the ground. And the other picture, the one he tried to hold in his head, the way he wished to remember her – astride Midnight, the horse's muscles rippling under his gleaming coat. He wouldn't say he didn't believe in *something*, but since that day he had never quite been able to abandon the notion that God, if He wouldn't take care of his twin, likely wasn't particularly interested in him either.

Eugenie's head was bent, an awkward silence between them. He tried to think what Kate would say in similar circumstances, offered, 'These things take time. Do not judge him by what you see in him today. Rather...' he felt a hypocrite saying it, but instinct told him that for her it was appropriate, 'rather pray for his healing, in mind and spirit.'

She straightened her shoulders, lifted her head. 'Netta? Can you fetch Father ... tell him the man who helped François is here.'

'Does he know...?'

'About the leg? No. Nor your hand, either, come to that. Only that François fell and you carried him home. It is perhaps best it stays that way.'

Her father had Eugenie's eyes, without the light in them, but his tone was cordial as he came forward and offered Robbie his hand.

'I believe we owe you thanks, M'sieur.'

It felt wrong to take credit, without also acknowledging blame, but Eugenie was staring at him, so he confined himself to bowing. 'M'sieur.'

'You have seen François?'

'Not yet.' He saw the first flicker in M Lavalle's gaze and the speculative glance he shot towards Eugenie.

'But did I not hear you arrive some time ago? Is François asleep?'

'I believe so.'

187

'Then we must waken him. It would not be polite to send ... Monsieur ... Munro is it? ... away without giving François the chance to add his thanks to ours.'

'If he is asleep, there is no need to...'

'Nonsense. Besides, if he is to doze all day, it will be all the harder for him to sleep at night.'

Netta skipped ahead of them. 'François!'

To judge by the unfocused look in his eyes as he turned his head, it was likely her clear, piping treble had woken him. He was lying on a low pallet jammed up against the wall, surrounded by piles of leather of varying qualities, which had clearly been pushed aside to make room for the bed.

'Excuse the untidiness,' M Lavalle said. 'This is but a storeroom pressed into temporary service while François is unable to climb the ladder to the chamber above.'

'And fortunate we are to have it,' Eugenie said. 'If we had not, he would have been forced to lie in the kitchen, and precious little rest he would have got there.'

François, seeing Robbie, tried to pull himself up, to his obvious discomfort.

'Don't move on my account. I am only here to see what progress you have made, that I may take word to my mother.'

M Lavalle said, 'And our gratitude also. It was more than kind of her to come out in the middle of the night to see to this scamp.' Robbie saw a shadow cross his face, imagined it was the lad's own mother he thought on as he rested his hand on François' head, his affection obvious. The feeling was confirmed as he continued, 'I trust he has learned his lesson and will not take himself off in the dark again…' He broke off. 'If you had not come upon him…'

'I'm glad I could bring him home safely.' That at least was true.

'Accidents,' said Eugenie, 'happen, and…'

'Sometimes,' M Lavalle said, 'accidents are not accidents at all, but a result of foolishness.'

And that also is true, Robbie thought, looking down at the floor, lest something of his own guilt was revealed in his eyes – if I had not been foolish enough to stand surety for Angus, I would not have become indebted to Del Sega. If not indebted to Del Sega, I wouldn't have stumbled into the funeral and François would not be lying with a broken leg. And hard on that thought, another one, refusing to be suppressed – I would not have met Eugenie.

It was as if she read his mind and was retreating, as a doe might when startled in the forest. 'Now you have seen François for yourself, you can no doubt set your mother's mind at rest that he is on the mend.' She was abrupt. 'Tell her she need not trouble herself to come back if it is inconvenient.'

A draught funnelling from the ill-fitting window was chill on his neck; the thought that she might be expressing her true feelings, that he might have been mistaken in the light he thought he saw in her eyes, equally chilling. He decided on a direct assault. 'It will be no trouble, for her, nor me. She would not rest easy without reviewing his progress, and it will be my pleasure to accompany her.' He paused, added another, less personal weight to the argument. 'She isn't used to wandering to about the

189

Paris streets on her own, and may therefore be glad of my protection.'

M Lavalle lifted his head, as if suddenly aware of the undercurrent in the conversation, so that Robbie, deciding he'd said enough, smiled at Netta and nodded to François. 'Next time I see you, young man, you will be hopping about on your crutch.' He took a step back. 'If you'll excuse me, M'sieur.' He bowed over Eugenie's hand. 'Mam'selle.' And as he left, he dared to think the faint bloom on her cheeks might be on his account.

Chapter 5

'You've escaped then?' Patrick Maxwell sprawled in an alcove at the rear of a tavern in one of the meaner parts of Glasgow, his tankard almost empty. 'It's taken you long enough. I thought when Yuletide came and went you'd decided to abide by your father's wise counsel.'

There was no mistaking the contempt in his voice, but William, himself still smarting, despite the passage of the months, at the summary manner of his father's dismissal of Maxwell, ignored it. 'Your treatment at Kilmaurs was none of my doing. Had it been, I would not be here now.' It was an apology of sorts, though he couldn't help adding, 'But your appearance uninvited served only to lengthen my confinement, not lessen it.' Looking around him, despite the poor light, he noted the bricks on the hearth were chipped and crumbling, the wall above, smoke-blackened. There was a man in the opposite corner with three tankards lined up on the table in front of him, which, to judge by the state of his dress, were all for himself. His breeches were held up with string, the cuffs of his jacket in threads, a dog lying like a moth-eaten rug at his feet. William dusted the stool opposite Maxwell with his hand, and, grimacing at the grime on his fingers, sat down. 'You couldn't find anywhere less salubrious?'

'Forget the sarcasm, William, it's you who doesn't want to be seen with me. I have no issue over our meeting.'

'No more have I, but I need to tread carefully.' He looked around again, acknowledged, 'I daresay there is no fear of recognition here.'

'It's eighteen months since you were forced to give up Broomelaw. How long will Glencairn nurse his anger? And more to the point, why should I bear the brunt of it?'

'Why indeed? As if you had no hand in that business with Mistress Munro. Had you left well alone, I might not be suffering now. Perhaps my father is right and you aren't the best of company to keep.'

'Your choice, William, no one's keeping you here … but the best of company can be gey boring, I can testify to that.' Maxwell waved his empty tankard in the air. 'This ale is passable enough, and since you're asking, I'll take another.' He waved it again, more impatiently, and received a bellow in response.

'Fancy clathes or no, ye can come to the counter for yer drink like onybody else.'

Maxwell leapt up, his hand going to his dirk, but William got there first. His grasp on Maxwell's arm was firm.

'I'll see to it.' The sarcasm was back in his voice. 'It may surprise you to know I didn't come here to get into a brawl with a tavern-keeper. Godforsaken hole or not, he may pay for friends in the watch.'

They were on their fourth round, the tavern-keeper, now that he saw they had money to spend and weren't slow about it, obliging them by providing refills of ale before they asked for them. William, in a more expansive mood, fuelled by the strength of the ale, waved away Maxwell's half-hearted offer to split the cost of their fifth. 'If I cannot buy a drink for a friend, what can I do? Nothing. And don' you worry. Glencairn may think he keeps me on short order, but I know where he hides the siller.'

'The money should be yours anyhow.' Maxwell, slumping further and further down on the bench seat, nodded his agreement, his head almost hitting the table top. He jerked upright, tapping the side of his nose. 'And what he doesn't know won't hurt him. That's what I say.' He lifted his tankard, took a long swallow and belched. A sly expression settled on his face. 'But what do *you* not know?'

William leant across the table and grabbed the front of his doublet. 'What d'you mean?'

'What I came to Kilmaurs to tell you. Why I suggested you meet me here.'

'Why didn't you say sooner?'

'You never asked.'

'Well you'd better tell me now, and it better be good.' He twisted his hand so that Maxwell almost choked.

'I will. If you stop throttling me.' As William relaxed his hold, Maxwell straightened the ruffle at his neck. 'The word at court is…'

'You're at court?' William slammed his fist down on the table, rattling the tankards. 'Since when?'

'Since I decided there was more sport to be had

there than with thon mulish creature I have for a wife.' He leant forward, became confiding. 'She hasn't been so welcoming of late, not since she dropped the last bairn. If that witch Kate Munro was still in Scotland I'd say she'd been colluding with her yet again to keep me from my rightful due.' He licked his lips. 'But if *she* doesn't find my attentions to her taste, there's plenty in Edinburgh who do, especially when they hear the clink of a purse. I could introduce you to a few.'

'I can choose my own doxy, thank you. But if it isn't too much trouble…' William tried to set down his tankard but missed the edge of the table, slopping ale over his hose and onto the floor. If he had been sober it would have annoyed him; as it was he swiped at his hose with the palm of his hand and tried again, repeating, 'If it isn't too much trouble, I'll thank you to tell me what word at court concerns me.'

'Braidstane is for Ireland.'

'Good riddance.' William was dismissive.

'And,' Maxwell paused, as if for emphasis, 'he's high in favour with James' merchant's daughter wife of his.'

'What do I care about Ireland? Polluted with wild Irish and woodkerns. Even dreicher than Scotland, if you can credit it. He's welcome, and may the bogs swallow him whole.'

Chapter 6

Elizabeth Montgomerie was seated in the window of the solar, catching the last sliver of the winter sun, her mending lying loose on her knee, the needle, still threaded, stuck though the heel of the woollen hose – a pity that Hugh was so hard on his clothes, so that she never seemed to get on top of the mending he produced. Pity also that she derived no satisfaction from it, however well done. There were wives, she knew, who took pride in a stocking well turned. But she wasn't one of them. Ishbel, had she been here, would have made a better job of it, but she was not here and her loss still keenly felt, for all that it was two months since the hectic had taken her off, despite all John's efforts. The girl who had replaced her was competent enough, but she lacked both the age and experience that would have rendered her companionable as well as a servant. It was a small step from thought of Ishbel to thought of Agnes, stubbornly resisting all attempts to draw her back to Braidstane, that she might live out her days in comfort. She had insisted that while John bided at Broomelaw, it was her place to see to him, though Elizabeth wasn't sure whether she sought to look to his comfort, or to protect the fabric of the tower from the likely carelessness of a bachelor tenant. Whatever the truth of it, his last letter had been blunt. *I fear Agnes will not see the winter out, but I cannot persuade her to rest. 'I shall die in harness, like the old nag I am,' she says whenever I raise the subject of taking things easy. And I don't doubt she'll get her wish.* Elizabeth didn't doubt it either, and she dreaded the task of writing to Kate when the time came – we are all getting older, however much we think to deny it. She placed her hand on her stomach – and the hope of a son slipping further away with each passing month.

Catherine's voice floated up from below and Elizabeth bent forward to try to see where she was, and more importantly if Mary had come to no harm from their walk on the hill. Catherine was only nine but already her voice was ripening from the high treble of a young child into the more mellow tone of a girl on the cusp on womanhood. Far from cheering Elizabeth, it served as another reminder of the passing of the years. And of the many losses she had suffered since her marriage to Hugh – not that he ever mentioned them, but she knew, deep down, it was a hurt that would only be healed with the birth of a healthy son.

She craned out the window, her mending sliding unnoticed onto the floor. The hillside below the tower was cloaked in the green-grey of frost-dulled gorse which clung stubbornly to the slopes, ever-ready to catch the unwary with its spikes. 'As good a defence as any, particularly in the dark,' Hugh aye said, when she protested the inconvenience of it. And that, she supposed, was true, though little consolation when it was her arms that suffered as she hunted for ripe brambles on the canes straggling among them. Hard to see and harder still at times to reach, they were a pleasure that generally came at a cost, both to her comfort and her clothes.

She thought of the gentler landscape of Picardie, of the farmhouse and the river flowing swift and smooth nearby, the water sweet. It was a pity the Munros had once again been uprooted, this time at the French King's command, when they had begun to find a peace. But as she well knew, Hugh's many absences a proof, kings were not to be gainsaid. She thought of each of them in turn: Kate, her health not what it was, but nevertheless enjoying the latest babe, the thought that he would have an inheritance in Picardie a consolation for the family's exile to Paris. Ellie, chattering non-stop, and more than halfway French. Maggie, for whom they all hoped the move to Paris might prove beneficial and restore her former confidence. Adam, who wore his position in the Gardes as easily as an old glove but found his recent elevation to a title less comfortable. And Robbie, effecting the careless elegance of a cavalry officer, the boy she remembered peering out from his eyes when he thought no one was looking. She trusted all was well with them.

Her attention was caught by a sudden wail, followed by Catherine's voice, this time soothing, and she stood up, pressing her face against the glass. Four-year-old Mary was sprawled in a clump of heather sprouting from a crevice in the rocks that protruded like bony knuckles among the swathes of blackened and rotting fern. Catherine lifted her up and dusted her down, and from the amusement Elizabeth saw her struggling to hide, it was clear Mary's cry had been one of outrage at the indignity of falling, rather than pain. No doubt her skirts would have borne the brunt of it, and likely be damaged as a result. Which brought her thoughts full circle and back to the mending at her feet. She would look to it tomorrow.

She was about to turn away from the window as a rider entered under the archway and drew to a halt in the barmkin, his horse skidding on the mossy cobbles. He slid to the ground and, looking up, saluted her, sweeping off his hat – news from Edinburgh. And Hugh. All thought of the Munros supplanted by her own family, she nevertheless resisted the urge to run down to meet him. A year or two ago she could have perched on a window seat for hours without ill effect, but now a single hour was enough to cause a twinge or two. Not something she would admit to anyone, least of all John Montgomerie, who might insist on a professional examination of the knee joint that troubled her most. Fine as it was to have a physician in the family, where minor ailments were concerned it could be more of a trial than a blessing. She waited for him to be announced, walking back and forwards along the length of the room to relax her leg, so that by the time he appeared in the doorway no one would have known she had suffered any discomfort. 'John! This is a welcome surprise.'

He hugged her, lifting her up and setting her down again with a thump and a grimace. 'Either you're growing heavier, or I weaker.'

She answered his speculative glance at her stomach by a shake of her head. 'No, I'm not. Though I wouldn't mind.' As much to suppress her own thoughts as to reprove his, she teased, 'And if you have nothing better to do than to speculate on my relations with Hugh, I might be tempted to retract my welcome and send you packing.'

'But then you wouldn't find out why I'm here.'

'Well?'

'I thought a visit to my brother's wife was overdue. Isn't that excuse enough?'

'Not normally, unless you are much changed. Your visits are not so frequent I can flatter myself it is for love of me.'

'The children then. They are my only nieces.'

For a moment silence hung between them, and she suspected they shared the same thought: four brothers and Hugh the only one with progeny, and only girls at that. Patrick: taken before his time on a battlefield in France; George: his only concern, it seemed, his career at the English court; and John himself, who kept his own counsel regarding his lack of a wife and family.

He relented. 'I came to bring news of Hugh.'

'Isn't keeping a check on Hugh normally Alexander's job.'

'So it is. He was intending to come, but when he heard I was making for Glasgow, he thought I might save him the journey. He doesn't wish to admit to it, but he is not as young nor as fit as he once was, and I think he feels it.' He flexed his right arm, cracked his elbow. 'I know I do, and I'm half his age.'

She had a moment's apprehension that perhaps he didn't come straight to the news from court because it wasn't what she would want to hear, but relaxed as he threw himself onto the settle and, stretching out his legs, linked his hands behind his head.

'Is there nothing to drink in this house? I have ridden long and hard to get here and taken a considerable detour besides, and have a drouth on me something terrible.' He grinned at her. 'I think the news must wait.'

'I think it must not.'

'A messenger is not worthy of his hire?'

She shook her head at him. 'Don't think by misquoting Scripture you can distract me. News first, refreshment second. If, that is, the news is good.'

'I'm not sure if it is good or bad…' He stopped, but his mouth twitched, as if he struggled not to smile.

'John!' She picked up a pine cone from the basket by the hearth and tossed it at his head. 'Just tell me.'

He ducked. 'The *bad* news is Hugh is well, though he chafes that the prospects for land in Ulster are long in coming. The *good* news is that, weather permitting, he is going to spy out the lie of the land there, so he won't be troubling you here for a while yet.'

She tossed another cone at him.

He caught it, threw it back. 'What? Married ten years and not tired of Hugh yet? I had no idea my brother was such a catch.'

She sat down at the table and, leaning on her elbows, rested her head on her cupped hands. 'I am tired of being alone here, with only the children and Joan for company. It has been a long winter and not over yet and once the children are abed the evenings are gey quiet. A husband is at least a distraction.'

'I'll tell him that, shall I? No doubt he'll be pleased to have some reason to rush home.'

She wrinkled her nose at him. 'Seriously, how long will he be delayed? We all miss him when he is away, however troublesome he may be when here.'

'A week or two, apparently. And if it's any consolation, the trip is one Alexander approves of, not some hare-brained scheme of Hugh's own. Now, am I getting that drink? Or must I fend for myself?'

The remnants of supper were removed from the table, only the glasses and a half-full flagon of wine remaining, the gossip from Renfrew and its surroundings all but exhausted, when Elizabeth thought to ask, 'Can *you* stay?'

'A day or two, no more. Renfrew is not an unhealthy place, as towns go, but there are aye bones to be set, bairns to be born, boils to be lanced…' His smile faded. 'And come the warmer weather who knows what ills may descend on us. Forbye that James wishes me to be also at his beck and call. It will be…' He broke off, and Elizabeth had the suspicion he almost said something he would have regretted.

Respecting his privacy, she said, 'This is a respite then? The calm before the storm?'

'Let's hope there are no storms. Last year we were fortunate, but ninety-seven, if you remember, was something else entirely, the plague on the rampage, leprosy also.'

'Let's not think of that year at all. There was too much of ill in it.'

He was worrying with his tongue at something stuck between his teeth, his conversation disjointed. 'Happily now past ... Have you news of the Munros? ... I can imagine Kate a lady at the French court, but "Sir Adam" takes a bit of getting used to.'

'Not since we returned from France. I do hope the move to Paris has been a good one, even though it wasn't looked for.'

'There is much in life that isn't looked for, and oftentimes it proves the best thing in the end.'

'You think they are well away from Ayrshire?'

'Don't you?'

'I suppose. For all that Glencairn seems to have a grip on William, he will not live for ever, and when he is gone, who knows? And for myself, that is the main reason for supporting Hugh's ambitions in Ulster. James' outlawing of blood feud is all well and good, but there are no guarantees folk will keep to it, or not this far removed from court at any rate. But I've not heard of any Cunninghame interest in Ulster, and it would be a fine thing to live amicably with our neighbours.'

She was aware John had stiffened and, sensing it wasn't a personal ill that it would be a politeness to ignore, felt a shiver run through her. If William Cunninghame had anything to do with it ... She had to ask. 'Did something else happen in Edinburgh?'

'Hugh had a run-in with the watch...'

Relief and irritation flared simultaneously. 'Does he forget altogether he has a family, who may suffer from his stupidities?'

John waved his hand as if to indicate it was trivial. 'It was weeks ago, and no harm done, bar a sprained ankle. It was as well I was about though, for anyone could have bound it up, but making him rest was a harder task. He recovered well enough, and faster than he deserved, and if it hadn't been for the sprain he would have been to Ireland and back by now.' Though his voice was hearty, his words, taken at face value, reassuring, his tension remained.

Fear of what she might learn by probing further warred with the likelihood she wouldn't be able to content herself unless she knew all. 'Don't hide anything on my account, John. What I imagine may well outweigh the reality.'

'All right. But I don't wish you to worry, for there really is no need. It is only that James Hamilton is back in Edinburgh, his character not improved, though his situation has. It seems he has weaselled his way back into James' good graces and now also looks to Ireland for advancement. It's a big enough island and they should be able to avoid each other, but nevertheless, when we heard of his presence we chose not to tell Hugh. Unfortunately, someone else did, along with the helpful information that he lodged in our vicinity. Hugh, being Hugh, instead of determining to avoid a confrontation, chose to be prepared for one. Which was why he disregarded the embargo on the carrying of arms and attracted the attention of the watch. I know it's important for your future benefit that he is seen about the court, but I have to admit it is easier on Alexander when he *isn't* there. Still,' he clearly intended to lighten the conversation, but the effect on Elizabeth was the opposite when he said, 'there is one blessing we can thank God for: William Cunninghame has not yet been reinstated, though it's rumoured he has been seen in Edinburgh. Whatever the truth of that we may pray the day of his reinstatement is long delayed. For when he is…'

There was a hard edge to her voice. 'Hugh will have the good sense to stay clear of him, or he'll have to answer to me.'

It was one of those awkward silences each tried to break at the same time, stopped, started again. It was Elizabeth, who finally said, with a smile, 'You said you were on your way to Glasgow. What's the attraction there?'

'Not attraction exactly, or not unless your taste in entertainment runs to studying pickled body parts and watching a chirurgeon wielding his knife.' His tension had been replaced by a suppressed excitement. 'There is to be a college of surgeons and physicians, and James has agreed to give it a royal patent. I am offered a place within it, alongside some of the foremost men of the day. We will be able to examine the living and cut the dead, and by so doing improve our understanding, and thus the health of everyone. It is an opportunity and an honour I will not refuse.'

Elizabeth rose, picked up her glass. 'Now that *is* worth a toast. To your good fortune and your new position. And…' she wrinkled her nose at him again, 'however much the thought of dissection revolts me, I wish you joy in it.'

Chapter 7

Maggie was also thinking of John Montgomerie, as she stood slightly apart in the group of students chosen by M Daumont. They had been summoned to witness the cutting of a newly arrived corpse. Her mind was filled with remembered images from the da Vinci drawings she had pored over at Braidstane, with John explaining the links between muscle and joint, and how it was the flow of blood that made everything work as it should. She took a deep breath: now she was going to see the real thing. She crossed her fingers behind her back – I mustn't faint. As M Daumont lifted a narrow blade and pressed it into the throat of the body on the marble slab in front of them, she noted, with surprise, the degree of pressure he had to exert, the thickness of the skin and the flesh that clung to it revealed as he peeled it back. Beside her, Anton de Vincennes dropped to the floor, his legs crumpling under him like a rag doll. Two of the others turned their heads away at the first sight of the opened chest cavity, their hands over their mouths, before following Anton's example. The final two lasted only as long as it took M Daumont to lift the saw and sever the ribcage. He looked up, and acknowledging with a nod that she was the last one standing, waved her closer, to peer into the corpse.

'Note the liver,' he said. 'This man drank heavily,

though I doubt it was that killed him.' He cut free a lung, handling it almost with affection, and pointed out the flattened lower portion. 'He would also have had a persistent cough, and though not especially painful, a considerable irritation, to himself and those around him.' As her fellow students rose, one by one, white-faced, and gathered again around the table, Maggie felt their antagonism towards her as a physical weight she was determined to shoulder, whatever it took.

'Glad you could rejoin us.' M Daumont's amusement was plain, his comments on the corpse pithy, punctuated by questions none of them could answer. If it is his intention to belittle us all, Maggie thought, he's making a good job if it. Sensing the others' growing irritation, she smothered her own annoyance. In her head she heard John Montgomerie talking of Allessandra Giliani – if studying meant she too could be a prosector, preparing bodies for dissection for men such as M Daumont, his brusqueness was not going to intimidate *her*. She had a lot to learn, yes, and if this was the way it was to be played, so be it. She held her head a little higher and, when the next pause came, risked a question. She pointed at the strawberry-like pitting on the section of intestine he was holding up for their inspection.

'Should it be like that? Or should the surface be smooth?'

'What do you think?' His question was directed at the whole group, but she jumped in before anyone else could respond.

'That it should all be one thing or the other. And as there is only a small area with the pitting, that is the abnormal state?'

A nod of approval. 'Indeed, Mam'selle. You have a good eye.'

She didn't dare look at any of the others, as he continued, 'But to see small variations from what is usual in a corpse is one thing. To be of any use at all as a physician you must learn to see oddities in a living body. Do not think it will be a quick process. It will take time and effort and,' he smiled as if he relished the thought, 'you will all make mistakes along the way.'

Maggie stifled her irritation again – perhaps over-confidence was a common problem, a bubble needing to be burst before any training became effective. He wiped his hands on a rag and indicated the partially dismembered corpse.

'I'll leave you to poke about. You will do him no harm and perhaps yourselves some good. But observe well, for tomorrow I will have questions for you all.' He paused. 'And it may profit you to share what you see, for six pairs of eyes … are better than one.'

As he left the room, Anton, the clear leader of the pack, elbowed his way in front of Maggie. 'Five will do me.' The others filled in beside him, blocking her view, every movement she made to attempt to squeeze between them countered. She was not tall enough to see over their shoulders, and it was obvious they had no intention of allowing her a place among them. For a moment she thought on the pleasure to be gained by a few well-placed kicks on elegantly clad shins, but discarded the idea. She had no intention of confirming their opinion of her as a petulant child, so she turned on her heel and left, her head high, ignoring the laughter following behind her.

She was waiting a few yards down a side passage, pressed into a window reveal to avoid being seen, when she heard the door of the dissection room opening, the laughter and snippets of conversation indicating the other students were spilling out. The bells had rung only once, for the quarter hour, while she'd waited, their examination of the corpse taking less time than she had feared, but all the better for her. It was obvious she was still the target of their humour, their satisfaction in thinking they had bested her, clear.

Anton's voice was loudest. 'We have suffered her presence long enough. Why should we have to share in our studies with a girl who is little more than a child? And a foreigner at that.'

A second voice, one she recognised as belonging to the smallest of the group, likely no older than herself. 'I say we protest to the college authorities.'

Anton again. '*I* say we threaten the withdrawal of funds. If there is no money, the college will suffer. My family I'm sure will be willing to make their contribution dependent on the removal of Mam'selle Munro from our class.'

There was a chorus of agreement. 'And mine.' 'Mine also.'

Maggie waited until she heard the click of the outer

door before heading back to the dissection room. A man was gathering up the organs spread around the corpse.

'Wait. Please.'

He turned and she thought she saw a hint of sympathy in his eyes, though his voice was brusque. 'I have a job to do and little enough time to do it.'

'You saw how they excluded me. I need to examine the corpse, and if I cannot work with the others, I shall have to work by myself.'

'Not my problem.'

'A half-hour will be sufficient. I promise you.'

'I have a job to do,' he repeated. 'And if I was to lose a half-hour every day, where would I be? I'd be out in the cold, that's where. Frozen out of me own house by a wife who thought I cheated on her on me way home.' He turned his back on her, lifted a kidney, gave it a cursory glance, set it to one side.

Maggie had another idea. 'If you help me, I'll help you in return, and between us I'm sure we can be finished in your normal time.' She took a deep breath. 'There will be much you know that I need to know.'

He humphed, but she sensed he weakened – flattery, she noted, with a glimmer of amusement, is a powerful weapon. 'I would value your expertise.'

He took a step back, waved at the body. 'You go ahead then. Look all you like. But if I'm made late today, I won't help you again.'

'Thank you.' She examined the organs he had set aside. 'These are to be kept?'

He indicated the jars of specimens ranged around the walls. 'The interesting ones we keep. The others,' he glanced down at the jumbled remains he had already dumped back into the body, 'are buried with the corpse.'

Her surprise must have shown on her face, for he laughed and said, 'Did you think we chopped them up and gave them to the Royal Menagerie to feed the lions?'

She coloured. 'I didn't think at all.'

'Like most of the young popinjays that Monsieur Daumont suffers. If you wish to make something of your studies, I suggest you start by thinking.'

It was the ideal opening. 'What makes the difference? Between an organ that *is* of interest and one that is not?'

'Disease, mostly. If you see enough of them, you'll come to recognise the difference between a good 'un and a bad 'un.'

'And by good you mean bad?' That brought a smile, and emboldened she picked up the lung M Daumont had removed and compared it to the one still in the body. 'This flattening Monsieur Daumont pointed out. What is it? And why would it have caused a cough?'

'Think about it.' He paused, as if to give her time to make a suggestion, then jabbed at the squashed portion of lung. 'When the air gets to here, it can't get through properly, can it?'

'I suppose.'

'Suppose nothing. It's but common sense.' He poked at the opposite lung. 'See the difference. Not that it's what killed him.' He took the lung out of her hand, put it back into the body. 'Two a sou, these are. Not worth keeping.' He grinned, and she saw that two of his front teeth were odd-sized and bound to those next to them by wire.

'Like me teeth, do you?' He clicked them together.

'Perk of the job. Salvaged last year. Cost a bit though, to have me own rotten ones pulled and these wired in instead.' He tapped the wire with his fingernail. 'Gold, that is, only the best. Me wife wasn't keen on the expense, but then she didn't like the smell of me breath either. Toss up, I says, two new 'uns that in't like kissing rotten fish, or an extra écu in the box.' He blew a puff of breath in Maggie's face. 'Sweet as honey, me mouth is now, and me wife reconciled to the loss of the money.' He clicked the teeth together again. 'Better than rotten ones, in't they? Even if they are a mite small.' He brought his lips over his gums and mimed trying to chew, then displayed the teeth again. 'Belonged to a child, see. Anybody much older and they'd likely 'ave been no better than me own.' He opened the mouth of the corpse on the slab and poked at the blackened stumps. 'Could do a decent trade in teeth, if folk would only die young enough.'

Maggie choked back a laugh, aware it wasn't amusement, instinct telling her she mustn't betray any squeamishness or all hope of help from him would be lost. The sun had moved round and was slanting in through the far end window. Mindful of the time and not wishing to risk his refusal to help her again, she said, 'What else should I be looking at here?'

He pointed at the heart, a tube on one side swollen. 'Valve's enlarged, see? That's what killed him, I reckon. If you mention that tomorrow to Monsieur Daumont as a question mind, tentative-like, you'll be all right.' He winked at her. 'Between us, we'll put those flashy fellows in the shade. You'll see.'

211

And, in the weeks that followed, so they did, but there was a price to pay. Maggie was leaning over the dissection table, scissors poised over a frog, which she had pinned out with care, his legs spread, his belly uppermost. She slit him neatly from throat to groin, taking care only to cut through the skin, leaving the muscle below intact, before making four more short transverse cuts towards each leg. The skin folded back as neatly as if she opened a letter. Animal dissection was a part of their studies she relished: the careful severing of muscles and tendons, the opening up of organs, the examination of bones and joints to discover their range of movement and the connections between them. She also never tired of watching M Daumont as he cut a human corpse, finding the tracery of blood vessels and arteries that wove their way around the body endlessly fascinating. She was looking forward to being allowed to assist him, for the more she studied, the stronger her ambition grew. It was no longer to be a prosector, but rather a surgeon, or at the very least a physician. The more she could learn of how the body worked, the better it would be, for her and her patients.

Only four of the original six students that had begun their training together remained, the other two dismissed by M Daumont, their lack of application clear in their careless attitude to time-keeping and disregard of the rules imposed upon them. The group was split over two tables, and Maggie felt the familiar frustration that she was still not an accepted part of it, despite, or perhaps because of, the enthusiasm she neither wished, nor was capable of hiding. The more she demonstrated her increasing knowledge, and her ability to retain all they were shown, the more it seemed Anton and his fellows went out of their way to cause problems for her. She knew M Daumont was aware of the situation and was pleased he chose to ignore it. For, as she said to Robbie when he enquired of her progress, 'If I cannot hold my own here, there is no chance for me elsewhere. And I am determined to succeed, whatever it takes.' She had watched his face for any trace of amusement, ready to fly at him should his mouth as much as twitch, his straight face a validation of her desire.

Anton was stationed beside her. She knew he was generally considered handsome, that there were many young girls about the court who envied her proximity to him, and indeed, if she were honest, she might have found him attractive, if it wasn't for the petty cruelties and deliberate attempts to sabotage her work he indulged in. And where he went, the others followed. An arm jiggled here; a foot tramped on there; a jar smashed, the spillage of iodine staining a segment of gut she was preparing for storage. Most irritating of all had been the candle knocked over, the flames igniting the paper on which she had painstakingly drawn the musculature of the forearm, so that it was all to do again. Several times she thought of requesting she be allowed to work at a separate table, but each time decided it would give satisfaction to her tormentors, a victory she wasn't prepared to concede.

Anton was pulling out the seaweed-like strands of fat

213

from the frog's chest cavity, and with an expert flick of his fingers he landed them on the back of her hand as she cut through the sternum. Concentrating on keeping the scissors angled upwards in order not to damage the organs beneath, the damp touch of the fat startled her, her scissors slicing through the liver, the point pressing against the heart. She shook the fat off her hand and bent her head to hide her frustration. The liver was in two pieces, the third segment severed, a puncture wound to the heart. Anton set his frog's heart to the side and looked over her shoulder. There was a malicious glint in his eye.

'What a pity, Mam'selle. Did your hand slip? Never mind. There is always tomorrow.'

M Daumont was at her other side, his face unreadable. She stepped back to allow him sight of the damage, but said nothing.

'Focus on the reproductive organs. Then neither your efforts, nor the frog, will be wasted,' he said.

Anton turned away, annoyance she hadn't received a stronger reprimand clear in the stiffness in his shoulders.

'I take it you can be more careful this time?' M Daumont's voice had a hard edge, but as she glanced up at him, he gave the smallest of nods, as if to say, *this is for his benefit.*

She examined the ovaries and the oviducts, the space surrounding them filled with a mass of eggs, and thought of the toads at Broomelaw, the sound of the males singing their pleasure as the spawn coiled out from the females beneath them. No wonder there had been so much of it. She could see the jellied strings now, the tiny eggs that would become the tadpoles, pinheads within them. Her

214

brow knotted and she looked up to see M Daumont on the opposite side of the table.

'You have a question, Mam'selle?'

'When toads spawn, the strings are thick, with ample jelly surrounding the eggs, and with frogs also the spawn comes in balls, but here…'

'Indeed.' He beckoned the others close, addressed the question to the whole group. 'Explanation, anyone?'

One offered, 'This frog isn't yet ready for spawning?'

'On the contrary. Look at the mass of eggs. They are healthy and mature.' He was looking straight at Anton, as if to challenge him. 'Anyone else care to offer a suggestion?'

Maggie felt a twinge of sympathy for Anton, for likely he had never seen toads spawning, as she had. It wouldn't be the most usual sight in the centre of Paris, but nevertheless, she took pleasure in answering. 'Is it to do with the water? Do the jelly sacs absorb it like seeds that swell if left in a bucket of water to germinate.'

'Well done, Mam'selle. We do not know exactly the process, but the analogy is good. And however it happens, the reason for it is clear.' He stirred the eggs with the point of his scalpel. 'As you see, they are in the thousands. Her belly couldn't have withstood the strain if the jelly sacs swelled inside her. So either she must produce many fewer eggs, or the swelling must happen after they are released. Which brings me to my next question.' He looked around the group again. 'Why so many? And why, if every frog produces a similar amount, is there not a plague of them?'

'So that's what happened with Moses and the Nile,'

215

Anton muttered, half under his breath.

'I commend your biblical knowledge, de Vincennes,' M Daumont's tone was dry, 'but it doesn't answer my question.'

'Perhaps,' Maggie said, relishing rubbing salt into Anton's wound, 'there were no appropriate predators in the Nile to eat the spawn.'

M Daumont nodded to her again, and she had the satisfaction of seeing Anton's increased irritation.

The question seemed innocent enough, but Maggie had the impression from the upward curl of Anton's mouth that it was not. 'How many eggs might a frog produce in its lifetime?'

There was mild surprise on M Daumont's face. 'A reasonable question, de Vincennes, which sadly I cannot answer for sure, but somewhere in the region of twenty thousand.'

'And a human female?'

Maggie felt the colour creeping up her throat and neck, staining her cheeks, as Anton said, 'Excusé, Mam'selle, I forgot there was a girl in the room.'

M Daumont took charge. 'That will do for today. Once you've cleared up you may go. But I wish to see your written notes by noon tomorrow. I expect them to be both clear and comprehensive.'

Maggie held back as the others left, preferring to have them where she could see them, rather than risk them behind her.

Anton's voice echoed back, loud, offensive. 'I wonder how many eggs Mam'selle Munro holds. And if they are mature?'

Chapter 8

Gabrielle, Duchesse de Beaufort, was stretched out on a day bed, a glass of Madeira at her side.

Kate, who had been summoned to the Duchesse's chamber, apparently for no other reason than that Gabrielle was tired of her own company and that of her ladies, was sitting on a chair beside her, wishing she could think of an excuse to leave. She chided herself and tried to put herself in Gabrielle's shoes, to think how it must be for someone who was the King's wife in all but name, and now, pregnant as she was, without the freedom to do as she pleased. Had it been boredom, she wondered, that drove Gabrielle to other affairs, short-lived as they were? Perhaps. Well, no fear of that in her current condition, and likely no desire either. She remembered how she had felt in the last months of carrying Patrick John, the frustration when she could neither move nor bend as quickly or as easily as normal, her only desire for her time to come.

It had likely been a long winter for the Duchesse, if Munro's assessment of her was anything to go by: more suited to accompanying Henri to the battlefield than to rest in the Louvre, surrounded by courtiers whose conversation was as vacuous as their faces. And not over yet, for though it was the beginning of March, it could be a tricky month, bringing all weathers in one day. If she could help to alleviate Gabrielle's boredom, she should be honoured. She thought of the children Gabrielle had borne to Henri. His daughter, Catherine, who at two, had already captured the heart of everyone who saw her, with her elfin smile and her inability to stand still even for a moment, constantly jigging from foot to foot, her head cocked to the side like a robin. The two boys, César and Alexandre, were both without the legitimacy that would give them a place in the succession, and a possible third to come. Which made her think of Marguerite de Valois, the King's true wife, a reminder she'd rather not have, for it was aye an uncomfortable thought.

Gabrielle said, 'I didn't bring you here just to share my tedium, welcome though your company is, but rather to show you something. Do you read French?'

Kate nodded. 'Enough to ensure I wouldn't have poisoned anyone at St Valery.'

'Good.' Gabrielle lifted a letter from the side table and passed it to her.

Kate turned it over and ran her finger over the broken halves of the waxed seal. It was one she did not recognise, but given Gabrielle's obvious excitement, she thought perhaps it came from the cardinal who had been charged with preparing a request for an annulment to take to Rome. It was not.

She lifted her eyes when she saw the signature, her astonishment matched by a discomfort at the idea of reading such private correspondence.

Gabrielle smiled encouragement at her. 'Go on. Read it. It will be a subject for gossip soon enough.'

Kate skimmed the parchment – however much she felt morally obliged to have sympathy for Marguerite de Valois, as the King's rightful wife, all she had heard of her in the past had been less than complimentary. Her dislike of Henri and of their marriage was common knowledge, her long-standing refusal to consider ending it and to allow Henri the opportunity to marry elsewhere, equally so. This about-face was as unexpected as hail in high summer.

'Elegantly phrased, is it not? And with a sympathy for Henri's predicament I never expected to receive from that quarter.'

Unsure what to say, Kate offered, 'It is gracious.'

'And more than welcome. I had almost given up hope, but now that de Valois no longer opposes Henri's wishes, indeed is herself willing to take steps to forward the annulment, it should be a formality a swelling of the Vatican's coffers will see safely accomplished.'

'And clear the way for you to wed the King, formally legitimise the children?'

There was no triumph in Gabrielle's voice, rather an unexpected contentment. 'We are to be married as soon as the Pope grants permission.' She tapped her stomach with her fan. 'Perhaps even in time for this young man's arrival.' The sapphire winking on her finger set a square of light dancing on the floor at their feet. 'You may wonder why I have chosen to share this with you, when the rest of the court is still unaware of the good news. It isn't known to any but the King and his closest advisors.' Gabrielle paused, then, 'Don't fret. This knowledge won't put you in le Grand Châtelet, though it isn't for general circulation. It is a lonely place sometimes to be the mistress of a King, and oftimes dangerous to have confidantes. But you I think I *can* trust, perhaps the more so because I have known from the start you do not altogether approve of me, or of my situation.'

Kate took a deep breath. 'It is not my place…' But Gabrielle waved away the apology she had intended to offer.

'I understand your reservations. Your religion is, I think, rather less forgiving than ours in these matters. Which makes your forbearance the more valuable as a result. I trust the regularisation of my relationship with the King will go some way to setting your mind at rest?'

It was one thing to be treated to a confidence, quite another to negotiate the pitfalls of a truthful response. Not least her reservations on the matter of divorce, and her desire that her own children should grow up with a respect for marriage hard to sustain in the lax atmosphere of the French court. Those feelings were at war with her sympathy for the Bourbon children, whose situation would be immeasurably improved by Gabrielle's marriage. She hesitated, trying to frame a suitable answer, but Gabrielle, looking towards the window and the clouds beyond, continued, talking more to herself than to Kate, as if it were she who needed to be convinced. 'It will be easier when I am a wife in truth, will it not? And my children able to rightfully call the King, *Father*. But I fear I shall find it hard to be a good Queen, for a husband has the right to demand faithfulness, where a lover does not.' She patted her swollen belly. 'Though that is not hard in the current circumstances, and I daresay I will find the advantages of my new position outweigh the disadvantages.'

This was a topic Kate did not wish to pursue, afraid that distaste at the lax attitude to marriage Gabrielle displayed even now, when it seemed within her grasp, might show on her face or in her voice. She looked down and clung to Adam's reminder that she stood or fell before God on her own merits, not those of Gabrielle d'Estrées.

Gabrielle's voice grew strong and confident again. 'I had not thought to need a wedding gown in this condition, but Henri has written to the Pope asking for the annulment to be expedited. He has set the date for the wedding: the Sunday after Easter.' A shadow flitted across her face. 'If all goes well and this little one is a boy, he will have the expectations of all of France on his shoulders. But such is the lot of a King's son. And such is mine to be fussed over as if I am a brood mare whose sturdiness is in doubt.'

'The King is no doubt seeking to ensure you have everything needed for your comfort. There surely cannot be anything wrong in that?' Too late Kate recognised the implied criticism, and she bent her head waiting for a rebuke.

It didn't come, Gabrielle clearly occupied with her own train of thought. 'It is not as if this is a first pregnancy. I have carried three children to war with me without ill effect. This peace, though I longed for it with all my heart, has its own irritations. I hate to sit here not allowed to do this, or that, or the other, lest something goes awry. Especially when Henri spends more time traipsing about the countryside than he does here.'

Kate risked an opinion. 'And by so doing is gaining the affection of his people. Everywhere he goes they flock to him, warmed by his informality, his willingness to talk to anyone, to show an interest in their concerns. It is a gift that cannot be measured.'

'If I could only be with him. Perhaps they would learn to love me too.'

There was a telltale brightness in Gabrielle's eyes, an understanding of what was said of her, and for the first time Kate felt a spark of sympathy. She had long known many considered the Duchesse a whore, and with good reason, and desire for a secure succession or not, would not wish to see her Queen, whatever the King wanted.

She brought the conversation back to safer ground. 'Every pregnancy, every birth, is different. Past history is no guarantee of future ease. It is as well to take care.' Weighing the value of sharing the experience of her own latest confinement against the danger of worrying Gabrielle unnecessarily, she decided to risk it. 'My first three births were as easy as the dropping of calves. Robbie was a twin, and they were both hale, right from the start.' She hurried on, not wishing to become involved in a discussion of Anna. 'Though we lost his sister when she was six. A needless accident.'

Gabrielle was clearly ahead of her. 'And Patrick John's birth was different?'

'Surprisingly so. And though all was well in the end, it was a lesson to me to take nothing for granted.'

'And I must do the same?'

'A month or two and it will all be over. What is that compared to the joy you will have thereafter.' It was the right note to strike.

'I suppose I must content myself then.' And with a laugh, 'Are you *sure* you are not in the pay of the King? For I think he would approve of your advice.' A pause, then, 'It is good of you to share in my inactivity. The value of having someone with whom I can talk about something of more moment than the latest width of sleeve cannot be measured.'

It was a suitable point at which to stop, and Kate toyed with the idea of seeking permission to leave but struggled to think of an appropriate excuse. Munro and Robbie were with the Gardes, Ellie with the de Bourbon children, and Maggie once again at the college, of which Gabrielle was undoubtedly aware.

Gabrielle, as if she followed Kate's thoughts, said, 'How does Maggie find her anatomy classes?'

'Interesting.'

Gabrielle hoisted herself higher on her cushions, frowned. 'I would have expected rather more enthusiasm. It is a rare opportunity she has been given.'

'I didn't mean to imply…'

'You didn't imply anything. That's the point.' Gabrielle took a sip of wine. 'If these studies are not to her taste, it is not too late to step back. And there is no shame in admitting to a mistake. For I had rather not encourage an experiment any further, if it is to go sour at the end.'

It was something that hadn't occurred to Kate, though, thinking back, she wondered if Munro had known. Of course someone would have to pay for Maggie's lessons, and if the money had not been demanded of them, then there was only one other possibility. 'Duchesse…'

Gabrielle waved her into silence. 'The money is nothing. All I want to know is if she is gaining benefit from the studies. If so, I am well repaid. Besides,' she raised her glass to Kate, 'you have not presented me with a bill for your services to date, so this is simply a favour returned.' She repeated her question. 'Are they all she hoped?'

'Everything she hoped for and more. Indeed, when they began she thought it would allow her to fulfil a long held desire to become a prosecutor, but her ambition has grown with every week that passes. It's just...' Kate frowned. 'I do not wish to dash her hopes, but I'm not sure the world is ready for a female surgeon, or not in France or Scotland at least. The others of her group are not welcoming.'

'There is always Italy.'

Kate nodded. 'We did think of it, once. Indeed, I would have welcomed the chance to go on my own account. There is a Montgomerie who spent some time at Florence, though he bides in Scotland the now. He told us many tales of the Santa Maria Nuovo Hospital. It seemed enlightened, as far as what women were allowed to do.'

'A brother of Patrick's?'

'Yes.'

'Then you must know, if it is a position he seeks, he would be welcome here.'

'The Scottish King would likely have something to say to that.'

'He is in service to King James? In that case I shall not try to tempt him away.' Gabrielle shifted and stretched upwards.

'You are not comfortable?' Kate said.

'Who is at this stage of pregnancy?'

'Is there any more to it? Anything new or different from previous times?'

Gabrielle shrugged. 'I did not suffer so with swollen ankles, nor spells of dizziness. But they are of no moment, I'm sure. As you say, in a few months I will be at myself again and will have forgotten the discomfort.'

Kate was sliding the slippers off Gabrielle's feet, palpating them, probing the ankles, seeking the bone – she had not seen Gabrielle before her pregnancy, but her general bone structure didn't suggest she would run to fat, or not at this age at any rate. 'This is not usual?'

'No. But I have perhaps been on my feet too much. César does not stay in one place for very long and I have not wished him to think me unwilling to play with him. He will be past playing with soon enough.'

Kate thought of Patrick John, still in swaddling clothes, who no doubt would also grow up too quickly, and likely the more so at court than if she could have stayed at Cayeux. She released Gabrielle's foot. 'I think there must be no more running about after César until this babe is safely delivered.'

Gabrielle slid her feet back into her slippers. 'I think so too, and so I have told him this morning. But I have promised it will not be too long, though two months is forever to a child.'

Kate wasn't sure whether Gabrielle's abrupt change of subject was an attempt at deflecting Kate's attention away from herself, or whether she wished to offer reassurance that Maggie's predicament was not forgotten, as she said,

'If the young men with whom Maggie is forced to study continue to prove troublesome, please, do not hesitate to tell me. I may not be able to move very far or very fast, but it does not mean my influence is less.'

Kate thought of Maggie, of her fierce independence. Of the need sometimes to be willing to accept help, especially when, as in this case, it came from a patron. 'Thank you. If the time comes, I will, though at the moment she insists she can handle them.'

Gabrielle echoed her thoughts. 'I don't doubt it, but sometimes even the most confident can do with a helping hand.' She raised her eyes to a portrait of herself as a young girl hanging on the opposite wall, her voice sober. 'I had an ambition once, and it wasn't to be the mistress of a King.'

Kate looked away, unwilling to intrude on the moment, but it was a new insight into the Duchesse's character, and her possible motive in championing Maggie, that made Kate at once more sympathetic, and less judgmental.

Gabrielle shook her head, as if to wake herself up. 'I think in some ways we are alike, your daughter and I, and if I can help her to realise her ambition, I will take pleasure in that.'

Chapter 9

Ambition was also the subject of discussion at Braidstane – John Montgomerie and Hugh both blown in on a March wind that threatened to lift rider and horse both from the valley floor and deposit them in the barmkin without the trouble of the climb. John was full of the opportunities the new college of surgeons at Glasgow might offer, Hugh of the situation in Ulster.

'Con O'Neill,' he said, stretching out his legs to the fire roaring in the hearth, 'is a fine fellow, if your idea of fine is for a companion who will drink you under the table at noon and be ready to do it all again by supper.'

Elizabeth, who had been nursing an ambition of her own but had once again been disappointed, was ready to be entertained. 'I trust you kept your wits about you, and your hand firmly on your purse, for I hear the Irish would fleece you as soon as look at you.'

Hugh threw his head back, his laughter loud and genuine. 'On the contrary, I suspect they are much maligned and indeed have the same tales of us as we have of them, for I found Con to be welcoming and hospitable, if somewhat wild, in appearance and behaviour.'

'Has he family?'

'They all have family, rather too many to keep track of, for the relationships appear a mite complicated and they seem to think as much of a fifth cousin, twice-removed, as they do of a brother.'

'And knowing it is his land you come for, he still gave you a welcome?'

'I didn't exactly trumpet that was my aim, but he cannot have failed to realise my interest. And I think perhaps there would be an accommodation to be made, for he seems an easy-going sort of creature, who has no ambitions to be a great man. And though his holdings are sizeable, happiness appears to consist of living in his own place, with plenty of peat on the hearth and a few cows in the byre and enough food and drink to cater for him and any who stumble by.'

'Not an altogether unworthy ambition,' Elizabeth said, her tone dry.

Hugh laughed again. 'Is that what you wish for me ... for us? That I drink myself into oblivion by day and snore my way through the night? It might be gey boring for you.'

A serious note crept into Elizabeth's voice. 'There is much to be said for a lack of ambition. I would not be sorry should you think less of advancement and more of the content to be had in small things.'

'No more would I, should we be allowed that luxury.'

She ignored the implication, sought to counter it. 'Surely we should be able to find much to take pleasure in within our own bounds.' There was a sound of scuffling from above their head, followed by a shriek and a succession of giggles. 'Family, for one. Our children healthy and happy and full of life.'

There was another shriek, followed by a wail. Hugh

nodded towards the ceiling. 'Rather too full sometimes. Should you...?'

Elizabeth made no move. 'No. If there is a leg broken no doubt they will come and tell us, otherwise they'll sort themselves out.'

It was John's turn to laugh. 'Our mother would have approved of you. That was her philosophy, exactly. And I often the loser by it, for that Hugh and George took advantage of their extra years and made me do their bidding whether I wished to or not.'

Elizabeth patted his arm, her voice dripping false sympathy. 'You were hard done by, I'm sure.'

'Spoilt, rather,' Hugh said. 'Allowed to do without question everything we had to fight for. It took all my powers of persuasion to be allowed to go to Holland, to join the army of the Prince of Orange, but when it came to Patrick and John, they were let slip without so much as a word of protest.'

There was a moment of silence, as if the spectre of Patrick stood in the room with them. Elizabeth, recognising it was better to speak than to have the shadow remain, said, 'He would not want us maudlin. He died as he lived, with energy and vigour and honour. The memory of him something to take pride in.'

Hugh nodded. 'Indeed. Father and Mother both would have applauded the man he became. Which is more than can be said of all those hereabouts.'

Elizabeth sighed. 'Are we never to be free of thought of the Cunninghames?'

'It is hard not to think of them, nor to desire to be beyond their reach. Having the Irish Sea as a barrier

229

between us would suit me very well. As I think it would you.'

Elizabeth was staring into the fire, seeing the farmhouse by Cayeux, the fields stretching beyond it on all sides, the river meandering close by, a glint of sea visible from the attic windows. She remembered the shame she'd felt at her envy of the opportunity the Munros had to start afresh in a new place – perhaps ambition was not such a bad thing after all. As much to encourage herself as him, she took Hugh's lead. 'What like of country is it?'

'Con's land? Gentle. Green. With little humps of hills all around, making it almost impossible to ride in a straight line except at the shore. His tower, Castle Reagh, looks towards the larger of two sea lochs, and the hills of Antrim beyond. And in the other direction there is another, smaller loch dotted with tiny islands scarce big enough to support a sheep. They go by the name of pladdies, and there are plenty of stories of how they came to be, and of the little people who inhabit them. He paused, as if a thought had just struck him. 'Come to think of it, I saw no sheep at all, so where the wool comes from for weaving I'm not sure. Not many dwellings either, but fertile ground by the look of it, so land ripe for the picking you might say. And plenty of woodland to provide timber for building.'

'I'd like fine to see it for myself.'

It was an impulsive comment, made without any prior thought, but once spoken, the idea took root. It was clearly a new thought to Hugh also, and with an instinct born of ten years of marriage, she said no more, content to wait and see what might come of it.

April arrived, and with it a week of good weather to welcome the new lambs. Hugh, his cheerfulness a result of the number of twin births, where mother and lambs both survived, surprised Elizabeth by breezing in waving a letter. 'From your brother. He will oblige us with the passage to Donaghadee, and though the harbour there isn't much to talk of, and horses a mite hard to come by, with luck we can cross to Ireland and be over to the Ards and back within the day.'

Elizabeth, who was once again pregnant but hadn't mentioned it, hid her concern for the new life quickening within her, for it had after all been her own idea. She put on her brightest voice. 'When can we go?'

Hugh grinned his satisfaction. 'The lambing will be passed within the month, and if there are any tailenders, no doubt they can be managed without me, and,' he touched her shoulder, as if to halt any protest, 'the house can take care of itself for a day or two without you.'

John Montgomerie, arriving just as Hugh was sketching a map of the Ards on the back of a pamphlet to illustrate how close everywhere was, raised his eyebrows at Elizabeth behind Hugh's back. And when Hugh had disappeared again to see to the stock, he hunkered down by Elizabeth's chair. 'Are you sure this is wise?'

She coloured. 'What do you mean?'

'I am a physician, Elizabeth. I can spot a pregnancy without it being shouted from the rooftops. I take it

231

Hugh doesn't know?'

'I didn't want to raise his hopes, not yet, and when he came with my brother's letter, he was so pleased he'd arranged it all I didn't want to spoil it. Besides, what harm can it do? I am but a few weeks gone, and feel more energetic than I have felt for a long time. I will be confined to quarters soon enough, as soon as Hugh knows of the babe. A day or two now won't make any difference. Will it?'

'You have had no bleeding or spotting, no twinges of any kind?'

'Nothing. And once we are home again I will tell Hugh. I promise. And in the meantime, you will keep my secret?'

'All right. If you promise *me* that if you feel any discomfort, any at all, you will say. Hugh's disappointment, should the jaunt have to be cancelled, would be nothing to his disappointment if you lost a child.'

Chapter 10

It was not how it was meant to be. The call came on 9 April in the hours before dawn, the messenger hammering at the door of their apartment, the servant who answered it grumbling at the disturbance. The messenger was brusque. 'Fetch Lady Munro. The Duchesse de Beaufort has need of her.'

It was a matter of minutes only before Kate was up and sufficiently dressed to pass, should she meet anyone as she flew along the corridors to the Duchesse's chambers. She had gauged instantly from the messenger's sombre expression that it was not the moment to be concerned about the niceties of layers of petticoats and had contented herself with pulling a skirt and bodice over her shift, dismissing the maid's disapproving mutter about the impropriety of it all. She ordered her to lace the bodice. 'The King will notice little and care less about my state of dress if I can but produce a living child for him and a mother who suffers no ill effects in the process. What is attire when compared to a life?' Her haste was justified by the fear in the eyes of the lady-in-waiting who met her at the door, a sheen of sweat on her face, a strand of hair escaping from her coif, words spilling from her.

'When the pains started she told us it was nothing. That we should not trouble you. That it was too soon

233

and they were phantom pains only, as she had before all three previous births. I was not here then, so had nothing to compare it with, no reason to think she was wrong.' There was a catch in her voice. 'No right to challenge her.'

And that, Kate thought, grimly, is part of the problem with the nobility: the deference servants feel towards them, which can so often be to their detriment. Had it been Agnes looking to Kate, she would have minced no words. Thrusting the thought away, she pushed the sleeves of the shift up over her elbows. It was too soon, but not seriously so, for many an eight-month child survived, with no apparent problem in either physical or mental capacity. She prayed it would be so now. She hurried through the salon to the bedchamber, throwing questions over her shoulder as she went. 'How long ago did the pains start?'

'Yesterday, in the forenoon.'

'And the interval between?'

'At first it was occasional twinges, sharp enough by the look of her face, but of a few moments' duration only. It wasn't until after supper they began in earnest.'

'And now?'

'There is no let up.' Her voice broke. 'But it isn't that...'

A group of ladies were clustered in the corridor outside the bedchamber and parted to let Kate through, their silence chilling. Gabrielle was not on the birthing chair but lying on the bed, her hair flowing loose, her skin the colour of parchment, a sheet tumbled about her. At the head of the bed one of her ladies paused in the wringing out of a cloth and turned, cold water falling unheeded onto the polished floor, the rhythmic drip, drip magnified by the silence.

The contractions were indeed constant, indicated by the arching of Gabrielle's back and the distortion of her mouth as if she screamed, yet without sound. She turned her head as Kate approached, and in a momentary gap between contractions, she struggled to acknowledge her. Kate knelt down, fighting her apprehension. She had never seen anything like this before, had no understanding of what might be the cause of Gabrielle's dumbness. She placed her hand on her forehead. 'Don't try to speak. Let us concentrate on bringing this little one into the world.'

Behind her, she was aware of the cluster of ladies who had followed her into the room and were now gathered in a huddle. Glancing across, she thought of dismissing them but, recognising in their faces genuine concern for the Duchesse, let them be. One said, her voice ragged, 'If there is anything … anything we can do…'

'If I have need, I'll ask. In the meantime, the best you can do is pray. For the Duchesse, and for the unborn child.' As the most senior of them moved to the prie-dieu and fell to her knees, her voice rising, she added, 'But silently, if you please.' She thrust aside the sheet and palpated the abdomen to check the presentation of the babe. It at least was normal, the head clearly engaged. She rummaged in her bag, found the slender ear trumpet, bent down to listen. There was a sob from another of the ladies, and fighting irritation, Kate made a chopping motion with her hand, the sound cut off midstream. She shut her eyes to concentrate, willed there to be a heartbeat. Finally she straightened, shaking her head. Another sob, hastily stifled, as the youngest of Gabrielle's ladies, placing her hand over her mouth, rushed for the door. Kate nodded but said, 'Not a word mind, to anyone. Not yet.' And then, as a crumb of comfort, 'For I cannot be totally sure until the babe is delivered. Which will likely not be long.' She turned her back for a moment on Gabrielle, spoke in an undertone to the woman at her side. 'The babe we may not be able to save, but the sooner it is delivered, the better chance there is for the Duchesse.'

The woman jerked her head towards the birthing chair, a question in her eyes. Kate nodded and, placing her arm around Gabrielle's shoulders, lifted her to a sitting position. Her tone was positive, encouraging, though inside she felt the customary sadness. It was never easy to lose a babe. 'We need to get you onto the chair. Can you stand?'

Gabrielle tried once again to speak, again without success, managed a nod. They had barely enough time to get her settled before another contraction, her fists clenched. Kate knelt in front of her, saw the crown of the babe's head, commanded, 'Please, Duchesse, one last effort and it will be done.' There was a rush of blood and the head was in her hand, the small body sliding out after it. Kate severed the cord, tied it, motioned to several of the women. 'When the afterbirth has come, help the Duchesse back into bed. I will concentrate on the babe.' The boy lay, blue and inert in her hands, but she wasn't ready to give up. She took the towel someone offered and leant her back against the bed for support, rubbing at the small chest, the buttocks, the limbs, praying for the pink tinge that would indicate hope. She gently prised open the mouth, checking for mucous and, finding it clear, blew in, paused, blew again, each breath punctuated by a renewed massaging of the chest.

From somewhere a bell chimed the half-hour, and Kate, lifting her head, saw with surprise the light outside the window, as dawn seeped into the sky. It should have been a good omen, but was not. The was a touch on her shoulder, hands reaching down to remove the babe, wrapping it up reverently, the towel a shroud. She heard herself saying, 'Go to Rosny. Warn him of what has happened. He will want to send to Fontainebleau, for the King must be told.' And as the whisper of skirts faded, she stood up and moved to attend to Gabrielle, who lay, eyes shut, her breathing shallow and fast. Kate touched her forehead. It was on fire, but dry as tinder, the colour, previously lacking, now spreading downwards across her cheeks, her neck and throat, her chest. Kate dipped the cloth in the basin of water standing by the head of the bed, found it tepid. 'Fetch fresh cool water, and more cloths. Her temperature must be reduced as speedily as possible.'

She bent to wipe away the trickle of saliva from the corner of Gabrielle's mouth, the realisation winding her. 'Oh, dear God.' It was scarcely audible, but it brought one of Gabrielle's ladies to her side.

'What is it?'

Wordlessly, Kate motioned towards the droop of Gabrielle's mouth, the slackness of one-half of her upper lip. She lifted the left hand, allowed it to drop onto the coverlet, her voice husky as if she had a cold. 'She has suffered a palsy, which, if it has affected her vocal cords,

237

may explain the lack of both speech and screaming.'

'Will she recover?'

Kate lifted her shoulders. 'Who knows. It is a little studied area of medicine, and though I will do what I can, there are no guarantees. And to be truthful, I have seen it in the old, but not in this circumstance. It is an added complication to the fever she could well have done without.'

The door opened as the youngest of the ladies-in-waiting returned to the room, her face still ashen. Kate looked up and nodded to show she thought no less of her for her earlier weakness, for the girl was barely fifteen, and likely with no previous experience of a birth gone wrong.

As she crossed to the foot of the bed, and gazed at Gabrielle, she blurted out, 'What of the King? He sets such store by beauty.'

It was likely in all their minds, but however much truth it contained, Kate felt the need to stifle it. 'That's enough. We must pray rather for the Duchesse's recovery, not waste our efforts on unseemly thoughts.' There was the sound of rapid footsteps on the gravel below the window, a knocking on the outside door, and a voice Kate recognised as Rosny. She asked, 'Is anyone with him?'

The woman nearest the window opened the casement a fraction, peered down. 'He's alone.'

Kate touched the wrist of the oldest of Gabrielle's ladies, who was hovering at her elbow. 'If you can delay him a little I will make the Duchesse more presentable.' She had only a few moments to straighten the covers and smooth the Duchesse's hair before the door opened,

Rosny filling the frame. She saw him glance towards the empty cradle, then to the bed where the Duchesse lay motionless.

His voice was unusually tentative. 'She sleeps?'

Kate hesitated. 'I have given her a sedative, yes, for the birth was not easy, and afterwards, with nothing to show for all the pain, I thought it more important that she rest.' She decided honesty was best. 'But there is something else, more troubling than the loss of the babe.'

Rosny took a step towards the bed, scrutinised Gabrielle more closely. 'Which is?'

'A palsy, of the left side, and perhaps of the throat also. It may only be temporary, but I cannot be sure. I thought the King should be advised of what has happened before he comes to see for himself.'

He was looking past her. 'Word must indeed go immediately, but I do not think it the job for a messenger. Someone more appropriate must be found.'

Focused on Gabrielle and her needs, Kate said, without any thought for the presumption of the suggestion, 'You are his friend, as well as his advisor. Are you not best placed to find the appropriate words?'

'You cannot give definite hope?'

Kate squared her shoulders. 'No. It wouldn't be right to promise what may not be brought to pass.' She placed her hand on Gabrielle's forehead once more. 'Aside from the palsy, a fever rages, and though that I can attempt to treat it, I likewise cannot give any guarantee of success.'

He was drumming his fingers on the cabinet beside the bed, thinking aloud. 'There are reasons why I cannot leave Paris at the moment...' He glanced at her as if

239

making a connection. 'Sir Adam is at Fontainebleau with the King, is he not? His value is far beyond that of bodyguard...' A settling of his shoulders, as if a decision made. He took a deep breath. 'I shall send a message to your husband. There is no one better.'

Kate bent her head, afraid her instinctive reaction might be noted, for it was not a task anyone would wish, and Adam as likely to flounder as anyone, perhaps more so, for a way with words wasn't his forte – if she could get a message to him ... suggest what to say ... she took a deep breath. 'Our son is also in the Gardes. Perhaps he could relay your instructions to my husband?'

'Excellent idea. I shall send for him directly.' And then, mirroring her own thoughts, 'It will be perhaps best if you can frame a message for your husband to take to the King. Your son can collect it en route.' He looked down at Gabrielle again, an odd expression in his eyes. 'She is asleep now. How long might she remain so?'

'The sedative is strong and will keep her settled for many hours yet. And if there is no improvement by tomorrow morning I shall administer it again. Complete rest sometimes goes a long way to allowing the body to heal itself, especially when there is no immediately obvious remedy available.'

With a nod he was gone, leaving Kate with the memory of his expression as he stood over Gabrielle, and the uncomfortable thought that perhaps he would not altogether mind her passing.

Chapter 11

There was a stiff breeze blowing from the west as Robbie
left Paris by the Versailles Gate heading for Fontainebleau.
Even without Rosny's authorisation to ride post-haste, the
few minutes he had spent with his mother, in the salon
adjacent to the Duchesse de Beaufort's bedchamber,
would have been enough to convey to him the urgency
of the letter he carried. She had shut the door firmly
behind her as she came to greet him, clearly to ensure he
saw nothing of the room beyond, and as she presented
her face for him to kiss, it seemed little more than an
automatic gesture.

Her instructions were equally abrupt, further evidence,
if any were needed, that the task he'd been assigned was
a vital one.

'Spare neither yourself nor your horse, Robbie, for
this is a matter that will touch not only the King, but all
of us, whichever way it turns out.'

Her eyes were shining with unshed tears, which took
him by surprise, for he had always been aware of her
unspoken disapproval of the relationship between the
King and the Duchesse.

As if she read his mind she said, 'I would not have
wished this on anyone, regardless of how irregular the
relationship.'

He had been spared the details of what ailed the Duchesse, but it was sufficient to know that the child was dead and she likely in grave danger also. As he spurred his horse into a gallop, he found himself thinking of Eugenie, of the feelings she stirred in him, of what might lie in store for her were their relationship to grow into something permanent – perhaps it would be kindest *not* to pursue her, not to ask her to run such risks. It was a thought that repeated itself over and over in his head throughout the long ride, between a growing appreciation of the mount Rosny had instructed he take. It wasn't every horse that could be depended upon to cover thirty-five miles without protest, even with the regular breaks he gave it, stopping every hour or so, and sliding from its back to allow it to crop at the grass and take a drink from a slow-moving stream. At least the weather was neither too warm nor wet, the ground soft enough for easy passage but not so soft they risked getting bogged down. Another month or two and it might be a different matter.

He was skirting the edge of the forest of Fontainebleau, and though he wasn't normally fanciful, the sound of the wind soughing in the trees as they bent towards him reminded him of his grandmother's keening as they laid Anna to rest in the hollow below Broomelaw. As always when he thought of it, the vision of his father, stony-faced, his body rigid, as if he feared to relax his muscles even for a moment, lest he collapse under the weight of his pain, rose up in his mind, as fresh today as it had been nine years since. In the months that followed, when it seemed no one could penetrate the barrier his father had erected around himself, Robbie had come close to hating

242

him, a memory he would rather not recall, despite that he knew it was the reaction of a child and therefore not something to be ashamed of. Now, with the benefit of maturity, he wondered what might befall France should the King be equally bereft if the Duchesse were to die.

Dusk had fallen by the time he arrived at the gates of the chateau, the gatekeeper who responded to his summons fumbling at the bolts and unsteady on his feet. Robbie was brusque, mimicking his father at his most authoritative, flashing the orders he'd received from Rosny. 'This is the King's business. Do not delay me or it may be the last time you open this gate.' His horse was lathered and showing signs of fatigue, and he relaxed his hold on the reins and allowed him to slow as they made their way up the long avenue towards the chateau. A minute or two more would make little difference.

Munro was sitting, his uniform undone, his legs stretched out towards the fire smouldering in the grate of the chamber occupied by the small contingent of Gardes who had accompanied the King. He rose to his feet, apprehension showing on his face as the servant ushered Robbie in. 'What brings you here? Is it your mother? Patrick John?'

Robbie shook his head. 'We're all fine. It's...' he glanced towards the other Gardes. 'I have a message from Rosny, which I was to deliver to you in person.'

Munro rose and hustled Robbie from the chamber. In the corridor he paused. 'It is not good news?'

'No. The Duchesse de Beaufort has been brought to bed but the child was stillborn.'

'And the Duchesse?'

'Not good, I think. At any rate, Mother thought the King should be sent for and Rosny agreed.'

'Munro was buttoning up his jacket. 'Why have you come to me rather than straight to the King?'

'Those were my instructions.' Robbie pulled out the letter Kate had entrusted to him. 'And these are yours. They thought it better the news be broken to him rather than have him read it for himself. The wording, I believe, is Mother's.'

Munro broke the seal, scanned the contents, his mouth tightening. He turned back into the room, nodding to two of the Gardes. 'There is news of the Duchesse. Go to the stables. Make sure there are horses prepared. If I know the King, he will want to leave straightaway. When the horses are ready wait in the courtyard. An escort of four will be sufficient.' He let them past. Then, gripping Robbie firmly by the shoulder, said, 'You're with me.' Once out of earshot of the guards he added, 'Henri may have some questions for you, which the letter doesn't answer.'

'I did not see the Duchesse, there is nothing...'

'You saw your mother. That must have given you some inkling of just how urgent this is.'

As Munro had predicted, they rode through the night, Henri pushing his horse as if the devil was at his heels, the others with no alternative but to do likewise. The horse

Robbie had been given to replace his own struggled to keep the pace, and he had to use his spurs constantly not to be left trailing behind. In front of him Munro rode beside Henri, the set of his shoulders mirroring the rigidity of the King. Dawn was breaking as they reached the outskirts of Paris, light beginning to emerge from a heavy sky, a few curls of smoke rising upwards, pale, wraithlike.

'Lost souls,' the woman who looked after his granddame had once said, when he woke early at Renfrew and knelt up on the window seat to look out over the town.

He remembered the uncertain note in his granddame's voice, as if she wasn't quite sure of herself when she retorted, 'Stuff and nonsense, Robbie. There is nothing out there but fires being coaxed awake from their slumber.' He hadn't quite believed her, and for a long time after Anna died had refused to look any higher than the ground floor of the tower, in case he accidentally caught a glimpse of her soul writhing into the sky above him.

'Robbie!' Munro's voice brought him back to the present and he reined in his horse a fraction to the rear of the King. A rider was galloping towards them, the hoofbeats echoing in the silence, and even at a distance they could tell he pushed the horse as hard as possible. There was not enough light to distinguish his livery, the Gardes shifting to form a protective cordon around the King and drawing their pistols.

'Hold fire, until I give the order,' Munro said. 'It may be another messenger from the Louvre.'

Robbie, his eyes still with the keenness of youth, was

the first to recognise the rider's colours. 'It's a Garde.'

They sheathed their pistols and waited in silence for the rider to reach them. He pulled up sharply, his distress visible in the tremor of his voice as he bowed to Henri.

'Sire.'

'You have word from the Louvre?'

Robbie, looking at the messenger's face, knew the Duchesse had gone. Munro, clearly thinking the same, reached out and placed his hand on Henri's arm.

The King took a deep breath. 'I am too late?' He shook off Munro and spurred his horse to a gallop.

Ahead of them the bulk of the city gate loomed, shadowed but solid. Munro cast a glance towards the King, who still forged ahead, and bent his head towards Robbie, his voice quiet. 'Did Rosny make any provision for the opening of the gate?'

Robbie fumbled in his jerkin. 'I should have given you the authorisation at Fontainebleau, but it slipped my mind.'

'No matter.' Munro took the proffered paper and urged his horse forward to catch up with the King. He turned sideways on to the gate and leaning downwards hammered on the sturdy planking. They could hear the guard on the inside grumbling as he pulled back the bolt.

'All right, all right, I'm coming. Give a body time.' The small inset door opened a fraction and a man appeared in the gap, bleary-eyed and yawning. Munro didn't need to hand over the paper, for the man looked up, his eyes opening wide, and bowed low.

Henri acknowledged his response, but there was an irritated nuance in his voice unusual in his dealings with the common folk. 'Yes, yes ... thank you. We are in haste, as you see.'

The door banged shut and they heard the thump as the beam securing the main gate slid back into its socket accompanied by a muffled oath. Then the screech of hinges as the gate swung inwards. The man who had first stuck his head out was over to the side, dancing from foot to foot, a hand in his mouth. Robbie shot him a sympathetic glance, for he well remembered the pain of fingers trapped in similar circumstances.

Chapter 12

Whatever Rosny's opinion might be, there was no mistaking the King's distress as he burst into the room, his doublet splattered with mud, mismatched boots on his feet. Not that it was unusual to see the King deshabillé, for his carelessness of dress had often been the subject of amusement among the ladies of the court, but there was an additional wildness in his expression that betokened an anguish far beyond anything Kate had seen before. He threw himself onto his knees by the side of the bed and gathered Gabrielle's inert form in his arms, holding her against his chest. For the first time since coming to court Kate understood the loyalty Munro had for Henri, the willingness to forgive him his faults for the sake of the essential goodness he saw in him.

She knelt down beside him. 'I'm sorry, Sire, that I could not save either the Duchesse or the child.'

He brushed one hand across his cheek, a crack in his voice. 'How could this happen?'

It was impossible to lie. 'I don't know, for I haven't seen anything like this before.'

He laid Gabrielle back against the pillows, smoothing her hair, stroking her face. As he ran his finger across her lips, halting at the still drooping corner, the gaze he fixed on Kate was that of a bewildered child. 'She was young and healthy. The other births...' He touched her mouth again. 'Aside from this, she does not look...'

With a heartfelt prayer of thanks that she had been able to smooth out the worst of the facial contortion with which the Duchesse had died, Kate said, 'It happened so fast ... there was nothing I could do.' As he struggled to his feet, she dared to meet his eyes, tears trembling in them. He looked down at his boots and began to laugh, great gasps of sound torn from his chest. Had it been a child she would have slapped him. As it was, she was powerless to stop it.

'You know I would have made her my Queen?'

Henri was standing, his back to the window. Kate sank in a curtsey. In the three hours since he had left Gabrielle's chamber, she had waited for and dreaded this summons. She had begun the work of preparing the body for burial, for though it was not her responsibility, she felt she owed it to the Duchesse, a way of assuaging her guilt: at her inability to save her, and for the personal reservations she had never been able to entirely ignore. The picture of Gabrielle's slide towards death, as first her speech, then her hearing, then her sight, deserted her, was an image that haunted Kate, the obvious agony of the final convulsion that left her face ugly and distorted rendering her last breath a relief to those who witnessed it. She almost wished Henri had been there, however distressing, for it might have helped him to accept her passing. But if what he wanted of her now was to describe the horror of it, she wasn't sure she could do it.

Adam was standing at the King's side, as if to support him should he break down, his nod for her fractional.

'Lady Munro.' Henri's voice, as he stretched out his hand to her, was calm, his eyes empty of expression, the lack of apparent anger or distress more chilling than his previous storm of feeling had been. He led her to a chair and sat down facing her. 'Tell me what happened. All of it.'

'I cannot explain … it defies explanation.'

'I'm not asking for an explanation, only to know what happened.' His voice broke. 'I missed her last moments and for that I cannot forgive myself…' There was another pause. 'She sent me away … that I might not smother her with cosseting. And when I protested my concern, my wish to remain until she was safely delivered, she laughed and said I would be of more use going to Fontainebleau to hunt, and take half of the court with me, and leave this business to women, for men were more of a trial than a support at such times.' He was staring at the rug on the floor, at the picture of the fallen stag, arrows protruding from its side, huntsmen and dogs milling all around. 'Did I do wrong?'

Her instinctive reaction, to place her hand on his arm and offer the comfort of touch, was unthinkable. She sought for suitable words. 'No. It has always been thus. In the last months, besides the discomfort, a woman often feels unattractive and desires to hide away, especially from those who matter to them most.'

Kate saw Henri's mouth move, as if he wanted to

say something, but the words wouldn't come. Beside him, Munro shifted, as if he meant to fill the silence, her fractional shake of the head enough to halt him. Henri began again.

'At the end, did she say anything … ask for me?'

Kate thought of the horrible truth of those last moments and hesitated.

'She did not speak of me.' His voice was flat, his heartbreak clear.

It was impossible to leave him in ignorance, to allow him to torment himself with false thoughts – would the truth set him free? Perhaps not, but she had to try. 'She did not speak of you because she *could* not.'

He lifted his head at her emphasis and swallowed. 'Go on.'

'By the time I was called she had lost the ability to make any sound and never regained it. But these last weeks I sat with her many times and her thoughts were always of you, and of the child. Her hope that he would finally bring peace and stability to all of France.'

'He?'

She nodded. 'Yes … I'm sorry.'

'I have two other sons and a daughter. If the Duchesse had been saved, that would have far out-weighed the loss of the child. She was … everything to me.' He fell silent.

For a moment Kate was tempted to leave it there, but recognising it was cowardice on her part and that it would not serve the King well in the long run, she took another deep breath. There was no good way to say it, no alternative but to be honest. 'Her speech was the first to go, I thought the result of a palsy, and possibly

251

temporary. But when it was clear that she could no longer hear, and her sight was also failing, I knew there was little hope. That was when I sent word. Perhaps I should have sent sooner.' She paused, the memory of Gabrielle's contorted face, which she had worked hard to straighten out, vivid in her mind. 'But I am not sorry I delayed.'

He stirred at that, a frown settling on his face.

'This I do know,' she continued, 'the Duchesse would not have wished for you to see her in that state, to have your memory of her clouded.' She paused again, aware she might be thought presumptuous to offer advice. She glanced at Adam and, encouraged by another small nod, continued. 'Better you remember her as you last saw her, shining with hope and anticipation and, above all, content. Better for you, and for the children also, that their memories are untainted.'

'They were not able to see her?'

'No. By the time we knew the end was coming, the opportunity had passed. When all the preparations for burial are completed, that is when to bring them to make their goodbyes. She will look as if she sleeps and it will be easier for them to believe she is at peace.' It was not how she had meant to say it, the implication of doubt clear, in her own mind at least, and to judge by his stiffening, in Adam's mind also.

It was echoed by Henri, but for a different reason. 'She died in a state of grace?'

That at least she could answer in a way that would satisfy a Catholic, and judging by the question, he had truly embraced the faith. She suppressed her own opinion of the proceedings. 'The priest was with her at the end and gave her absolution.'

His relief was palpable, obvious in the settlement of his shoulders and the unclenching of his hands. 'Thank you. Whatever the circumstance, I am grateful for all you tried to do, and that you were with her at the end, for I know she considered you a true friend, and they are not always easy to find in a court such as ours.' There was another moment's silence, then, 'Your son also deserves my gratitude, it is not an easy thing to bring ill news to a king.'

'It was but his duty as a Garde, Sire.' Munro said.

'Nevertheless, I shall not forget it. Or him, for the Duchesse thought well of him and I have always respected her judgement.' He turned back to Kate. 'As for my children, they are fond of you and yours. If you can be of help to them through this time I will be doubly grateful.'

This time Kate had no reservation. 'Of course. We will do all we can.'

Henri looked towards the window as if noticing for the first time the rain slanting against it. 'This is an ill day. Thank you for seeking to soften it.' It seemed a dismissal of sorts, and so Kate took it, rising and curtseying before retreating to the door. But as she rose to leave, Henri halted her. 'And if you have need of anything, you have only to ask.'

Chapter 13

Portpatrick was shrouded in a thick sea haar as Hugh and Elizabeth picked their way around the litter of torn nets and damaged lobster pots stacked against the harbour wall. There was little wind, and Hugh, raising his head as if to sniff out a decent breeze, said, 'I'm sorry, Elizabeth, I trust this won't be a wasted journey, I'd hate to have inconvenienced your brother for nothing.'

'How much wind do we need?'

'More than this,' John Shaw said, 'or there'll be no point in trying. The last thing I'd want is for us to be marooned on the other side.'

She swayed in the saddle, feeling a little light-headed, but whether with her pregnant condition or the excitement of the journey, she wasn't sure, made an attempt at a joke. 'Pity we can't whistle for a wind.'

'If it would be effective, I'd be whistling my heart out right now and urging you to do the same.' As if to demonstrate, Hugh began to whistle a folk tune a fiddler had played for the children at the Michaelmas Fair.

She laughed, remembering his outrage at the price that had been extorted from them afterwards. He had been for haggling, but she had placed a restraining hand on his arm and whispered, 'Pay the man. We don't want the bairns to feel guilty that they pleaded for it.' Now she said, 'Maybe if you could whistle in tune it might do the job.'

'I am perfectly in tune.'

'With yourself, perhaps, but not recognisable to anyone else, far less the wind.'

As if to prove her wrong, they felt the stirring of a breeze, and a rat's tail of rope came birling along the quay at their feet, causing Hugh's horse to shy. He held it in check. 'Easy now, easy.' And to Elizabeth, 'Maybe we will be lucky after all.'

John Shaw's boat was moored at the seaward end of the harbour, the preparations for sailing already made. He climbed up from the deck and, helping Elizabeth down from the saddle, hugged her, then stepped back. 'You're looking well.' A pause, his eyes widening.

With a glance towards Hugh, who was busying himself removing the saddles, she pulled John out of earshot. 'Please, don't say anything. If Hugh knew he wouldn't let me come.'

'So you are…'

She placed her hand over his mouth. 'Only just.' And then, as Hugh turned back towards them, 'Will there be enough wind, John?'

'Out in the open sea, yes, but we may have to row first.' He nodded at Hugh. 'If you can still manage an oar?'

'How do we load the horses?' Elizabeth said, seeking distraction.

'Ah. Watch and learn.' John grinned and indicated a rickety-looking contraption mounted on the harbour wall. A beam, attached to a collection of ropes and pulleys,

255

protruded from it, much like a swee they swung round to place pots over the fire, only bigger.

Hugh was leading both horses, now saddleless, towards the beam.

There was doubt in Elizabeth's voice. 'Will it take the weight?'

'It's a lot sturdier than it looks. We often have cargo to load and unload and it's never failed us yet.'

It was clear they'd done it many times before, for in a matter of minutes the first horse was secured in the sling and swinging out over the edge of the harbour wall, legs dangling. John was working the pulleys, Hugh leaning over the edge directing him. Elizabeth hadn't realised she was holding her breath until she heard a voice calling up from the deck, 'Slowly ... slowly ... that's it!' accompanied by the ring of horseshoes on timber.

As they were nosing their way out of the harbour, she asked, 'Will it be the reverse process at the other side?'

'No. The harbour at Donaghadee, if such it can be called, is little more than a jetty, protected by a low curve of wall. If we time it right it will be a simple matter of leading the horses up a short ramp.'

'And if we're wrong?'

'Don't worry. We have the tides right ... so long as we don't have to row the whole way...'

It's a joke, she told herself. It has to be. And so it proved, for there was plenty of wind, in fact rather too much for Elizabeth, and with it a driving rain that, though it dispersed the haar clinging around the rigging, similarly blotted out all possibility of seeing anything of the crossing. Not that Elizabeth was caring, her main concern to hold onto her breakfast. She remained below deck, the roll of the boat sufficient to explain her queasiness, had Hugh questioned her, and despite her own discomfort, she envied him as he breezed in and out of the small cabin, his hair windblown and glistening, his relish in the conditions easy to see.

'Is it always like this?' She gestured towards the small scuttle, which was above the water level one moment and below it the next.

'Not always.' He grinned at her. 'They say it can be as calm as a millpond, though I have to admit I've not experienced that. Only a bit of a swell, as now.'

'A bit of a swell?' She struggled upright, her stomach lurching in response. 'I'd hate to see it rough.'

Hugh's grin broadened. 'This was your idea, remember.' He stretched out his hand with a smile. 'Come on. The rain has all but stopped, and the fresh air will do you good. Besides that, you won't want to miss the first sight of the Irish coastline.'

In truth, Elizabeth would willingly have been spirited back to her own bed at Braidstane, should such a thing have been possible, but she reached to take his hand and allowed him to haul her to her feet. At the foot of the companionway he paused and indicated for her to go first, joking, 'I'll be able to break your fall, should the need arise.'

She devoutly hoped it wouldn't arise, for she was having enough trouble as it was, and nice as it had been to have a breakfast set in front of her that she hadn't had a hand in preparing or serving, she rather wished she hadn't eaten at all.

As if he read her mind, Hugh said, 'We will be on dry land soon enough and you will feel yourself again, I promise you.'

'You promised the crossing would be easy. Should I trust you this time?'

He placed a hand in the small of her back. 'Up you go. We have little enough time to spend before we'll have to come back.'

'That's what worries me. That we have all this to do again. And next time I may not be able to stop my stomach rebelling.'

He smiled down at her. 'The first time is always the worst. On the way home you may be standing with me at the rail enjoying every minute of it. In the meantime, I wish to show you as much of the countryside as I can. A pity we won't make it to Castle Reagh, for I think you might find Con O'Neill entertaining. He has a charm to him that is hard to explain, halfway drunk or not.'

The countryside *was* green, startlingly so, even for someone used to the dampness of the west of Scotland. The grass sprang fresh under the ponies' hooves and the gentle hillsides had an emerald sheen to them indicating Ulster might beat even Ayrshire in the rain stakes. As if to confirm her suspicion, the rain started again as they left the small harbour and skirted the cluster of cottages ranged along the shore. Looking at them, Elizabeth wondered why they had been set gable-end onto the sea and was just about to ask when Hugh nodded towards them.

'The gable-ends of the houses aye take a battering.'

'The winters can be harsh here too?'

'Not harsh, exactly, for they get very little snow or frost, but the winds can be wild, and if they coincide with a high tide, the sea does a good job of washing the cottage walls. That's why they don't have any windows facing it.'

Elizabeth lifted her face to the rain, the dampness refreshing. It felt more like mist, except that, unlike the Scottish haar that blotted out the landscape as if it had never been, this was a fine dusting, pearling their shoulders and sparkling on their cheeks. She found it hard to imagine rain like this battering anything, and breathing in the clean mix of the rain and air she found, as Hugh had predicted, that her stomach settled. They struck across country, weaving in and out of the small hills, the hollows dotted here and there with bog cotton, the stems waving in the breeze. In the distance, a range of mountains, their slopes purple-black, their tops obscured in cloud, making it impossible to gauge their true height.

Hugh said, 'They are the only hills hereabouts, and a steep enough climb, I believe, if that was your wish, but not likely to be of much importance to us, for they are further away than they look.'

'To us, maybe not, but the children may think differently. Kate has a fertile imagination and will likely see them as the lair of giants, which we should take very good care not to awake.'

'The children? Or you? They must get their imagination from someone, and I don't think it's me.'

That, she couldn't argue with, and stifling any superstitious thoughts, she settled to taking in as much of the surroundings as she could. It was unlikely she'd have another chance to gauge the lie of the land, for once Hugh knew of her pregnancy, that would be the last of her gallivanting until the babe was safely delivered. There was something itching at the edge of her brain, a lack that to begin with she couldn't pinpoint. It wasn't until they approached the head of a loch, and she saw a second cluster of cottages clumped together close to the water's edge, that she realised what troubled her. She thought back to the countryside they'd come through, the land almost untouched by habitation. 'Surely it wasn't always this empty?'

'There is the occasional cottage, tucked away in the shelter of a hollow, if there is a water source near at hand, but they are few and far between. Word is it's a result of the English Queen's attempt at plantation. She parcelled out land to those who were interested in making their fortunes on this side of the water, but the venture proved a failure, though not before the majority of the native Irish fled southwards, burning down all they left behind them. At least so Con boasted, as if it were the best tactic in the world. And perhaps it was, for it seems it worked.'

'The people still lost their land.'

'Yes, yes, they did. But that is long since, and we stand to benefit from it, for as you saw, the countryside is so sparsely populated none need to be displaced. I believe it is different further north.'

260

Elizabeth's thoughts were already elsewhere. 'What of tenancies? If you were to be granted land, would the few cottagers there are be able to stay?'

Hugh shrugged. 'I have no idea of their existing arrangements, but if they can pay their way I would not be driving them from their homes.'

'What if they don't have to pay at the moment, if they aren't tenants, but own the land?'

He swept his arm in a wide arc. 'There are no fields to speak of, no strip farming, only the scraps of garden ground with a few vegetables, and a pig or two tethered outside the wall. From what I can gather, they look more to the sea for their food than to the land. You might not credit it, but they find seaweed a delicacy. Hardly what you'd expect of a landowner.'

The thought of it was enough to turn Elizabeth's stomach. 'A good job we brought our own provisions.'

'Speaking of food…' Hugh indicated a stump of a building set back a little from the loch shore, the roof gone, the walls no more than single-storey, punctured by a few narrow window slits. 'That,' he said, 'is the remnant of a castle, and will, I hope, provide us with sufficient shelter to take a rest and a bite.' They walked the ponies round to the landward side of the ruin and found the remains of an inglenook fireplace, with a stone seat inset below the partial arch that was all that survived of a broad curve of chimney. Hugh, with a glance at the sky, as if disappointed he'd been unable to conjure up a glimmer of sunshine, swung himself down from his horse and grasped Elizabeth around the waist. 'This is likely as good a place as any, and it's a long time since breakfast.'

Someone had been there before them, a few half-charred sticks lying in the hearth amidst a crumbling of ash. He rummaged in his saddlebag and produced a flint. 'There's a bit of burning in those yet, we might as well make use of it.' As he knelt down, Elizabeth had the uncomfortable sensation of being watched, but when she turned saw no one. He criss-crossed the sticks, struck a spark and held it under them until a curl of smoke became flame. A second stick took light, then a third, and when it was burning steadily he smiled up at her, and scrambling to his feet, he stretched out his cloak over the seat and bowed. 'Welcome, to what may be your new home.' When she hesitated, he said, 'You needn't worry about the fire, it was likely nobody of importance, children perhaps, playing at living in a castle.'

As if conjured up, a boy appeared by the stump of wall, and though his breeches were frayed and his collar likewise, he had a dignity to him, his unaccented English a surprise. 'This,' he said, coming close, 'is O'Neill land, and you're trespassing.'

'We have but stopped for a bite,' Hugh said.

'I see you lit a fire. A sensible precaution.'

'Against what?' Elizabeth wanted him to say wolves, for they were to be expected, but from his expression she suspected he wouldn't.

'Not what. Who. Cathal Airt O'Neill. This was his, until the English came.' He spat. 'They drove him out, hanged him for it. But that very hour,' his voice took on the dolorous quality of a death knell, 'while they watched him dance, a fire started. The O'Neill says it was an accident, a spark setting the straw alight, but other folk

262

think different.' He stopped, as if unwilling to say more.

'What do they say?'

'That he was seen setting the fire. Cursing the stones.'

Hugh was clearly amused. 'And our fire?'

'If he sees smoke he thinks it still burns and rests content.'

Elizabeth stood up. 'I think we've lingered here long enough.'

The boy inclined his head. 'Perhaps.'

They headed further along the shore. 'Stuff and nonsense,' Hugh said, 'and typical of papists, aye seeing ghosts were there are none. Those ruins may not look much, but I think we could start there, make a temporary home within the walls until we could build on a grander scale.'

Elizabeth turned in the saddle and saw the boy, now standing on top of the remnant of wall, watching them. She shivered. 'We are not welcome here.'

'We will be,' Hugh seemed unconcerned, 'if we treat folk right.'

She looked past him to where, at some distance from the shore, a single hill reared above the surrounding landscape, the lower slopes heavily wooded, the upper slopes outcrops of bare rock punctuated by swathes of gorse and heather. It dominated the skyline, a site that would, for generations of Ayrshire lairds, have been considered the ideal location for a tower house. 'Why not build up there?' she asked.

'No need. Here we can spread out, have all the conveniences of flat ground, close to the shore, and to land easily tilled.' There must be a source of fresh water nearby.'

'It is all Con O'Neill's land?'

'It seems so. He fell heir to it under some strange Irish system I didn't even try to get my head around. Not that he pays much attention to this area. He looks more to the north and east of his castle. And only to what is close to hand. If we want this, I see no problem in coming to terms with Con.'

A new thought struck her. 'There is no fear of flood?'

'If the cottages we passed can stand, then a good stone house surely can. Besides, though this is a tidal loch, we are a long way from the sea. It would be a flood of Genesis proportions to reach here.'

'The cottages aren't stone?'

'They may look like it, but no. They're wattle and daub, on a simple frame, and I daresay the whitewash is an extra protection from the rain, which, as you can see by the colour of the grass and the thickness of the thatch, is not an uncommon occurrence.' He reached across and touched her hand. 'You will not mind the rain?'

She looked up at the hill again and then all around. From the loch shore she heard the lapping of water and the call of a reed warbler, attracting a mate. She took a deep breath, and in an attempt to convince herself, said, 'I won't mind anything, if we can all be here, together, and at peace.' She took another breath, decided it was as good a moment as any, and placed her hand on top of his. 'All six of us.'

Chapter 14

Maggie was sitting with Kate in the anteroom of the chamber at the Palais de Justice. It had been three weeks since Gabrielle d'Estrées' death, three weeks in which rumours had grown wings and taken flight. In an attempt to silence the gossipmongers, Henri had insisted a commission of inquiry be set up to examine the circumstances surrounding her death and Kate was one of the first witnesses to be called. The image of Gabrielle's distorted face was something she had not yet been able to dispel from her mind. For the hundredth time since the death she pondered whether it would have been easier for Henri had he seen the Duchesse before she died, or if it was a blessing he hadn't. There was no doubting the depth of his distress at losing her, the whole court plunged into mourning, the King himself wearing black, something which, so Rosny said, no French King had done before. It was as if Gabrielle had truly been his queen. Her funeral was a sensation, not only within the court, but in the entire country, her coffin followed by a procession of nobles to Saint-Germain-l'Auxerrois for the requiem mass and then to Notre-Dame-La-Royale de Maubuisson Abbaye for the interment. It was unprecedented for a mistress to be accorded the honour of a state burial, but Henri would not be gainsaid. It was the first time Kate had seen for herself his stubborn streak, and it caused her to consider how much choice Gabrielle might have had in the matter of their relationship, or if at the start she'd had any at all.

There were plenty at the court who did not mourn her passing, but few had the courage to voice their thoughts. Sully, who, like Rosny, was one of the King's closest advisors, was the most outspoken. He expressed sincere condolences for the King's bereavement, but also said 'he hoped His Majesty recognised that providence had intervened in a just cause.'

Kate had whistled when Munro reported the comment to her.

'How did he dare to speak thus?' she asked.

Munro's admiration was clear. 'He is a brave man and an honest one, and has been close to the King for many years. What he said was borne out of love for Henri and for France. But he must have known it was a risk, especially in the King's current mood, when his likely reactions cannot be anticipated or guessed at. The fact that he wasn't arrested immediately is a sign Henri, however broken he might be by Gabrielle's death, is neither vindictive nor unable to recognise true loyalty.'

Now, as they waited, Maggie asked Kate, 'What will you tell them?'

'The truth. That I cannot precisely establish the cause of death, but that it seems to have stemmed from some kind of seizure brought on by the premature birth.'

'Or the other way round?' Maggie's interest was professional, her thoughts less of the tragedy of it than of the potential medical interest.

'Perhaps, it's difficult to say which came first, the onset of labour or the palsy, but whatever the case, I saw no indication of poison or other foul play. And that is what I must state, clearly and without equivocation. Whether there is a medical reason for what happened, or if indeed it was the "hand of God", as many believe, is rather more challenging to sift.'

'Monsieur Daumont might be able to shed light on it, were he to be allowed to examine the body.' Maggie sounded almost hopeful.

'Cut it, you mean?' Kate shook her head. 'The King supports all manner of new developments, including in the medical sphere. If he did not, you would not have had the opportunity to learn alongside Monsieur Daumont these last months. And, in principle, he favours the examination of the dead, to see what can be learned from them for the good of all, but in the case of the Duchesse? No. It would be tantamount to sacrilege in his eyes.'

'But he wishes to know the truth, does he not?'

'He wishes to know she was not murdered. Beyond that, he will want her to be left to rest in peace…' And then, injecting a brisk tone into her voice, 'As I do. As do we all. For the sake of the children if nothing else.'

Maggie picked up the new thread of thought. 'Will there be changes that will affect them, now that she is gone?'

'Changes are inevitable, but who they will effect, and in what way, is less easy to gauge.' In the back of Kate's mind a troubling thought surfaced; that Maggie also stood to lose from the Duchesse's death. She was debating with herself whether she should forewarn her, but decided against. If it was going to happen they were powerless to stop it, and if not, she would have worried Maggie for nothing.

The door of the audience chamber opened, Rosny beckoning to Kate. She took a deep breath.

He was leaning forward, his gaze fixed on her, the others of the commission equally intent. 'Let me ask you one more time, Lady Munro. You are sure you saw nothing, nothing at all, to indicate anything other than a mischance of the birthing process?'

How many times must I say it? Kate thought. Either they believe me or they don't. Repetition will not change anything. She squared her shoulders, stifled her irritation, gave her answer for the third time. 'Nothing.'

'No sense of another presence … a devilish one?' The man who had posed the question had narrow eyes, set deep in an olive face, so that Kate was momentarily distracted, thinking of his possible origins. 'Nothing,' she repeated, more firmly. 'It was a tragic misfortune, that is all.'

'And could it have been averted had you been called earlier?'

That was a more difficult question, one she has asked herself over and over again since Gabrielle's death, without reaching any conclusion. She knew he was asking in an attempt to tease out if there had been any intent to delay treatment for the Duchesse, any possibility that malice had contributed to her passing, even if no one had administered a fatal potion or struck a fatal blow. If that were true, she had no evidence to prove it, and it would serve no purpose to suggest it. 'No,' she said, 'there was nothing I could do. Nothing anyone could have done.'

Chapter 15

April bled into May, May into June, rain-soaked days following one after the other, the misery of the weather outside in tune with the atmosphere within the Louvre. Henri had declared a period of three months mourning for Gabrielle, and the courtiers went about their business avoiding any laughter or unnecessary chatter in the corridors for fear of censure, the entire building echoing with the silence. Even the children were unusually subdued, scurrying from apartment to apartment like mice being stalked by a cat. Henri saw Alexandre, César and Catherine daily, but at set times, their nursemaid bringing them into the salon and lining them up like toy soldiers for inspection. He ruffled their hair, asked what they were doing, and complimented their schoolwork, as he had done in the past, but Kate, watching in the background, ached for him as he spoke to them as if by rote, and though clearly he was trying hard to make no difference, it was no longer the easy relationship it had once been. When she shared her concerns with Adam, his response was unequivocal.

'If the King has not asked for advice, you cannot give it, however helpful you think it might be.'

'You know how I struggled over his liaison with the Duchesse. How I still do. I knew he cared for Gabrielle, perhaps more than for anyone, but I did not expect this outpouring of grief. And I cannot but respect him for it. But the children have lost one parent, and as things stand are halfway to losing the other. It is hard to stand by and say nothing.'

'Hard or not, you have no choice.' He cupped her face in his hands, 'You are there, as he asked. Who knows, perhaps an opportunity will come.'

Come it did, two days later, when, the weather having turned, the children were brought to meet the King in the garden. Once the formalities had been observed, he gave them leave to run along and play, the formality in his tone belying the words. Turning to Kate, he indicated they walk together. When they were out of earshot of the children, he said, pain in his voice, 'When I look at them, I see her face, in Catherine especially, and I fear to look too long lest I break down. Will it always be thus?'

'It is but part of normal grieving, Sire. In time, you will look at them and be comforted by the resemblance. For now, it is enough that you don't shut them out, but...' She hesitated, aware of the presumption in the advice she wished to offer.

'Whatever it is you wish to say, say it, for I am sorely in need of sound counsel.'

Bolstered by the thought that her advice, should he act upon it, would be of benefit both to the King and his children, she said, 'When the children look at you, they see a father with his emotions firmly under control, and so they try to emulate you. It is the way of a king, but not the best way for a child. Grief must be released if its sting is to be drawn.' She hesitated again, searching

271

for the right words, decided to be blunt. 'Let them see your pain. It will give them permission to cry, and in time those tears may bring healing to you all.'

The Munros weren't the only people in the court to be surprised at the depth of feeling Henri exhibited. The new Spanish ambassador was overheard to say to one of his retinue, 'I had not thought to see the King so distracted. If we were not so set on peace, now would be a good time for war.' A remark that, when it was reported to Sully, earned the ambassador an instant return to Madrid.

Maggie, who had previously shown no interest in politics, asked, 'If the ambassador but spoke the truth, why should he be sent away?'

'Because it was neither the moment to express such thoughts, true or not, nor an appropriate sentiment at any time.' Munro came and stood behind her, and rested his hand on her shoulder, as if to keep her within bounds. 'As he should have had sufficient wit to realise, for an ambassador, above all people, should know when to speak and when to be silent. He is no loss. Besides…'

Kate, her mind running ahead of him, said, 'Is there still a possibility of war?'

'There is always the possibility, but the dangers are at present somewhat reduced. At home at least, for the economic benefits peace brings are not something many of the nobles would wish to threaten. The King's safety, however, is harder to ensure when, as now, his preoccupation renders him careless of any potential dangers.'

'The risk of assassination? Surely now with the Edict of Nantes finally ratified by the parlements he should be safe?' And when Munro didn't answer straight away, 'Have there been more recent attempts?'

'A few. But none made public, for it is thought better to conceal them than to put the thought in the mind of other crackpots and hotheads, of whom there are no shortage in Paris.'

'But he is popular.'

'As kings go, yes. But not everyone is in favour of kingship, and it is the job of the Gardes to remember that and act accordingly. And as for his outpouring of grief, that too is a problem, reducing him in some eyes from a king to an ordinary man. The kings of France have aye had their mistresses, the populace, for the most part, tolerant of them. The Duchesse d'Estrées was regarded by many as a whore, and thus acceptable as a mistress if one was not overly fussy about such things, but to accord her the honour of a state funeral and to continue to mope about for months thereafter is a different matter. We may sympathise with his grief, but there are many of the nobles who resented having to walk behind her coffin as if she were a queen. As for the people, they want a legitimate heir to the throne, and for that there must be a suitable marriage. Sully isn't the only person to feel the death of Gabrielle was a fortunate mischance, even if the only one with the courage to say so. But all that is of no value at all if Henri will not marry. He may not be old, but his life has not been easy, as his appearance testifies, and who knows what is to come. There are many, Catholic and Huguenot alike, who, for the good of France, wish the period of mourning over and Henri returned to his senses, and were I French I might find myself among them.'

The danger, when it came, was not a risk to Henri's life, but it was equally serious nonetheless, and from an unexpected source. Kate was entertaining Ellie and the Bourbon children with a game of spillikins, when she heard footsteps in the corridor outside their apartment – early for Adam to be home, but welcome nonetheless. Her smile froze on her face as he entered, banging the door against the wall. He halted when he saw the children, and she recognised the effort it took for him to summon a smile and speak quietly. He nodded towards the window, which framed a square of blue, dotted with bog-cotton clouds. 'Take the children out please, Ellie. It's little enough sunshine you've had in the last months to waste it. You can play the game outside as easily as in. I want to speak to your mother.' He nodded towards the Bourbon children. 'And what I want to say is not suitable for their ears.'

The game was almost at an end, Ellie set fair to win, and Kate, seeing her mouth tighten, as if she was about to protest, pre-empted her, gathering in the remaining spillikins and announced her the winner by a good margin. By way of mollification to them all, she added, 'Perhaps,' she nodded to Alexandre, 'in the next game it will be your chance to win.'

'And mine.' Catherine's high fluting treble had a determination in it, her mother evident in her voice, her father in her stance, her chin tilted upwards.

Kate concealed a smile. 'And you.'

The children dispatched, she turned back to Munro. 'The news is not good?'

'I should have been careful what I wished for.' The enforced delay had given time for his anger to subside a fraction, but his frustration was still visible. 'So much for Henri's protests that his heart was broken, that he would not look at a woman again. Eight weeks. Eight weeks since Gabrielle's death and he is infatuated all over again.'

'With whom?'

'Henriette d'Entragues.' He spat out the name, as if it was a sour plum.

'Who is she?'

'Only the most notoriously immoral woman in the entire country. Or at least within a hundred miles of the court. And avaricious with it.' He strove to control his breathing. 'She could not be worse, for Henri or for France, if she were a child of the Devil. As indeed she might as well be, given her parentage.' He was pacing up and down the chamber. 'It's well known Henri is susceptible to a pretty face, and no doubt her father counted on it when he put her in Henri's path at Blois in March.'

'Before…? I had not thought…'

'No. To do Henri justice he had no thought then of anyone other than the Duchesse. But Henriette was paraded in front of him all the same, and if d'Entragues did not have a hand in the Duchesse's death, he has certainly taken advantage of it.'

Kate moved to the door onto the corridor, which stood ajar, and closed it firmly. 'Adam, you cannot libel a man because you do not like him. You know there was no evidence of anything other than natural causes in the Duchesse's death.'

He took a deep breath, as if to calm himself. 'I know, but he is odious, and in the queue of folk who wished for the Duchesse's downfall he would have been first in line.'

Against her better judgement, Kate was curious. 'What's Henriette like?'

'Her mother's daughter. A witch if ever I saw one.' It was a thoughtless reference she knew he had not meant to make, a sign of his strength of feeling. He continued, oblivious to her tension. 'She's young, pretty, provocative, and rotten to the core, with an over-developed sense of her own value.' His voice was rising again. 'Without even the pretence of any affection for the King, she demanded a fee for her favours – a hundred thousand écus! And got it too, however much Sully protested. No woman should be worth that.'

'Thank you.' Kate's tone was dry, but Munro still wasn't listening, still focused on his own frustration.

'And her ambition does not stop there. She has demanded a title and wrung a signed promise from Henri that he will make her his queen should she bear him a son within the year.' He was pacing up and down, scarcely pausing for breath. 'Can you credit it?'

She thought of the King, prostrated across Gabrielle's deathbed. 'Does he mean it?'

'I suspect not, but even if he did, none of his advisors would have any intention of letting him keep to it, but it's a mess they would rather not have to sort out.' He was staring out over the gardens, drumming his fingers on the sill, so that she knew something else was eating at him.

'Adam…'

He was like a coiled spring, ready to burst its restraints. 'I did not join the Gardes to escort a strumpet such as her to his chamber. Nor should any of my men be ordered to do so. It is an affront to the regiment.'

'The regiment,' she said, stilling his fingers, 'is the least of it. Can no one speak sense to him?'

'They can speak, and some do, risking their own positions in the process, but they cannot make him listen. There is a line even his closest advisors cannot cross.'

From the gardens she heard Ellie's voice, and though she couldn't make out the words, it was clear from the forceful tone that she was intervening in some dispute between César and Alexandre. 'Those poor children. They have lost one parent. Is he to deprive them of the other also?'

His shoulders relaxed a fraction. 'Infatuated he undoubtedly is, but his love for those children is strong.' His gaze once more fixed on the view through the window. 'It may need to be.'

She was about to ask what he meant, when, as if in an attempt to avoid being questioned, he changed the subject. 'Have you noticed anything different about Robbie recently?'

'His interest in Eugenie Lavalle? That's understandable, if not altogether wise, for she's a pretty girl and, I think, a good one. If we let it run its course without comment, it may come to nothing.' She straightened her shoulders. 'But if it proves serious, we must do our best to help him, however difficult it becomes.'

'Whatever the problem is, it is of longer standing. His distraction was obvious long before he helped the Huguenot boy.'

'His conduct in the Gardes is in order?'

'I cannot fault him there, but it is as if he tiptoes around me, lest he let something slip. I'd like to know what it is.'

She thought of Robbie's evasiveness when she'd asked how he came to be in the Huguenot quarter. 'Whatever it is, if he needs our help or advice I trust he will have the courage to say so.'

'Courage he has in abundance, but it needs to be allied to good sense, which I very much fear may be sorely lacking.'

'Are you not too hard on him? Perhaps this problem is not of his own making. Perhaps it is a result of generosity and thus something we could be proud of.'

'If it is generosity, it is likely misplaced. And that is never something to be proud of. If I could only direct him…'

'Adam, we cannot live his life for him, however much we may wish to. Nor do we want to risk driving him away by trying. You bailed him out once before, we may pray God that particular lesson is learned and won't be necessary again, and whatever this is, that we have the means to help.'

There was another commotion below the window: a series of thumps followed by a whoop of laughter. Kate craned her neck to see what was going on, her stomach shifting as she saw Alexandre and Catherine laid flat out on the grass with Ellie and César leaning over them. She

278

hadn't realised she was holding her breath until Catherine started to giggle, Alexandre's shoulders also shaking. Catherine scrambled to her feet and danced away, Alexandre sitting up and crowing, 'I won, I won.'

'What did you mean,' she asked Munro, 'when you said Henri's love for the children would need to be strong?'

'Only that it is hard to be the bastard child of a king, forever dependent on his continued interest and goodwill.'

For a moment Kate saw the months and years stretching ahead of her, her continued presence at court a necessity if she was to keep her promise to the King. She leant against Munro, burrowed into his chest, her voice muffled. 'Hard on us too.'

Part Three

October 1599 – June 1600

Virtue itself turns vice, being misapplied,
and vice sometimes by action dignified.

Romeo and Juliet Act 2 Scene 3

Chapter 1

The dismal spring had progressed through a summer of long, warm days into a breathless autumn, even the birds listless, their song subdued. As Elizabeth's waist thickened, her condition showing much earlier than in her previous pregnancies, John Montgomerie became a frequent visitor. He took time out from the college at Glasgow despite her protests, for though she seemed hale enough, the dangers in pregnancy increased with age and he knew how much this child meant to both of them, so was determined to look after her throughout. As to their shared, but unexpressed, desire for a son, that was not in his gift, but given the progression of the pregnancy, he had hopes. As she approached her third trimester her stomach ballooned. John saw the unspoken question in Hugh's eyes and risked, 'The babe is big. There's a good chance it will be the boy you hope for.'

A smile spread across Hugh's face, tempered with, 'Don't say it. Or not in Elizabeth's hearing at least. I know it is superstition, and foolish besides, but I have a fear that to talk of it might lessen our chances.'

'I won't. But not for any fear of affecting the outcome. That indeed is superstition. There are better reasons for not talking of it.'

'That Elizabeth is not disappointed if it is a girl?'

'That she doesn't feel she fails you.'

'She could never fail me. Even if she produces a quiverful of girls.' Hugh was uncharacteristically reflective. 'Rather, I think, it is I who sometimes fail her.'

'That much is true.' John grinned at him. 'Though she seems to suffer you well enough, failures or no. It was a good day when Father insisted on you going to college in Glasgow, despite your protests. A good day too when John Shaw took to you.' There was a serious note underlying his laughter. 'Don't squander it, Hugh. Elizabeth may have the patience of a saint, indeed she must have to put up with you, but exploits like that ruckus on the Canongate are not designed to help her keep calm, and quiet and lack of excitement is aye beneficial for those in her condition.'

He was circling his horse, waiting for Hugh and Elizabeth to finish their farewells. They had none of them expected a call to court so soon, but when the King called there was little choice but to obey. He would have much rather been returning to Glasgow, but the summons had included him. There were times when he regretted, on his own behalf, the offer made to James to take Kate Munro's place as midwife to the Queen, but it had released them and that he could not regret. He thought of the Queen, and if she had particular need of him, trusted he wouldn't have to stay long. If it was for but a day or two, it would be little more than a detour, riding two sides of a triangle, rather than one.

He moved out of earshot to give Hugh and Elizabeth a semblance of privacy, but could guess at what Hugh was saying as he placed his hand on the bulge of her stomach. She was smiling and nodding, but he very much suspected she had no intention of following any instructions or admonitions Hugh was offering. For, as she had predicted when John had questioned her on the wisdom of travelling to Ireland, once he knew she was with child, he had cosseted her. And encouraging as it no doubt was to see his care, it was clear that however hard she tried to hide it, she found it suffocating. This opportunity to make her own choices as to what she could and couldn't do, welcome. He had seen her swiftly concealed relief when the summons arrived, followed by her dismay as initially Hugh expressed his intention of sending apologies. She had left no room for discussion, insisting, 'I am not alone here. I will be fine,' and this with a glance of apology for John. 'Women are better at these things. Besides, you have been away before, Hugh, and much farther than Edinburgh. When the time comes I will send. If this one is anything like his sisters he won't be in a hurry to be born and you will likely be back long before he's out.'

Especially as it will be a child of the new century and not the old,' John said.

'What on earth do you mean? I may feel and even look the size of an elephant before I'm finished, but I've no intention of carrying this child any longer than the nine months, give or take, that we humans suffer. The birth will be January.'

283

'Didn't Hugh tell you? The King has decreed that we are to start the new year on the first day of January, rather than on March twenty-fifth as it has aye been.'

'Why?'

'We are out of step with the rest of Europe,' John said, 'and James wishes to bring us in line.'

'We are out of step with England,' Hugh corrected, 'which is more to the point. For what is no more than a minor inconvenience now, despite the possibilities for confusion, will become serious once James is king of both countries. I think it a sensible move.'

John agreed. 'I also, though there is the troubling issue of lost days.'

Elizabeth looked puzzled. 'What?'

Hugh was laughing. 'Credulous folk, women, mostly.' He stepped back in an unsuccessful effort to avoid the playful punch she directed at his chest. 'If you'd let me finish, I'd have said, credulous folk, of which you are not one,' he gave her a squeeze, 'are frightened that they will lose twelve weeks of their life when the new year starts ahead of time. And I have heard better men than John, here, struggle to explain how it isn't so.'

'I like the thought,' she smiled up at Hugh, 'that this child will belong to the new century. It is…' she seemed to be struggling for the right word, 'fitting.'

John could guess at what she was thinking, but was afraid to say, that it would be fitting for a son and heir, and a glance at Hugh's expression suggested it was on his mind too. He brought the conversation back to safer ground, adding his weight to Elizabeth's argument that there was no need for Hugh to refuse a call to court on her account.

'This is your fourth child, Hugh, and the first three birthed without complication. There's no reason why this time will not be the same.' It was an intervention he saw Elizabeth appreciated, though he noted the momentary shadow that flickered on her face and suspected she was remembering Kate's last confinement, which had gone very differently indeed. Thankfully, Hugh had not been in France to see it. And the circumstances had been different. Elizabeth was not likely to be attacked at the crucial moment. Nor, he imagined, would she take risks.

Now, as Hugh swung up into the saddle and turned towards the gateway, John stopped for one last word with her. Mindful that Hugh was within hearing, he confined himself to an oblique reference to Kate's fall, which he hoped she would recognise. 'Take care, especially on the stairs, and, should the need arise, when climbing into a cart.'

Her comment, 'Uncomfortable things, carts, I take care to avoid them whenever possible,' was enough to convince him that his warning had been understood.

For the first hour of the journey, Hugh's concern for Elizabeth was all he talked about, until John, exasperated, said, 'If this is your plan, to be sent home early with a flea in your ear, it may very well work, for I suspect James will no more want Elizabeth's pregnancy to be the whole sum of your conversation than I do. Remember, you are going to Edinburgh to court James' favour, not to bore him with your domestic issues. He would no doubt understand your feelings, for it isn't so long ago he himself almost despaired of producing an heir, but there is a world of difference between understanding and having an interest. His interests, as we know, are firmly focused on his own concerns.' He had settled into his stride, dispensing his advice without hesitation. 'For the next weeks or months or however long the King wishes you to remain, you must contain yourself. And when you are tempted to talk of Elizabeth, think instead of Ireland. Of the plans you have for Con's land and your future there. A week or two played aright may lead to a lifetime of opportunity and prosperity. But it isn't in the bag yet, and a wrong move might still spoil everything.'

They were skirting the edge of a wood, John's horse restive, shying at every rustle of leaves and scuffle in the undergrowth, when the sky began to darken and the wind to pick up. Hugh tilted his face upwards and breathed in, sniffing the air. 'I think we should stop at the next available tower. There is a storm coming and we'd be as well to wait it out.'

'Fine by me.' John was struggling to hold his horse in check. 'This beast is as skittish as a kitten, and I'd rather arrive in Edinburgh a day late than with a broken leg or not at all.'

They pulled to a halt. Hugh gestured to their right. 'There is a Boyd house not far from here. I think it may be the other side of that hill. If I'm right, it will be a fifteen minute ride perhaps, no more.'

'Let's hope so.' John looked up. 'Any blacker and we might as well be travelling at night. Never a good move, especially,' he glanced down at the track that stretched ahead of them, 'when the condition of the road is as poor as now, with as many holes in it as Dutch cheese.'

The rain came as they passed under the archway into the barmkin, rivering across cobblestones free of moss, the horses skidding as they came to a halt. John had a moment to note that the doors of the outhouses were freshly painted and the barmkin wall newly pointed. 'Well kept, I see. Let's trust their hospitality matches the appearance.'

A boy appeared at the entrance to the stable, and ducking his head against the rain, he ran towards them to grasp both bridles.

Hugh nodded his thanks. 'We have come a distance and will go no further tonight, so you may groom and settle the horses and give them a feed before bedding them down. Is your master at home?'

There was a slight hesitation. 'My father is not, sir, but my mother is, and will be happy to receive you ... You aren't the first to seek shelter from the storm, and as she is otherwise alone...' He faltered, clearly unsure how to phrase something.

John rescued him. 'Your other visitor is a man? Then our presence will preserve her reputation.' He reached over and tousled the lad's hair. 'My apologies that we took you for a groom, but don't worry, we will do our best to provide protection for your mother should she need it, and if not...' He avoided looking at Hugh lest he laugh out loud. 'Braidstane here is well versed in many topics of interest and will help out by keeping the conversation flowing.'

As they headed for the tower door, Hugh said, 'I am well versed? Good of you to reassure the boy, but you'd better be prepared to fulfil the task yourself.'

They were both smiling as they surrendered their cloaks to the girl who opened the door, but the flash of relief in her eyes, which mirrored the uneasiness he had sensed in the boy, gave John pause – something is not right. He was turning to ask Hugh if he felt the same when a door above them opened. The voice was clear.

Hugh's reaction was instinctive. He hissed at John. 'We cannot stay. To bide a night under the same roof as William Cunninghame is impossible.'

John was matter of fact. 'It is perfectly possible, if you can but contain yourself. We are all guests here and can surely manage a modicum of civility. What would you rather do? Trust yourself to the storm and risk injury, or worse? Or swallow your tongue for an hour or two in order to stay safe and well? I know what I shall choose, and if you have any thought to Elizabeth's well-being, you will do likewise.'

They had reached the entrance to the hall, William's voice, dripping with honey, rolling out through the open door. The girl stepped to the side to let them through. Mistress Boyd stepped forward to greet them, her momentary relief replaced by a quiver of apprehension, quickly concealed. She curtseyed. 'Braidstane. And…?'

Hugh was like a coiled spring, but he bowed in return, then drew John forward. 'My brother John, physician to the King.' The emphasis was clear.

John stepped forward, bowed over her hand, prayed that William wouldn't rise to the bait that Hugh dangled in front of him. 'Your hospitality is much appreciated. Five more minutes in that rain and we'd have been completely drookit.' William was standing behind her, his expression indicating regret, but John was sure it wasn't for their plight, but rather for their escape.

She curtseyed again, her smile genuine and her words sincere, if, John thought ruefully, somewhat unhelpful. 'You are welcome here, and though we have never met, your name is not unknown to me. The word is everywhere that we have you to thank for the safe delivery of a healthy heir to the throne. But I forget myself.' She half turned, tension visible in the rigidity of her back. 'No doubt you know the Master of Glencairn?'

This time it was William who baited Hugh. 'Indeed. We are near neighbours.' There was a contemptuous twist to his mouth. 'Though we do not see as much of each other as you might expect.'

'A pity,' said Hugh, taking up the challenge, 'you have not been at court of late, or we might have crossed paths.'

John rushed in. 'It is easy, is it not, to be so concerned with our own affairs that it leaves little time to be sociable.' He bowed to Mistress Boyd, but his comment was aimed equally at William and Hugh. 'Perhaps tonight, when nothing else is pressing, we will have opportunity for neighbourly discourse.'

She took his lead. 'I shall call for food and drink. You will all be hungered I'm sure.' And to John and Hugh, 'And you will no doubt want to change from your wet clothes, lest you take a chill.'

John looked down at his feet, at the damp stain that spread outwards around him. Sought once more to lighten the atmosphere. 'Or your floor suffer.'

Chapter 2

They limped through the evening, Hugh and William sniping at each other at every opportunity, though to anyone who did not know the background to their situation it might have seemed no more than a variation of the 'flyting' which was so popular at court. By the time the candles burned down and were beginning to gutter, John felt as taut as an over-tightened bowstring that might snap at any moment, and looking at Hugh he feared he was equally strained. He didn't know William well enough to be able to judge to a nicety his breaking point, but he knew it couldn't be far away. He stood up, turned to Mistress Boyd. 'My apologies, but at the risk of you thinking me feeble, I must beg to be excused. We had an early start this morning, and meaning no disrespect to your hospitality, hope for an equally early one tomorrow. The King…' He hadn't meant it as a parting barb, though it was clear from the frown on William's face that he took it as such, but there was no way back. He continued as if he hadn't noticed any reaction. 'We were expected at court yesterday, and the King is not always sympathetic to excuses, however genuine they may be.'

'You are all going to the court?'

It was an innocent enough question, but unfortunate nonetheless.

William snapped. 'I do not care for toadying to anyone, even the King. My inheritance is secure, and of good standing. Others, less fortunate in their birth, may not be so scrupulous.' He drew himself up.

John placed a warning hand on Hugh's arm and turned to William, his voice betraying only mild interest. 'You are heading for Ayrshire?'

'As it happens, no.' William was beginning to bluster. 'It is filial duty takes me to Edinburgh, and where my father commands, there I go.'

'I'm sure your father is glad of it.' Hugh's rejoinder was barely more than a mutter, but judging by William's expression, he heard it.

Mistress Boyd directed a smile at John. 'If I have the servants prepare breakfast for seven in the morning, will that be early enough for you?'

'Perfect.' Placing his hand on Hugh's arm again, he said, 'Come, Hugh. I've no wish to have to shake you awake tomorrow. Nor to have to tie you to your horse because you aren't fit to sit upright on your own account.' He smiled back at Mistress Boyd. 'Your wine I imagine has come from France,' a wider smile, 'legitimately of course. The quality is particularly fine, but I think we have both had enough for tonight.'

William's raised eyebrow eloquently expressed agreement ... and contempt.

Hugh resisted John's pressure on his arm. 'Speak for yourself, John. I am no lightweight and would be good for another hour or more, with no fear of ill effect on the morrow, whatever your weaknesses.'

'And I to match you. That is...' William raised one

eyebrow again, 'if you are up for the competition?'

Hugh sat down again, Mistress Boyd, clearly uncomfortable, looking to John as if for guidance.

'I think not, Hugh.' John's tone was cordial, laced with an underlying steel. 'We will retire together. In deference to my weakness, as you so kindly put it. You may be good for another hour, but I have no wish for you to disturb my sleep by stumbling to bed, whether the worse for wear or not. Nor, I'm sure, does Mistress Boyd. It would be a discourtesy to her and to this household.' John gripped Hugh's arm for the third time, pulled him to his feet, and this time, with a shrug, Hugh acquiesced.

'Mistress Boyd, Cunninghame, we bid you goodnight.'

There was just enough insolence in William's bow to cause Hugh to stiffen, but John kept a firm hold of him and steered him to the door.

Once in their chamber Hugh exploded. 'I could kill him. One day I *will* kill him.'

'And if you do? What then? Go to bed, Hugh. It was an ill wind that brought us to the same door, but we do not have to be driven by it.'

Ill wind or not, by the morning it had abated. They woke to a world rain-washed and fresh, the damp cobbles in the barmkin sparkling under a clear sky. John's expression radiated satisfaction as he turned from the window. Hugh, though awake, was still sprawled across the bed, his hands

292

clasped behind his head. With one swift movement John stripped away the covers and nodded towards the square of blue visible through the narrow casement. 'The weather is kind. It should be an easy journey today if...' he prodded Hugh, 'if you can stir yourself. With luck we might manage to sup and be away before William is up, if, as I suppose, he drank himself into a stupor last night.'

When they stepped into the hall, John was relieved to see that it was indeed empty. His smile for Mistress Boyd, who appeared at his shoulder, her tray laden, was unforced.

'Here. Let me.' He took the tray and turned towards the table.

'Well, well, I had not thought to find you so proficient at serving.' William was framed in the doorway, and though the whites of his eyes were flecked with red, his speech was clear. 'I take it your household at Broomelaw does not stretch to servants.'

John held himself in check, though his grip tightened on the tray. 'My household is adequately served, as, no doubt is Mistress Boyd's. But there is no shame in lending a helping hand.'

'For those who have no position to maintain, perhaps.'

It was discourtesy of the worst kind, hitting as hard at their host as at the Montgomeries, Mistress Boyd flushing a deep red.

Hugh stepped in. 'Those who have attained their position have no need to flaunt it.' The reference to William's subservience to his father was clear, as was Hugh's assertion of his own status: salt in an old wound. John steeled himself for the explosion as Hugh

293

continued. 'Nor does a man demean himself by knowing how to treat others, of whatever station.'

The explosion didn't come but John was left feeling on edge, certain that William wouldn't leave it at that, uncertain of how he might respond, or when.

Mistress Boyd intervened, waving them to the table. 'Please, sit down. Though what we can offer may not match an earl's table,' her smile for William was disingenuous, giving him no scope to take offence, 'what we have is yours and welcome.'

They ate in silence, and despite the strain it put on the atmosphere, John was glad of it, for no conversation was preferable to the dangers of a careless word spoken in William's company. Talking to him had aye been akin to treading on eggshells, and the events of the past two years had not improved matters. Unlike William, who ate as if there had been nothing untoward in his earlier behaviour, John had little appetite, but there had been discourtesy enough already, so that he forced himself to make decent inroads into what had been put in front of them.

It was Mistress Boyd who broke first, clearly unable to bear the silence any longer. Her comment, safe enough at her own table, would have amounted almost to treason if voiced in Edinburgh. 'They say the King is more concerned with his future prospects than with what is happening in his own land. That he spends so much time looking to the English and their doings that he has little to spare for his own folk. Is it true?'

John was matter of fact. 'True enough. And hardly surprising. He has been schooled all his life to think of the English crown as his likely inheritance, and now it is within his grasp, no other concerns can match it. We are but small beer compared to what is to come to him.'

'Will he forget about us altogether?'

William dared the others to contradict him. 'At his peril. Getting the English crown will be the easy bit. Keeping it, something else again. For that he will need the support of his own nobles.'

The emphasis on *nobles* was unmistakeable, and John, afraid of how Hugh might react, trod on his boot under the table. To no avail.

'However much the *nobles* may cluster around James, it is the *laird* class he favours,' Hugh said. 'He recognises, and rightly, that their loyalties are more to be trusted.'

William stretched backwards, rocking on the legs of his chair, as if he considered Hugh's obvious challenge amusing, but little more. 'You of all people cannot claim to be more trustworthy...or less self-seeking, come to that.'

Hugh was terse. 'Prove it.'

'Was it the act of an honest man to present a women masquerading under a false name to the King, claiming a family connection? I think not. Is it a disinterested desire to serve James that has you running to court with every morsel of gossip that your brother can supply? I think not. And as for your designs in Ireland...' He smiled as Hugh's eyes widened. 'Oh, do not think your intentions there have gone unnoticed. Hamilton, for one, is watching you.' William paused as if to give emphasis to his next words. 'Or is it that you want to go to Ireland because you are afraid to remain in your own place? Afraid to be bested by your neighbours?'

Hugh was on his feet, his hands pressed on the table,

his stance combative. 'I am afraid of nothing and no one, certainly not you. And why would I be? It wasn't me that lied to send an innocent woman to trial for witchcraft, that sought to deprive her family of a wife and mother, and to take their home for himself? The King judged between your actions and mine, and as I recall it wasn't me he banished from the court.'

They were facing each other across the narrow table, their faces almost touching. William was the first to draw back, his bow to Mistress Boyd perfunctory. 'Thank you for your hospitality. A pity it was tainted by poor company.'

Hugh lifted his arm, his fist clenched, but John grabbed hold of it. 'Let it go, Hugh. Let him go. He isn't worth it.'

That might have been the end of it, but for William's parting shot. He turned at the door. 'Give my regards to your good lady, Hugh. I hear she expects again. Perhaps this time she will oblige you with a son. However poor your property, it is no doubt galling to lack an heir, forbye the drain of finding settlements for a clutch of daughters.' Another deliberate pause. 'Though I have heard it rumoured that the gender of a child is to be laid at the man's door. A weakness in you, perhaps, that no amount of trying will sort. I hope she does not come to regret her choice of husband.'

Hugh covered the distance to the doorway in two strides and was gone, pursuing William down the stair, roaring for satisfaction. The distance between them was minimal, their footsteps echoing in unison, and to judge by the sound of metal striking the wall, Hugh had drawn his sword. John spread his hands in a gesture of apology and plunged after them.

They spilled into the barmkin, Hugh springing towards William, sword raised.

William half turned. 'I know you for a hothead. Are you a coward also, to strike at an unarmed man?'

Hugh skidded to a stop, facing him. 'Draw, damn you. Unless *you* are the coward.'

'What? And abuse the hospitality of this house? I think not.' William adopted a sanctimonious tone, before turning his back to grasp the bridle of the horse the lad held ready for him by the mounting block.

Hugh was too fast for him. Flinging aside his sword and grabbing William by the collar, he spun him round, ignoring the tearing sound. 'I will have satisfaction.'

William had his hand at his throat, his face puce. 'Damn you, Braidstane.'

John was between them, thrusting them apart. 'Let him go, Hugh. To brawl here would be ill done.' And to William. 'If you know what's good for you, I suggest you take the coast road to Edinburgh, that we do not meet again. Next time, I may not be able to stifle my own instincts, for it would give me nothing but pleasure to see Hugh skewer you like the weasel you are, save for the consequences for both our families.'

Hugh was attempting to shove John aside, but Mistress Boyd squeezed herself between them, the measure of her distress obvious in her disregard for convention, as she placed her hands against Hugh's chest to hold him back.

'Please. Not here. Not now. This is a peaceable house and I wish to keep it so. I do not want anyone's blood spilt on our cobbles.' She gestured towards the entrance to the tower and to the children clustered there, wide-eyed. 'Nor for them to see it.'

Her intervention gave enough time for William to mount and spur his horse towards the gate. She dropped her hands to her side, colour blooming on her cheeks again.

John was gentle. 'You need have no embarrassment on our account. Rather it is us who should feel shame. It was not well done to cause you grief.'

She waved away his apology. 'I do not blame you. The Master of Glencairn's reputation preceded him, and I see it is well deserved.'

'Nevertheless, we owe you an apology.' He was staring at Hugh, daring him to remain silent.

Hugh bent to retrieve his sword, thrust it back into the scabbard. His attempt at an apology, whether sincere or not, equivocal. 'I did not intend for any of this.'

John sought to redeem the situation, looking up at the children and raising his voice a fraction. 'Your mother is a brave lady, and a sensible one. You will do well to follow her example.'

He noted a brightness in Mistress Boyd's eyes that indicated she held back tears, but she was brisk. 'Your breakfast was disturbed. You will finish it before you go?'

It was less a query than a command, and one that John was minded to accede to, for it demonstrated both a tolerance of Hugh's behaviour and an astute assessment of the circumstances; better by far they put distance between William and themselves, and thus remove the temptation to finish the business so narrowly averted.

Chapter 3

Autumn was starting to bite, the leaves on the trees in the Bois de Boulogne curling and the colours changing. Despite his mother's admonition, in the eight months that had elapsed since Robbie's meeting with the Lavalles, he had slipped often to the Rue Colin Pochet to visit the cobbler's house, drawn by Eugenie's shy smile and soft voice. Her conversation, at first stilted and largely confined to François' progress, gradually developing to include flashes of humour at his expense. A teasing that gave him hope that she too valued their friendship beyond the circumstances that had brought them together. It was clear to him that his mother's reservations regarding the wisdom of the friendship remained, but he was grateful that she did not continually remind him of them. They had talked of it only once, at Eastertide, when, François fully recovered, Robbie had no further excuse to continue his visits. She had elaborated on her earlier caution.

'Grief takes many forms and when you lose a parent,' she hesitated and he had the sense that she chose her words carefully. 'There is the danger of turning for comfort to whoever is nearest at hand. Her father has his own struggles, which leaves her the more vulnerable.' Another hesitation. 'And remember, she is very young. As are you. In six months or a year you will both be better placed to know your own minds in this. Promise me you will wait and I shan't speak of it again.'

Had it not been for the ongoing issue of Angus' debt to Del Sega, he would have protested; as it was, guilt on that score made him acquiesce. The arrears of pay had come, not at the time promised, but several months later, and when they had returned to the moneylender, it was to find, as Robbie had feared, that the delay had added to the debt to the tune of another twenty écus each. Del Sega had been disarmingly obliging, professing himself delighted at the repayment of the original loan and giving them further time to settle the remaining charge. Angus was optimistic that at the next quarter they would be in the clear, but Robbie wasn't so sure, the spectre of a continuing debt a constant shadow hanging over him. And the longer it went on, the harder it became to think of confessing the problem to his father.

The Gardes quarters were abuzz when Robbie sauntered through the gate, intending to give the impression he'd merely been for a stroll to stretch his legs. At first no one displayed any interest in him. The soldiers were clustered in groups of threes and fours dotted around the courtyard, the conversation on all sides animated. Whatever the news was, it evidently met with universal approval. His first thought was that the arrears of pay had come. The men were exuberant, and why not, for few among the Gardes didn't have debts, even at the best of times. And for many of them these past months had not been the best. He attached himself to a group, raised an eyebrow at Angus. 'What's happened? Is it the arrears?'

The nearest Garde said, 'No, but…'

'Are we on the move? If so, I trust we will carry a good field kitchen with us.' He patted his stomach. 'For my mother's cook has given me a taste for fine food.'

'Henri has ratified the naturalisation of all Scots.' He gave Robbie a dig in the ribs. 'So those of us who can bed in with a French lass stand to gain in more ways than one.'

'Hey, lads.' A second Garde draped his arm about Robbie's shoulder. He raised his voice to carry across the courtyard. 'Munro here has been absent much of late, so maybe this news is especially timely for him.'

Other men drifted over, scenting entertainment.

Robbie forced a laugh, though it felt like a betrayal. 'Chance would be a fine thing.'

He was surrounded by a dozen Gardes, all chipping in with an opinion, none of which he wanted, but it was imperative he listened and laughed with the rest of them, if the truth was not to be discovered. Neither Eugenie nor her family deserved that. Forbye the danger for them that drawing attention might entail. Many of the Gardes were Protestant, by birth if not conviction, but not all, and there was money to be made in denouncements.

The badinage continued. 'Leaving it to chance are you? I wouldn't. Not if the lady is willing … and wealthy. A useful combination in any circumstance, but with this news, all the more appealing.'

'Maybe she's a pauper.'

'Or a whore. Not much chance of inheritance there.'

Robbie tensed. Should anyone learn of where he had been, Eugenie could be laid open to gossip, her reputation tarnished.

'On the contrary, get in with a Madame at the right moment and who knows what pickings may come your way.'

'There are a few of Henri's discards around…' The first Garde who'd spoken gave Robbie another prod in the ribs and with an exaggerated wink said, 'With your connections, Munro, you should be well placed to make something of the opportunity.'

'Maybe he already has.' There was a burst of ribald laughter and a few crude gestures.

Something snapped in him and he swung round, his fist connecting with the Garde's jaw, knocking him down, his head hitting the cobbles with a crack. The person nearest reached out to help him to his feet, but he remained sprawled in the dust, a trickle of blood running down the side of his head.

A third Garde, on the perimeter of the circle, slow clapped. 'Out cold. Well done, Munro. No doubt you'll have a good excuse at the ready, should the captain hear of it.'

The man Robbie had knocked down stirred and lumbered to his feet, spitting out a mouthful of blood and a couple of teeth. He faced up to Robbie again, but Angus grabbed Robbie's arm.

'Don't be an idiot, Munro. Felling a man once in the heat of the moment is likely inconsequential, but to

302

continue to brawl would be folly. Think of your father.'

Another Garde called out, 'Never mind his father, it's his mother he should worry about. They are aye the more troublesome, and his, I believe, up there with the best of them.' His comment was greeted by another burst of laughter, cut off midstream.

Robbie was stepping forward again, his fists raised. Once again Angus restrained him, his warning glare and fractional sideways nod insufficient to alert Robbie to the danger behind him.

Adam Munro reached the centre of the circle, his voice a whiplash. 'Anyone else wishing to make a jest of Lady Munro?'

There was a shifting of feet, ten pairs of eyes focused on the cobbles. 'No? I thought not. You are dismissed. Before I decide to take this further.'

Robbie was turning with the rest, cursing the ill-luck that brought his father at exactly the wrong moment.

'Not you, Sergeant Munro.'

'I…'

There was no softening of tone. 'Any excuses you might have can wait.' Munro turned. 'Follow me.'

The courtyard emptied as Munro strode towards the main building, Robbie on his tail. He took the stairs two at a time, the few soldiers he met squeezing themselves against the wall as he passed. Robbie caught a few sympathetic glances, grimaced in return.

In the privacy of his quarters, Munro turned. 'Well? What was all that about?'

'Nothing much. Someone made a joke about French lasses and…'

'And that is sufficient cause to lay a fellow Garde out?'

'I didn't care that an innocent girl should be talked of in that way.'

'Who is of such importance? And how innocent?'

'The sister of the boy Mother treated for a broken leg. She doesn't deserve to be made the butt of soldiers' jokes.'

'It doesn't do to take barrack-room humour too seriously. You should know that.'

'You didn't appreciate the reference to Mother.'

'That was too close to home and I have a position to uphold.'

Robbie refused to give ground. 'The girl should be accorded respect. Just as Mother should.'

'Your mother would no doubt be pleased to know you are ready to champion her. As I am.' There was a curve to Munro's mouth. 'The boy has recovered fully, I believe. Yet you are still in contact?' His smile broadened. 'By the way, how did you come to be involved? I never did hear that part of the story.'

It was the perfect opportunity to confess to the difficulty with Angus, the paper he had signed on his behalf, but Robbie, still clinging onto the hope that when the arrears materialised no one in his family need know of his folly, said, 'It was an accident. The boy was out late, and when he stumbled into me in the dark, I reacted, knocked him down. And having broken his leg, it was the least I could do to take him home. His sisters were alone in the house and I knew Mother would not refuse to help.'

'What were you doing in the Huguenot quarter?'

He avoided a direct answer. 'I didn't know I was, not at the beginning. And afterwards … the boy needed medical attention. Besides, Mother would say it doesn't matter who or what they are.'

'So she would.' There was a new dryness in Munro's tone. 'But that doesn't answer my question.'

It was important to respond, dangerous to leave the way open to further probing. He settled for, 'It was a shortcut. Or so I thought. That's all.'

Munro's gaze sharpened. 'To where?'

It was a second chance for confession, but Robbie found the words stuck in his throat. 'A little business I had to do.' He took a deep breath, justified it by the thought it was half true. 'To help out a fellow Garde.'

'Be careful, Robbie. You were lucky to escape from your own problems, do not take on too many for others. I cannot always be bailing you out.' A pause. 'Is this anything to do with Angus? Has he allowed himself to be gulled? I thought he looked a mite uncomfortable…'

This was treacherous ground. Robbie was trying to think how to respond when they heard hoofbeats in the courtyard. Munro, distracted, turned towards the window.

'A messenger from the King. See yourself out, will you? And take word to your mother – I may not be home in time for supper tonight, or not at all.'

Chapter 4

In the event, Adam, though he missed supper, did return to the Louvre in time to find Kate still up and sitting in the salon. He leant against the mantleshelf, warming himself at the fire. She could tell from his demeanour that the news he brought was of importance.

'The Parlement of Paris has made petition to the King.' A flicker of a grin. 'Not that you can truly call it a petition, more an ultimatum, which thankfully it seems the King will accede to.'

'Regarding Henriette?

'Yes, though that is not to be apparent to her.'

'What hold does she have on him? She does not seem to have any of the redeeming qualities that Gabrielle, for all her sins, had. He has tired of many such in much less time in the past. Why should she be different?'

'Why indeed. There are many in parlement and in the country at large that think she has bewitched him and are the more eager to see her supplanted as a result.'

'What has parlement demanded?'

'That Henri renew his application to the Pope for an annulment of his marriage to de Valois to leave him free to marry Marie de' Medici.'

'But doesn't that play straight into the hands of d'Entragues? If he is to be free and she were to bear him a son ... what of his promise then?'

'Henri plays both sides.' There was reluctant admiration in Munro's voice. 'He has convinced d'Entragues that he agreed to parlement's request as a means to pacify them and that if his signed promise of marriage to her is taken to the Vatican, the Pope will surely uphold it and prevent the Medici marriage.'

'And is that likely?'

'Who knows what might happen should the Pope get to see the document, but although Henri has arranged for it to be taken by a monk that Henriette trusts, he has also taken steps to ensure that it will not reach His Holiness.'

Kate, attuned to the slightest nuance in Adam, sensed there was something he was *not* saying. 'How...'

'The details cannot be spoken of, but there will be no lives lost, though I suspect d'Entragues will be spitting blood when she realises how she has been tricked.'

Kate's thoughts moved to the children. 'The marriage with Marie de' Medici is certain?'

'As certain as these things can be. The contract isn't signed, but she has suitable credentials and is favoured by both parlement and Henri's closest advisors. She may not be a princess, but money aye speaks, and beyond an unsullied past, the dowry she will bring will be substantial, for her family are among the richest in Europe, and France is sore in need of an injection of capital.'

'France? Or the King? Does d'Entragues cost so much?'

'What she demands is trifling compared to what will shortly be required. For there is no doubt that war is coming.'

Kate pushed away that unpleasant thought, replaced it with a more pressing worry. 'Will de' Medici treat Gabrielle's children kindly?'

Adam shrugged. 'If she has any sense she will.'

He fell silent and again Kate was aware of something unsaid. 'This war you speak of. Will it be soon?'

'It would be folly to begin a campaign when winter approaches, and Henri is no fool. But it cannot be avoided next year, for he is determined to bring Savoie to heel. As indeed he must, if France is truly to be at peace.'

He was tap-tapping his fingers on the mantleshelf, betraying unease.

Kate rose to stand beside him and placed her hand on top of his, stilling his fingers. 'Whatever it is that disturbs you, Adam, I need to know. It cannot be worse than I can imagine for myself. Is it Robbie? Have you discovered what troubles him?'

He placed his arm around her shoulder, drew her back to the couch. 'It isn't worse, and no, it doesn't concern Robbie. It is only that it is I who have been ordered to take a message to the ambassador in Rome to intercept the d'Entragues letter and extract Henri's promissory note. I will be away some months.'

The relief made her laugh, and when she saw the way his face fell at her reaction, she laughed again, but this time in genuine amusement. 'I'm sorry, Adam. It isn't that I wish you away, and I promise you, while you are gone I *will* worry: about the dangers of the journey; the risk of vagabonds; of bedbugs or bread with weevils, or worse, in the inns; and the many sicknesses for which Rome is famous. But I will remind myself daily that most who take that journey return safe.' She caught both his hands in hers. 'But there are worse things than your absence, and if you do not delay unnecessarily, you will find us largely unchanged on your return. Aside that is, for Patrick John, who seems to sprout like a weed every time I turn my back.'

It was the right note, Munro slipping one hand free of hers to pull her close. 'I shall not take a day longer than is necessary, that *I* promise you, and at least I shan't have to worry about *your* safety. Not much fear of vagabonds here.'

They were at supper when Adam announced to Maggie and Ellie that he had business to conduct and would be away some time.

Ellie displayed only mild interest, Maggie none at all, which surprised Kate, but demonstrated clearly that she was caught up in her own concerns – and just as well perhaps, for it might have been difficult to field her questions.

Ellie said, 'You will be back in time for the Yule festivities?'

'Of course. And with presents.'

Kate found herself remembering a previous return, when the presents he brought had pleased them all and had begun the thaw that allowed them to rebuild their relationship fractured by the business at Annock.

Unaware that she had shivered, she was taken by surprise when Munro leant across the table and cupped her face in his hand.

'What is it?'

'Nothing. Just a memory that is so far in the past as not to concern us any more.' She lifted a glass and raised it as a toast. 'To Yuletide then. And to your safe return.'

It was much later, in the privacy of their own chamber, that she thought to ask when exactly he'd be leaving.

'In a day or two, no more. There are some arrangements that must be made for the oversight of the Gardes while I am away, but I need to steal a march on the monk who is to carry the d'Entragues letter and make sure I have plenty of time in hand.'

It was the first time she noticed that he said 'I' and not 'we'. She turned, her hair half-unbraided. 'How many will be in your party?'

'Only me, bar a boy as my servant.' He hurried on, as if to give her no time to protest. 'It was thought better that I travel alone so as not to draw attention to my journey. It will be rumoured that I have private reasons for the trip, and I will travel not as a Garde, but as an ordinary Frenchman.' He grinned. 'It's to be hoped I'm not quizzed on my antecedents, for as you know, my accent isn't the best.'

'I wish…' she began.

'This is for the best. I shall slip in and out of Rome as easily as a wraith and be back before you've had time to miss me.'

'Never that,' she said. 'Never that.'

Chapter 5

Snow had been falling at Braidstane for almost two weeks without any respite. Although it was only the beginning of December, and the babe not due until January, Elizabeth began to worry that if there was no let up in the weather she would be birthing with no one other than Joan to help. And though Joan was competent enough as far as housekeeping went, her experience of childbirth was limited. It was at times like these Elizabeth most missed Grizel and Kate, and it was hard not to wish them back at Braidstane, for a visit at least, however selfish she knew that desire to be. Looking out as the snow swirled down, the flakes drifting against the windowpanes and gathering into L-shaped sweeps in the corners of the wooden frames, she thought of Flekkefjord and the little wooden house that Grizel had described, which, by the sound of it, though a mite cramped for their growing family, would at least be cosier than a tower house. As she poked at the logs that slumbered in the open fireplace, stubbornly refusing to flame, she imagined the tiled stoves burning night and day in every room, the chairs pulled close so that Grizel and Sigurd could toast their toes on the warm hearth. The sweeping roof would already be heavy with snow, and the windows shuttered against the biting winds that nipped at your cheeks until they ached.

'The hardest bit,' Grizel had said on her last visit, when they talked of the trials of the winter to come, 'is that folk close over the shutters in November and often don't open them again until March, so that we are forced to live in semi-darkness. It seems wrong not to derive benefit from the sun when it shines, or the additional light it gives when it is reflected back from ground blanketed with snow.' She had been silent for a moment before continuing. 'No doubt we would have heat also, could we have sun without wind, as you have here, but a still day is a rarity in Flekkefjord's winter and so we retreat into our houses and hibernate like animals until the spring.' There had been a note of mingled regret and resignation in her voice as she finished. 'It has always been so, and to flout traditions that go back generations would be to shame Sigurd in the eyes of our neighbours. However much I long to, however much the children plead, I cannot do it.'

Isabella, leaning against Grizel's knee, had tilted her head and pinched her nose, her comment so sage it was clearly a repetition of something she'd heard, her high nasal treble in sharp contrast to her words. 'The light from tallow candles is poor at best, but preferable to the smell of fish oil burning in the lamps.'

They hadn't been able to avoid laughing, and Isabella had taken it badly, stamping her feet and shaking her curls, her hands clamped on her hips, which made them laugh all the more. Elizabeth sighed. It was a little thing perhaps, but significant nonetheless and a sign that even in the best of marriages there were compromises that had to be made. No doubt Sigurd had made some also, for the house they lived in was set back from the seaboard, rather than the family home at the docks, so that at least their front door wasn't washed with seawater by every high tide. 'If Scotland's weather is harsh, Norway has it beat,' he'd always said; Grizel's 'True,' a heartfelt echo. They were likely already frozen in, and making the best they could of it. *At least they are together,* Elizabeth thought, *and have each other to keep them warm in bed at night. Whereas I have neither husband nor physician to aid me…*

The heavy sky was lifting, the sun filtering through, and Elizabeth, leaning on the windowsill, was momentarily dazzled by the beam of light hitting the glass. Below her she heard the bang of the tower door as Catherine and Mary erupted into the courtyard. She pressed her face against the cool of the glass to watch as Catherine stepped carefully through the fresh snow, making one line, then hopping sideways and zigzagging backwards until she was level with her first step. A bigger step, then a diagonal line of footprints, and another in the opposite direction. Mary was trudging up and down, mimicking her, and Elizabeth held her breath. If Mary were to spoil Catherine's spelling out of her name there would be ructions, and she didn't relish having to trail down the stair to sort them out. Better perhaps *not* to watch.

She turned back to poke at the fire and rouse it into flame – it wasn't Hugh's blame that he was not at home, not this time at any rate, and surely he wouldn't be kept in Edinburgh for long. The King, now that he was a family man himself, was said to be more sympathetic to those who wished to be at home for a birth than he had been in the past. And as for John, he had promised to return early in January and bide until the babe was safely delivered, and he had never yet broken a promise. The children's voices drifted up, their squeals of laughter indicating that whatever they were now doing, they were enjoying it. She glanced back at the window, at the snow that sparkled against the glass, and ran her hand over her stomach – there was plenty of time yet. Which brought to mind the King's latest edict: that the new year would start on 1 January. Thinking of it made her smile. In the normal run of things she wasn't superstitious, but nevertheless, it was surely a good omen that this babe, who she had thought would be born in the old century, would now be a child of the new.

And so perhaps it might have been, were it not for a series of unfortunate events.

At first it seemed a blessing when, after two weeks in the grip of a frost that made travel all but impossible, there were two days of unbroken clear skies and sunshine. The temperature rose just enough to allow the snow to settle, though it remained crunchy underfoot. On the second day, Elizabeth, counting it prudent, called the factor and ordered him to go to Irvine and bring back a midwife. She was somewhat hesitant in her request, given the conditions, but he waved away her concerns, looking down at her stomach.

'This is a window of opportunity that may not come

again in a hurry. And better by far a firmness underfoot than a skim of slush on top of frost. That really would be treacherous. If the weather closes in again, we will be ready for it.'

As she watched him dwindle into the distance, the sunlight glancing off his stirrups, she was tempted out into the barmkin to enjoy a moment or two of fresh air with the children. No doubt John had thought only of her safety when he'd charged her with taking care, but who knew when the sun would come again, and it would be a shame to waste the opportunity. Catherine and Mary, who had tired of the slide they'd made, were scooping snow into balls to toss at each other. Elizabeth stepped backwards so as not to be caught in the crossfire, the heel of her boot skidding on hard-packed snow so that she almost fell – perhaps it would be more sensible to remain indoors after all. Returning to the solar she contented herself with flinging open a window and thrusting her head out to breathe in the scent of pine. She was not unduly worried when dusk fell without the factor reappearing, reasoning that he'd likely had to wait for the midwife's return from aiding some other child into the world, and had chosen not to travel in the dark with a woman on his pommel.

Unfortunate then, that when they woke the following morning it was to howling winds and a blizzard so thick they couldn't see the barmkin wall, far less the valley beyond. She dismissed a twinge of unease with the thought that the storm would surely be a temporary thing and the factor and midwife both safely with her in a day or two at most. She was not uncomfortable, save for the babe riding high against her ribs, and as that was a sign he wasn't yet ready to be born, there was no need to fret. The blizzard raged for the best part of a week, and when it did abate it left an unrecognisable landscape sculpted in snowdrifts, some of which the stable lad, sent out with a pole to investigate, estimated were eight feet or more deep. Elizabeth resigned herself to being cut off for some weeks to come and daily thanked God, both that she had time in hand, and that ample food supplies had been moved from the storeroom at the bastle house into the tower cellars, for even to attempt to cross the barmkin was an expedition. She was thankful too, in the absence of the factor, for the presence of the lad, who normally resided in a cluster of cottages in the valley foot but who had remained to look after an ailing cow and was likewise trapped at the tower. He dug a track daily to the well in the corner of the courtyard and kept them supplied with fresh water. Catherine agitated to be allowed to help him, but Elizabeth fobbed her off with the promise that she would think on it when the snow stopped. But when it did, there was something else to distract her, or rather someone.

Elizabeth, having decided that, however much she detested the task, she couldn't continue to ignore the pile of mending which had accumulated in the chest under the window, was stitching a tear in one of Mary's petticoats. It was as good a job as any in this weather and no doubt she would feel better once it was done.

Mary herself, who was curled on the window seat, her face pressed against the glass, let out a squeal and fell backwards onto the floor. Elizabeth dropped the mending and levered herself to her feet, but Mary was already up and clambering back onto the seat.

'Come and see. There's a snowman coming up the hill.'

'Catherine, engrossed in a puzzle, barely lifted her head, scorn in her voice. 'Snowmen can't walk, silly.'

'This one can.' Mary was insistent. 'Look.' She shifted sideways to leave space for Elizabeth, and pulling her sleeve down over her hand, she wiped a larger circle in the condensation on the glass. 'See.'

Elizabeth did see. A boy, that she judged to be about thirteen, was battling up the hill on makeshift snowshoes, which, though it was impossible to tell for sure because of the snow that crusted them, were likely formed from woven willow. Snow lay thick on his head and shoulders and stuck to his clothes, his face and eyebrows likewise frosted, so that he did indeed resemble a snowman.

Catherine, her curiosity getting the better of her, was on tiptoe, peering over Elizabeth's shoulder, her attention focused on the ovals attached to his feet. She jiggled Elizabeth's arm to get her attention. 'Mama, can we make snowshoes like that? Then we could go out too.'

'Perhaps.' Elizabeth, pre-occupied with the reason for the boy's visit and where he might have come from, answered automatically, without listening to Catherine's question – wherever he'd come from, he'd be exhausted by the time he reached them. And likely soaked to the skin and needing a change of clothes while his own dried. She turned away from the window, mentally rummaging through the contents of the chest in her chamber – a shirt of Hugh's might serve.

Catherine, her nose pressed against the glass, said, 'He

isn't there any more. What if he's fallen into a drift and can't haul himself out?'

'It's just the wall hiding him.' Elizabeth squeezed her shoulder. 'We'll see him again in a minute.'

Mary tugged at Elizabeth's arm. 'How will he open the gate?'

Elizabeth looked over their heads towards the gate, the bottom half obscured by piled snow that filled the gaps between the metal spars. It opened inwards, and would be impossible to shift until the snow was dug away. The boy had stopped just short of it, clearly also realising the problem. Even from this distance she could see he was shivering. She thrust open a single casement, glad that it still moved, and called down. 'Go round to the right. We'll put a ladder over the wall.'

'We won't be able to see from here,' Mary protested.

'You can watch from the gable window in the hall. I'll get the lad.'

He was emerging from the kitchen, pulling on his boots just as she reached the tower entrance. 'I s-saw h-him. L-leave it t-to me.' He ploughed his way across to the outhouse and opening the top half of the door clambered inside. She could hear him raking through the jumble of materials and equipment, before reappearing with a rolled rope ladder draped over his shoulder. Instead of dropping back down into the courtyard, he swung himself from the half-open door onto the thatch and edged along to the crow-stepped gable, climbing up to where it met the top of the wall.

He put his fingers in his mouth and whistled, the sound piercing in the still air, then hooked the ladder over

318

the ridge. He was leaning outwards, one leg over the wall, one braced against the gable, steadying the ladder and offering encouragement to the boy below.

Elizabeth held her breath until first the boy's hands appeared, then his head and shoulders, then the rest of him. He was a comical patchwork of white and dark, where snow had rubbed off him as he climbed, his mouth a red gash in an otherwise white face.

He swung himself over the top of the wall and, with a glance at the ground, pushed himself off the ridge, sliding down the thatch and off the edge to land in a plume of white. He trekked across to the tower and stamped on the steps, shaking himself to dislodge most of the snow. His glance moved to the swell of her stomach. 'Begging your pardon, mistress, I had no idea…'

Elizabeth placed her hand on his shoulder, the bones sharp beneath her fingers, and propelled him towards the kitchen. 'No need for an apology. You can tell me your reason for braving these conditions while we dry you off and get some hot food in you.' He reached almost to her shoulder – Hugh's clothes would be a mite big, but warm at least. Joan was at the hearth, working the bellows to get the fire roaring. 'Strip yourself off, while I bring you something to wear.'

He looked doubtfully at Joan.

'You don't need to worry about her. She has a ween of brother's and you've nothing she hasn't seen before.' When he still didn't move, she said, 'But if it troubles you, she will turn her back. You'll hardly want to waste the effort getting here by dying your death of cold before you can tell us why. And a name wouldn't go amiss.'

'Andrew, mistress, Andrew Baxter, but I'm aye called Dand.'

When she returned, her arms full of shirt and hose and stockings, he was hunched on a stool by the fire, wrapped in a towel, still shivering. She dropped the clothes at his feet and said, 'Here. Put these on. They won't be the best of fit, but will do as a temporary measure.' Joan was ladling soup from a pot hanging on the swee. 'We'll soon have you heated up, and then you may tell us all.'

It was a familiar story, but nonetheless moving for all that. An absent father, who clearly drifted in and out of their lives. 'Working away, my mother says,' there was a defiant tilt to Dand's chin, 'and likely would have been home long since, were it not for the weather.' He swallowed. 'The babe had colic and we had insufficient money for the medicine. Mother sent me, with all that we had, to ask of the apothecary in Irvine.' His voice broke. 'I told him Father would be back soon, that we would pay him the rest as soon as we could, but he refused. He refused.'

Elizabeth was gentle. 'What did you do then?'

'I was on my way home when I met a pedlar. And when I told him my story, he said he had just the thing and wouldn't mind how much I could pay, seeing as it was for a bairn. I gave him everything I had.' His voice broke again. 'But when I got home, it wasn't medicine he'd given me, but a wee poke of flour, nothing more.'

Elizabeth saw that tears threatened.

'The babe never stops crying, and now Mother...' he took another long shuddering breath, 'Mother won't wake, not properly. She tosses and turns and moans, and though I've covered her with everything we have, she will not warm.' He stared into the fire, his shoulders slumping. 'I had to come. I didn't know what else to do.'

'You did right.'

'I hoped you could help, but...' He glanced at her stomach.

'Of course we will help,' Elizabeth said.

By the fire, Joan shifted. 'Mistress...'

Elizabeth motioned her to be silent, focused on the boy. 'How long is it since your mother took ill?'

'Since the snow came back.'

'And the babe?'

'Two weeks, three perhaps. I can't remember exactly...'

'No matter. He is no worse than at the first?'

'She.' For the first time a flicker of a smile crossed his face. 'Mother was so pleased when she was born, for she has had three girls and all of them born dead. But Annie is a sonsy wee thing and, until this, hale.' He balled his hands into fists. 'I have to save her, for if I cannot, I think Mother will die of a broken heart.'

Elizabeth turned her head away, afraid that he would be able to read her thoughts – if she has not died already. She was running through the possibilities – could she send the lad with Dand? Or send Joan? Should she wait until the factor returned? But each time it came back to the same thing. Without seeing mother and child it was impossible to know what must be done for them. Neither

321

the stable lad nor Joan had sufficient experience. And even a day's delay might be too late. The boy had risked his life to seek help and his bravery could not be refused. She squared her shoulders, commanded Catherine. 'Call for the lad to clear away some of the snow inside the gate. Two feet should be enough to allow for squeezing through.' And to Joan, 'Gather every medicine we have. Bread and cheese and milk also. A flint.' She turned back to Dand. 'Have you firewood, kindling?'

He shook his head. 'I haven't been able to gather anything since the first snow. I hoped it would last out, but…'

'We will take logs then, enough for a day or two at least. By then our factor should be returned and can bring you more. We'll need the sledge.'

Joan, still hovering at Elizabeth's shoulder, spoke up. 'The lads can't manage all this between them?'

Elizabeth's voice was firm. 'I will carry the medicines and the milk. The rest can be pulled on the sledge.'

'You can't!' Joan moved to stand in the doorway, as if by blocking it she could stop Elizabeth.

'I must.' She drew her aside from the door. 'They may not be our own folk but they are our near neighbours, and we cannot turn our backs on them, especially at this season.'

'Let me go then.'

'I wish I could, but I need to see them for myself, to judge what it is that ails them.' She forced a smile. 'And I need *you* to look to the girls.'

It was not an easy journey, Elizabeth slipping and slithering on the makeshift snowshoes that the boy had insisted she wear, the two boys ahead of her, one on each side of the sledge, holding it back to stop it running away from them on the slope. Watching Dand tramp through the snow in the factor's spare boots, at least two sizes too big for him and reaching part way up his thighs, he reminded her of Straparola's great cat. Not an unworthy comparison, though a fairy-tale end to this mission was far from likely. And the possibility of him losing his footing as a result of the over-sized boots an additional concern. The depth of the snow was perhaps a blessing, slowing both their steps.

They were halfway down when her right snowshoe caught the edge of the run of packed snow left by the sledge. It shot away, the jerk taking her leg from under her, throwing her sideways. She fell heavily and slid twenty yards before fetching up against a birch sapling that snapped under the impact, the jagged shard of trunk snagging on her skirts and halting her downward progress. Dand was ploughing up the slope towards her, fear in his eyes.

She edged herself to a sitting position and taking his outstretched hand struggled to her feet. Despite a pain in her side and at the base of her spine, she was quick to reassure him. 'I'm all right.' He conjured up a smile. 'Nothing broken.' She released his hand and waved him back to where the stable lad waited with the sledge – concentrate, she thought. Concentrate on staying on my feet.

Steady once more, she tried to avoid any thought of the possible consequences of the fall, or, indeed, if she would manage the return journey. Downhill had its own hazards, but the haul up to the tower was something else again. But if the boy had managed it, so could she. She thrust away the niggling voice in her head, *He is not eight months gone*, countered it with: *He is but a child. And you carry one. What of the risk to it?* She laid her hand on the swell of her stomach, and as if an apology, murmured: *I have no choice.*

The house, if such it could be called, was almost invisible, cloaked in snow and tucked into a fold of the hill near the foot of the slope – damp, likely, with no mortar between the stones, Elizabeth thought. The snow had drifted against the door and she was glad she had thought at the last minute to add the shovel to the pile of logs on the sledge. Even so, her teeth were chattering by the time the doorway was clear. Inside was scarcely warmer than out, the only sound a hoarse rasping coming from the rear of the single room – someone still alive at least. Elizabeth struck the flint and lit the candle she'd brought, and taking a firm grip of the holder, she raised it to head height. In the circle of light she could make out a central hearth formed of rough stones, a pile of snow in the middle of them. She passed the flint to the lad. 'Clear the hearth and light the fire. And scoop the snow into a pan, there must be one somewhere about, we'll need water.' Holding the candle higher still, she turned towards

Dand. He was kneeling on the floor by what looked like a bundle of rags piled against the back wall. Setting down the candle, she knelt beside him and gently peeled back the top piece of cloth. The woman's face was grey, her breathing ragged and shallow, and the small body curled into her side was white and still.

Dand reached out to touch the babe's head, swallowed hard. 'Is she...?'

Elizabeth held her finger to the tiny nose and felt a puff of breath. It was so light she couldn't be sure she didn't imagine it, so to check she lent her cheek against the child's, the coldness of the skin causing her to recoil. But she hadn't been mistaken; there was breath. She touched Dand's shoulder, and, undoing her cloak and the lacings of her bodice, she offered the encouragement she knew he needed. 'She lives.' *If* she was to survive, and Elizabeth acknowledged to herself, if not to the boy who crouched at her side, that it was a big *if*, she must be warmed up, and speedily. She placed the babe inside her shift, skin to skin, refastening the bodice around her. Beside her, the boy's shoulders began to shake, the tears he had valiantly restrained since arriving at the tower house leaving a clean trail on his cheeks. Elizabeth, pretending she hadn't noticed, gestured towards the fire beginning to flicker in the hearth, the criss-crossed sticks catching, flames licking around the pyramid of logs. 'Warm some milk while I look to your mother.'

The babe stirred against Elizabeth's breast, moving her mouth from side to side questing, and finding nothing she began to mewl like a kitten. 'You see.' Relief flooded through Elizabeth, and this time her smile for Dand was genuine. 'She's hungry, and once she's warm and fed I shall let you hold her. Do you have a spoon?'

Dand scrambled to his feet and stepping around the fire came back with a wooden box. 'We hae three,' he said, holding out the box to Elizabeth, pride in his voice.

Two were wooden and rough, the third made of horn, small and smooth, with a narrow cup and a curved handle. Elizabeth, thinking of the set of salt spoons in Braidstane's kitchen, felt a constriction in her throat but forced herself to smile at him again as he said, 'Father brought it, for Mother. On her naming day. He said...' Dand broke off, 'he said that when next he came back he would bring one for each of us.'

It took almost an hour to feed the babe, dribbling milk into her mouth from the horn spoon. At first she gagged, but gradually she began to manage without choking, and towards the end was sucking from the edge. It wasn't until she had almost finished, her eyes beginning to drift and lose focus, her eyelids to droop, that Elizabeth noticed the silence in the room. She motioned to Dand to sit cross-legged on the floor close to the fire and, wrapping her shawl more tightly around the babe, placed her in his lap. Then, taking his finger, she stroked it across the smooth, pink-stained cheek. 'She'll sleep now. Hold her gently and don't worry if she startles from time to time, all babes do.'

In the corner of the room she bent down and placed three fingers against the woman's throat. Nothing. She looked back at the boy highlighted in the glow of the fire. His head was bent over the babe, his mouth curved into a smile, his crooning, 'Annie, Annie, little mannie', as tuneless as it was nonsensical. At least his efforts hadn't been all loss. And perhaps there had never been any chance for his mother. A shame to spoil the moment for him, but there was no point in waiting any longer. The sooner they left, the sooner they would reach the safety of the tower. She placed a cover over the woman's face and returned to squat beside Dand, resting her hand on Annie's head. 'This is your doing. Your mother would be proud of you.'

He looked up, and she saw the flash of comprehension in his eyes.

'Mother's gone?'

'Yes. And you two must come back with us.'

He turned and looked at the bundle in the corner, then tightened his arms around Annie so that she whimpered. 'We can't leave her like that! We have to bury her.'

Elizabeth was gentle. 'We can't. Not now. When the steward returns he'll sort it. But you have saved the bairn and we must see that you are both well cared for.'

'But my father? He will expect to find us when he returns.'

Now was not the moment to destroy his illusions. Bad enough to lose one parent, but not two. 'When I send the steward, I'll make sure he leaves a note, so that he'll know where to find you.'

'He cannae read.'

'A picture then, and an arrow to show the direction. Everyone knows our tower house hereabouts. You found us. He will too.'

Chapter 6

The first pain came as they started up the slope to the tower. A poker was boring into her spine and Elizabeth recognised it instantly, halting to grab onto the trunk of a nearby tree, her nails biting into the bark. It had been almost an hour since her fall and she had just begun to think that it had been of no consequence, the realisation of the danger she now faced correspondingly more bitter. Annie was lying against her chest under her cloak, supported in her shawl. She must protect her and she couldn't lose Hugh's child. She focused on breathing through the pain, long, slow breaths that drew cold air into her mouth and caught at the back of her throat – it would last no more than a minute or two and then they could go on. The boys stopped beside her, Dand placing one hand under her elbow, as if he thought she needed the support – as I do, she thought, but I cannot let them see it. She straightened. 'It's nothing. I just need to catch my breath.' And when they still registered uncertainty, she added, in an attempt at levity, 'I am much older than you, remember. And this is a steep hill.'

She was forced to stop for a second time to ride out the pain, and though she struggled to conceal it, it was clear Dand at least now realised what was happening. She said, 'I'm fine, it's just there is another little person eager to enter the world.' And to the stable lad, who looked terrified by her announcement, 'You needn't worry. It won't be a snow baby, for we will be home well ahead of time.'

As she clung to the tree, Dand rubbed his hand along her arm, a sympathetic gesture that moved her – of course, she thought, he has seen this before and understands what is to come.

'The babe,' he began, and she knew it wasn't his sister he spoke of, so sought once more to reassure him.

'Will not be lost. My bairns are aye lusty.'

It began to snow again as they reached the barmkin wall, large flakes drifting down and settling on their heads and shoulders. Elizabeth, looking at the swirling sky, sent up a silent prayer of thanks that they had made it home and without major mishap. She gestured for the boys to go in front of her, Dand slipping through the gap between the gates first, the stable lad following. Once through they attempted to open the gate further, to give Elizabeth more room, but despite their combined efforts, it wouldn't budge.

'I'm sorry…'

Elizabeth's laugh was a mixture of hysteria and relief. 'Despite your sister, Dand, I'm no fatter now than when we left.'

Catherine met them at the door, her eyes widening as she looked at the bulge at Elizabeth's chest. 'What…'

'Let's get inside, before we all become snowmen.' She put her arm around Catherine and pulled her close. 'We have a little surprise for you.'

It was the best possible distraction for the girls as Elizabeth's long labour progressed. There were moments when she feared for the outcome. Slow, she had anticipated, even hoped for, as a sign that the fall had not affected her normal pattern, but not three days of dragging pains that stopped and started and stopped again, as if the babe, having been jolted into beginning his journey, was determined to demonstrate his reluctance to come early into a world of ice and snow. If it would only halt altogether, she would happily wait a week or two for her expected time, for the midwife and for Hugh. But if not, she was prepared to make the best of it, if it could only be over and the child safely delivered. It was Joan's first experience of assisting at a birth, and Elizabeth could see that she was nervous, and so, burying any misgivings of her own, she put herself out to reassure her. 'It is my fourth child and the previous three were no trouble at all, if somewhat slow in coming. If you follow my instructions we will do a fine job of bringing this young man into the world. And by the time help arrives, our need for it will be over and you will be able to take pride in that.'

Between contractions she supervised the girls, as first they washed Annie in a basin set in front of the fire in the solar, then dressed her in one of the garments set aside for their own new arrival. She was a wee scrap of a thing, but with a fine set of lungs and a willingness to use them that augured well for her survival. Catherine lined the makeshift crib, made of a shallow willow trug, with a piece of velvet covered in a remnant of linen, and Mary sacrificed a doll's blanket to tuck in around her. Elizabeth, seeing both Catherine's grimace of distaste when Annie's own ragged and soiled gown was removed, and Dand's reaction to it, ordered her, 'Take this down to Joan. The poor bairn had the most of a day without anyone to see to her, but she'll be needing it again once it's laundered and dried.' She followed Catherine out onto the stair, shutting the door behind her, one finger held to her mouth. Turning Catherine to face her, whispered, 'It's a wonder Annie had any clothing at all. We cannot embarrass Dand by throwing away her only gown as if it is of no value. With a little repair here and there it can be made to do for a while at least. The world is ill-divided. This child will be both well fed and well clad, but it isn't so for everyone. And though as good Christians we should share where there is need, there is a danger that generosity may heal the body but crush the spirit.'

She could see that Catherine was struggling to understand and was about to try to find easier words when another pain hit. She put out her hand to the wall for support, said, 'Put the gown to steep in some soda and lavender. Let Dand help. He needs to feel of use. She is all he has left.'

It was the middle of the third night when the pains set in with a ferocity she hadn't experienced before, so that she thought she would be torn apart. And though she did her best not to scream so loudly as to frighten the children, it was too much for Joan, who collapsed on the floor by the birthing stool, shaking. Elizabeth, feeling the urge to push, grasped her shoulder. 'I need you. Now! The babe is coming. When you see the head, you must guide it out, and the rest will follow.'

She began to pant and gave one final push, rewarded when Joan cried out, 'A boy. It is a boy.' She laid the child on her lap and wiped her hand across her nose to catch the drip that hung there.

For what seemed like an age, he made no sound, Elizabeth ordering, 'Lay him on his side and hook your finger in his mouth to see if there is mucus to clear, and if not, then slap his buttocks.'

There was a wail of outrage, the babe's face screwed up, his mouth opening wide, sucking in air to fuel another howl. Hearing him, Elizabeth found herself crying – Hugh would be so pleased. She indicated the knife and the candle. 'Hold it in the flame. Then cut the cord and tie it in a knot. And when you are done, wrap him tight and give him to me.'

'Shouldn't he be washed?'

'In a while, but for now, what is important is that he is kept warm and secure.'

Joan's hand was trembling as she made the cut, and as she fumbled with the knot the babe startled, his arms flying out, his face crumpling again.

Elizabeth gestured towards the bed. 'For a while

332

he will be easily frighted. This is a very different world from the warm sea he has been used to. Lay him down and make sure his arms and legs are swaddled.' Her face contorted as pain gripped her again, and she grabbed the edge of the stool.

'The afterbirth is coming.' She remembered Kate's instructions to Maggie. *Check that the placenta is intact. Once you're sure of that, a sedative will do no harm and indeed may help, for to sleep through the after pains is often a blessing.* 'You must see that it's all there.'

Joan looked doubtful. 'How will I know?'

Elizabeth gasped again, and when she felt the final contraction that expelled the placenta, said, 'Show it to me.'

Young Hugh was three days old before Elizabeth brought him down from her chamber and settled him in a crib on the opposite side of the hearth to Annie. In the absence of the factor, the stable lad had fashioned a trestle for the trug, so that it too was raised off the floor, Elizabeth sitting on the settle hearing snuffles from both sides. Although Annie was Hugh's senior by a month or more, to go by size they could almost be twins. And, she decided, if Dand would allow it, would be raised as such. Her appreciation of the boy, begun when he had risked his own life to seek help for his mother and sister, had grown in the few days since into an admiration that made

333

her determined to do all she could for him also. The birth had taken more out of her than expected. A fact that Dand, with experience beyond his years, seemed to recognise, evidenced by small acts of kindness: shutting doors that the girls left open, so that neither she nor the babes would suffer a draught, and fetching and carrying for her without being asked. She found he had an instinct for anticipating her needs, and when she was at her most tired, he took it upon himself to distract the girls by involving them in the care of the latest arrivals.

Catherine was hanging over the edge of the crib, Hughie's hand wrapped around her little finger, while Mary knelt beside the trug, drawing circles on the top of Annie's head. Sybie toddling back and forwards between them, tapping the sides of each in turn in some kind of game of her own devising. Dand hovered behind them, watching over them all, his expression less guarded than usual. It was a rare glimpse of his private pain, and Elizabeth, seeing it, shelved the plan she had thought to put to Hugh. Now was not the right time to absorb him into their family, however much he deserved it. Later, perhaps, when his father did not return and when he had become comfortable in their company and with their lifestyle. As, pray God he will, she thought.

Hughie stirred. Dand, gently detaching Catherine and lifting Hughie from the crib, suggested she might like to hold him. Although she affected an *'I am an old hand at this'* look, she betrayed a nervousness as he laid Hughie on her knee, and was quick to hand him back as soon as his mouth opened in a wide yawn and he arched his back, stretching his limbs.

Elizabeth turned her laugh into a cough, and Dand, with a conspiratorial grin, handed him over and disappeared, and by the time she had Hughie settled on the breast, he was back with a cup of mulled wine.

'Won't it make Hughie drunk?' Mary asked.

'No.' Elizabeth smiled her thanks to Dand. 'Though it may keep him asleep for a while longer than usual, which will be all to the good.' She leaned back on the chair with a yawn, feeling her eyelids flicker. 'For I could do with a decent rest myself.'

Dand set aside the empty cup and replaced Hughie in the crib. 'You rest then. I can watch them.'

'I know you can.' She smiled at him again, risked, 'I cannot be glad of the circumstances that brought you to our door, but I am grateful for what you have done since.'

His fingers clenched into fists. 'It's me owes the debt. Me and Annie, and I doubt we'll never can repay it.'

Elizabeth wanted to take his hands and unfurl them, tell him there was no need, but she wasn't sure if he was ready for that yet. There was an awkward silence before Mary scrambled up onto the settle beside Elizabeth.

'When will Father be back?'

'Soon, I hope. When the weather clears. The roads are treacherous at the best of times and doubly so just now, and I'd rather he arrived in one piece.'

She was bouncing up and down. 'Can I tell him?'

'Tell him what?'

'That we've got two new brothers and a sister all at once!'

Elizabeth risked a look at Dand, but this time his hands hung loose at his side.

Chapter 7

Alexander and Hugh were standing in the attic chamber of a house at the castle end of the High Street. Below them, the snow, funnelled through the tall tenements that bounded either side, lay piled in drifts at the entrances to every close, frosting the front of every building. It was unlike Hugh to be poetic but even he found the scene attractive, however frustrating it was to be forced to stay indoors. Especially now, when, the main business done, he was free to return home and to Elizabeth. For once he would like to be with her as she counted off the days to her confinement and be around to welcome the latest Montgomerie into the world.

He leant on the windowsill, his boredom apparent. 'How long are we going to be trapped here?'

'Content yourself, Hugh.' Alexander clearly sought to be encouraging. 'January it may be, but according to John, Elizabeth isn't due for several weeks yet and your bairns are aye slow to push themselves out.' He looked out over Hugh's shoulder. 'If this one has any wit he'll hold off until the weather is kinder.'

A sudden gust rattled the casement and a dusting of snow found its way around the frame and settled on the inside window ledge. Hugh thought back to childhood winters at Braidstane, when Alexander had been a frequent visitor. A favoured uncle, who aye had time for the children. 'Do you remember me trying to see how the snowflakes stuck together, and quiz you as to why they were different from rain?'

Alexander grinned. 'What I remember is you scooping up great handfuls and trying to stuff them down your brothers' jerkins and getting grief from Ishbel for your pains.'

'I never understood why she made such a fuss – we got wet enough other times without censure.'

'There is one thing clothes being wet on the outside by the rain, which you cannot help, and them being soaked on the inside by deliberate intent.'

'They dried.' Hugh shrugged.

'Yes, in her kitchen, and it cannot have been easy to cook with clothes hanging from the pulleys stretched out in front of the fire and draped over every available surface for days on end.'

'She managed.'

'She managed lots of things, you children included, and I think, though she wouldn't have admitted to it, that she enjoyed having a houseful of boys who could be depended upon to make mischief and took pleasure from making a fuss. She reached a good age, but I miss her when I visit. The place isn't the same without her.'

'That's for sure.' Hugh was pensive. I could do with some of her homespun wisdom right now.'

Alexander raised his eyebrows. 'In relation to what?'

'Something William Cunninghame said when we ran into him on our way here…' Hugh held up his hand to stop Alexander interrupting. 'John thought it best not to mention it to you, for we survived it without coming to blows.' Honesty forced him to admit, 'But it was a close-run thing. We were driven to shelter overnight at a Boyd tower, to ride out a storm. William said that our having only girls is a fault to be laid at my door.'

'What does John say?'

'That it was a deliberate barb intended to annoy me. And based on nothing more than malice. That only God knows why some families are overrun with boys and some by girls.'

'Well then.' Alexander traced his initial in the dusting of snow on the ledge, reflective in his turn. 'Mind, there are many poor women who would sleep easier in their beds if they could be guaranteed a son, however unfair that may be.'

'Or not sleep.'

It was a flash of humour to which Alexander responded with a grin. 'Indeed.'

Hugh became serious again. 'Do you think Elizabeth minds?'

'Elizabeth has more sense. As I hope have you. Of course you wish for a son, who wouldn't, for the world is tilted in our favour, but neither, I imagine, would you change the bairns you have. And that's as it should be. Pray God for a son, by all means, but be grateful, be it male or female, if it is hale.'

'But if there is any truth in what William says...'

'Truth is hardly William's strongest suit. Forget him. You may not be the best of friends, but you are near neighbours, and though you have been fortunate only to meet once this past year, there is no guarantee that will continue. You need to learn to live and let live, and besides...' Alexander broke off and Hugh pounced.

'Besides what?"

'Nothing. Or, nothing confirmed at least. It was a rumour only and likely untrue.'

'He is back in James' favour?'

'Favour would I think be pushing it, but I have heard it said James has expressed himself willing to receive him again at court, if he can behave in a fitting manner. Which perhaps explains his presence in Edinburgh. Though, as you're aware, he has not been seen about the court yet.'

'If there is any likelihood of that, it's time I was away, ill weather or not, for I couldn't stomach exchanging pleasantries as if there was no bad blood between us. I am no hypocrite.'

'It isn't hypocrisy, Hugh, it is common sense. A commodity that at times you seem to be sorely lacking. What price is a little civility measured against a renewal of the enmity that has cost more lives than can be counted. James is becoming increasingly intolerant of family feuds, and with good reason. A countryside at peace is an ambition we should all share.'

'The time will come when William'll try me too far.'

'Right, well, let me know when and I shall ensure I'm well out of the way. And you'd better warn Elizabeth too, and your children.' Alexander dropped the sarcasm. 'How many people do you think would be caught in the crossfire, Hugh, were the old enmity rekindled? Did Annock teach you nothing?'

'It taught me, if I hadn't known already, that the Cunninghames are a treacherous lot, and everything I have seen since convinces me that William is the worst of them all.'

'And the bloodbath afterwards? What did that teach you? Atrocity breeds atrocity and we none of us benefit.' Alexander's voice hardened. 'Nor are we blameless.'

Hugh's mouth was set in a stubborn line. 'The world would be a better place without him.'

'Agreed, but the same could be said of twenty folk or more of our acquaintance, Montgomeries included. That does *not* mean it is your job to rid the world of them. You are here to further your own ambitions, concentrate on that. And on keeping safe the family you already have, and the one to come.'

'She will be all right?'

'No reason why she shouldn't.'

On the opposite tenement, yesterday's snowfall hung from the gutter in a frozen swathe, like a blanket about to slip to the ground. Hugh was pulling on his boots and doing up his jerkin, in preparation for an attendance on the King – if he must be stuck in Edinburgh, it was as well to make good use of the time. His thoughts strayed again to Braidstane – how would Elizabeth feel were he to invite James to visit to take the chase? He hadn't realised he was speaking aloud until Alexander responded, his tone thoughtful.

'That's not a bad idea, Hugh, but best leave it for

a month or two perhaps, until the babe is well settled and the weather likewise. It will do no harm that he be welcomed by the King. In fact, it would likely be to his advantage, and yours.'

They found James, not in the audience chamber as expected, but in the bedchamber. Maitland was perched on a stool opposite him, cards spread out on the table between them. Hugh bowed over the King's outstretched hand.

'Ah, Braidstane and Montgomerie.' James was jovial. 'How are you at cards? Maitland here lacks the killer instinct, which makes for a dull game.'

Hugh flashed a glance at Alexander, and seeing the infinitesimal shake of his head, said, 'Not my forte, Sire. As you know, the hunt is more my game.' It was an opportunity and best not wasted. 'Indeed, I came to issue an invitation to Ayrshire, when the weather lifts sufficiently to allow for it. The woods around Braidstane are well stocked, and no doubt fresh venison would be welcome.'

James swept up the cards and flipped them at Maitland. 'No doubt it would.' He moved to the window and, scraping a hole in the film of ice on the inside of the glass, peered out. 'Though it likely won't be today or tomorrow.' When he turned back his smile was wry. 'More's the pity. But rest assured, when the weather improves, I will be happy to join you. A good chase is aye the thing to dispel boredom. But now…' His expression was unreadable, and Hugh, looking to Alexander for guidance, was dismayed to see his shrug. 'Tell me of Ulster. You paid a visit there last spring, I hear … yet did

341

not see fit to enlighten me.'

There was a hollow feeling in the pit of Hugh's stomach. 'It was a day's jaunt only, Sire. From Portpatrick to Donaghadee in the county of Down. To entertain my wife. We saw little but mist and a few cottages. An empty country by the looks of things.'

'One that you think to populate?'

Alexander's expression signalled that it was as good a time as any to introduce the subject of plantation.

'If it were to please you, Sire, yes.' He took a calculated risk. 'I could guarantee to take a goodly number of loyal subjects with me.'

The King raised his eyebrows. 'Please me? Is it not the old Queen's territory?' It was clear James was toying with him, a capricious gleam in his eye.

Hugh played safe. 'I meant, of course, in the fullness of time … when you have come into your own.'

'We must both hope you don't have too long to wait then.'

Hugh bowed, relieved to be off the hook, but his relief was premature, James continuing to play him like a fish he wished to tire before landing.

'And the Irish chieftains? They will pose no problem?'

'It is O'Neill land, Sire, and Conn O'Neill a lazy, good-natured sort of fellow. I think we could come to some accommodation.'

'And so you court him now, that the groundwork may already be done when the opportunity arises?'

It was as accurate an assessment as any. Hugh nodded, hoped it would be left at that. He was partly right.

'Well, well.' James nodded. 'You can count on my

blessing.' A pause, a half-smile. 'But next time let it be done openly and in order. I do not care for my lairds to be sniffing around in my inheritance without so much as a by-your-leave.'

Alexander's intervention was smooth. 'I shall see to it, Sire.'

'Make sure that you do.'

The dismissal was clear. Once back in the open air, Hugh expelled his breath. 'That was tricky.'

'That was dangerous.' Alexander was abrupt.

'Any idea who told him of our trip?'

'I can hazard a guess. Hamilton and Fullerton arrived yesterday and were closeted with James half the afternoon. It would be like Hamilton to seek to stir up trouble for you.'

The trouble when it came, however, was not from Hamilton. Hugh and Alexander woke to a clear sky, bled almost white by the reflection from the previous day's snowfall that still carpeted the pavements, though the stairs leading up to most of the doorways seemed clear. As they opened the street door to make for the pie shop, Alexander said, 'Looks like James might be wrong, and you may be able to make for Braidstane today.'

Hugh squeezed past him and stepped out onto the top step of the stair. 'Come on, I'm famished.' He half swivelled, the heel of his boot skiting away from him, and when he stuck out his arm to grab the handrail, he missed and fell down the steps, landing awkwardly at the foot.

He sat up rubbing at his spine.

Alexander was laughing as he trod gingerly down to Hugh and reached out his hand. 'Perhaps today isn't the best for travelling after all.' He slid his foot along the bottom step. 'Black ice. Aye the most treacherous.'

'Better a day or two longer here than a broken neck, I guess.' Hugh stepped into the street, the snow firm underfoot. 'If we take it canny, that is.' They were not the only folk looking to break their fast, the queue from the pastry shop stretching around the corner. 'Here's hoping they've made plenty,' Hugh said. 'For I've no wish to wait my turn and then find we're out of luck.' They had been waiting for about ten minutes when a boy came scuttling along the queue, fragrant steam from the parcel he carried drifting towards them. 'You, boy.' Hugh grabbed his arm and gestured towards the parcel, the boy tightening his grip on it as if he feared to lose it. 'Is there plenty where that came from?'

The boy glanced along the queue, hesitated.

'You needn't be feared. We won't take your pie. Only, we've no wish to waste our time waiting here, if we'd best try elsewhere.'

'I can't say, sir.' The boy hopped backwards out of reach, looked towards the corner. 'There are a lot of folk ahead of you, it might be best.'

'Come on, Hugh.' Alexander swung on his heel. 'There's another stall at the foot of the Cowgate. We can try there.' The queue was shorter, the smell issuing from the stall rather less appetising than the first one had been, so that Hugh was for moving on, but Alexander said, 'They may not be the best of pies, but they'll fill a hole.' He stamped his feet on the snow and blew on his fingers. 'Better fed than frozen.'

The pies bought, they headed back the way they'd come. The queue at the first shop had gone and the few stragglers that appeared as Alexander and Hugh reached it were turned away empty-handed.

'Good job we didn't wait,' Hugh said. 'Else we'd have starved.'

'Hardly starved.' Alexander grinned. 'But disappointed I grant you.' They approached the open area in front of the Holyrood gates and turned onto a beaten track heading for the Canongate. There was a group of men a few paces ahead of them, and though Hugh couldn't have named them, they had a familiarity about them that itched at his memory – courtiers for sure, and with the swagger that suggested they considered themselves important. They were laughing, their comments ribald, neither Hugh nor Alexander paying much attention until they heard Hugh's name. Alexander put out his hand and held Hugh back, but it was impossible not to hear the conversation.

'They say Braidstane's wife is about to pup again.'

'Not before time. Any betting on the bairn?'

'Dalgleish is offering odds on a boy.'

'Did you take them?'

'Not likely. With three girls so far, it seems a fair assumption Braidstane isn't up to the job. Unless...' the second speaker made a crude gesture, 'his wife has tried her luck elsewhere.'

Hugh sprang forward to grab the shoulder of the speaker, swinging him round, almost knocking him off his feet.

'Mind your tongue! That's my wife you're maligning.'

The man staggered, then, straightening, shook Hugh off. 'Well now, if it isn't Braidstane himself.' He oozed insolence. 'Perhaps he can enlighten us.' And then, as if talking to his companions, 'Who knows what a wife will get up to when a husband is away. Especially if an heir is hoped for and boys seem in short supply.'

Hugh lunged for him again, Alexander restraining him for just long enough to allow the man to twist sideways, avoiding Hugh's grasp.

The mockery was unmistakeable. 'Cunninghame is a neighbour of yours, is he not, and has been stuck at Kilmaurs these two years or more. How better to be neighbourly than to see to the needs of a lonely wife… '

With a roar, Hugh was on the man again, attempting to wrestle him to the ground.

Alexander grabbed Hugh once more and pulled him away, the other man similarly dragged back by his friends. 'Don't be an idiot, Hugh. To brawl here, in public view, is insane. You've had one narrow escape from the watch. To expect such luck for a second time is a foolishness I thought even you incapable of.' He turned to face the other men. 'We make for the Canongate. I suggest you take another route and have a care in future who you traduce.'

Once in their lodgings Hugh rounded on Alexander. 'She is my wife! How could I stand back and listen to such comments?'

'They weren't worth it, Hugh. You know that. William's lackeys likely, and with nothing better to do than to cause trouble by malicious gossip.'

'All the more reason you should have helped me teach them a lesson, not thwarted me.'

'And be both of us clapped in the Tolbooth? What good would that do? Another day or two and you will be home and free of all such aggravation.'

Hugh stopped his pacing. 'I will be free of it today.'

Chapter 8

It was a hard ride and a dangerous one, Hugh forcing the pace despite the conditions. Alexander had tried to convince Hugh to wait at least until things improved, but Hugh had been adamant in his refusal.

'You can say what you like but I will not be dissuaded.'

'It was not my plan to leave Edinburgh so soon, nor do I have permission from James.'

'Stay, then. I have my permission.'

'It would be madness for you to travel alone, Hugh.'

'I do not need to be watched over like a child on a leading rein.'

It was impossible to argue with him. Reckoning the potential hazards of the journey the lesser evil, when weighed against the difficulties of containing Hugh within their lodgings in order to avoid another confrontation, Alexander had given way. 'It isn't your capabilities I question, Hugh, but the weather. Allow me an hour to speak with the King and I will come.' A decision he hoped he wouldn't regret. Or be forced to explain to Elizabeth, should disaster befall them.

In the event it wasn't Hugh who came near to disaster, but Alexander himself. At times they rode on fresh snow that rose up in soft clouds around their feet, at others the ground crunched and splintered beneath the horses' hooves, scattering shards of ice in all directions. Most treacherous of all, the tracks where sledges had polished the hard-packed snow to a shine, so that it was hard to get any purchase at all. Alexander had given up urging caution after the first few miles and was concentrating on steering his horse away from the most hazardous sections, all the while keeping Hugh in his sights. When they breasted a hill and saw Braidstane silhouetted against the sky ahead of them, it was as if a weight had been removed from his shoulders. He relaxed his grip on the reins, and in a moment of inattention failed to notice the snow-covered boulder in the track ahead. His horse stumbled and fell heavily, casting him out of the saddle.

Ahead of him, Hugh halted and turned, clearly hearing the horse's whinny of distress. Alexander was already on his feet and, ignoring the pain in his back, urging the horse to stand. It took three attempts before he managed to help it scrabble to its feet, and when it did it stood with one hoof resting on its edge.

He ran a practised hand down the foreleg and straightened.

'Well?' Hugh already had his pistol out and was priming it.

'No need. He's lamed, that's all, thank God, though,' he looked past Hugh towards Braidstane, still a mile or more away, 'it'll be a long enough walk leading him.'

'You'd best ride with me, slow as we will be riding double, it will be faster than you could tramp.' He gestured westwards. 'There's little enough daylight left, and I've no wish for either of us to be caught out in the dark.'

It was the first sensible comment Hugh had made all

349

day, and Alexander, grateful for it, unbuckled the reins to turn them into a leading rope.

They covered the last part of the climb up to the tower under a sky heavy with cloud. The sun was well down, and though they had caught a glimpse of a sliver of moon as they approached the valley floor, both it and whatever stars might have been visible on a clearer night had disappeared again. It was a relief to see the gate standing open and the flicker of candlelight in the solar window. They slid to the ground, Alexander leading both horses towards the stable while Hugh thundered on the door of the tower, calling for assistance and lights.

There was a creak as the main door was scraped back, the stable lad stumbling down the steps, hopping on one foot as he hauled on his other boot. Behind him Elizabeth, newly slim and smiling, the girls crowding beside her, and behind them John and another lad, a stranger, hesitating in the doorway as if uncertain of his standing.

Alexander relinquished the horses to the lad, who bent and ran his hand over the leg, probing gently, then straightened.

'Ne-needing a p-poultice, ah r-reckon, and st-strapping. L-l-leave it t-to me. Wi' l-luck a w-week or two w-will s-see him r-right.' He jerked his head towards the tower. 'Ye'll b-be w-wanting t-to go up, th-though they ma-managed f-fine w-without ye.'

'I can see that. The babe?'

'A b-boy, wi' l-lungs on h-him l-like a f-foghorn.' He grinned. 'Th-though th-the wee l-lass isna f-far b-behind.'

'Twins?' Alexander looked across at Elizabeth. 'What…?' He turned back to question the lad, but he was already halfway to the stable.

Hugh lifted Elizabeth off her feet. 'Missed it again, I see. I'm sorry. I really did mean to make it this time.'

'I know. And had it not been before time, you would have done.'

He gestured at the snow. 'The weather…'

'I know,' she said again. 'And unlike his father, this Montgomerie heir…'

'A boy!' Hugh lifted Elizabeth again, swung her round, his delight obvious. He looked towards John. 'I take it you were here?'

'The way to Glasgow was likewise blocked, and I arrived two days ago expecting to be in ample time and instead found…'

Elizabeth cut in, with more than a hint of pride in her voice. 'He was two weeks late. We had neither doctor, nor midwife, but managed fine on our own.'

Hugh set Elizabeth down and took a step back to hold her at arm's length, a teasing note creeping into his voice. 'He is half-grown already then. And you halfway to a figure.'

Mary was bouncing up and down, hanging on Hugh's arm. He released Elizabeth and picked her up. 'I hope you've been helping to look after your little brother.'

'Yes,' she said. 'I've held him. But he's awfie wriggly. Annie is too.'

'Annie?'

Hugh looked at Elizabeth and then at John, whose face registered nothing. 'You never suggested…'

There was mischief in Elizabeth's expression and a hint of something else that Alexander couldn't quite fathom as she took Hugh's arm and said, 'Come inside and you'll see.'

Hugh was lounging on the settle, one arm about Elizabeth's shoulder, his other hand resting on Hughie's head as he lay at her breast, his sucking vigorous and noisy. John was sitting cross-legged on the floor, playing spillikins with Catherine and Mary, Sybie using the two she'd been given to keep her occupied as drumsticks, tapping them on the leg of the table, while Alexander leant against the mantleshelf, content to watch.

Hugh tugged at an escaped strand of Elizabeth's hair. 'That was unkind. Leading us on like that. For all you knew my heart might not have stood the shock.' He looked across at John. 'You at least could have given an inkling.'

'And spoiled Elizabeth's surprise? It was more than my life was worth.'

Elizabeth reached up and covered Hugh's hand with hers. She took a deep breath. 'Would you have welcomed twins, had it been so?'

'Of course. Why not? Though I imagine it would have

been harder on you.' Hugh stroked the soft down on his son's head. 'Keeping this one satisfied is work enough, I imagine.'

Alexander saw her gaze flick towards the trug where Annie slumbered, her expression half-guilty, half-defiant. The realisation – she's feeding them both – at once surprising and yet not. He looked at Hugh, as yet clearly unaware of the undercurrent in the conversation, and at John, his head bent over the spillikins, as if he had no wish to be part of the exchange.

'You are eating well and resting plenty?'

'Yes and yes.' Her hand found Hugh's again and squeezed.

'Good.' Alexander abandoned subtlety. 'I'm no expert, but isn't milk for two difficult?'

Hugh shot upright. 'You're feeding both of them?'

'You don't mind, do you? It was less a question than a statement of intent to continue. 'Annie is but a wee bit thing and sorely in need of sustenance. In truth, it is less effort feeding her myself than from a spoon. That was a lengthy business.'

"Cept,' Mary said, her mouth pursed, 'now I can't help.'

Hugh's shout of laughter was the release they all needed, Elizabeth relaxing against him, John looking around with a smile and Catherine hugging Mary and consoling her with, 'No more can I.'

Elizabeth looked across at Alexander. 'It was good of you to accompany Hugh home. Can you bide a while? There is aye room in our house for family, and things are quiet in Edinburgh at present, are they not?'

'Yes, yes they are. But though I have James' permission to be away, his indulgence will stretch to a day or two only...'

'A pity,' she said, settling Hughie to her other breast.

John said, 'But while you are here, perhaps you can handle being tormented by the children and let me off the hook.'

There was a chorus of protests from the girls, silenced by Alexander scooping up Mary and winking at Catherine. 'I may be out of practice, but I daresay I can survive.' He shifted her onto one arm. 'I see you don't have a snowman to guard the gate. That is an omission I could rectify in the morning ... with a little help.'

Alexander left two days later, the snow still crunching under foot. As the others assembled at the tower gateway to give him farewell, he looked up at the sky, a cloud the size of a man's hand on the far horizon. 'The sooner I'm away, the sooner I'll arrive, for though it may not look like it the now, I suspicion the weather may yet take another turn for the worse.' He grinned at John, standing at his stirrup, and gestured towards the girls clustered on the steps. 'If it does, you may be snowed in here till the spring. Could you cope?'

'I may pray I don't have to.' John became serious. 'It is a privilege to have been invited to join the College of Surgeons. Indeed, I relish the work.'

As Alexander reached down to take Elizabeth's outstretched hand, she said, 'You would be welcome to stay longer, you know that.'

'I know. But with Hugh safely home you have no need of me, and I will do better for all of us if I can stay in James' good books.'

His parting shot was for Hugh's ears alone. 'Enjoy your family, Hugh, and don't go looking for trouble. And whatever the aggravation, for their sake and your own, do nothing to jeopardise the present peace.'

It was advice that Hugh, uncharacteristically, seemed minded to follow, and Elizabeth, seeing his growing affection for Annie and Dand as well as their own latest arrival, was well content.

Chapter 9

In Paris, Yuletide came and went, the old year ushered out, the new one in, and still no sign of Munro, much to Ellie's displeasure, and it took all Kate's powers of persuasion to convince her it was not her father's fault. Had she been able to say it was the King's business he did, it would perhaps have mollified her, but preserving the fiction of 'private business' made that impossible. She hesitated to make new promises, for if the weather turned severe she knew he might be longer delayed, and as January bled into February, she watched anxiously for signs of snow. And blessed the lack, no matter how much or how often Ellie and the Bourbon children bemoaned it.

By March Maggie appeared to have reached some kind of accommodation with the other students in M Daumont's anatomy class. The name Anton de Vincennes was still mentioned from time to time, but without the previous edge of irritation, an indication of a more tolerant attitude on both sides that made Kate privately wonder if it might grow beyond tolerance. Whatever the situation, Maggie blew in and out of the apartment, her enthusiasm for her studies undiminished. Kate had never seen her happier, nor more determined to make the most of the opportunity, and with it an increase in maturity and a perception beyond her years. All of which would have pleased Kate, had it not been for the persistent niggle at the back of her mind regarding payment for the tuition. There had been no mention of it and Kate had no idea how much or for how long Gabrielle d'Estrées had paid M Daumont, but she feared for the consequences if the money ran out and they had not the funds to allow Maggie to continue – telling her would not be easy. It was a problem she returned to again and again when she was alone in her quarters, but so far she hadn't reached a conclusion.

She was running possibilities through her mind for the hundredth time when Robbie burst in, his uniform dishevelled, dark stains on the jacket and arms. He didn't give any greeting, nor present his cheek for a kiss, instead demanding, 'When *will* Father return? And what is this *private business* that has detained him so long?'

Inwardly Kate feared for what had brought him to the apartment in such a state; outwardly she sought to settle his agitation. 'Nothing to worry you. Nothing to worry any of us. He will be back soon. I'm sure of it.'

'The rumour among the Gardes is that he is on the King's business, not his own, so which is it?'

'Robbie, please.' She hesitated, weighing up her promise to Munro not to tell Robbie the true nature of the business he was undertaking lest it got out among the Gardes. Her main concern was that left to himself he might worry at it like a dog at a bone and come to some conclusion more dangerous than the truth. Concern winning, she said, 'It is a mission for the King, but not to be spoken of. So you must swear to me that you will not be drawn into any discussion of it when you are in quarters.

357

Nor indeed to let anything slip, here, or anywhere else. The story is that he had some business to transact, that is all.' She paused. 'A hint that it has to do with the property at Cayeux, with legalities that must be sorted now that we are free to inherit, might suffice.'

He slumped into a chair and dropped his head into his hands, his breathing fast and shallow. She gave him a minute to compose himself, but when he lifted his head again she saw a pulse still throbbed in his neck. 'Robbie, what is it? Your father may not be here, but can't I help?'

There was despair in his eyes, anguish in his voice. 'I thought it would never come to anything, but instead...'

'Robbie.' She slid to the floor beside the chair, grasped his arms and shook him. 'You're not making any sense. Thought *what* wouldn't come to anything?'

He closed his eyes, a shudder running through him. 'Standing surety for Angus.' Another shudder. 'I trusted him.'

It was her turn to shiver, but she kept her voice even. 'Start at the beginning. I cannot help if I don't know everything.' She forced him to look at her. 'There is little in this world that cannot be helped, in some way or another. Tell me all. I will not judge.'

He gave a deep sigh, and when he began to speak his voice was husky, hard to hear. 'Since Father bailed me out I have not wagered at cards, nor taken loans, but Angus did, and as a result found himself indebted to Del Sega, and that partly my fault.'

Kate shut her eyes, struggled to control her own breathing. 'Del Sega! He is a Shylock.'

'Modelled on him, that's for sure.' Robbie ran his

hands through his already dishevelled hair, increasing his wild look. 'It was the arrears that originally caused Angus' problem, but when we were promised we would have them soon, I signed for him as a guarantor. He had no connections, while I...'

'Are the son of a colonel in the Scots Gardes.' Kate tried, but failed, to keep the bitterness out of her voice. 'How could you play on that, Robbie, after your own narrow escape?'

'If the arrears had come when they first should, he would have been able to pay without any call on me. But despite Angus having repaid part of the loan twice in these last months, the interest kept mounting, and two days ago, Del Sega called it in.'

In her mind, Kate was running through her resources: jewellery, clothing; the gifts from Gabrielle – they would fetch something, surely. Adam's strongbox, to which she had a key. 'How much do we need to find?'

He was shaking, his mouth working, but nothing coming out.

'Robbie.' She took hold of his shoulders. 'We can sort this.'

He swallowed hard. 'It isn't the money. Del Sega is paid. Only...'

'Only what?'

It came out in a rush. 'Angus denounced them, for the money. He denounced them ... how could he do that?'

She didn't need to ask who it was Robbie referred to, white-hot anger replacing her fear. She struggled to remain calm, however, for to lose control now would help no one, least of all the Lavalles.

'How could he,' Robbie repeated. 'He was my friend.'

'He is sixteen, without resources and afraid.'

'But the Lavalles…'

'Are just names to him. He doesn't know them.'

'He knew me.'

'Where are they, Robbie, what happened to them?'

'They were taken. All of them.'

'On what charge?'

'Practising their religion within the boundary of the city. Inciting others to flout the law. Burying their dead by Protestant rite.'

'Is there evidence?'

'Other than what can be tortured out of them? I don't think so. Unless some who have reason to know can also be bought. But who can withstand interrogation?' He was staring at the floor as if he saw their image reflected in it. 'Their father might, for a time at least, but Eugenie? Netta? François? I could not bear to think of it.'

Unbidden, the memories resurfaced. Of Irvine, her own incarceration and torture, her narrow escape. This time there would be no king to come to the rescue, for whatever Henri's private sympathies, the Edict of Nantes was too precious to jeopardise. And though he had turned a blind eye to their own religious adherence, it was on the understanding that when they travelled out of Paris to meet with others of a similar persuasion, the reason for their journey was neither openly acknowledged, nor spoken of, and occasional public attendance at mass remained an expected part of Adam's duties. The King would not publicly ignore the terms relating to Paris for anyone, far less an unknown Huguenot family to whom he owed nothing. She was shaking her head to dispel her own demons and focus on what could be done for the Lavalles when the tenor of Robbie's words penetrated. *He was my friend. He knew me. I could not bear to think of it.* Past tense. She reached out her hand, grasped his shoulder. 'Robbie?'

She felt a tremor run through his body, his sentences disjointed, each one sharp as a shard of glass. 'I was so angry ... I couldn't think of anything other than that he had betrayed them, betrayed Eugenie...' Another shudder ran through him. 'I didn't mean to kill him ... I don't know how ... he was always the better swordsman ... When I challenged him I thought it would be me would die ... And with Eugenie taken, and likely as good as dead, I didn't care ... But there was so much blood ... I didn't know there would be so much blood...' He was picking at the stains on his jacket, as if they would come away by scratching, his voice so quiet she could hardly hear it. 'I never thought my first kill would be my friend.'

She wanted to gather him in her arms, to rock him as she would a child having a nightmare, to tell him it would be all right. Except that he wasn't a child, and it wasn't a nightmare, but real, and couldn't be easily swept aside. And likely could never be made right – if only Adam were here. She forced herself to think clearly. To consider what he would do in this circumstance. What must be done today? What could wait until tomorrow? She could do nothing for Eugenie and her family on her own; that would require more thought, more time. She prayed they might have time. But Robbie's situation was urgent, for with every moment that passed, Angus' absence might be noted and questions asked. She steeled herself to ask, 'What have you done with the body?'

'We were by the river when we fought. I rolled him into the water and the current took him away. If it hadn't been for the blood on my hands and my clothes, I might have thought it all a dream.'

– Downriver, then, and unlikely to resurface anytime soon. She hated herself for the momentary sense of relief. Considered another angle. 'Were you seen?'

'No. At least,' he rubbed his hand across his eyes, 'I don't think so.' Then, 'What shall I do?'

There was only one thing to do. One person to approach. She sent up a silent prayer, *Please God let this be the right decision*, strove for an even tone. 'You will stay here. And say nothing, to anyone. Not even Maggie when she returns. I shall go to Rosny. You will not be the first Garde to kill another in a duel, and no doubt you will not be the last. In the absence of your father, we must put ourselves in his hands.'

'It isn't myself I'm concerned about. It is the Lavalles. I am to blame for their arrest. What can be done for them?'

'I don't know yet, but I will think of something.'

'There may not be much time. The conditions...'

She cut him off. 'Believe me, I know.' She was back in the Tolbooth at Irvine, her clothes in tatters, slipping on the slime of vomit and faeces, fighting off the men that leered at her, beating at their clutching hands, turning her face away from the foetid breath that rolled over her in waves. It was unlikely that any Paris prison would have better conditions. 'You will not be able to help them if you yourself are imprisoned. Once we have dealt with your situation we will look to theirs. I promise.'

Rosny looked up as Kate was announced, surprise registering in his eyes. 'Lady Munro? To what do I owe this pleasure?'

She swept a deep curtsey. 'I am in need of help, and with my husband away on the King's business, I had no one else to turn to.'

'Whatever it is, if it's in my power, I will do it.' He poured two glasses of wine, gestured towards the pair of chairs beside the fire. 'Let us sit down and be comfortable and you can tell me all.'

Not quite all, Kate thought, just enough to enlist his help. She took a sip of wine, rehearsed what she wanted to say. 'My son…' She hesitated, at this last moment unsure if it *was* a wise move to look for help in this quarter. For the story once told could not be untold, and if there was no evidence linking Robbie to the disappearance … it wasn't unknown for a soldier to abscond, especially when debt was involved. Robbie's anguished face swam in front of her eyes, his words reverberating in her head. *'I didn't mean to kill him.'*

'Yes?' His voice and expression were kind. 'You and your husband have done much for the King, past and present, your loyalties clear. If that can be repaid in some measure, His Majesty will be glad of it, I'm sure.'

Angus was dead and nothing would change that, but he didn't deserve to have his reputation destroyed also. She took a swallow of wine to bolster her courage, plunged straight in. 'Robbie got in a fight with another of the Gardes, a personal matter that angered him, and unfortunately...' she took another swallow, 'the other Garde was killed. We do not know what to do.'

There was what felt like a lengthy silence before Rosny asked, 'It was a fair fight?'

'So Robbie said, and I believe him, for whatever his faults, cowardice isn't one of them. But there are no witnesses to corroborate his story.'

Rosny's hands were pressed together as if in prayer, his fingers resting against his lips. 'No witnesses, eh?' He nodded. 'That makes it easier. For it means that your son's testimony can stand without fear of contradiction. Nevertheless ... it is a delicate problem and must be approached carefully.' There was another pause, before he began to speak as if to himself. 'That might serve. Yes that might serve very well.'

For a moment Kate wondered if he had forgotten she was there, until he asked, 'Where is your son now?'

'In our apartment. I thought it best he stay there until I had consulted with you.'

'A wise move. This ... predicament is not without precedent, but if we are to cover his tracks he must go back to his own quarters as if nothing has happened.'

'His uniform...' She swallowed, thinking of the dark patches on the jacket.

'The streets are covered in muck and walking in them treacherous at the best of times. And even more so just now. If he was to fall on the way back, no doubt that would suffice.'

She thought again of Robbie's distress. 'And if he cannot act as if nothing has happened?'

Rosny's voice hardened. 'He must.' Then, as if to offer some comfort, 'Tell him it will only be for a day or two. I am instructed to Florence to finalise the marriage contract between the King and Marie de' Medici. Naturally, I do not go alone. And who better to accompany me than a select group of the Gardes. I will ensure your son is among them.' He refilled her glass. 'Who is it that he has killed?'

She had to steel herself to reply. 'Angus Muir.'

'If your son is not here when Muir is looked for, he cannot be suspected of involvement. I will send for him tomorrow, that arrangements may be made. No doubt there will be plenty of frustrations on the journey to Florence to try the patience of all of us. If your son is morose, it will scarcely be noticed.'

Kate set her glass down and rose, ready to express her thanks, but he waved her back into her seat.

'This *personal* matter? You know the cause?'

She would have liked to be able to deny it, but the lie stuck in her throat. 'There is no need to trouble you with it.'

'No need, perhaps, but I suggest you do.'

It was not a suggestion.

She lifted the wine glass again, drained it. 'Robbie had acquaintance with a Huguenot family.'

She saw his indrawn breath, anticipated the next question, and sought to forestall him. 'How they met is not important … but Angus, who was his friend, knew of it, and when he had a debt to discharge with Del Sega, he denounced the family to the authorities and was paid for his pains. That was the cause of the fight.' She straightened her shoulders. 'I do not condone the killing, but I understand, indeed sympathise, with the reason for the fight.'

His eyes narrowed, and she hurried on. 'I treated one of their children for a broken leg and found them to be honest and loyal citizens. Robbie's defence of them, whatever the outcome, was justified, for they were badly used.'

She thought she detected a flash of sympathy in Rosny's eyes, but couldn't have sworn to it, and his reprimand was clear.

'Take care, Lady Munro, that you do not share such thoughts widely. They would not be universally popular. And as the proscription of the Protestant religion within the bounds of Paris is an edict of the King's, they could be considered treasonable.' A hint of softening. 'For myself, in the light of your husband's undoubted loyalty, I shall forget I heard them.' He looked past her, and she wondered what was still to come.

'This Angus Muir, has he family?'

She felt a stab of guilt for her thankfulness. 'Not as far as I'm aware. His parents fell victim to the plague in '86. Robbie said…' Her voice broke. 'Robbie said Angus joined the Gardes because he hoped to make a life here, having nothing to keep him in Scotland.' It was close to their own reasoning, and thus the more painful to think on.

'So much the better.' He reached out his hand and drew her to her feet. 'Leave this with me. Your son's reputation will remain intact and if there is a way of saving Muir's also, I will do it. For the standing of the Gardes must be maintained and scandal avoided if at all possible. As for those other poor unfortunates caught up in this trouble, I can do nothing for them. If the charges brought against them prove to be true, that will be the end of the matter. If the charges be false they will have lost nothing bar a week or two of confinement in less than ideal conditions.' A pause. 'Does your son know where they are held?'

'Not for sure, though neighbours suggest it is the Palais de la Cité. I told him it was not safe for him to seek to enquire…'

She allowed her sentence to tail off.

Rosny lifted one shoulder. 'Perhaps. Perhaps not.' And then, as if an aside, of no particular moment, 'The conditions in the Palais are not always as bad as is thought. At least so I'm led to believe.' The emphasis in his next words was so slight as to be almost imperceptible. 'There is a captain in the watch who is well placed to know, having charge of the tower where many of those arrested are first taken. They say he is an honest man, with a soft spot for a pretty face … and a liking for drink that puts a strain on his purse. Should you wish to find him, I believe he frequents a tavern on the right bank close to Les Halles.'

Chapter 10

'I won't go.' Robbie was standing in Kate's quarters, his fists clenched tight by his side. 'How can I save myself and leave the Lavalles to suffer?'

'Rosny's offer is generous. You must see that. He thinks to preserve your reputation, to save you from the consequences of your actions.'

'He thinks to preserve the reputation of the Gardes. Had I been other he would not have cared.'

True as it was, Kate refused to be distracted. 'Maybe so, but you must be grateful nonetheless. You cannot help Eugenie if you are in prison yourself.'

'And how am I supposed to help her if I am in Florence?'

'It is but the finalising of a marriage contract that has been years in the making already. The King's advisors will have no wish for any further delay. I do not think you will be away for long.'

He cut her off. 'The travel alone will take weeks, not days, forbye the negotiations. How can I bear it with no means of knowing how she is treated or whether...' his voice cracked, 'she survives at all.'

'She will survive.' Kate injected a certainty she didn't feel into her voice. 'We will find her and will use all the influence we have to urge her release. When your father returns…'

'When…? Yuletide is past, despite his promises, Epiphany also and still no sign of him. What if it is Eastertide before he is home?'

It was a memory she had never shared, not even with Adam and Maggie, who had witnessed the ghastly finale, a memory she had no wish to share with anyone and which she had hoped would remain forever buried. The nightmare of the torture, the sleep deprivation and the endless rounds of interrogation that at first she had thought could not be borne. Even the strength she had found, which ensured she hadn't been broken by the experience, was something she hadn't talked of. She grasped Robbie's arm, pressed him into a seat, and, sitting down beside him, took a deep breath. If it would help him to know, he must be told the bones of it, if not the detail.

The bell in the clock tower was tolling six when she came to an end, and she looked up in surprise. She had not thought to speak so long. Robbie was silent, carved from stone. She took hold of his hand, held it within both of hers, repeated, 'I survived, Robbie. I survived. And so will Eugenie.' She swallowed. 'She will find the courage, as I did. And though you may not think it now, believe me, she will be the stronger for it.' He looked up, a flicker of hope in his eyes, and before he could retreat again into despair, she added, 'I will move heaven and earth to ensure her safety. You have my word.'

Robbie rode out beside Rosny, his mouth set in a thin line, his shoulders stiff, his hands clenched so tight on the reins that his horse pulled against them and showed the whites of its eyes. Kate, who had visited the quarters, ostensibly to see him off, but in reality to make sure that he went, willed him to relax. And as they disappeared along the Quai de Louvre, heading east, she consoled herself with the thought that he couldn't maintain such tension for long.

Her own was another matter. Rosny had suggested she seek information from a captain of the watch who could be found in a tavern on the right bank of the Seine. As she had no description to offer, she thought to visit them one by one, to question the bartenders and, if that failed, to sit in a corner and watch the clientele come and go in the hope that she might strike lucky. She should have known better.

For her first foray, she slipped out after Maggie and Ellie were both asleep. She took the precaution of borrowing a cloak and gown from one of the maids, to avoid being conspicuous, and that too proved a mistake, for it was neither one thing nor the other. Not good enough to indicate real quality, nor poor enough to allow her to blend in with those who frequented the docks. All along the quayside she was hustled and jostled, snarled at and spat upon. The sailors looking to have a quick fumble in the shadow of an alley she had anticipated, and to that end had brought a slim dagger, which she brandished at all comers. When, despite the shaking of her hand, she drew blood from the first assailant who tried to force her against a wall, she felt both satisfaction and revulsion and had to steel herself to continue.

The antagonism of the whores she had not expected, thinking, wrongly, that if she kept her head down and didn't loiter, she would be ignored. Instead, they came at her, with rouged cheeks and white faces, pulling back her hood and threatening to cut her pretty face and weigh her down with stones and throw her in the river if she didn't go elsewhere to ply her trade.

'Looking for a nob, are ye? Wi' yer fancy clothes and yer piled-up hair?'

'I seek only information. I have no wish to sell my favours.' It had been the wrong thing to say.

'Think yourself better than the likes of us, do ye? We'll soon sort ye.'

They tore at her clothes and pulled pins from her hair, running greasy fingers through the sections that came loose so that they fell in an untidy tangle around her face. And when she escaped their clutches and fell through the door into an alehouse, she had just enough time to note the low-cut dresses of the women before the bartender grabbed her by her breast and twisted, the pain of it taking her breath away. Her head was swimming as he flung her out, sending her sprawling on the cobbles, growling, 'Be off with you. I keep a good house. We want no street doxies here.'

She fled back to the Louvre and collapsed into their apartment, grateful that she had escaped with nothing worse than scratches and bruises.

It was clear she couldn't wander in the dock area alone but would have to find another way. Once again she wished Adam was at home. As a Garde he could have gone where she could not, and with impunity. The plan was audacious in its simplicity. Uncomfortable perhaps, and with some difficulties, but surely less than she had already suffered. Munro's spare uniform hung behind a curtain in their chamber. A tuck here and there in the shirt and breeches, and the buttons moved on the jacket, should do it. There was a pair of Robbie's boots that had been laid aside to be resoled: they would fit well enough. And if it rained, the worst she would get would be wet feet... Her hair. Before she could change her mind she found the shearing scissors and, holding it section by section, chopped it close to the nape of her neck. It wasn't the tidiest but would have to do. She turned to replace the scissors, but catching sight of her head in the mirror, began to laugh.

Maggie, clearly having been disturbed by the sound, appeared in the doorway behind her. 'Mother! What are you doing?'

'Cutting my hair,' Kate said, her laughter dying.

'Why?'

'I need to.'

'And I need to know why.' Maggie refused to be fobbed off. 'Something is wrong. You can pretend all you like with others, Mother, but I'm not stupid and I won't stop asking until you tell me what it is. Is it Father?'

'No.' She couldn't allow Maggie to think that.

'I don't understand then. Father loves your hair.'

'I know.'

Kate was hesitating, wondering how much to say, when Maggie interrupted. 'This is to do with the Lavalles, isn't it? I heard about their arrest.'

'How?'

'One of the students was talking of it today, after class. He had it from his uncle and he from one of the archers. He thought it amusing.' She paused. 'But then he thinks anyone's trouble amusing so long as it doesn't touch him.'

'Anton?'

'No, though he confirmed the rumour. I meant to ask you about it, for I hoped it was false, or at least that the tale had grown in the telling, but Ellie prattled away so long at supper it slipped my mind. It is true then?'

Kate nodded. An unlikely source perhaps, but with his connections, de Vincennes' information might be good. 'Does Anton know where they're being held?'

'If he does, he didn't say.'

Kate sighed.

Maggie sat down beside her. 'But surely Robbie...? He will not stand back and...'

'He's not here. He left two days ago as part of the delegation to Florence seeking the marriage agreement between the King and Marie de' Medici, and he won't be back until that job is done. In the meantime...'

'*We* need to help them.'

'*I* need to help them. You should not get involved.'

'I am already involved. We all are. Robbie's friends are ours also, and Eugenie, as we both know, is more than a friend.'

'All right then. You can help by first tidying my hair. I need it to look like Robbie's.'

Maggie took the scissors. 'Sit down, but while I'm doing this, you need to tell me what you intend to do.'

Kate spent a week scouring the taverns in the streets on the right bank of the Seine, looking for the captain who might be able to give her the information she sought. The hardest part was borrowing a horse from the stables and slipping the noose of the Louvre without being seen. A risky business for a real Garde, doubly so for Kate. She practised dropping her voice an octave and prepared a story, should she be stopped, of a lady who welcomed her attentions but dared not risk a daytime liaison. As she rode towards the docks, she thanked God for her childhood in Ayrshire, when she had borrowed breeches from the stable lad and riding astride had been able to match the speed of the Munro brothers. The horse she left in the care of an ostler a ten-minute walk away from the river. It was certainly easier to move about the docks as a Garde, especially on foot, the worst attentions she received those of the whores who offered their services. Recognising some of them as ones who had previously attacked her, she had to bite her cheeks not to laugh and took some pleasure from spurning their advances.

Each evening she slipped out, her hopes high, and each evening returned, tired and dispirited, to Maggie, who waited in the salon. Kate had tried to get her to go to bed, for she needed to rise early for her classes with M Daumont, but she had refused on the grounds that she wouldn't be able to sleep anyway until she knew that Kate was safely home again. And knowing that in Maggie's shoes she would likely have said the same, Kate let her be. By the start of the second week she was beginning to fear that it was fruitless. If the captain had frequented the area in the past, it seemed he did so no longer. For all her efforts there had only been once that she thought she was getting close. The man in question did indeed wear a semblance of a uniform, but he turned out to be a simpleton, who favoured her with a gappy smile, winking and nodding and touching his nose, and repeating 'At your service, sir. Capt'n Jacques, at your service', accompanied by a series of elaborate bows.

There were only a few taverns left to try, but she was determined not to give up until she had exhausted them all. One more night would do it. And pray God she would be lucky this time. She was stepping out of her gown, ready to put on the Gardes uniform for one final time, when there was a rap at the apartment door. She heard Maggie open it and the voice of the maid.

'Pardon, Mam'selle Marguerite, but Mam'selle Ellie has disappeared. I left her tucked up in bed and well on her way to sleep...'

Kate pulled her gown up over her shoulders and holding the back together emerged from her chamber. The maid was standing on the threshold, her face white.

'Pardon, milady, I do not know...'

'How long ago did you leave her?'

375

'An hour, no more.'

As Maggie laced her gown, Kate's mind raced, but she strove to hide her panic. The girl was afraid enough without adding to it. 'It's probably a childish prank, some game she's playing with the Bourbon children. Have you checked on them?'

'Yes, milady. They are still in their own beds and sound,' she took a deep breath, 'aside from…'

'César? He is missing also?'

It was no more than a whisper. 'Yes.'

'They cannot be far. Have you called the Gardes?'

The maid was trembling, her silence answer enough.

Kate grasped her by her shoulders. 'It is not your blame.' She turned to Maggie. 'You go. Tell them to search the gardens while we search inside.' She gave the maid a gentle shake. 'Get help and search this wing first, and if you've no joy here, then fan out further.'

The girl's eyes were dark, her voice cracking. 'And the King?'

Kate released her. 'I shall inform the King.'

It was two long hours before they found them, two hours during which Kate struggled to remain calm as the search parties scoured both grounds and palace. She found it impossible not to think of Anna, the only consolation that she had still been in the Louvre when the maid appeared and that there were no horses missing from the palace stables, so they could rule out an accident of that kind. She was returning to the King's apartment to report on an unsuccessful search of the west wing, when she heard rapid footsteps in the corridor behind her and turned to see two Gardes, each carrying an inert child. She felt her legs sag beneath her and reached out to grasp the door handle for support, but as she did so it opened, Henri catching her as she stumbled forward. She was aware of his hands under her elbows, and the buttons of his doublet pressing against her chest, and his steadying voice.

'They are found. Merci le bon Dieu.'

He pulled her gently to the side to allow the Gardes to pass into the apartment and she felt her legs give way again, this time in relief. As he steered her into the salon, they heard the regular breathing of children deep in sleep, and he smiled down at her. 'All is well.' He motioned the Gardes to wait and whispered to a servant, 'Put warming pans in a bed. They will sleep here tonight.'

'I should…' Kate began.

'Better we don't disturb them.' Henri touched César's head. 'We can be stern with them on the morrow. For tonight, let us be grateful for their safe recovery.'

Neither child stirred as they were settled in the bed in the adjoining chamber, the warming pans at their feet. Kate tucked the blankets around them and straightened the brocaded coverlet. She turned to find Henri at her shoulder.

He gestured towards the Gardes who still stood in the outer chamber. 'No doubt you will wish to know where they were found, as I do.'

The story told and the Gardes dismissed, Henri said, with a rueful moue, 'A night in a folly. We have adventurous, if foolish, children.' He waved Kate to a seat at the side of the fire, and though she would have preferred to return to her own apartment and take Ellie with her, she had no choice but to obey, an apology springing to her lips.

'Ellie is the older and should have had more sense...'

He waved away her apology. 'Do not blame her, at least without good reason, for if César makes up his mind to something, an angel could scarcely dissuade him, far less another child.' He paused to pour a glass of wine for her. 'It is inevitable perhaps for the son of a King, but I have heard him trade on his privileged position, and command obedience, even from those much older than himself.'

Kate sipped the proffered drink, feeling the warmth trickle through her. 'Even so...'

His voice was gentle. 'Tonight is for celebration, not censure.' He raised his glass. 'Let us drink to the mercy of Providence and the diligence of the Gardes.'

They sat for a moment in companionable silence, warmed by the wine and the fire and linked by shared gratitude. Kate, now that the crisis was past, found her thoughts returning to the problem of the Lavalles and, unaware of Henri's scrutiny, sighed.

'Lady Munro?'

She started. 'I'm sorry, I...'

'Was abstracted. I know. Something else is troubling you. If I can be of help...'

She would not, in any other circumstances, have

dreamt of approaching Henri about the Lavalles, but whether it was the loosening effect of the wine or the shared experience of the evening, she found herself spilling out the whole sorry tale, finishing, '…If only Adam was here. He would know what to do.'

There was a prolonged silence in which she feared she had over-stepped the mark, that to bemoan Adam's lack could be construed as criticism of the decision to send him away, and thus of the King. And as for Robbie and the possible consequences for him as a result of her revealing his actions… When she dared to look up, it was to see that Henri appeared deep in thought, without any trace of anger on his face.

He tapped his fingers together and then reached out and pushed back her hood, revealing her cropped hair. 'You are very brave, Lady Munro. Perhaps Ellie takes her adventurous nature from you.'

She was unsure of how to respond, but it seemed no response was needed.

'It is in my service your husband is detained at Rome, therefore his responsibilities are mine … but as you will be aware, there are certain difficulties.' He took the empty wine glass from her hand and rose to refill it. 'Does anyone else know of this?'

'Rosny. It was to distance Robbie he chose him as one of the party accompanying him to Florence.'

'So … for the moment your son is safe. Your primary concern now?'

'Is for the release of that innocent girl and her family.'

'Are you sure they are innocent?' He held up his hand. 'Do not answer that. There are some things it will be best I don't know.' He paused, and she heard the note of sadness in his voice. 'For the father it's likely little can be done, but the children could be considered helpless pawns in this.'

'Eugenie is fifteen, her sister thirteen, and the boy, François, ten.'

There was another, much longer pause, during which Kate drained her glass and stood up, instinct prompting her that more might be accomplished if she left Henri to his thoughts.

He stood also and bowed her to the door. 'Come to fetch Ellie in the morning, and we will tease out what she and César were doing at the folly.' It was clear he was choosing his words carefully. 'I will give some thought to this other matter.' He pressed her shoulder. 'The girls are rather old for pawns, but something may be able to be done.'

Chapter 11

Maggie was dozing on the couch, her legs curled under her when Kate returned. She thought of covering her up and leaving her there, and had gone to fetch a blanket, when Maggie stirred. She hurried back through and dropped onto the floor in front of her. 'They are found, perfectly safe, and are sleeping in the King's apartments.'

'What was she thinking of?'

'That, we don't know, for they were already asleep when they were found, and Henri insisted they were not to be woken.'

'Well I hope when she does wake there will be someone to tell her how stupid she has been.'

'I shall retrieve her tomorrow when she wakes, and no doubt be cross with her then. But we have all done foolish things in our time and this prank likely less dangerous than some.' It was not meant as a reprimand, nor to remind Maggie of her own jaunt to Broomelaw, that had so nearly brought them all to grief, but so it came out. There was no point in trying to pretend it hadn't been said, instead, ignoring the colour flooding Maggie's face, Kate focused on the positive. 'However difficult this night has been, good may come of it. I spoke to the King...'

'About the Lavalles?'

'Yes. I didn't mean to, for it was hardly proper, but it

381

slipped out. He was surprisingly generous in his response.'

'He will sort it?'

'He will think on it, and we must pray God he will find a solution. For in all my traipsing these last weeks I have found none. Nor any hope of one.'

'And Robbie?'

'What do you mean?'

'There is a rumour that a Garde denounced the Lavalles and was killed for it. Is that why Robbie was sent away?'

'Yes. They fought. Robbie says he didn't mean to kill him. In fact, he expected to be killed. And I believe him. But the Garde died. Nothing can change that.'

'You told the King that?'

'It came out. And what will be the end result I'm not sure.' She rose and pulled Maggie with her. 'There may not be much of the night left, but we should get some sleep. You have a class in the morning, and from what you've said, Monsieur Daumont does not tolerate tardiness.'

'Monsieur Daumont wouldn't be the problem. Laziness he cannot stand, but a genuine problem would be met with understanding. It's my fellow students I have to be concerned about. My acceptance among them has been hard fought, and I don't wish to give them any opportunity to criticise.'

382

Ellie was suitably penitent when Kate went to collect her, and it was clear that the King had given both she and César a severe talking to. She flew at Kate and wound her arms around her. 'I'm sorry, Maman. We didn't mean to frighten anyone. It was…'

'It was a dare. And as I thought,' Henri looked sternly at César, 'originated with this young man. I have spoken to them both and impressed upon them the thoughtlessness of their actions, in causing, not just concern for their welfare, but also wasted time and effort for half the palace staff in searching for them.' Over their heads his eyes met Kate's, and she saw the twinkle in them and had to struggle to keep her own face straight.

'It will not happen again?' she said, looking down at Ellie and biting hard on her cheeks.

Ellie shook her head, darted a glance at the King.

'Until I see that they are to be trusted,' Henri waved towards a tall, middle-aged woman who stood by the door, without even a flicker of a smile on her face, 'Marie here will accompany César at all times and will sleep in his room.'

Once again Kate smothered a smile, thought – no fear of indulgence there. 'A fitting response, Sire, to such foolishness. I trust she will drum some sense into them.'

'I have no doubt of that.' Henri motioned to Marie. 'Take your charges into the gardens. They like fresh air. You can teach them the names of all the plants, and Mam'selle Ellie's mother and I shall quiz them later.'

The King waited until their footsteps had faded away, before gesturing Kate to a chair. The laughter had gone from his face – this is it, she thought, he cannot help.

383

'You have heard of André Ruiz?'

She trawled through the names of everyone she had ever met at court but came up blank. 'I'm afraid not, Sire.'

'Your husband did not mention him?'

'No. Not that I remember. He is…?'

'The Spanish merchant in whose house the Edict of Nantes was signed.'

'Adam did mention the Maison de Tourelles, but what…?'

'Ruiz is here, in Paris. He comes from time to time, and your husband is tasked with all liaison between us. Ruiz has long sought to be of some use to me, for his own ends of course, but now might be the time. He has connections but is sufficiently distant that his actions will not be laid at my door. I cannot speak directly to him, of course, and as your husband is away, the normal channel is not open to us. But as someone who has entertained your husband in his house, it would not be inappropriate for you to return the compliment.'

Kate thought of Munro's description of the Maison de Tourelles. Her apartment in the Louvre would stand against any in elegance terms, but as to food… It was impossible to refuse, and what was a meal after all?

As if he read her thoughts, Henri said, 'If you were to arrange a supper for him, I shall provide the cook.'

'Thank you, Sire, that is…'

'A relief?' He smiled. 'Remember, I too have been entertained by André Ruiz. It was indeed an experience, which even the best of the cooks from the royal kitchens may not be able to match. But I shall instruct them to try.' His expression sobered again and she wondered what

384

was to come. 'If he is willing to facilitate this family's release, it is likely there will be certain expenses required. That too…'

She made a move to protest, but he ignored it.

'In that too,' he repeated, 'I will be of assistance. I owe my life to your husband, several times over. And that, money can never repay.'

There was something about André Ruiz that made Kate uneasy, though she couldn't explain it, even to herself. He was the epitome of courtesy, as he bent over her hand, the pressure of his lips exactly what could be expected of a gentleman meeting a lady for the first time. His conversation also. He paid her compliments on the meal that the King's cook had produced, and expressed his regret that Munro was not at home, and especially that his lodgings in Paris were not of a sufficient size or elegance to allow him to return the invitation.

'Perhaps one day you will be able to visit Nantes?' There was pride in his voice. 'My house there would not disappoint.'

'My husband speaks well of it.'

'When does he return? I would very much like to renew our acquaintance. I mean, of course, socially. Your husband and I do meet from time to time,' he leaned forward, as if to indicate that what he was about to say was confidential, 'in a, shall we say, professional capacity.'

After supper he broached the issue of the Lavalles, setting his empty wine glass on the table in front of him and placing his hand over it when the maid came forward with a flagon. 'No thank you. Good as it is, a clear head I think is called for.'

Kate, knowing they had come to the nub of the evening, dismissed the servants and, with a meaningful look at Maggie, suggested she saw to Ellie.

He came straight to the point. 'You have, I believe, some little difficulty that I may be able to assist you to resolve?'

She was unsure how much to tell him and confined herself to the matter of the arrest of the Lavalles, omitting the reason for it – best that she keep Robbie out of it if at all possible.

'You have a personal interest in this family?'

It was a perfectly reasonable question, but nevertheless it reinforced her sense of unease – he knows about Robbie. She stifled her concern, told herself – I have no option but to trust him. And the best deceptions come cloaked in a kernel of truth. 'I was called to treat the boy for a leg fracture. And found them to be a loyal and honest family. Of course,' her smile was disingenuous, 'we are ourselves of the Protestant persuasion, though we do not flaunt it, so are minded to be sympathetic to their plight. If they can be got out of Paris, we have a house at Cayeux, near St Valery, and there they could exercise their conscience without issue.'

'Where are they held?'

'We cannot be sure, but it's thought they may be in the Palais de la Cité.'

'You wish me to ascertain the accuracy of that report?'

'Yes.'

'And once that is done, make a scheme for either their rescue or release?'

'Is it possible?'

'Anything is possible, in the right circumstances, and for the right price.'

It should have been reassuring, and for a day or two it was, but as time passed and Kate heard nothing from Ruiz, she began to be concerned that either he had decided not to help her, or had found it impossible to do so.

For once, it was Maggie who was the voice of reason. 'It is little more than a week, and there could be a hundred and one reasons why he has not yet contacted you.' She tilted her head. 'From what you've said, he is not the kind of man to wish to appear less than confident, or to come with a plan still in the making. Give him time.'

'There may not be time. Eugenie and her family have been in prison for almost three weeks now. For all we know they could be...'

'Dead, or worse. I know. But it does no good to think it. We are in André Ruiz' hands on the King's recommendation. He does this to improve his standing with the King. If that does not inspire him to move heaven and earth to accomplish our ends, nothing will.' Maggie was plucking at a loose thread in the weave of her skirt, and when she looked up at Kate, her eyes betrayed an uncertainty. Then, 'You have not talked of it, Mother, and I know you may not wish to, even now, but how long were you imprisoned, before you were finally set free by James?'

'Several weeks. But it felt like ... I don't know how much longer I could have held out, for they came daily to try to force me to confess. If that is what Eugenie suffers...'

'She is not held for witchcraft. None of them are.'

'As good as. They have broken an edict from the King. And as such it will not be taken lightly. Tolerance of religion in this country goes only so far, and in Paris, as you know, not at all.'

'We practise our faith.'

'In the privacy of our apartment, yes, for the King turns a blind eye so long as we are discreet. It was a concession given when he requested our presence here. But even for us the privilege is fragile at best. If we did not have servants also sympathetic to the Protestant cause, we might have been denounced a hundred times over. And sympathetic as the King is to us, as a result of the debt he owes your father, if that were to happen, I wouldn't be entirely confident of the outcome.'

'What did the King say?'

'That children may not be held responsible ... Eugenie is not a child.'

'She is petite and may pass for such. If they have the sense to conceal her age.'

'It isn't just the authorities I fear, but their fellow inmates. Prison does something to people, and perhaps understandably so, for the conditions are...' she shut her eyes to blank out the memories 'not of a kind to encourage compassion, or any sense of fellow-feeling. It is everyone for themselves, and as a result the weakest go to the wall.'

'Eugenie is not on her own. She is with Netta and François and her father. He will protect them.'

'If we only knew that for sure. They may have been separated.'

'Ruiz will discover it.'

Kate squared her shoulders. 'Yes, of course. But I wish Ruiz would come.'

A voice behind her. '*André Ruiz?* I'm not sure that I like the idea of my wife waiting for André Ruiz.'

'Adam!' She was in his arms, crushed against his chest, and though he smelt of horses and sweat and dirt, she didn't care. His boots were mud-streaked, his jerkin likewise, his hair tousled by the wind and curled with the damp, and when he bent to kiss her, the stubble on his chin scratched her cheek.

'This is a welcome. I should go away more often. And stay long.' He took a step back. 'You look different.' Then, one hand straying to her neck, 'Your hair. What happened to your hair?'

'I cut it.'

'I can see that, but ... why?'

'It's a long story.' She was rubbing a finger against her other palm. 'And not a happy one. When you've changed and eaten, I'll tell you all then.'

'Tell me now.'

Dusk had fallen before she finished, interrupted occasionally by Maggie.

Munro was silent.

'Robbie didn't mean for any of this,' she said.

'Intentional or not, his foolishness has cost others dear. And he killed a man. He will have to live with that. As will we.' There was a longer silence, then, 'And Ruiz? How does he fit in?'

'He was the King's idea.'

'You told the King?'

Kate heard the surprise in Munro's voice. 'I wouldn't have, only...'

'It was Ellie.' Maggie had come to settle at Kate's side. 'Ellie?'

'She and César scared everyone near to death with a night-time adventure, and in the aftermath, it just came out. Henri was...' Kate examined her hands, 'more understanding than I could have expected, and than Robbie deserved. And Angus' death... Whatever the provocation, I still struggle to think on it.'

Munro focused on the practical. 'How do things stand now?'

'We have heard nothing at all from Ruiz for over a week, I had thought...'

'I'll meet with him. It would be no more than anyone would expect, given my prolonged absence.'

'You don't think...?'

'He will not have forgotten you, or the Lavalles.'

'He is Spanish and therefore Catholic. I had begun to fear he might have changed his mind about helping them.'

'He wishes to be in Henri's confidence. From what I know of him, that will trump any religious quibbles he might have. There will be a reason for the delay, and a good one, I'm sure. He knows the dangers of a spell in a Parisian prison, and the need to move as quickly as possible.'

'You don't think I...'

'Did wrong?' He shook his head. 'You did what you thought was right and in that you should take pride. For it is all any of us can do.'

And now...' he touched her cheek, 'there will be three of us on the case and not just two.'

It was her undoing. She relaxed against him, and with the release of the pent-up tension of the past weeks, the tears came. She tried to rub at her cheeks with her sleeve, but he caught her hand and, turning her around, wrapped both arms around her.

'It will be all right,' he said. 'I promise.'

Chapter 12

It was a sentiment that Elizabeth echoed as the days moved into weeks and no trouble came to disturb their peace. She wrote long, gossipy letters to Grizel and to Kate, happy that for once the news was good. No matter that they wouldn't receive them until the spring, the process of writing was sufficient to bring them closer to her.

...Alexander spent two days with us, the girls enjoying the attention, even little Sybie toddling around after him like a puppy with a new master. If she had a tail it would wag. I think he also enjoyed their company. Hugh shuttles back and forwards to Edinburgh, drip-feeding James information from George regarding the situation at the English court, but never stays away for more than a day or two at a time, professing himself far happier at home than he could ever be at court. I do not know if, or for how long, it will last, but I am determined to make the most of it. John is an irregular visitor, his work in Glasgow keeping him busy and, I think, content, however gruesome it appears to be, for when he does come it is with a cheerful countenance and an enthusiasm for everything that is infectious. It was a happy day for him when you gave him the tenancy of Broomelaw, and should you visit, I know you would find him worthy of it. He and Agnes

rub along well together, though I cannot help thinking a wife
would be a fine thing, but that he seems determined to avoid.
Hugh, in the spirit of brotherly encouragement, continues
to suggest it from time to time, but something in John's eyes
each time the subject is broached, a memory perhaps that he
doesn't care to share, but which still causes him pain, stops
me adding my support. Who knows, perhaps changing the
calendar has given us all a fresh start, the new year a chance
to look forward, not back.

It seemed she was right, though the weather remained
inclement. In March, melting snows flowed down the
slopes below the tower and gouged fresh stream-beds
where none had been before. The river filled to bursting
point, the fields that bounded it becoming shallow lakes
that lapped at the outcrops of rock dotted along the valley
floor. Despite the floods, the family and farm prospered,
and although the stock had to be retained longer than usual
in the pens adjacent to the tower, the autumn servicing
had been effective, ewes and heifers both growing plump
with the promise of new life to come. The month crept
by them almost unnoticed, a succession of days of pale
sunshine drying up the streams and driving the waters
back into their rightful place, leaving the valley springing
with fresh grass and the trees bursting into leaf.

Elizabeth was sitting in the shelter of the gable wall,
enjoying the spring sunshine and thinking over the
events of the last months and the good fortune they had
brought, and for the first time since she had returned
from France she felt no longing to leave Ayrshire. Hughie
was thriving and set fair to be as sturdy as his father,

393

and though Annie remained a wee mite and as light as a feather, the roundness of her cheeks and the pink blush on her skin were evidence of her good health also. In the months Dand had been at Braidstane he had changed from a child who startled like a frightened deer at the slightest noise into a boy mature beyond his thirteen years, and clever too, already able to write his own name and to read a simple primer. And, most pleasing of all, with a sensitivity that fully justified her decision to adopt him into their family.

She had talked of it to Hugh. 'Once or twice I've seen a longing in his face when the stable lad rides out to exercise the horses, but though I asked if he wished to work with them too, he refused. I think it is that he doesn't wish to put the lad out, or to usurp his position, a generosity of spirit that should be rewarded.'

'It will be,' he said. 'When he is of an age to know where his interests lie. In the meantime he is proving himself useful in many practical ways. It was indeed a good day when you brought him home.'

'He reminds me of Robbie Munro in the last months before he ran off to France. He has an affinity with animals and a sixth sense for when they might be in difficulties. Perhaps he could be given the task of looking to the stock.'

'Hmm.' Hugh was non-committal.

'Do you have another plan for him?'

'Yes. As you say, he is bright and clear-thinking, and his bravery and loyalty are not in doubt. Important as the animals are, he would be wasted as a stockman. I thought to take him to Edinburgh when next I go. He could be valuable to me there.'

'Valuable, how?'

'A messenger. A go-between, if you like. Someone who can be trusted to carry information, without fear of selling out to the highest bidder. An honest man at court is like gold dust. And young Dand here is shaping up well to fit that bill. Besides, that status, or at least the trappings of it, is everything there, and to go without a following diminishes our standing.'

'You have done fine in the past.'

'I have trodden on Alexander's coat tails and I think perhaps it is time I stood on my own.'

'This is about the Cunninghames and the fight for precedence.' It was an accusation. 'Is it not enough that you have the King's ear.'

'That's exactly the point. I have it now, and our standing increased as a result. But the King expects a certain display from those around him. Not to rival him, of course. It is a delicate balancing act. But if I am to further our ambitions in Ulster I must be able to demonstrate I can command a following, and not only among those who bear our name.'

Elizabeth, with a silent apology to Dand for demeaning his mother, was dismissive. 'A following among cottagers? That *will* increase your standing.'

'Who in Edinburgh will know where he came from? Who even in Irvine? I did not see him at the first, but I imagine he is already a world away from his beginnings. And that is your doing. What is so wrong with giving him the chance to rise further?'

'He is young, Hugh. Is Edinburgh really the place for

him?'

'At his age I had been away from home for two years, and well on the way to serving in the army of Maurice of Nassau.'

She shivered, thinking of Patrick. 'Please, Hugh, do not encourage him in that direction.'

'Trust me, Elizabeth, I've no intention of it, but he shows promise, and deserves the chance to develop.'

'You attend the court on sufferance. If he is happy here, why make him suffer too?'

'He is happy here because it is a vast improvement on what he knew before. That doesn't mean he wouldn't relish a different challenge.'

She made one last objection. 'I do not think he will wish to leave Annie.'

'I do not think he will have any fears on her account, for she is well looked after. You have seen to that.'

He placed his hand on her arm. 'Let me take him once at least and see how he does. If he is not happy, I will bring him home again, I promise.'

And so it had been arranged, and though Elizabeth would have preferred it to be different, it was clear that Dand relished the prospect, standing taller and with an added sparkle in his eyes – watching him, she thought again of the Munros. Strange how things worked out. Robbie's flight to France, which had seemed like a disaster to Kate Munro at the time, had ended up happily for all concerned. Perhaps her worries for Dand were equally misplaced.

It was the end of the last week in March when Alexander blew in again on a warm east wind, full of apologies that he hadn't returned sooner to see how they all fared. He smiled at Catherine, tousled Sybie's hair and lifted Hughie to dandle him on his knee. 'He has a stare on him would best an obelisk. I wonder what he's thinking?'

Elizabeth laughed. 'He can certainly outstare Mary, and that's saying something. I don't think she's overly pleased, though that aside, she likes him well enough.'

'She hasn't yet told you to send him back then?'

'No. Nor Annie either.'

'Of course, the little sprite.' He moved across to lean over the trug. 'Hugh seems quite taken with her.'

'We all are. Whether it's that she had such a difficult start, or that compared to Hughie she is tiny, I don't know, but if anyone were to come and claim her now, I think we'd all be bereft.'

Alexander peeled back the blanket and looked down at her. 'Unlikely, surely?' He rubbed her cheek with his finger. 'Sonsy though she undoubtedly is.'

'Isn't she? And to be truthful, it isn't her I fear for.' Her smile faded. 'If her father, who, as far as we can tell, is the only person with a claim, were to come for anyone, it would be for Dand, for he is useful. She is not.'

'Who's not useful?' Hugh had stopped in the doorway to kick his boots against the wall, clods of dry earth dropping onto the flags.

Alexander raised his eyebrows at Elizabeth. 'Hugh, taking account of your floors?'

'If he'd stop to clear his boots at the scraper outside it would be more helpful, but better something than nothing I suppose.'

'Better a wife who answered my questions,' Hugh said, coming to Elizabeth and dropping a kiss on her head.

'I was but asking how Annie fares. Aren't you going to ask me of the latest from court?'

'I suppose. If there is anything of real moment. The old Queen's death, for example. Or Glencairn cut down to size.'

'No such luck. But this *will* interest you. And you, Elizabeth. Not only has James outlawed the bearing of arms on the street, but it is rumoured that the old laws against single combat without express permission from the crown are to be ratified again in Parliament and that this time they will be strictly enforced.'

Elizabeth's tone was tart. 'Not before time.'

'Indeed. It has become endemic, the first resort when there is the slightest of affronts, and James is sick of it.'

Hugh shrugged. 'Severe penalties or not, it will only push it out of town.'

'I think not, Hugh. The new edict is not just for Edinburgh, but for the whole country. You'd best behave yourself in Irvine or you might find yourself up before the bailie.'

Hugh stretched his legs out and leaned back, his hands linked behind his head. 'Have you seen the current bailie of Irvine? Anyone who needs to worry about him is either too old or too infirm for duelling.'

Elizabeth had a mental picture of the bailie, bandy-legged and as broad as he was long, with a head as shiny as a new-born, the over-sized cap he aye wore in a vain attempt to conceal his lack slipping sideways over one ear. She struggled not to laugh. 'Troublesome as you sometimes are, Hugh, I'd rather keep you than lose you. And incompetent bailie or not, it's a risk I'd prefer you not to take.'

Alexander had barely time to change his clothes before a messenger arrived from Edinburgh. He scanned the letter and, with a moue of apology for Elizabeth, tossed it onto the table. There was a genuine note of regret in his voice. 'I had thought to stay for a week or two, but my presence is required at Holyrood by the first of the month. Hugh also.'

'What for?'

'A smart move by James. He wishes to have a full attendance of his nobles and others who might be minded to disobey, to be present at the forthcoming sitting of Parliament. The edict against duelling will be ratified, and thus, no one will be without excuse.'

'Sorry as I will be to see you go, I am happy for the reason. I am not naïve enough to think it the end of all such senseless fights, but if it saves the life of even one person, it will be worth it.'

Hugh accepted the summons without protest. 'At least there will be something of interest for Dand's first jaunt to Edinburgh. No doubt James will turn it into a spectacle, and the burgh poorer as a result.'

They saw them off from the barmkin gate, Alexander and Hugh relaxed, Dand betraying his excitement by a tremor that shook the reins he held, causing his horse to sidestep on the cobbles. Hugh leant across, patted the horse's neck.

'Easy, now, easy.' And to Dand, 'He senses your excitement, which is no bad thing, for he will give of his best as a result, but if you can calm a little it will be helpful, for I want us to reach Edinburgh without mishap.'

Elizabeth had Hughie in her arms, Catherine holding Annie, Mary clutching Sybie's hand. Hugh bent down and touched Hughie's head, then Elizabeth's cheek.

'We will be back before you know.'

Dand echoed Hugh, smiling at Catherine and clicking his teeth for Annie, receiving a gurgle in return. And then they were gone, picking their way down the slope. Mary let go of Sybie and climbed onto the barmkin wall, hopping up and down, waving a napkin, which flapped like a miniature flag in the breeze.

Elizabeth called up, 'Come down before you fall.'

'When I can't see them any more,' Mary said.

'Be careful then.' They were heading east and Elizabeth shaded her eyes against the early morning sun, wanting to catch the last glimpse of them before they became so small as to be indistinguishable. The Parliament was two days hence; she did a quick calculation: another day perhaps to pass himself, and another for the journey home – they, or at least Hugh and Dand, could be back in little more than a week.

Chapter 13

The chamber was nearly full when Hugh and Dand entered with Alexander, and it was sufficiently warm to be uncomfortable, despite the chill in the air outside. They were directed to stand by the rear wall, from where they had a clear view of the whole company. Hugh whistled. The nobles were arranged in groups, but not of their own choosing. He turned, his voice too low to be heard by anyone other than Alexander. 'Caprice? Or a desire to reinforce the point?'

'Both, likely. And typical of James. It is to be hoped the edict will not be honoured more in the breach than the observance. Or that such close proximity does not engender trouble rather than the reverse. For there are many here who look none too comfortable in the company they are being forced to keep.' Alexander nodded towards the far side of the dais, where Bargeny had been placed next to Cassilis, Lindsay to Lord Glammis and Scott of Buccleugh to a Ker. On their own side, near to the front, The Earl of Montrose was with Sandilands, and beside them, Moray and Huntly.

Eglinton and Glencairn were close to the seat set aside for James and stood conversing with every appearance of civility. 'If we can all manage that,' Alexander said, 'perhaps the edict may stand, for a day at least.'

Hugh grinned. 'With luck it may be enough for James to place them together without concerning himself with lesser mortals.'

'Such as yourself and the Master of Glencairn? Don't be too sure.'

Dand, in new clothes bought for the occasion, was juking from side to side, trying to see past those in front of them, his eyes alight. He tugged at Hugh's arm, whispered, 'There's your brother. He's seen us.'

Hugh followed his pointing finger. It was John Montgomerie, right enough, and he raised his bonnet in acknowledgement, mouthed, 'I'll see you later.'

John Cunninghame was next to him, and he too looked across and, after a swift glance towards Glencairn, nodded also.

'See,' Alexander said. 'We are being placed with counterparts of equivalent standing.'

'Is there anyone James hasn't called?' Hugh was mentally ticking off all those of the nobles that he knew and a sizeable number that he recognised only by their colours.

'It's a goodly company, that's for sure. It's a rare spectacle to see the Parliament so well attended, and a sign of the importance James places on the outlawing of illegal duelling. There will be no one without excuse.'

There was a stir by the door, as William appeared with several others in the Cunninghame livery and with him Hamilton and Fullerton. Amidst the general hubbub they couldn't hear what was being said, but it was clear from the set of his shoulders and the glower on his face that William was not best pleased they were being split up.

Alexander put his mouth against Hugh's ear. 'Prepare to be civil. He's been directed this way. Inconvenient as your placing may be, no doubt you can take some comfort from being matched with an earl's heir.'

'As you would in my position, I'm sure.' Hugh oozed sarcasm, barely managing to wipe his face of all expression before William reached him.

'Braidstane.' His bow was the least that could be deemed civil, as if he dared Hugh to take offence.

'Cunninghame.' Hugh dipped his head in return.

Alexander leant forward, a fraction more warmth in his voice. 'You have come from Kilmaurs?' It was not intended to be offensive, but nevertheless William flushed, his hand going to where his missing scabbard should have hung.

'I have been in Edinburgh this last month or more. It is a pleasure to be back at court.'

'No doubt,' Hugh raised his voice just enough to cause some of those closest to him to turn round, 'when you have been away for so long.'

William flushed again. Alexander, with a frown for Hugh, cutting in with, 'This is a good day and we should all be glad of it.' He gestured towards Eglinton and Glencairn. 'As our respective heads clearly are.' He held out his hand to William. 'Let us shake to happier times.' It was one of those moments in any company when there comes a pause in conversation, so that Alexander's invitation rang out in the surrounding silence. Glencairn turned and fixed William with a look that left him no option but to take the proffered hand.

There was a ripple as the crowd parted, opening a

path for the King. Hugh, inwardly irritated by Alexander's conciliatory efforts, smiled and bowed with the rest, his irritation mitigated as he noted James' hat, the pearls catching the light from the candles in the sconce behind him. It was the one William had been forced to gift to him on the day when the truce between the families had been signed and was clearly still a favourite. He glanced sideways and saw William stiffen – clearly he still resented the gift.

The King ignored the provided seat and remained standing, surveying those around him with obvious pleasure, in which Hugh suspected a tinge of malice. 'We are pleased…' he began, and Hugh rested his hand on Dand's shoulder and bent down to whisper.

'We do not always have to suffer such long speeches. But it is a privilege of a king to bore his subjects.'

Alexander frowned at Hugh again. He bent in his turn to Dand. 'Long speech or not, this is a serious matter and we should not mock it. We shall all rest easier in our beds if order can be kept.'

The speech wore on and Hugh was amused to see that there were many among the throng who attempted to conceal their yawns behind their hands and struggled to remain focused on the King. He found himself drifting, and was brought back to attention by a sharp jab of Alexander's elbow in his side. The speech was building to a crescendo, and at the last, when he called for ratification, the response was deafening.

'He aye likes the sound of his own voice,' Hugh said afterwards, in the safety of their lodgings, 'and could have got agreement to anything by the time he came to an end, even a quadrupling of taxes. Just to ensure that the ordeal would be over.'

'It wasn't the only ordeal I was glad to see the finish of.' Alexander flung himself into a chair. 'Being placed next to William was trial enough, without you baiting him.'

'I wasn't the one who started it. You were the one asked him if he'd come from Kilmaurs.'

'That was *not* intended to offend. Your comments, however, were.'

'I can't stand to see his swagger and hear him crow about his reinstatement to grace.'

'Well you'd better learn to. Now that he is back I imagine he won't pass up any opportunity to remain. Nor to keep himself in James' line of sight.'

'I know. I know. If…' Hugh lifted his shoulders, dropped them again, 'when we meet, I shall be civility itself.'

And so he was. If a lack of deliberate goading classed as civility. He crossed paths with William on several occasions over the next few days and each time passed on with no more on either side than a cursory bow and a murmuring of names.

On the third morning, Alexander returned from an audience with the King and bounded into their lodgings beaming. He tossed his bonnet on the table. 'Well done,

Hugh. You've made it through without incident. You've permission to return to Braidstane. Elizabeth will no doubt be relieved to see you home safe and sound.' His smile, if that were possible, widened. 'Though I can't see the attraction myself.' He dodged the punch that Hugh aimed at his shoulder. 'Remember, before you try to injure me, that you've me to thank for your release. I convinced James that any word from George in London would be sent to Braidstane and that if you were on hand to receive it yourself, it would reach his ears more speedily. And undertook for your immediate return thereafter with any news. He is becoming increasingly impatient.'

'As are we all.' Hugh winked at Dand. 'It will be a good day for us when the old Queen dies, as you'll see. We none of us expected her to be such a tough old bird.'

'No more we did.' John Montgomerie was standing in the doorway, haloed in the sunlight spilling in behind him. 'And when James goes to London, I intend to stay here. If London physicians can keep Elizabeth standing well past her prime, James will have no need of me there.'

'Perhaps they have pumped preserving fluid into her veins to replace her blood. That might explain the whiteness of her face.'

John snorted. 'Arsenic paste, more like, and it's a wonder the cosmetics haven't killed her, though they might yet.'

'And not before time.'

Alexander placed his hand on Dand's shoulder. 'Take Hugh home, lad, we'll all lie safer in our beds knowing he's well out of harm's way.'

They were approaching the West Port when they spied
William and two of his men coming from the opposite
direction, and it was clear they were likely to meet within
the gateway. Hugh pulled his horse to one side of the
road.

'Best we go in single file. I wouldn't wager on their
horsemanship, and an accident is the last thing we want.'

William, it seemed, shared his thought, urging his own
horse forward and waving his men back. As they passed
under the archway, he bowed to Hugh, his greeting
pleasant enough as far as the words went, his intention,
betrayed by the upward curl of his mouth, rather different.
'Heading home, Braidstane? To your good lady and your
son and heir. What a pity. I had thought we might have
had more time to become reacquainted. '

Hugh ignored the implied mockery, bowed in his turn.

He was through the gate, Dand just entering the
archway, as William's men crowded in, two abreast. The
lad pulled sharply on the reins, meaning to hold back to
let them past, but it had the opposite effect, his horse
starting sideways and rearing, his front hoof catching one
of William's men a glancing blow on the leg. That should
have been the sum of it, had William's man not jerked
back, pulling on his reins in turn, his horse also rearing,
the flailing hooves locking like competing stags in the rut.
Hugh, hearing the commotion, turned round in time to
see the Cunninghame horse taking a blow on the cannon

407

bone, the front legs buckling, spilling the rider onto the ground. He curled into a ball and rolled towards the wall, covering his head with his arms, while above him his horse struggled back to its feet and bolted.

The second man drew his sword and slashed at Dand as he also fought to regain control of his horse. The strike sliced through his cloak and doublet and as he toppled sideways and went down Hugh saw him clutch at his arm above the elbow, blood oozing through his splayed fingers. Hugh flung himself from the saddle and grasping the reins of Dand's horse pulled the head down and led it out to the grass verge beyond the gate, where his own horse munched contentedly. One hand still on the reins in case it should take off, he patted its neck, murmuring into its ear until it stood still, sides heaving. And when it bent its head and began to chew, he turned back, expecting to see Dand emerging from the gateway behind him.

The lad was lying crumpled against the wall, his eyes shut, his hand limp at his side, blood still pumping from his arm. Hugh knelt by his side and, thrusting aside the cloak, took his dirk and cut the doublet from shoulder to wrist; then, ripping out the shirtsleeve, he formed it into a wad and pressed hard on the wound, binding it up with a strip of cloth torn from the shirt tail. Behind him, he heard a muttered order and half turned, in time to see one of William's men urging his horse in pursuit of the runaway, while William himself pulled the other man up behind him and trotted away without looking back, as if nothing of moment had occurred.

John was emerging from the lodging as Hugh reappeared, Dand in his arms, a boy coming along behind leading the horses.

'What in heaven's name…?'

'William.' Hugh ground out the name. 'He has a sword cut above the elbow … deep, I think. I tried to stop the bleeding but haven't been entirely successful.'

'Lay him out on the table. And send for vinegar. I will need you to hold him down. I will do what I can to minimise the pain, but it is going to hurt.' John worked swiftly, carefully peeling away Hugh's makeshift bandage. He tied a string around Dand's upper arm to staunch the flow of blood, then trickled a distillation of poppy seeds onto a wad of gauze. He leant over Dand. 'I'm going to cover your face with this. Don't fight it, please, for with luck it will make you dozy. If, in five or ten minutes, it does not, I will give you something to bite on.'

Hugh's face was surprisingly white.

John glanced at him. 'I trust you won't faint on me, Hugh. You are no stranger to wounds such as these.'

'In war, no. But when it is your own…'

'It's different, I know. But you must try to think of it as a task that must be done, and not of the person.' Dand's eyelids began to flicker, his breathing to deepen. John lifted a flagon of wine, nodded to Hugh. 'Keep a firm hold. Asleep or not, his body may react.' He poured the wine into the wound, staunched it with gauze, and taking tweezers he gently probed the raw flesh. He paused in his examination, stiffened. 'There is a tendon almost severed.'

Hugh was at his shoulder, looking down. 'Can you do anything?'

John shrugged. 'I can try stitching it, but there are dangers in leaving thread inside him. I have seen cases where the solution has ended up worse than the problem. There may be enough of a link to do, but I've no way of telling.' He was staring at the arm, his lip caught between his teeth. 'I think I must try.'

He was snipping the end of the thread he had used to stitch the tendon as a girl entered with a basin of steaming water and a knob of soap. He straightened. 'Wash your hands, Hugh, then,' he indicated a flagon on the table, 'rinse them with the vinegar. I cannot hold the wound together and stitch the skin at the same time, and the risk of infection is great enough as it is, without us adding to it.'

He worked swiftly, and when he stood back he looked at the row of knotted stitches puncturing the wound and said, 'Would that I had been trained as a seamstress, but that's the best I can do.'

'Or a butcher.' Hugh attempted a laugh. 'They make a neat job of trussing a stuffed chicken.'

He wrinkled his nose as John smeared ointment over the wound. 'What's in that?'

'Oil of roses, egg yolk, turpentine. Another of Paré's inventions, developed when he was serving as an army physician. And found to be much more effective than cauterising wounds – the death rate of his patients much

410

diminished.' He covered and bound the wound, released the tourniquet and lifted the gauze from Dand's face. The lad was beginning to stir. John looked at the gauze, as if considering whether to sedate him again, decided in favour. 'Let's get him to bed. But we're going to need to tie him down, for if we cannot keep him still there is a risk the wound will reopen. He has lost enough blood already, any more and…' he lifted his shoulders, 'I couldn't guarantee the outcome.'

Afterwards, as John poured a mug of ale for them both, Hugh said, 'What will I tell Elizabeth? She didn't want me to bring him here.'

'What happened, Hugh?'

'I didn't see it all. We reached the West Port and met William with two of his men. I told Dand to hang back, so that we were in single file, and William did likewise. I was through when I heard the commotion behind me. I don't know what the start of it was, but I saw the end, an attack on Dand by one of William's men.' He gestured towards the bed. 'The result as you see. And do you know the worst?' His voice rose, suppressed anger eating at him. 'William called his men and rode on, without any thought to Dand lying bleeding in the gateway behind them. I cannot forgive him that.'

'If you didn't see the whole, perhaps…'

'Dand? Is he likely to provoke anyone? And on our way home to his sister! Whatever it was, it wasn't his blame.' He put out his hand and smoothed Dand's sweat-soaked hair away from his forehead. 'He will be all right?'

'He's young, and having spent three months in your household is healthy and strong. All that is in his favour.

411

But the wound is deep and the blade carried some of the sleeve in with it, though I think I was able to remove all traces. I certainly hope so.' He lifted the lad's hand, curled and uncurled the fingers. 'The problem of the tendon is another issue altogether. I am in uncharted territory...' He moved through to the main chamber. 'I have done what I can. The rest is down to good care and providence.'

'And if the tendon doesn't hold?'

John hesitated. 'The usefulness of the arm will be much reduced. If indeed it is useful at all. But that we won't know for some time. The sedative I've given him should let him sleep till tomorrow perhaps. When he wakes, if he is coherent, that will be a good sign.'

'You will stay with him?'

'Of course.' John attempted a smile. 'You don't think I would leave him in your hands?'

'Good.' Hugh strapped on his sword and flung his cloak across his shoulders.

'Where are you going?'

'Where do you think?'

'Hugh, you don't know what happened. At least wait until Dand can give his side of the story.'

'I don't need to *know*. One of William's men was down, thrown from his horse, but he dusted himself down and rode off behind William. If he has a bruise or two for his pains, that will be the height of it. While Dand...' He slid his dirk into his boot, repeated, 'I don't need to *know*.'

The door to William's lodging was standing half-open, the sound of voices and muffled laughter rolling down towards Hugh. He took the stairs two at a time and thrust back the inner chamber door, the handle banging against the wall. William's two men were lounging in chairs by the fireside, their boots discarded in the corner, their jerkins undone. One was lying, his head back, his mouth open, snoring. The other looked around and waved a hand at Hugh.

'Whad'ye wan wi us?' His words were slurred, the tone insolent.

Hugh grasped his shoulder, hauled him upright. 'Satisfaction.'

'For wha?'

'For the boy you left bleeding at the West Port.'

'Wha boy?'

'My boy.'

The man shook Hugh off, narrowing his eyes as if to attempt to focus them. 'Yer boy? The word a heard is ye dinna hae a boy, or no yer ane anyroads.' He tapped the side of his nose. 'If ye tak ma meanin.'

Hugh was ready to take his meaning and thrust it down his throat, or grind the man's face into the spilt ale on the table top, or take his tongue and twist it till he screamed like a stuck pig, but as he reached for him again, he felt the draught on the back of his neck and a hand on his own shoulder. He spun round, his fist raised, expecting William and found Alexander instead. He was breathing fast as if he'd been running. He grasped Hugh's arm, pulled him towards the door.

'They aren't worth it, Hugh,'

'Let me go!' Hugh lunged sideways, throwing Alexander off-balance, his hold breaking. His dirk was in his hand. 'I have unfinished business here.'

Alexander launched himself at Hugh again, grasping his sword arm and twisting his wrist, the dirk flying across the room and landing in the ashes in the hearth. 'What are you going to do? Kill them in cold blood?'

'An eye for an eye. Or in this case an arm for an arm.'

'And then what? God's truth, Hugh, but you are a fool.' Alexander took a firmer hold. 'Do I have to disable you myself? If there is a charge to answer, take it to the bailie, not into your own hands. If you do this, no one will win, not Dand, not Elizabeth, and most certainly not you.'

'Do you think I care about me?'

'No. But you should care about your family, about your son.'

There was a moment of silence before Hugh wrested free once more, and going to the hearth he rooted for the dirk. He thrust it into his belt and turning to the table grabbed the man who was awake by his hair, pulling his head back. 'Tell your master there is an innocent lad who may lose his arm as a result of this day's work, and if he does, I *will* have satisfaction.'

Chapter 14

Munro had been home a week when he finally tracked down André Ruiz and brought him back to the Louvre.

Ruiz bent over Kate's hand. 'Lady Munro. You have my apologies that I have not been back sooner. I did not wish to trouble you until I had something to report.'

'And you do now?' Her hand was shaking as she poured him a glass of wine, the spill that dribbled onto the table glinting in the candlelight. At any other time she would have sent immediately for a cloth; as it was she wiped at it with her handkerchief, the resulting stain turning the lace border blood-red. 'Please, sit down.'

He relaxed in the chair, raised his glass as if he came for no better reason than to be sociable. 'Your good health, milady, and yours, Sir Adam.'

She couldn't bear it. 'What news do you have? Is Eugenie...?'

'Eugenie is fine. That is...' He paused. 'She is alive, beyond that, as yet I have no further details.'

'And François and Netta?'

'They likewise.' He hesitated again, and she felt a chill in her stomach, as if a plateful of ice had melted and pooled there.

'Their father?'

'He is condemned. And with others will be taken to

415

the cathedral square for a public confession and then to the Place de Grève.'

'Executed?' She felt the weight of it as a pain in her chest, and, 'It isn't a capital offence surely?'

'The word is the authorities wish to make an example, that others might not be tempted to breach the rules in future.'

'They have not convicted the children?'

'Not as yet.' Ruiz set down his glass and leant forward, as if now, the social niceties concluded, they could come to business. 'But we should get them out and soon.'

'When?'

'Two days' time. Early. All attention will be on the executions, and there is safety in crowds. Many will come for the spectacle, for who wouldn't want to witness the death of a heretic?' There was no trace of irony in his voice, no distaste.

As if he wished to excuse Ruiz, Munro said, 'There is no room for emotion in what we seek to do, Kate. If we are to succeed we must treat it as a military exercise.'

'What can I do?'

Munro covered her hand with his. 'See that the girls are occupied here. And ensure that someone is with them.' He turned her hand over and traced the line of the scar at the base of her thumb.

'You want me to go to the execution?' It came out as a whisper.

'Yes.'

'Adam, I...'

He turned her to face him and she saw her own pain reflected in his eyes.

416

'I know this will be difficult and I wouldn't ask it of you if I didn't think it necessary. When the escape is discovered, suspicion may be directed at us. There were many among the Gardes who knew of Robbie's attachment.'

The memory of Angus' treachery was like sour wine in her mouth. 'But surely no one else...'

'They have wives, mistresses, creditors. Any one of which might be prepared to share such information if the inducement is right.'

His grip on her hands was firm, his voice likewise. 'It will behove us all to be distanced from suspicion, and be safer for the Lavalles also.'

She took a deep breath. 'If you think it will help, I will go. But...'

Again he pre-empted her. 'I will send one of the Gardes to accompany you.' There was an implied apology in both his tone and the extra pressure on her fingers, as he added, 'One whose sympathies lie with the authorities and not the victims.'

Oblivious of Ruiz, she collapsed against him, burying her head in his chest.

'You want me to...'

He tightened his arms around her, gave her time.

She shut her mind against the horror of it, forced herself to think of Eugenie, said, 'I shall scream with the rest.'

Munro released her and she subsided onto the chair. He refilled her glass. 'I will tell you when it is done.'

'Will you bring them here?'

'We cannot risk implicating the King, even by

417

association.'

'Where will they go, then?'

'Better you don't know. Better no one knows, other than André here.'

Ruiz met her gaze, and for the first time she noticed his eyes, the untroubled blue of a summer sky. As if he knew what she was thinking, he said, 'There is Viking blood somewhere in my ancestry, or so I've been told. Something I'm rather proud of, as it happens.'

A hawk, not a dove, she thought – and perhaps what is needed.

Ruiz had been right. Despite the early hour, the streets were crowded with people, all hurrying, it seemed, in the one direction: towards the Place de Grève. There was an air of suppressed excitement, as if it was a feast day and it was to a fair they headed. As indeed it might as well be, Kate thought, every hawker and peddler in Paris likely preparing to take advantage of the throng to sell their wares. She was in a carriage with Maggie, who had insisted on coming, despite all Kate's pleas to the contrary, the Garde that Munro had assigned to her riding alongside. They were at the tail of a short cavalcade processing along the Quai de Louvre, the King and his phalanx of Gardes, Munro included, at the front, his foremost courtiers following close, and behind them sundry other members of the court, showing their approval of the coming spectacle and thus their loyalty to the King and to the Parlement of Paris.

'Must we be so public?' she had asked, when Munro had come from the King with details of the arrangements.

'I think you must. As must the King, and believe me, it does not lie lightly on him either.'

She had believed him, but it hadn't made it any easier, nor had his instruction that she dress as if for a celebration, not a wake. They were approaching the new Pont Neuf, the construction work clearly abandoned for the day to allow the workers to attend the executions, and as the quay narrowed, Kate caught glimpses of Munro keeping pace with the King's carriage.

'If you lose sight of me during the proceedings,' he had said, 'do not concern yourself. I will be somewhere about.'

A coded message, from which she gathered that he had some part to play in the rescue, and though she feared for his safety, his presence increased her confidence in a satisfactory outcome. The cavalcade reached the point at which the quay dwindled to a narrow path. She saw the King's carriage swing to the left, leaving the riverside, and when their carriage too turned into the wider thoroughfare, she looked ahead, to find that Munro had disappeared – dear God, she prayed, let them be successful. And keep them all safe.

The carriages drew to a halt as they reached the Place de Grève, lining up on the perimeter of the crowd, sideways on to the scaffold, so that their view was clear. There was a chorus of jeering and catcalls as the prisoners were marched up the short flight of steps to the raised platform, some of those nearest spitting on them as they passed. There were three men, including M Lavalle, and one woman. Their clothes were torn, their hair unkempt, and their skin grey and slack. Trails of spittle glistened on their cheeks, but despite it all they stood upright, facing the hostile crowd, their dignity intact. Kate, knowing from her own experience the effort it cost, encouraged Maggie. 'We dare not show our partiality openly, but only God sees our hearts. Let us pray that they will not falter, that their courage will not fail.'

M Lavalle stepped forward first and began to address the crowd. There was a brief moment of silence before his '…Good people, know this. Our only crime is to worship…' was drowned out by renewed howls and whistles. Someone threw an egg and it broke against his forehead, bits of shell snagging in his hair, the yolk trickling into his eye and merging with the spittle on his cheeks. The executioner grasped his arms and pulled him back towards the scaffold, to where a priest stood. The priest raised his hand, the crowd falling silent as he cried out, 'Enough. We know your crimes. You do not only defy God, you defy the King. To God your soul is forfeit, to the King your body.' He dropped his hand and there was a third, more prolonged roar as the trapdoor beneath M Lavalle fell away, his body jerking and twisting as the rope around his neck tightened and held.

There was a stir at the front of the crowd, an anguished cry of 'Papa' as a small figure hurled himself up the steps and grabbed the jerking body, trying to force the legs upwards.

'François,' Maggie said, sagging against Kate, who put

420

her hand under Maggie's elbow to hold her upright, her own body rigid.

There was a surge towards the steps at the foot of the scaffold platform as the executioner caught hold of François and lifted him, kicking and sobbing, and displayed him to the crowd.

A voice rang out. 'Heretic child! Hang him too', the cry taken up and echoed all around. Kate pressed her fist into the hollow beneath her breast, powerless to act – was this how it was going to end?

Out of the corner of her eye she saw a snaking movement in the crowd, as if someone too small to be seen above the heads was attempting to squeeze through. A gap opened briefly and they caught a glimpse of a girl in ragged clothes and bare feet elbowing her way forward,– Netta. Kate closed her eyes, and then, aware of Adam's instructions, leaned from the carriage, as if she didn't wish to miss anything of the spectacle.

Ruiz, barely recognisable in the garb of a blacksmith, thrust past Netta and leapt up the steps. He faced up to the executioner, reaching out for François. Soldiers were closing in towards the scaffold, the roar of the crowd reduced to murmurs, Ruiz shaking his head, gesticulating, occasional words audible. 'My sister … idiot child … night terrors … imaginings…' The executioner hesitated, and Kate saw him look towards the King's carriage. The door was open, Henri on the top step, his hand outstretched. Those nearest to him sank to their knees, the action spreading like a ripple across the Place de Grève. Ruiz was looking directly at Henri, his words clearly audible above the reduced murmurings of the crowd as he repeated,

'He is but an idiot child.'

Please God, Kate thought, let him recognise Ruiz.

The King spoke with the bored quality of someone who wished business completed that they might return home to a good meal.

'I am come to see heretics hanged, not a simpleton. Release the child and get on with the job.'

The executioner thrust François at Ruiz, and turning his head he spat as if to indicate contempt, or perhaps as an attempt to ward off the evil eye. François was wriggling, Ruiz pulling him tight against his chest, bending his head over him. The boy slumped, his protests silenced, and Ruiz turned to push his way back towards the edge of the crowd, Netta following. For a moment they were the focus of attention, before a renewed roar heralded the second hanging as the woman was dragged forward and the noose placed around her neck.

'It was a close-run thing.' Munro was standing in their salon, running his hand through his hair, the lines in his forehead emphasised by the light from the candle sconce above his head.

'Surely it wasn't part of the plan they should see their father hanged?'

'Of course not. The intention was to melt away so soon as we crossed the bridge onto the mainland, but though we had dinned into them to follow our instructions exactly, we couldn't afford to have it look as if they were our prisoners, so we had to trust them to stay close. When François gave us the slip we tried to convince Eugenie and Netta to stick to the original plan, and promised we would find him, but,' Munro shrugged, 'Netta ran off too and we had two children to chase, not just one.' A glimmer of a smile flitted across his face. 'She has courage and spirit, I'll give her that. And without her instinct, Ruiz might not have reached him in time.'

Maggie, interested to hear the whole tale now that the immediate crisis was past, said, 'What happened at the prison?'

'That was the easy part. Ruiz had done his groundwork well and, money spent, we slipped into the Palais without opposition and were able to spring them as easily as releasing hares from a trap. Once out, it was simple enough to mingle in the crowd. The population of the Île de la Cité was, like all Paris, focused on getting to the Place de Grève, and no one gave us a second look. Not until…'

Kate said, 'We know the next bit, but what now?'

'For the moment they are safely stowed, and must remain in hiding until the dust settles.' And as if in answer to her unspoken question, 'Not long. A day or two, a week perhaps, and we can think of moving them.'

'Who will take them to Cayeux?'

'That, I do not as yet know. But we have time in hand and they will need to be tidied up a little in any case before they go.'

'Can I see them?'

'Best not. Ruiz has reason for visiting the Maison

d'Ourcamps, but if you or I were to venture, it would likely draw attention we'd rather not have.'

'Is there anything I can do?'

'Clothing for them all and soap and a comb and scissors ... Oh, and if you could wheedle a pastry or two they wouldn't go amiss. I believe the food at the Palais wasn't exactly gourmet.'

Chapter 15

It had been just over two weeks since the Lavalles' escape. The King visited the Munros' apartment, on the pretext of consulting Kate on an issue regarding Catherine, and waved away the thanks she offered on François' behalf.

'Without your intervention...'

'He is a child whose only sin is to love his father. Hardly a crime deserving of death.' He accepted a glass of wine and indicated for her to sit. 'I am not an ogre to relish the death of a child. Even if I hadn't suspected who he was from the start. Though I couldn't be entirely sure until Ruiz turned, for he made a surprisingly good French peasant.'

She spoke with conviction. 'God answers prayer. Or at least He did mine, for I feared you wouldn't recognise Ruiz.'

'Indeed. But it is not the Huguenot family I have come to discuss with you. It is better I know nothing of them. Your son's future, however, is my concern.'

'He must leave the Gardes?'

'I am afraid he must, but not for the reason you think.'

She looked down at her hands, unsure of what to say, afraid of what might be to come.

'I have had word from Rosny. I expect his return in the next day or two, your son with him. Which makes the decision of what to do with him an urgent matter.'

'I thought the time away would be enough…'

'Had it been only the matter of the duel, it might have done, but the escape of the Lavalle children has not gone unnoticed, nor has your son's connection to the family. There have been rumblings of favouritism, of your husband trading on his position, and sending Robbie with Rosny has, I fear, only served to convince the malcontents. Something must be done, or your husband's standing may suffer, and I have too great a need for him to let that happen.'

'Robbie was but a child when Adam first came to France, but all he ever dreamed of was joining the Scots Gardes. I do not know what else…'

'He has had a taste of diplomacy in Florence. We may trust it was to his liking, for I intend to send him on another mission.' Henri set down his glass and, putting his hand under Kate's chin, lifted her head, forcing her to meet his eyes. 'It will be necessary, however, to play out a little charade first. He will be publicly censured for his connection to a Huguenot rebel, and condemned to be sent home. Your husband must be the one to mete out the punishment.'

Kate felt the colour drain from her face.

'The reality, of course, will be rather different. I have a wish for eyes and ears at the Scottish court that will not be viewed with suspicion. And who better than a native Scot and from a family that your king favours.'

'A spy?' It came out as a croak.

'An observer. And one who may be a conduit for private messages between myself and James. There have been times in the past when the official channels proved less than satisfactory. An alternative will be welcome.' He paused. 'And if he should wish to travel to Cayeux en route to see how your farm fares, that will be permissible.'

Kate was standing at the door, staring along the corridor, when Munro appeared. 'When do you think the Lavalles will be able to leave Paris?' she asked.

'As far as practicalities go, I think they could be moved anytime. Indeed, the sooner the better, for with every day that passes the likelihood of word getting out that they are hiding in the Maison d'Ourcamps increases. It would not be to anyone's advantage should they be discovered. And I suspect the patience of the boatmen wears thin. Netta seems to be recovering, in spirit as well as body, but...'

'What?'

'I am less certain of Eugenie and François. They get up, and go to sleep, eat when food is put in front of them, but aside from that there is no life in them. It's a long road to Cayeux, and as to who is best to take them there...'

'Robbie,' Kate said.

'Robbie? He's not here. And even if he was...'

'He will be, in a day or two. The King has had word.'

'But he cannot be released from normal duties again so soon. It would smack of favouritism to give him leave.'

It would have been amusing, if it hadn't been so serious. 'On the contrary,' she said, 'it will serve to counter the charge of favouritism.'

'You're not making any sense.'

'The King was here. You just missed him. Robbie is to be dismissed from the Gardes. And you are to do it.'

Munro sat down.

'You will send him home to Scotland, apparently in disgrace.'

'Apparently?'

'He wishes to have an extra pair of eyes at James' court. But he has said he may visit Cayeux on the way.' Her voice broke. 'We will not see him again for months, maybe years.'

There was a draught on her neck and she spun round. 'Robbie! You're back. I didn't expect you so soon. The King said…'

'Rosny received a message from Henri just over a week ago, and whatever it was it caused him to push on as fast as possible, so here we are.'

After the execution, she thought, with reluctant admiration. He planned this. 'How long have you been listening?' she asked.

'Long enough to know that the Lavalles are out of prison, and that is the best of news, but,' his face clouded, 'where are they now?'

Kate was rubbing her hand up and down Robbie's arm, as if she wasn't quite sure he was really there and needed the touch to confirm it. 'They are still in Paris but are to be taken to Cayeux as soon as possible. Madame Picarde will be delighted to welcome them.'

'When were they freed?'

'A week ago, but they're not free exactly. They're in hiding until they are all fit to travel.'

'Eugenie?' There was anguish in Robbie's voice.

Munro poured him a drink and handed it over. 'They are fine, but taking it hard. Especially François. He saw his father hanged.'

'Hanged?' Robbie sank onto a seat. 'For being a Huguenot?'

'He knew the rules, Robbie. You can be as Huguenot as you like outside of Paris, but not within the bounds of the city.'

Robbie's voice cracked. 'If it hadn't been for me, for Angus…'

'It does no good to dwell on that, Robbie. Monsieur Lavalle took risks daily. If it hadn't been Angus it might have been someone else who exposed him. And once he was taken, there were others queuing up to save their own skins and more than willing to testify to the clandestine services in his workshop and to the burials. Fear of a noose is a great tongue-loosener. But a hanging is something no child should see, and certainly not when it is their father.'

Kate struggled to keep her voice even, devoid of emotion. 'It is all arranged. You will take them to Cayeux and leave them with Madame Picarde.'

'And then?'

'Go to Scotland.'

'On whose orders?'

'The King's.'

'But why?'

'Because it's impossible for you to remain here, and ... difficult for your father.'

She took a deep breath. 'Henri has a task he wishes you to perform. But first you must be dismissed from the Gardes.'

'Because of Angus?'

Munro was at the window, staring out, his back rigid.

'That ... and other reasons best not talked of. Suffice it, we must all be grateful for Henri's forbearance and do as he commands.'

Chapter 16

The Montgomeries were still in Edinburgh. Hugh, who normally hated to remain indoors, had spent the best part of a week pacing up and down, wearing a track in the rushes that covered the floor of their main chamber, raising dust with every tread. He hovered in the bedchamber every time John cleansed the wound and replaced the dressings, craning over Dand, his shoulders hunched.

John had tried to convince him to return to Braidstane. 'Go home, Hugh. You are no use here, pacing about like a caged lion. The arm will be no better or no worse for your presence. And I'd prefer not to have you hanging over me, watching my every move and getting in the way. Besides that you unsettle the boy with your tramping. It is quiet he needs.'

Alexander had added his weight to the argument, focusing on the practicalities. 'With you here, who will look to the stock? You're aye complaining there aren't enough hours in the day, or hands to the pump at calving time.'

'How can I go to Elizabeth with the outcome for Dand's arm still uncertain? She pleaded with me not to bring him.'

'What happened was not your blame. Elizabeth will

understand that.'

'I know very well who is to blame, and if it comes to it, I have vowed he will pay. I hope Elizabeth will understand that.'

On the morning of the tenth day Hugh went into the bedchamber and found John dozing in a chair by the bed. It was clear he had been up all night, and looking at Dand, Hugh understood why. He was barely conscious, his face flushed, beads of damp standing out on his forehead and his arm was swollen from elbow to wrist, green pus seeping through the gauze. John stirred, and with a curt nod at Hugh, he bent over Dand before disappearing to return with a basin of tepid water. He soaked the dressings and peeled them back. The skin around the line of the wound was swollen and red, streaks of colour spreading outwards, like the branches of a tree. Hugh watched as John pressed around the wound, the skin unyielding, but though his touch seemed gentle, Dand jerked into consciousness and screamed as if it had been a hot poker touched to his arm.

Stooping, Hugh held his hand over the arm and felt the heat radiating from it. He touched John on the shoulder. 'Is there nothing you can do?'

John shook his head. 'I tried, God knows I tried, Hugh, but the infection has too strong a grip, beyond the body's ability to heal it.' He motioned towards the upper arm. 'If I leave it any longer, if it spreads as far as the shoulder,' he swallowed hard, 'it will be all over for the boy.'

'And if…' Hugh couldn't get the words out.

'If I amputate, there is a chance he will live. Slim perhaps, but still a chance.'

'Do it then.' Hugh's mouth was set in a tight line. 'What do you need of me?'

'Go to the flesher at the foot of the Cowgate. He has a reputation for meat that is disease-free, and with premises as clean as we are likely to find. Beg or borrow … or steal, if you have to, his best cleaver. And if it does not draw blood when you touch it to your finger, insist he sharpens it. You were aye good at persuasion … and force. Use whatever you must to ensure it is as sharp as it can be.'

When Hugh returned, Dand was stretched out on the table top, once again unconscious, makeshift straps formed of rope padded with cloth pulled tight over his belly and legs and chest. There was a tray on a stool at John's side, heaped with wads of gauze and neatly rolled strips of linen, and the pottery jar of ointment covered in muslin. John, with a glance at the cleaver, jerked his head towards the fire where a kettle steamed. 'Put it in the kettle.'

'Will the heat not cause more hurt?'

'It will be agony whatever I do, but boiled, the instruments will at least be clean.' He wrapped a strip of linen around his hand and removed the forceps from the kettle, laying them on the tray, followed, a few minutes later, by the cleaver. Motioning to Alexander to grasp

433

the boy's arm and indicating to Hugh to stand at his shoulder, he applied a tourniquet close to the armpit and picked up the cleaver, testing the weight of it in his hand. He squared his shoulders. 'It must be one clean strike. That is my responsibility. There is an artery that must be compressed quickly, tourniquet or not, or he will bleed out in minutes. That is your task, Hugh.' He indicated the forceps. 'We may be grateful for this latest invention, but do not hesitate or we'll lose him for sure. Ready?'

'Ready.'

John raised his arm. There was a flash of silver followed by a spurt of red. Dand was screaming as Hugh applied the forceps to the artery, while John looped linen thread around it twice and tied it off. He nodded to Hugh to release the forceps and nodded again as the ligature held.

'So far, so good.' John turned his attention to dressing the stump, Hugh passing him ointment and gauze and bandages, all the while his eyes fixed on Dand, who lay corpse-like on the table, his face alabaster-white, the severed arm beside him, blood pooling around it.

'Let's get him to bed.'

The boy stirred as they lifted him, his face twisting in pain.

'Easy, lad. This will only take a minute and then you can rest.'

They propped him up against the bedhead, a folded blanket at his back, a sheet covering him to chest height. Hugh saw him look at the stump, then as quickly away again, a shudder running through him. His eyes were huge, his face pale.

Hugh perched on the edge of the bed and took Dand's remaining hand. It wasn't the first time he'd had to speak to an amputee, but this was personal. He summoned a smile. 'You're a brave lad, none braver. I have seen many soldiers who could not endure as you have done.' He indicated the heavily bandaged stump, the dressing already spotted with pink. 'This is a badge of honour, which you may wear with pride. You left Braidstane a boy, with little experience of the world. You will return with the courage of a man. It was not what any of us would have wished, but when you are fully recovered, we will think on what to do with you.'

It was a poor choice of words.

'I will be useless, at Braidstane or anywhere else.'

John was brisk. 'No you won't. I have seen plenty of men that are twice as useful with one arm than others are with two. It is all a matter of determination, and that I'm sure you will have. But, if you are to manage it, you need rest.' He jerked his head at Hugh. 'Come on. We should leave him in peace. You have done your part, and well. Leave me to do mine.'

Hugh followed him out of the bedchamber. 'How long...?'

'Before we know if he will pull through? If no fever develops within a week, we may begin to hope. In the meantime, I will keep him fully sedated and stay with him.' Then, as if to pre-empt any protest. 'And best if you leave him entirely to me. Visitors, however well intentioned, will only serve to tire him. All that can be done at present is to keep the dressings clean and him quiet. And quiet is not your best quality.'

435

'Will you need help?'

'The girl will bring me all that I need.' John gestured towards the arm on the table. 'The best help you can be is to get rid of that. Take it out to the moorland below the crags and bury it deep enough that the dogs won't get it.'

Hugh picked up the arm and wrapped it in a spare piece of linen, his mouth set in a thin line. 'Don't worry. I'll get rid of it.'

He opened the bedchamber door a fraction and looked at Dand, the image he carried away as he ducked through the doorway and headed down to the street, the slow seeping of blood through the bandages, and a low moaning that seemed to come from far away.

Chapter 17

Hugh hammered on the door of William's lodgings, the girl who answered drawing back, her eyes fixed on the loosely wrapped, bloodstained parcel in his hand. She tried to push the door shut, but he was too quick for her, shoving his foot in the opening.

'There's no one here, sir,' she said, a trace of desperation in her voice.

Hugh pushed the door wider. 'I have no interest in you, girl. Only in the Master of Glencairn. Where is he?'

'I don't know.' And then, as if she decided any answer was likely better than none, she lifted one shoulder. 'He went out, an hour ago maybes, with Maxwell of Newark.'

'For Maxwell's lodgings? Or to the palace?'

She looked down at her feet. 'I've tellt you all I know.'

'They said nothing else?'

Colour stole into her cheeks, a defiant note in her voice. 'Not that I'd repeat.'

'A tavern then. Of the meanest sort.' He was watching her face for a reaction, decided she really didn't know, but considering the hour, his guess was as good as any. He waved the parcel at her. 'When he returns, if he's sufficiently sober to understand, tell him I have something for him…' her eyes were fixed on the bloodstains on the linen and he took pity on her, 'that I intend to deliver

437

myself.'

It took him no more than an hour to find William and Patrick Maxwell in a tavern down a close leading towards the Nor' Loch. It was clear from the narrowing of the bartender's eyes when Hugh asked after them that the man was weighing up which would provide him more gain: admitting to knowledge of them, or hiding it. After a moment he jerked his head towards a corner to the rear of the room and Hugh, tossing a coin onto the counter, thrust his way through. Maxwell and William were lolling at a table made of planks set on barrels, clearly well on the way to being drunk and, to judge by the glitter in the eyes of the doxies who were sprawled over them, to being fleeced also – a pity I have to spare them that, Hugh thought.

William was fondling the younger of the whores, one hand inside the wide neck of her blouse, the other squeezing her buttocks, her giggle clearly forced. A jug of ale and three tankards stood on the table, Maxwell with the fourth in his hand. He looked up, his eyes widening in recognition.

'Braidstane.' His mocking voice was over-loud, attracting the attention of those around them. 'Come to join us? That wife of yours proving unwelcoming? She was aye a tease … if I recall.' He waved at a serving woman passing the table. 'The ladies here are more accommodating.' He gave Hugh an exaggerated wink. 'And not hard to pay, neither.'

Hugh sucked in his breath, refusing, despite the obvious provocation, to be distracted from what he had come to do, promised himself – someday I will make him pay for that. Ignoring Maxwell, he slapped the parcel down on the planking in front of William, sending the mugs rolling off the edge and causing the jug to tip, ale spilling in all directions.

'Wha's this?' William looked up, his eyes red-rimmed.

'Your doing.' Hugh took the edge of the linen and pulled it aside, exposing the arm. The girl on William's lap sprung up, her hand over her mouth, but she was unable to stop herself spewing over William's doublet before fainting at his feet. The second woman was backing away from Maxwell, pulling the lacings of her blouse together, hiding her breasts.

William poked at the arm. 'Wha's it to do wi' me?'

'Everything,' Hugh said. 'Your man, your responsibility. This belongs...' he corrected himself, 'belonged to the boy your man attacked in the West Port. Not that's it's much use to him now.'

'If I remember correctly,' William became combative, 'your boy attacked us first, not the other way round.'

'There was no attack and you know it. A simple accident, no more. And if your man had been enough of a horseman, he could have ridden on without mishap.'

'His horse was spooked, reared up. Small wonder he drew his sword. Who wouldn't? No doubt he feared for his life.'

'Who wouldn't?' Hugh was incredulous. 'Any man with a shred of decency and a morsel of control. Only a coward would pick on a lad of thirteen, leave him lying bleeding and ride off without a backward look. The boy has already lost a limb, but his life may also be forfeit.'

William shrugged, looked across at Maxwell. 'If he

439

couldn't control his horse he should have been left at home. No doubt he will be now. A pity he had to learn the hard way.'

'It was an outrage, and one for which you will pay.' Hugh drew his sword.

The tavern-keeper, a club in his hand, was pushing his way through the group of onlookers who had gathered round to enjoy the spectacle. He swung the club at Hugh's sword arm, but missed, catching him on the ribs instead. 'Not here you don't. I keep an orderly house. Any fighting will be done elsewhere. Or I shall call the watch.' He raised the club again.

Hugh held one hand against his side, his sword still in the other. He pointed it at William's throat. 'Your man. Your responsibility,' he repeated. St Leonard's Hill. Six o'clock tomorrow. Unless you are too feart to defend his honour. No doubt Maxwell here can be your second. Unless he is feart also.' He sheathed his sword, spun on his heel. 'You can keep the arm.'

Dawn was breaking as Hugh climbed St Leonard's Hill, the man he had found to be his second toiling behind him. He had taken a last look at Dand before he slipped out, his boots in his hand. The boy's breathing remained ragged, and the fresh bandage, which John had applied the previous evening, was once more stained with a yellowish discharge. He hoped John was right when he said some oozing was to be expected. But recovering or not, he would never be the man he could have been. In his clearer moments in the night that had passed, Hugh recognised that fighting William would accomplish little, and might very well cause more harm, but he owed the boy.

Edinburgh stretched out before him, mirage-like in the half-light. A mist had settled in the valley, above which the castle seemed to float like something in a bairn's tale. At the other end of the High Street a flag fluttering on the flagstaff of Holyrood indicated the King was in residence. Would he understand the need for this? Perhaps. Perhaps not. Hugh looked at his reluctant second, wondered if he could trust him, whatever the outcome. Somewhere below them a bell tolled six, and he stationed himself where he had a clear view of the track leading up the hill. William was not above treachery and he didn't wish to find himself facing half a dozen Cunninghames without warning.

He waited an hour, pacing back and forwards, his frustration growing, the hill remaining as empty as if the world had come to an end. The man with him became increasingly nervous with every passing minute, and on the stroke of seven Hugh said, 'It seems the Master of Glencairn is not coming. So I have no further need of you. But if I hear word of this from any quarter, I will know who is to blame.'

He waited on the hill, his thoughts alternately on the boy and on William, nursing his anger, until the man had dwindled into the distance, then began to make his own way down. The sensible course, the course that John and Alexander and Elizabeth would favour, would be to return to the lodgings and sit it out until Dand, supposing he did recover, was well enough to travel to Braidstane. At the foot of the slope he saw a boy ahead of him, reminiscent of Dand in weight and height and similarly tow-headed. Two younger children swung, one from each arm, their laughter ringing out in the still air. He thought of Annie and of young Hughie and of his own two girls, of how Dand had blended into their family as if he were the older brother of them all; and how he would never be able to swing two children at once again. He headed to William's lodgings.

This time he didn't stop to question the girl who opened the door, thrusting past her and storming up the stairs. The main chamber was empty, the bedchamber behind it, likewise. He stood in the centre of the room, realisation washing over him – it wasn't just empty, it was deserted. He turned to find the girl standing in the passageway.

'He's gone,' she said. 'Last night. Left in a hurry.' Her voice rose in indignation. 'And without paying what he owed.' She came into the room and stood in front of a chest, defiant. 'You shan't have it.'

'Have what?'

'The clathes. If he hadn't left something behind we would be well out of pocket.'

'I've no interest in anything of the Master of

Glencairn's. Only in knowing where he has gone. Tell me that, and the clothes are yours to dispose of as you wish. Refuse me and I will take them.'

'London,' she said. 'I couldna help hearing, for the Master was stamping up and down and shouting his mouth off about some jumped-up laird ... and that other looby who canna keep his hands to his self agreeing wi' him. But I dinna remember much else. Oh...!' Her eyes widened and she folded her arms around herself as if in protection.

'I suggest you try, or this jumped-up laird may not take it kindly.'

She slid her tongue around her lips. 'In the end the Master of Glencairn bundled him out and followed after him, wi' talk of horses and the need to be speedy, night or no, and that was the last I saw of them. I swear it.' She was still standing in front of the chest as if she feared Hugh would dispossess her of whatever it contained. A sly look crept into her eyes. 'I doubt I'll still be the loser, even once his leavings are sellt.'

'I doubt you won't.' Hugh stared her down, weighing up the likely truth or otherwise of her information, decided it was worth a groat. He flipped her a coin.

'Thank'ee, sir. Much obliged.'

Chapter 18

It was John Cunninghame who brought the news.

Alexander, who had come to check on Dand's progress, opened the door to him, his 'Hugh, where the devil have you...' cut short. He stepped back to usher John past him, apologising. 'You've caught us at a bad time, I'm afraid, Cunninghame, but come in, nonetheless. We have an injured lad, though it seems he will pull through and could now be taken home, but Hugh has disappeared when he is most needed, and gone God only knows where.'

'I know where. At least I think so. That's why I'm here.' He took a deep breath. 'I had hoped never again to come in such circumstances, and am deeply sorry for the part my nephew played in the lad's injury. Oh...' He registered Alexander's surprise. 'The confrontation at the West Port is the talk of the court. The sympathies all with the lad. Not that it will be any consolation to him.'

'Including the King?'

'That I don't know. But as far as others go, William does not come out of it well. Glencairn isn't best pleased.' He sighed. 'But that isn't the news I came to bring.'

John Montgomerie had joined them, closing the door to the bedchamber behind him. He too registered surprise, swiftly followed by concern. 'Cunninghame?

What has Hugh done now?'

'He accosted William and Maxwell in a tavern. Threw a severed arm on the table and was for fighting with William there and then, but that the tavern-keeper intervened. It was there he issued the challenge.'

Alexander gripped hold of the mantleshelf. 'They fought a duel? Despite James' edict? With what result?'

'It didn't come to that, for William didn't show. And cowardly or not, I might have applauded the action, except the end result is he fled Edinburgh and Hugh after him.'

'To Ayrshire?' There was a tinge of relief in Alexander's voice. 'Surely the earl will not allow them to come to a fight.'

'Unfortunately he hasn't gone home. He's gone to London, or so the girl in his lodgings says. She overheard him talking to Maxwell, just before they took off.'

'Why London?'

'I don't think he intends to stop there. I think he makes for the Low Countries until the dust has settled: there is plenty of scope for miscreants to hide out there. But if Hugh catches up with him first…'

'There will be bloodshed.' John Montgomerie looked towards the bedchamber. 'Has there not been trouble enough? Why could Hugh not be content to wait until the lad was able to travel and take him home?'

'Why indeed.' Cunninghame was grim. 'The lad was ill done by, and if I could get hold of William I would whip him to within an inch of his life myself, but a confrontation between him and Hugh risks the peace of every Cunninghame and Montgomerie in Ayrshire.

And everywhere else, come to that.' There was silence for a moment, the demons he raised a tangible presence between them. 'I intend to follow and see if this madness can be stopped once and for all. I thought you would wish to know.'

It was a frustrating journey. Five days during which John Cunninghame, accompanied by John Montgomerie, pausing intermittently to change horses and snatch a few hours' sleep, played catch-up all the way to London. At every place they stopped, careful enquiry revealed they were on the right track, but despite their speed, they remained a day behind, so that it was clear those they chased also wasted no time. William and Maxwell had left a trail easy to follow, their demands for bed and board and fresh horses delivered in a manner that had caused offence to all but the most phlegmatic of hosts. To their surprise Hugh had been more circumspect, his desire for haste, and refusal to rest for more than an hour or two, night or day, the only thing which made him stand out. The closer they came to London, the more hopeless the quest seemed.

Alexander had wanted to be the one to accompany Cunninghame, but as John Montgomerie pointed out, it would be one thing to ask the King's permission to take Dand to Braidstane, quite another to ask leave to follow Hugh. 'Only a fool would let you go to London without asking why, and James is no fool. If this thing is to be kept secret, then it better be me who goes. You can put it about I've returned to the college in Glasgow and there will be no one to say otherwise.'

'And Dand?'

'Take him to Agnes. I'll send instructions for his care. She lived long enough with Kate to know what to do... Send to the college, to Peter Lowe. He will check on him.'

'Elizabeth?'

'Send word that Dand has been injured, and that we are all staying in Edinburgh until such time as he is fit to ride. Tell her he's on the mend, but not quite ready yet, and leave it at that. With any luck she'll assume Hugh is staying in Edinburgh with him.'

Now, as they approached the fringes of London, the smoke from a thousand chimneys a grey pall hanging over the city, John Montgomerie voiced the concern that had lain over him like a shadow throughout the journey. 'If we cannot find them. What then?'

'Someone will know where they are, or where they have been. The Scottish contingent in London is a small pond. William's arrival will likely have caused a ripple, whatever story he tells. He and Maxwell made no effort to conceal themselves on the road down, quite the reverse. Why would they start now? A beggar may be invisible, but the Master of Glencairn? I think not. Besides, they have no idea they are being followed. My concern,' Cunninghame's grip tightened on his reins, so that the horse baulked at the touch, 'is not where William and Maxwell are, but where Hugh is and whether he has found them.' He relaxed his grip. 'Where would he make for first?'

'Our brother George I imagine. He keeps his ear close to the ground. I doubt many ripples in the Scottish pond pass him by.'

John Montgomerie was right, though the news George gave them was not what they wished to hear. They were ushered into his rooms by a manservant in livery and offered a choice wine – rich pickings at the English court, Cunninghame thought. No wonder he stays.

'John?' George rose to greet them. 'Word travels fast. How did you know Hugh…?'

'Don't ask. Is he here? We followed to try to stop him but were always just too late to catch him.'

'Well, I'm afraid you've missed him again. He took passage on a ship this morning, heading for Veere and, I suspect, The Hague. At least, that's where the Master of Glencairn is headed, if the rumours are to be believed.' Belatedly, he turned in John Cunninghame's direction. 'I'm sorry, this is…?'

'The Earl of Glencairn's brother.' John wasted no time in preamble. 'With equal reason to try and stop a confrontation. We travelled together.' He frowned. 'Why didn't you stop Hugh?'

'Believe me I tried.' George took a sip of wine. 'And indeed I thought I had succeeded. We argued the toss last night and he appeared to accept my reasoning, but I woke this morning to find the bird had flown. Short of tying him down or locking him in, I don't know what I could have done else, and I had no reason to suspect he hadn't made the sensible choice.'

'When does he ever?' John Montgomerie said.

Cunninghame set his glass down. 'When do either of them?'

They discussed it at length over a breakfast of soft white bread, cold cuts of meat, and a firm cheese that George said came from the Cheddar Gorge, where he had his living. George did the meal justice, the others no more than picking at it.

Cunninghame returned to the lodgings after a fruitless two hours at the docks trying to buy a speedy passage to Veere. 'There isn't a ship to be got before Thursday at the earliest, and with three days start, no chance at all of finding William before Hugh does. At best we might arrive in time to pick up the pieces.'

'If there are pieces to pick up,' John said.

'Are you sure it's worth the trip?' George sounded doubtful.

'I have to go. I cannot go back to Elizabeth without…'

Cunninghame cut in, deliberately harsh. 'You have lost one brother. How would Elizabeth feel if you made it three? I will go, and if I am there in time, I'll knock their heads together and bring them both home. If not,'

449

he spread his hands, 'it is the best we can do.'

'Hugh is my responsibility.'

'And William mine.'

'I have no family,' John began.

'If anything happens to Hugh, you will have charge of his family and of Elizabeth.'

'There is Alexander.'

Cunninghame made a dismissive gesture. 'Who is twice your age and approaching his allotted span, and though he seems hale enough, who can tell?'

George weighed in. 'He's right, John. I cannot go, and you should not. We can trust Cunninghame, surely?'

'It's not a matter of trust. We learned to trust him long ago. It's a matter of obligation. To Elizabeth, to the children, to our family name.'

'As to obligation,' Cunninghame stood up, closing the conversation, 'there has been plenty of that over the years, on both sides, and high time we made an end of it. This current trouble can be laid at William's door: it falls to me to sort it.'

Chapter 19

The sun was dipping below the horizon as Robbie and the Lavalles approached St Valery. The weather had been kind to them in the five days since they left Paris – the only thing that had, Robbie thought. They had slipped away from the Maison d'Ourcamps under cover of darkness, a boatman rowing them west along the Seine. Eugenie sat in the bow of the boat watching as the silhouette of the Palais de la Cité faded into the shadows behind them, her eyes clouded with tears. They landed well past the city walls, Munro waiting in the shelter of a copse of trees with horses to send them on their way. He handed François up first, then Netta, and finally Eugenie, resting his hand for a moment on hers as he passed her the reins. He gripped Robbie's arm in farewell.

'Take your time. Remember, they none of them have experience of riding, and though these ponies are as gentle beasts as we could find, there is always a risk if they are startled. Look after them. Look after yourself, and fulfil your duty to the King.'

'Which king?' It had been a genuine question he hadn't dare ask in the presence of his mother for fear that it might raise questions in her mind, for which there might be no comfortable answers. His father had been equivocal.

'Both, if you can. As a conduit for messages, you are not obliged to favour one over the other. Indeed, it may be to your advantage if you are seen to be impartial. It would lend a credence to your reporting.'

'And if I must pass on something to James that he will not want to hear?'

'Tell the truth. James has many failings, but in my limited experience it seems he favours honesty over sycophancy.'

It had been an encouragement of sorts, and one he would have liked to share with Eugenie, had she shown any signs of a desire for conversation. After his father's warning, he had expected silence from François but had hoped that five days in Eugenie's company would have served to restore their friendship. Her retreat was disheartening. Several times, as they paused to eat, or stopped for the night at a wayside inn, he attempted to draw her out, hoping that if he could get her to speak of what she had suffered he would gain an understanding of it and thus be better placed to offer comfort. But each time she shrank away from him, shaking her head. He lay on a pallet bed unable to sleep, suffering the snoring of a merchant lying on his back beside him – perhaps she knows, he thought ... if she were told a Garde had denounced them ... surely she couldn't think...? He remembered the way she had looked at him each time he'd called at her home, of how she avoided looking at him now – perhaps keeping a distance between us is her way of showing she blames me for her father's death. And with justice. The other thought that haunted him, that she knew about Angus and had taken the guilt for his death upon herself.

Netta was the only one of the three who made any attempt to talk, commenting on the landscape and the young crops and especially the animals in the fields as they passed. She had never seen a live cow before and was fascinated when they passed a small herd, which chased alongside them for a minute or two on the other side of the ditch that separated them from the track, clearly expecting something from them, the plaintive moos following long after they'd left them behind. 'They have such sad eyes,' she said. 'D'you think they know they will soon be slaughtered?'

'I think,' Robbie said, 'if they are well fed, and those were, to judge by their size and the healthy look of their coats, they are content enough. And why wouldn't they be – they have no worries to disturb them.'

'Like the sparrows,' Netta said.

'Exactly like.'

Eugenie, riding beside Robbie, stirred briefly. 'Lucky them, if food is all they need for happiness.'

He wanted to reach across, to touch her hand, to find some way of bridging the yawning gap between them, but she rode on, her back ramrod-stiff, looking straight ahead, as if she took this journey alone.

When we reach the farm, he thought, when she has had time to begin to feel safe, perhaps then she will talk. *Except that you won't be there to see it*, the voice in his head said. *And by the time you return there may be some other young man who takes an interest in her. One of the Bachellerie perhaps.*

Ahead of them he saw the twin towers that protected the St Valery gate and decided to skirt the town rather than riding straight through. 'It is the longer road,' he said, 'and with a hill or two, more effort for the horses, but though we should be far enough removed from Paris to be perfectly safe, it is as well not to attract undue attention. Once you are settled at the farm it will be easy to pass you off as the orphan children of some faraway relative…' Beside him, Eugenie dropped her head and he cursed himself for his choice of word. 'I'm sorry, I…'

'You spoke but the truth as far as orphan goes. But it is something I'd rather Netta and François are not reminded of at every turn.'

And you, he thought, but didn't risk saying. And you.

Madame Picarde was at the gate as they arrived, her plump face and even plumper figure a welcome sight. Robbie dropped down first and lifted the others to the ground, the stable lad coming forward to take the horses. He had a familiar look, but Robbie couldn't place him, until he noted the slight limp as he led the horses away.

'He's the lad that Mother…'

'Yes. He and his own mother are with me now. Since his father lit out without so much as a word. And though he left them more poverty-stricken, if that were possible, than when he was here,' she sniffed, 'if he never returns it'll be too soon.' She reached up to Robbie and standing on tiptoe planted a kiss on each cheek, then turned to the Lavalles and did likewise. 'But what am I thinking of, chattering on about Pierre, when what you all need is a seat and some food in you.' She bustled them into the kitchen, the woman who bent over the fire coaxing it into a blaze turning and bobbing a curtsey. Since Kate and Maggie and Ellie and the wee fellow deserted us,' Madame Picarde's smile belied the word, 'we have rattled around like peas in a half-empty pod and will be happy to have the place full again. Besides, there is always work to do on a farm and not enough hands to do it.' She touched François' shoulder. 'And this young man may be exactly what we need.'

It drew a flicker of a smile from Eugenie. 'Merci, Madame, we are grateful for your hospitality. And will repay it in any way we can, will we not?'

Netta nodded, but François studied his feet, remaining silent.

Robbie stayed two weeks at the farm. The letter he carried from Henri to James was propped up on the window ledge of the chamber he shared with François, staring at him accusingly every morning when he woke. He was standing with Madame Picarde leaning on the fence that separated the yard from the paddock, his eyes fixed on the track to St Valery that wound around the edges of the fields. A light northerly wind was blowing into their faces, carrying on it the smell of the estuary at low tide, and he thrust away the thought of Le Crotoy and the ship-owner he had been instructed to find there. Above their heads bats dipped and swooped as dusk fell.

'How long do you intend to stay, Robbie?'

'Do you wish me to go?'

Madame Picarde sighed. 'What I wish or don't wish is of no matter. You are on a King's mission. To remain here beyond what is reasonable is a denial of that.'

'How can I leave them like this?' He was gripping the rail, his knuckles white. 'If you had known them before…'

'I have known others suffer similar traumas, their recovery not measured in days or weeks or even months. But recover they did. And so will the Lavalles. Trust me.'

'Eugenie…'

'She matters to you. I know. And in the will of God, that too may come right in time.'

'God?' he said, his voice rising. 'The same will of God that put them in the prison?'

'God is not a doer of evil, Robbie, men are.'

'If he is God at all, he could have spared them that.'

'True. But he does not always choose to intervene. And if he does not, he has a reason.' She unfurled his fingers from the rail, turned him to face her. 'He helped them to escape, remember that.'

He wrested his hand free. 'The escape was Ruiz' doing and my father's. It is to them I owe gratitude.'

She lifted one shoulder, said, 'Of course.'

Despite her acquiescence, he had a feeling he hadn't won a victory, so changed tack. 'She will not talk to me. She talks to you, and with Netta and François she makes an effort to be almost herself. But not with me. Not with me. I want…'

Madame Picarde placed her hand over his. 'You must have patience, Robbie, and understand that when a girl suffers, as it is likely she has, there is often a feeling deep down that she is in some way to blame, a sense of shame, of being unclean.'

'Whatever happened in the Palais de la Cité was not her fault!'

'You know that. I know that. And in time, she will come to accept it too. But for now, do not press her...' She hesitated.

Robbie was adamant. 'I would never blame her.'

'Perhaps not blame, but ... if she were to speak of the horror of it, it might become an image of her neither of you would be able to escape.'

'Do you think she blames me?'

There was a pause as if Madame Picarde was weighing up her answer. 'She is ... not comfortable with you just now.' Another pause, shorter this time. 'That is not a bad thing, rather a sign that you matter to her. When she is herself again, that is when you will know if you have a future.'

'I will be in Scotland and she here and...'

'With but a stretch of water between you and boats plying back and forth constantly. As near to each other as if you were in the south of France.'

'I cannot go without a word.'

'You are young, Robbie, and so is she.'

It was his mother all over again.

'Do not set your heart on something that may never be. Nor attempt to tie her to you when she is not ready. If none of this had happened, perhaps you could have had an understanding. As it is…'

He knew her intention was good, and that what she said was truth, but it didn't make it any easier to hear.

Her voice was quiet but firm. 'Don't wait here any longer, Robbie. Aside from your duty to the King, with every day you linger it will only get harder.' Then, as if she understood the battle going on inside him, 'One day your head and your heart will be in agreement. Until then … it is your head you must follow.'

He slipped from his chamber the following day in the half-light before dawn, and carrying his boots, crept down the stairs, holding his breath with every creak. It had rained overnight, the damp cobbles gleaming dark against the honey stone of the farmhouse. He looked down at his feet – noisy or not he couldn't cross the yard in his stocking soles. Each step was a war: one voice in his head saying *'Leave. Now.'* Another equally insistent, *'Go back. While you still can.'* The door of the stable scraped across the cobbles, loud in the silence, and he looked across at the farmhouse, unsure whether he wished the sound would waken them, or whether not. He was saddling the horse, bending down to tighten the girth, when he heard the door scrape again. He swung round smiling, his eyes dark. 'Eugen…'

'I'm sorry.' Netta was framed in the doorway, her feet bare, a shawl thrown over her night-rail. 'I heard a noise.

I thought…' She stopped and he filled in what she didn't say, that noises in the night still held terror for her, as for them all.

'I hoped not to disturb anyone.'

'Why would you go without a farewell?'

'Because,' he willed her to understand, 'if I went when you were awake, I feared the last memory I would have of Eugenie would be of her looking everywhere but at me. This way I can pretend a better goodbye.' He took both her hands in his. 'Tell her I'm sorry for all that has happened, and that to me she will always be the Eugenie I first met. Tell her that as soon as my duty is done to the King, I will come back. Tell her…'

'She knows,' Netta said. 'But I shall tell her anyway.'

Chapter 20

They were heading for the open sea, tacking back and forth across the river, beating into a strong north-westerly. Robbie leant on the top rail, breathing in the salt air, fascinated by the process required to turn the ship at the end of each leg. When Du Bois had said they could leave, despite what appeared to be a contrary wind, he had not imagined anything like this. The officer of the watch shouting orders, his 'Ready about' the signal for them to prepare to change tack. The helmsman, spinning the wheel, and the men below working in concert, the bo'sun bellowing at anyone out of step. There were men to each side of the yardarms, hauling on the braces, others loosening and tightening the sheets that served the sails, a momentary flapping as they crossed through the eye of the wind before the canvas filled again.

Pierre Du Bois appeared at his shoulder. 'You're impressed. You should be, for it's a complicated manoeuvre, in which a single mistiming can spell disaster. But with a good crew there is nothing more beautiful than seeing a square-rigged ship tacking.'

'How long will it take to reach the Channel?'

'Longer than I'd like.' Pierre looked up at the sky. 'But, we have three or four hours of daylight left, and with this wind, once out in open water we should make good time.

Two days to Calais and a chance to take on water and rest out a night there.' He bared his teeth in a grin. 'If rest is what you're after.'

'I have a girl,' Robbie said stiffly. 'At least, I hope so. And I will do nothing to jeopardise that.'

'I hope she's worth it.'

Robbie found himself saying, 'If I haven't ruined everything already.'

'Women,' said Du Bois. 'Hard to understand and harder to please. We've all been there, lad, don't worry yourself. You'll have absence and time on your side. Which I've always found to work in my favour.'

They were on the leg facing the St Valery shore. 'I never intended for it to be this way.'

'Maybe it isn't as bad…' There was a call from the helmsman. Du Bois made a gesture of apology and, his expression seemingly serious, said, 'If you have a need to talk, I'm a good listener.' The grin reappeared. 'With my wife, I need to be.'

Robbie stayed at the rail until they reached the Channel, watching as the length of the tacks was adjusted in their approach to the estuary mouth, so that on the final leg they slipped into the open sea and with little more than a heel to starboard caught the wind. The sails filled and they continued parallel to the French coast, far enough out to have a clear run, but close enough, Robbie imagined, to be able to make for a safe haven should the need arise. He knew little about sailing, but understood well enough the risk of piracy, and though, as instructed, he hadn't boarded the vessel until it was fully loaded and ready to sail, he had a suspicion that the contents of the hold were of sufficient value to attract interest in the wrong quarters.

They made Calais without incident, reducing their sail at the harbour mouth and nosing into a berth beside a fishing vessel, which rose and fell on the incoming tide and bumped against rope fenders hanging from the harbour wall. Once they were secure, with the upper masts set down, Du Bois disappeared along the dock, returning with a parcel of fresh fish, his forehead lined.

Robbie was surprised. 'We eat on board?'

'Yes.' There was no trace of Du Bois' earlier light-heartedness. 'There is a rumour of brigands straying much further east than usual, and we have no wish to become a target. A group of fishing boats will be leaving early with the tide and we with them. A cargo of fish is of little interest, empty fishing vessels even less so. They are heading towards English waters, which will suit us very well. And though we are bigger and will stand out among them, there is some safety in numbers. The further we travel in a group, the better.'

And so it was. At first it seemed all was going to plan, though Robbie, staying out of the way at the stern of the brig as they cast off and slipped along in the middle of a line of small craft heading out, noted Du Bois' expression was not the relaxed look of the first stage of the journey. Several times as he stood at the binnacle Robbie saw him glance upwards at the shreds of white cloud that trailed across the bruised sky, like bandages come adrift. He had no idea if it was word of the pirates that had unsettled him or if it was the sky itself that gave him concern. There was little wind, but more warmth in the air than

Robbie expected for the time of day – the possibility of thunder, perhaps? He hoped not.

The fishing boats spread out and prepared to cast their nets, Du Bois steering a course around them and heading north and east. They were hugging the coastline, but making slower than expected progress, when Robbie felt the wind pick up, veering beam on, and with it the first rumbles of thunder. One minute the sky was a pale purple, shot with yellow, the next it was pewter, heavy clouds pressing down on them. Du Bois was calling for the ship to be turned into the wind, and the sails reefed, boys scrambling up the rigging, when the rain came, heavy and slanting, blotting out sea and sky both. A sailor made for Robbie, moving along the rail, hand over hand, leaning into the wind that threatened to throw him across the deck.

He put his mouth against Robbie's ear. 'Ye need to get below. Now. And take a hammock, not yer bunk. It's going to get rough.' Clearly seeing Robbie's doubtful expression, he continued, 'It's getting in that's the tricky part, but once ye are it wraps around ye like a blanket and we'd have to be near to being overturned before ye'd fall out. It's by far the safer option.' There was a crack, a jagged line of lightning splitting the sky, the boat canting as a gust of wind hit them beam on. Robbie lost hold of the rail and went down, sliding across the damp planking. A rope uncoiled on his right and he stretched out to grasp it, but it shot through his fingers, burning his palm. Another crack, another lightning flash, the deck illuminated as a wave rose above the top rail and crashed down, washing towards him in a rush of spume. There was nothing close enough to reach to halt his slide, instinct causing him to twist so that he hit the opposite bulwark sideways on, the uprights catching him on the ankle and waist and chest. He scrambled onto his knees, reaching for the top rail with both hands, the last thing he remembered, a second wave, lifting and couping him, smashing his head against the deck.

When he came to, he was lying in a hammock, the fabric wrapped around him like a cocoon. The boat was bucking like an unbroken horse, the timbers creaking and groaning. All around him, the howl of the wind and the whining of rigging and the sound of rain lashing on the deck above. The unlit lantern hanging from the deckhead swung crazily on its chain, as if it were trying to break free. He looked at the scuttle, alternately submerged by sea and sky, and felt his stomach revolt. Unable to control it, he turned his head sideways and vomited, leaving the taste of metal in his mouth. He was struggling against the hammock, consumed by an irrational desire to be free of it, when the beam above his head cracked. His last thoughts as the lantern fell – Eugenie will never know why I didn't come back. Perhaps it's no more than I deserve.

Chapter 21

It was a similar thought that troubled Hugh in the two days following his arrival at The Hague. The enforced delay as he waited for information allowed Elizabeth's face to intrude upon him, her expression accusing. In all the long journey he had refused to think of her, or of the children, focusing instead on the last sight he had of Dand: his sweat-dampened hair plastered on his forehead; the empty sleeve of his nightshirt pinned above his elbow; and of his own blame in bringing the boy. William's contemptuous comment – *He should have been left at home. No doubt he will be now* – fuelling his anger and giving him the needed strength to hammer on with little respite, when in other circumstances he would have broken his journey.

It had been an increasing frustration to him that he had been unable to catch up with William and Maxwell, and an impossibility that he should give up the chase, even when he discovered they had left for Holland. He had followed the rumour to The Hague but had been frustrated in his early efforts to track them down. It was on the second evening he ran across a Montgomerie cousin with connections in the town.

'Leave it to me,' Robert said. 'If they're here I'll find them.' And so he had, bringing word the next day.

Hugh was incredulous. 'They spend their mornings strolling in the Binnenhof, without a care in the world, as if the boy isn't lying in Edinburgh, his life hanging in the balance?' He was buckling on his sword.

'Perhaps,' Robert suggested, 'it might be best to send word and issue a private challenge. Duelling here is not uncommon and attracts no censure if it is done in the proper manner.'

'And run the risk of William taking off? Not likely. He refused once, I'll not risk it again. This time the challenge will be public, his cowardice also public should he fail to meet me.'

Public it was. The Binnenhof was crowded. Hugh scanned the constantly moving kaleidoscope of people, old and young, tall and short, civilian and military, their presence an indication they either were, or wished to be thought, gentlemen. The sound rose and fell, a polyglot mix of languages in which Hugh could hear snatches of French and German, Dutch and Spanish, English and Scots. Over to his left William's voice, rising above the general hubbub, accompanied by appreciative laughter from the small group surrounding him.

Robert placed a restraining hand on his arm. 'Are you sure this is wise, sir?'

'Wisdom is much over-rated. I didn't come all this way to be dissuaded from confronting William because it may not be wise.' Hugh began to thread his way through the crowd. 'You may accompany me or not, as you wish.'

He came up behind William and grasping his shoulder spun him round. 'Well, well. The Master of Glencairn, a coward and a fugitive!' He addressed those with William.

'Has he told you why he is here? Why he fled Scotland in such a hurry? No? Well let me enlighten you. I sought satisfaction for a boy, whose only crime was that his horse accidentally dunted another. And for that he lost an arm and very nearly his life. The Master of Glencairn and his men carry swords but are afraid to use them against any but a child. When I issued a challenge, he ran.' He poked William on the chest. 'You thought you had escaped. Well you were wrong. It would take more than a stretch of water to make me lose the scent. You refused my challenge in Edinburgh. Will you meet me here?'

William clapped three times. 'An orator, Braidstane? I had no idea.' His tone was contemptuous. 'And no. I will not take your challenge. Your boy wasn't worth spilling ale for, never mind blood. It was to save *your* life, not my own, that I chose to leave Scotland.'

Hugh cast aside his cloak, drew his sword. 'And I choose to risk it. Fight me now!' He pointed his sword at William's chest, waited. A space had opened around them, those closest to William falling back, others joining the circle. Hugh took another step forward, spat at William's feet. 'Coward,' he repeated.

William threw off his jacket and drew with a snarl, launching himself at Hugh, their blades clashing. It was an exhibition match, Hugh standing his ground, parrying William's thrusts as easily as if he were a tutor testing the metal of a student. William became increasingly erratic, lunging and twisting but failing to make contact, his face puce. Then it was over, Hugh making one forward thrust. It caught William in the stomach, penetrating his doublet and laying him out, a ribbon of blood leaking from below

467

his belt. Hugh stood over him, his anger cooling, and sheathed his sword. Maxwell was on the ground bending over William, slapping at his face, calling out, 'He's killed him.'

Officers of the guard were breaking through the circle, pinioning Hugh's arms from behind. He struggled to free himself, but another guard stood in front, a blade at his throat.

'Where are you taking me?' Hugh asked.

'To answer to the provost marshall. On the charge of affray.' The guard nodded towards William. 'You may hope he isn't dead or it will be murder you face.'

Chapter 22

It was the talk of The Hague. And the last thing John Cunninghame wished to hear. He arrived as dusk was beginning to fall and found an inn that looked, by the clientele, halfway to being clean, and somewhere he might not be robbed while he slept.

'You'll be wanting a bite to eat, I daresay?' The woman who bustled to meet him was homely, the apron tied around her ample waist white, aside from some splatters of gravy, clearly fresh. Her face was as round and as brown as a russet apple, her smile genuine.

He smiled back. 'Thank you. And a room?'

'To yourself?' Her laugh was hearty but lacking in malice. 'We're a mite busy, but we can squeeze you in, and it's only one person you'll have to share a bed with. Unlike some other places I could mention, where you'd be lucky to get off with three.' The stew she brought was hot, the meat tender: the first decent meal since he'd left Edinburgh. The ale too was good, not the usual watered offering of an inn that catered to travellers passing through. She hovered at his shoulder, nodding at the clean platter. 'Good?' she asked.

'Very good. Very good indeed.'

'What brings you from Scotland?'

'I have some private business. Someone I need to

469

find,' he said.

There was a twinkle in her eye. 'I recognise the burr, see. I knew a man once, from the west coast, he said. A gentleman. I might have gone to live in Scotland myself, if he hadn't gone and died on me.'

He felt the need to respond. 'I'm sorry…'

'Ah, it was a long time ago. When I was but a slim thing, if you can believe it. But for all that I'm well settled now,' she jerked her head towards the man at the counter, 'I still like to hear the burr.'

He looked around the room – it seemed a mite too orderly for William and Maxwell's taste, but if she favoured Scots, it might be worth enquiring of Hugh. He was about to ask, when she said, 'Strange thing, Scots are all the gossip today. I hope it wasn't any of them you were looking for, for one's in prison and the other one dead, or so they say.'

'Do you know the names?'

Her forehead creased. 'Braid … Braid … something.'

'Braidstane?'

'Yes. He's the dead one. And something … home perhaps?'

'Cunninghame?'

'That's it He's in prison. Or the other way round.'

It was the worst possible news. 'Prison?'

'In the hands of the provost marshall. And if he has money to spend, they will be generous hands. A room to himself, a servant and as many visitors as can buy their way in.'

He shifted, about to rise, but she shook her head at him. 'You needn't rush yourself, you'll not gain admittance

470

till the morn. And if you want my advice, I wouldn't try too early, the turnkeys have a reputation of enjoying a good night at visitor's expense and suffering for it the next day.'

He woke the next morning to a pale sunshine warming one side of his face and the ring of horses' hooves on the cobbles of the inn-yard, accompanied by the creaking of cartwheels, the jingle of harness, a tuneless whistling and the shouted orders of an ostler. He hadn't expected to be able to sleep at all, but to judge by the noise, he had, and well.

The innkeeper's wife had been right. The turnkey opened the gate to him, rubbing at his eyes, his shirt tail hanging out, his jacket unbuttoned. 'Cunninghame, you say? No one of that name here. You could try the Prison Gate.' He bared his teeth in what John imagined was intended to be a grin. 'We only have the best of prisoners, see.' He rubbed his fingers together, 'Those with means.' He was about to shut the gate, but John held it open.

'Montgomerie, then?'

'The Scot that was brought in yesterday? He's here. Claims he used to be in the service of the prince, not that I believe him, or that it'll do him much good if the word be true that the man he injured died.'

He felt a twinge of guilt at the relief that surged through him. 'Can I see him?'

The turnkey rubbed his fingers together again. 'I daresay...' He waited, hand outstretched, palm up.

John dropped a thaler onto his palm, the turnkey stepping back, pulling the gate wide.

'John Cunninghame? Where did you spring from?' Hugh stood up.

'From Edinburgh. Following you. And a devilish inconvenient journey it was too. Forbye the wasted effort. You do choose your moments. To attack William in the Binnenhof, with half of The Hague as witnesses? He may have deserved to die a hundred times over, but so publicly? How do you expect to get out of this?'

'For one thing, he struck the first blow. And for a second, he's not dead.' Hugh was dismissive. 'If I'd killed him, I'd know. It was but a prick ... though I did lay him out cold.' He grinned, relish in his voice.

'You'd better be right. And even if you are, where does it leave you?'

'Detained at the provost marshall's pleasure, but not for long I hope. I have former comrades here, who will no doubt come to my aid and intercede on my behalf.'

'Fourteen years is a long time, Hugh. There may be none left in Maurice's army who remember you.'

'Long in the tooth, maybe, but with memories to match, I trust. And if not...' Hugh shrugged, 'I have another plan. A mite costly perhaps, but, with luck, effective.'

'Do you need money?'

'I wouldn't say no.' Hugh looked Cunninghame straight in the eye. 'A loan. Which will be speedily repaid when I make Scotland.'

'I believe you.' Cunninghame went to the door, stuck his head out, and satisfied, shut it again. 'This plan?'

'*If* it proves necessary, the less who are party to it the better. Suffice it I will need passage to Scotland ... for three.'

'Give me a week and it will be done.'

John Cunninghame found William in rooms on a street leading away from the Binnenhof. He was stretched out on a padded bench, his head on a cushion, doublet undone, Maxwell in a chair opposite him, a drink in his hand. As the girl announced him, William straightened, his obvious surprise equalling that of Hugh Montgomerie.

'Nursing your pride, nephew? Or have you any other hurt?'

William pulled open his shirt, displaying a broad bandage. 'Braidstane will suffer for this. See if he does not.'

'An impressive binding for a scratch. How much did that set you back? Or has Maxwell here turned nursemaid?'

'I am the victim, Uncle, and there are plenty to testify to Braidstane as the aggressor. He cannot rely on friends

473

in high places here.'

'And others, I hear, who will testify to provocation.'

William stood up, wincing. 'A passing comment is hardly grounds for attack, and a sword thrust a disproportionate response.'

'A fight, I heard,' Cunninghame said, 'fair and square.'

William looked at Maxwell, as if for support. 'An inch lower and who knows what the outcome would have been.'

The corner of Maxwell's mouth lifted. 'An inch lower and it could have been the end of William's line.'

William glared at him, placed his hand on his midriff as if to protect it.

Cunninghame swallowed his smile, the idea of William with damaged tackle not unpleasing. He stepped forward, as if responding to William's pained expression. 'Let me take a look. I have some experience in dressing wounds...'

'Thank you, Uncle,' William said stiffly, 'but I'd prefer to leave it to those with qualifications.' He sat down with exaggerated care.

Cunninghame abandoned any pretence at sympathy. 'Go home, William. Or I might be tempted to finish the job Braidstane started. If, of course, you are fit to travel.' The sarcasm was clear. 'Leave me to sort this mess out.'

William's face was flushed. 'Finally, Uncle, support for our family and not our enemies. My father will be pleased.'

'Your father may not favour the Montgomeries, but he is intelligent enough to know where and when to draw the line. A pity you do not.'

'A man to see you, sur.' The girl stepped back to allow the visitor past, her face registering speculation. 'I can bring you both a drink, sur.'

John Cunninghame shook his head. 'No thanks.'

She hesitated on the landing. 'Anything else you might need?'

'Nothing.' He moved to shut the door and added sternly, 'Nor do I wish to find you eavesdropping, or your mistress will hear of it.' He turned to his young visitor, whose uniform had the fresh look of a relatively recent recruit. 'Have you been in Maurice of Nassau's service long?'

'Six months, sir.'

'And already placed in a difficult situation.' The lad shifted from one foot to the other. 'Don't worry. I'll not make it more so.' He waved at the room. 'I'm sorry I can't offer you a seat, but feel free to perch on the bed. It's little more than a board, but better than nothing, and it appears to be flea-free, always a bonus.' The lad remained standing, as John leant against the window ledge, his legs stretched out in front of him, ankles crossed. 'Perhaps you can start with your given name. I do not require your family name if you don't wish it.'

'I'm not ashamed of my name.'

'I didn't mean to suggest you were.'

'It's Montgomerie, sir. Robert Montgomerie.'

'Ah.'

475

'A cousin of Braidstane's. Third, I believe, but family nonetheless, and thus with obligation.'

'He sent you?'

'No.' The lad coloured. 'I followed you. To The Master of Glencairn's rooms and then to here.' He placed his hand on his sword hilt, his tone fierce. 'To ensure you don't play Braidstane false.'

For the second time that morning John swallowed his amusement, but this time it was tinged with admiration – the lad was loyal, if foolhardy. 'I assure you, Hugh's well-being is as important to me as to you.'

Perhaps it was his use of Hugh's given name that did it, the lad's shoulders relaxing, his hand dropping back to his side.

'Sit yourself down.' John waved at the bed again. 'And let's discuss this plan of his and see what must be done to make it work.'

Chapter 23

Robbie woke to a throbbing head and a dull ache in his stomach. Grey light was filtering through the scuttle, the horizon beyond moving up and down gently – the storm was past then. He looked up to see the crack in the beam where the lantern chain had hung and put his hand to his head. It was tightly bandaged, the edges of the cloth crusted.

'Ye're lucky ye weren't killed.' The boy ducked his head as he entered, and Robbie thought he detected a ghoulish disappointment in his voice as he said, 'Ye only took a glancing blow. An inch or two to the right and ye'd have been done for, for sure.'

Robbie tried to sit up, the hammock swaying and tumbling him out, depositing him on the floor at the boy's feet.

He laughed. 'Lubber, in't ye? Never mind. Now the storm's past ye can go back to yer own bunk. But not now.' He held out a grubby hand. 'Ah've to bring ye above, if ye think ye can manage?'

He followed the boy onto the deck. The ship was riding at anchor, the entire crew, it seemed, occupied in clearing the ravages of the storm. He stumbled over to stand beside Du Bois, who was watching the carpenter and the bo'sun, one either side of the yardarm, binding wood to the topmast with stout rope.

'Change of plan.' Du Bois was matter of fact.

'What happened?'

'The topmast's sprung. That's split to you. They're fishing it. A temporary repair, a bit like splinting a broken leg.'

'We'll be able to go on?'

'Limping along, I'm afraid. Jury-rigged we cannot set full sail. Instead of carrying on, we'll make for Veere. It would be a foolishness to try and go much further without a replacement topmast. And Veere's as good a place as any to get one.'

'Will it delay us long?'

'If we have no trouble getting the topmast, no. Replacing it's a task we can do ourselves.' He gestured towards the mainmast. 'We got off lightly. Had we lost her lower down it would have been a different thing altogether. And likely cost lives. As it is, a few sore heads and empty stomachs, and a bit of work for the carpenter, to keep him from getting bored, is a small price to pay for riding the storm.' Robbie heard the relief in his voice. 'The cargo is safe and we'll be ship-shape in no time. Now, d'you think you can manage a bite?'

Robbie nodded, then winced, lifting his hand to his head.

'Still sore?'

'As if someone was jumping on it.'

'A drop of brandy will help, once you've something in your stomach. You took quite a crack and may suffer for some days yet. But by the time we get to Veere you'll be well on your way to recovery.'

'How long will it be till Veere?'

'Four, five days, perhaps. If the wind is kind. And if the repair holds, which it should. They're good men and know their job.'

They made it in four, both weather and wind kind, though to Robbie's surprise they steered a course mid-Channel. He would have liked to ask for an explanation, but decided he'd rather not show any further ignorance, so kept his curiosity to himself. He spent most of his time on deck and was pleased to find that after the first day he could now walk from bow to stern without having to hold onto the rail.

They were nearing the narrowest section of the Channel, the tall cliffs of England and the softer coastline of France both clearly visible. The ship's boy appeared at his shoulder. 'Cap'n's asking for ye, sir.'

He entered the cabin to find Du Bois leaning over a chart, whistling.

'Robbie. I thought to show you where we're headed once we leave Veere. We'll cross the Channel here.' He tapped at the chart. 'And head up past Suffolk and around the curve of Norfolk, staying close inshore.'

'Why,' Robbie said, plucking up courage, 'aren't we doing that now?'

'A combination of the prevailing wind and the jury-rig. Too close in and we'd run the risk of being driven ashore. At least out here it's just other vessels we need to avoid. Though as you can see there are plenty of them and we aren't at the narrowest point yet. Traversing the English Channel's a bit like heading to St Valery on market day, with boats to look out for instead of carts.' He was tracing a line on the chart up the English coast, 'Once past the Wash it becomes much quieter.' He straightened. 'Are you looking forward to being home?'

'I won't be home, exactly. I've never been to Edinburgh. When I came to France it was from Irvine on the west coast of Scotland.' He felt a stirring of excitement, which he was unable to conceal. 'I've never seen any of England. I pray the weather is clear for us.'

'Pray away.' Du Bois' tone was dry. 'But for more than the view, if you please.'

They slipped into Veere on the evening tide, Du Bois sending Robbie ashore to get accommodation for the time it might take to sort the topmast. 'No point in you hanging around,' he said, 'for all that you might find it interesting to watch.' Perhaps sensing Robbie's disappointment, he placed his hand on his shoulder. 'I'm sorry, lad. I'm afraid you'd be in the way, and the less distraction there is, the quicker we'll be sorted and can get going again. I know you're not wanting a girl to warm it, but I daresay a proper bed for a night or two won't go amiss.'

It was a sensation Robbie hadn't felt for three years. He disembarked onto the quay and found himself weaving across the cobbles, unable to keep a straight line, to the amusement of a boy perched on a bollard watching the comings and goings.

'Lost your landlegs?' he called with a grin.

The sailor who'd volunteered to direct Robbie to an inn, where he wouldn't be fleeced nor suffer bedbugs, aimed a slap at the boy's head. 'Don't mind him. Impudent pup.'

The St Julian, situated several streets back from the quay, was narrow and tall, squeezed between two broader buildings as if there had been a miscalculation on the architect's part. The façade was punctured with small windows, one above the other, the gable facing the street crow-stepped.

'It may not look much, but the food's good and it's far enough away from the docks to avoid trouble ... unless you cause it yourself,' the sailor said, 'but near enough that we can rescue you should the need arise.'

'It won't.' Robbie said, looking at the brightly painted shutters and the freshly brushed entrance. 'All I'm after is a good meal and decent ale and a mattress to lie on.'

Chapter 24

Hugh was getting restive. His initial plans for escape had been moderated by John Cunninghame's more measured approach, which meant he'd now been confined for almost a month. Night after night he entertained the provost marshall in his rooms, plying him with food and drink and regaling him with tales of his service as a young man under Maurice of Nassau and of life at the Scottish court, the marshall thawing to the point of almost friendship. He leant back on his chair, linking his hands behind his head.

'I take your point, Braidstane. But what is acceptable, or even usual, on the streets of Edinburgh, is not common practice here. Had you fought a duel outside the city boundaries, few would have known and none cared. But you put me in a difficult position. The Binnenhof is not the place for a public brawl. More lives were endangered than the Master of Glencairn, for these things have a habit of getting out of hand. My officers had no choice but to arrest you. It's what to do with you now is the issue.'

Robert Montgomerie was standing by the window looking out onto the courtyard below. 'Wouldn't a simple reprimand do?'

'Unfortunately not, there were far too many witnesses

to the aggression. Oh, I know,' he held up his hand, 'it was not one-sided, but ill-considered nonetheless. Though now that we know Braidstane's opponent has suffered no ill, should the prince be disposed to pardon him, it would be another matter.' He was looking directly at Robert. 'You are in the prince's service are you not?'

Robert opened his mouth to say, 'Only in a very min…' but Hugh cut in. 'Indeed, and is set fair to rise through the ranks.'

The marshall stood up. 'Once again, Braidstane, thank you for your hospitality, I always like to see my best prisoners are being well looked after.'

Hugh picked up the flagon from the table and turned it upside down.

'Dear me, did we finish the wine?' The marshall looked apologetic. 'That must be rectified. I shall send my daughter to get more.' He waited.

Hugh nodded to Robert, who reached inside his jacket and produced a purse. Handing over a florin, he said, by way of an explanation, 'My cousin has much land in Scotland and the rents are good.'

'Well, well, anything you need, anything at all, you know you have only to ask.'

'My freedom?' Hugh said.

The marshall coughed. 'Very good, Braidstane, very good. If I could, I would.'

'End of act one,' Hugh said with satisfaction, as they listened to his retreating footsteps. 'Though it's cost a pretty penny. If John Cunninghame hadn't obliged, I'd not have been able to keep up the façade for this long. Act two is the pardon.'

'You know I can't get…' Robert began.

'Of course not. We don't actually have to *get* a pardon, just promise it's on its way. How are you getting on with act three, by the way? Enjoying your starring role?'

There was a knock at the door, the marshall's daughter coming in with the refilled flagon. She curtseyed to Hugh, and, as she turned to go, cast a sideways smile at Robert.

'Pretty well, then,' Hugh said, when the door shut behind her.

'Robert flushed. 'I think so. I've been meeting her in the mornings, when she goes for bread. The basket is heavy and she's grateful for someone to carry it.'

Hugh noted his flush, but decided not to comment. The lad was young and perhaps not altogether comfortable with the subterfuge. 'And the keys? Have you found out yet where they're kept at night?'

'Generally in the marshall's desk.'

'Which is?'

'In his bedchamber.'

'Roll on act four then. I trust you have a good head for drink?' Hugh saw the doubtful look on Robert's face. 'Don't worry. Whatever else, we will remain sober, just *appear* merry. Can you manage that? By the way, have you heard from John Cunninghame? All the best plays have five acts and ours is no exception.'

'He received word yesterday. There is a Scottish ship

due in Veere in five or six days' time, which aye carries passengers. He thinks we should aim for it.'

'We?'

Robert looked down at the floor, then up again. 'I've resigned my commission. Though it isn't common knowledge.' His voice rose as if he expected opposition. 'I intend to come.'

'I take it you'll be returning to Braidstane with me, then? I can always use another pair of hands.'

'You don't need to feel obliged.' There was a new stiffness in Robert, a holding back, which Hugh noted but dismissed as unlikely to be crucial to their plan – the lad was trustworthy, he'd wager his life on that.

'Let's worry about what happens at home later. We have to get there first.'

Chapter 25

'So this is what you were hiding from me?' Hugh gripped Robert by both shoulders. 'And I thought it likely unimportant.'

'You don't disapprove?'

'How could I? It's ideal.' The smile that spread across Robert's face faded as Hugh continued. 'A perfect addition to the plan.'

'He means,' John Cunninghame interrupted, glaring at Hugh, 'he's pleased for you. As I am. She's a fine lass and will be good company on the road home. Even if the courtship has been a mite fast.'

'It isn't a sham.' Robert was defensive. 'I do truly care for her, and she me.'

'I believe you,' Hugh said. He filled three glasses. 'Here's to you, lad. And to your bride-to-be.'

Their glasses drained, they sat down at the table. Robert, clearly feeling the need to explain further, said, 'She will miss her father, of course, but we both think it better in the circumstances that she comes away with me now. There will no doubt be a ruckus when the deception is discovered and her father likely suffer considerable embarrassment. When the dust is settled we will return and hopefully receive his blessing.'

Hugh nodded. 'No doubt.' He became brisk. 'But to

business.' He was thinking aloud. 'Sixty-five miles, give or take, to Veere. Three, four days. The most direct route involves crossing several inlets, so we have to allow for tides.'

He turned to John Cunninghame. 'And you reckon it's best not to send word ahead to the ship?'

'At the moment only we ourselves know of our intention. I say we keep it that way.' John leant forward, elbows on the table, leaning his chin on his hands. 'But we shouldn't delay. William and Maxwell are gone, the marshall has swallowed the story of the pardon and for the moment folk have lost interest in you. Not to mention,' he grimaced, 'my pockets may be deep, but we're getting gey near the bottom of them. Entertaining the marshall these last weeks hasn't been cheap.'

'A betrothal ceremony,' Hugh said. 'The perfect act four. We can invite everyone: marshall, turnkeys *and* guards. Tonight. No one will wish to miss the opportunity to drink to your future. Especially not when the drink is flowing and free.' He turned to John. 'You still have at least one florin left, I trust?'

'Yes, and I know someone who can cut it in two.'

Robert was looking bewildered, as if the conversation was moving too fast for him. 'The betrothal "penny",' Hugh said. 'Only this time it will be gold, so guaranteed to impress.'

The ceremony was brief. Robert was beaming and his bride-to-be smiling shyly as Hugh presented them each with half a gold coin, which joined together made a perfect whole. He crossed to the barrel of ale brought in for the occasion and filled the first mug, lifting it high and draining it in one, his 'To Robert and to Griet' drowned out in the chorus of cheers.

Cunninghame was the first on his feet to offer his good wishes, making an effort to conceal his tension – it was a tight schedule. Two hours to get the entire company, barring themselves, sufficiently drunk as to render them incapable.

Hugh's own speech was long but spiced with wit, so that he carried the company with him, raising and draining their mugs in unison, while Griet and the maid circled the table replenishing them. Besides the ale, flagons of the finest Rhenish wine, which Griet had assured them was the most potent available, lined the centre of the table, within easy reach of everyone, though the Montgomeries chose to ignore it. The maid served the guests while Griet served the Montgomerie contingent. Cunninghame saw Hugh wink at her as she made a good show of pouring his ale, leaving his mug less than a quarter full – essential in this circumstance, Hugh was no doubt hoping it was an art Elizabeth would never master.

By the time the marshall rose to his feet he was already unsteady, and leaned on the table, his speech also long, but rambling. It was a cross between a maudlin eulogy to his daughter and to his dear but long-departed wife. He paused to pull out a handkerchief and wipe at his eye, offering an effusive welcome to the 'fine lad' who was going to make both his daughter and himself so happy. John Cunninghame saw the look that flashed from Griet to Robert and willed them not to get cold feet. No doubt he and Hugh could leave without them, but however happy the marshall was tonight, tomorrow would be a very different story, and it was best they weren't left to bear the brunt of it.

The evening wore on, and as the ale flowed, conversations degenerated into mumbled tales of previous debaucheries, women who were willing, those who, devil take them, were not, accompanied by nods and gestures and raucous laughter. Cunninghame, nodding and grinning with the rest, was beginning to feel concern, and as a clock tower struck one, he saw Hugh turn his head towards the sound and wince. The marshall was mumbling into his mug as Griet took his arm.

'Come, Father. Robert and I will help you to your chamber.' She nodded to those of the men not already slumped over the table. 'Thank you, I shan't forget your good wishes. But I think it time we all retired.' She smiled. 'Some will need a little help.'

It was the signal for them all to leave, those still able to stand pulling those already well away onto their feet, stumbling down the stairs and weaving their way across the courtyard clutching onto each other. Hugh followed them.

'Lock them in,' John Cunninghame said. 'No point in taking any chances.'

The streets were deserted and John Cunninghame was beginning to think it was going to be plain sailing, when a group of Maurice's soldiers rounded the corner. They were on foot but strung out across the street, their gait unsteady. Robert slowed, and leaning towards him, John whispered, 'D'you know them?'

'Yes, unfortunately. And one recently promoted.'

'Can you talk us through?'

'Montgomerie!' The foremost soldier was in the middle of the road and he grasped Robert's bridle, forcing him to pull to a halt. The other soldiers formed a circle around them, and though they seemed relaxed enough, John knew that only a hair's breadth lay between freedom and recapture.

'Where are you going?' the soldier said, keeping a close hold of Robert's bridle. He peered at the horse. 'That's not your horse.' His gaze slid to John and Hugh. 'Not aiding fugitives, I hope. Or I'd have no choice but to turn you in.'

It was a signal for the other soldiers to close in, taking hold of one bridle each.

Robert hesitated and, with an apologetic gesture towards Griet, forced a laugh. 'The only person we are fugitives from is this lady's father. And these men are fellow Scots who volunteered to see us safely on our way.'

'Running off, are you?'

He took a calculated risk. 'Just until I get her safely

490

settled at Veere. There are Scottish houses there where she'll be welcome, and a minister to wed us.'

The leading soldier turned to look at Griet, who threw back her hood and dipped her head in acknowledgement.

'Tis true, sir.' She bit on her lip, displaying small white teeth. 'If my father knew what I was doing he would lock me up, or send me away, or…' She manufactured a sob and stretched out her hand as if in appeal. 'Please, sir, do not send me back to him.'

There was a moment of silence before the first soldier said, 'Hidden depths, Montgomerie. Not that I blame you, she's a pretty piece.' Another pause, then, 'When you return, I'll ask for your transfer. I could use someone with your mettle.' He released Robert's bridle and stepped back. 'Good luck.'

Once out of the city they rode for an hour without stopping, pushing the horses as hard as they could. When they neared a small wood, John Cunninghame, with a glance at Griet, pulled to a halt. 'The horses need a rest, and I daresay we could all do with a break.' He slipped from the saddle and reached up to hand Griet down, aware of the tension in her, like an instrument strung too tight. 'Our King James,' he said, with a smile, 'could make good use of you. It's said there are female spies in his pay. And you have a gift for acting that would match the best of them.'

'It was almost true.'

'As the most convincing lies always are.' He looked at Robert. 'You make a pretty pair. Though whether either of you'll ever be able to believe a word the other says is another matter.'

It had been his intention to make several stops en route, so that Griet, in particular, would be able to rest, for onboard ship it would be none too comfortable, even if the crossing was smooth. The encounter with Maurice's men changed everything.

'We need to press on,' he said. For it's likely the alarm will be raised first thing, and it won't be hard for those soldiers to work out who we really were.'

Griet coloured. 'Not so early perhaps ... I drugged the wine. It seemed a useful precaution.'

Robert turned towards her, his surprise obvious.

Hugh was laughing. 'In danger of being drugged as well as duped. I hope you realise what you've taken on, Robert, and are up to the challenge.'

'Right,' John Cunninghame said, 'we'd best not waste our advantage.' He put his hand on Griet's arm. 'When I told Robert you'd be good company for the journey, I had no idea just how good.'

They reached Veere mid-afternoon on the fourth day, weary and stiff, to find the tide out and ships lying low at anchor all along the dockside.

John Cunninghame took charge. 'There'll be no movement for some hours yet, so I suggest you three make straight for the inn. I'll join you there once I've found the ship and booked our passage.' His smile was for Griet, and he thought he detected an especial thankfulness in her. And no wonder, for she wasn't a horsewoman and would have suffered much more than they did from the days in the saddle. 'It's called the St Julian and set two streets back, but easy to find: the narrowest building in the row and tall to compensate. I stayed there on the way to The Hague and the landlord is used to folk going in and out with the tides. I'm sure he'll oblige with a room where Griet at least can rest.' He swung down from the saddle. 'Take my horse with you. I'll be better on foot.'

He was working his way along the dock, checking the ships, searching for the name he'd been given. It was near the end of the line, a ladder hanging down from the quay. He was just about to step onto it when a hatch opened on the deck.

The man emerging had his head turned away, speaking to someone below him, but his voice was unmistakeable. 'High tide at three in the morning you say? We'll be here. I trust there'll be no delay. Nor any other passengers, for we have paid plenty for the privilege of a bunk to ourselves.'

John Cunninghame froze – William and Maxwell, the worst of all possible luck. He looked around, and spying a narrow alleyway between two of the buildings bounding the quay, he melted into its shadow, prayed they wouldn't come in his direction. For though it would have been a pleasure to knock them both off the quay into the mud below, it was a pleasure he'd have to forgo – why weren't they halfway to Scotland by now. He waited until they were well along the quay – thank God they were making in the opposite direction from the St Julian, the others at least should be safe. He continued his search, looking for another Scottish vessel, but found none. He had reached the end of the quay, the harbour mouth yawning in front of him, and he leaned back against the wall, staring towards the channel that led to the sea. There was a stray float lying against the wall at his feet and he picked it up and hurled it as far out as he could, hearing the faint splash as it landed in the thin ribbon of water that remained in the centre of the harbour even at low tide – Dear God, what a mess. Why, when there were so many Scots merchants who used the harbour at Veere, was the only ship here the now the one option they didn't have.

The cellar room at the St Julian was crowded, and it took John a few minutes to spot Hugh and Robert. He squeezed his way through to them and sat down heavily, waving away the girl who came to offer him a drink.

Hugh leaned forward to make himself heard. 'The ship's not there?'

'It's there all right, but we can't go on it.'

'Why not? Is it not due to sail?'

'Oh yes. On the morning tide, I believe.'

Robert said, 'We can wake Griet. She will be grateful

494

for even a few hours' sleep.'

'We can't take it, because she already has passengers. William and Maxwell, to be precise.'

'It can't be. Are you sure? Did you see them?'

'I saw them. Narrowly missed running into them, as it happens.'

'What about another ship?' Hugh was swirling the ale round and round in his mug.

'None. I checked. No Scottish, no English. Not that an English one would have been much use.'

'We could have gone overland once we got there.'

'With Griet?' John shook his head. The ride is arduous for a practised horseman, never mind a girl unused to the saddle. Anyway, there wasn't one, so it hardly matters. We'll have to lie low until a ship comes in that we *can* take.'

'And run the risk of being recaptured? The marshall's men may not be long behind us. Believe me, our end would be worse than our beginning.'

'What choice do we have? If we must wait, risky or not, this inn is the best option. We can keep to our rooms. We do *have* rooms?'

'Griet has a room. We were offered the share of an attic with a young lad who's been here for the last ten days.'

'There was nothing else?'

'Apparently not, and as it was across the landing from Griet, and we were only expecting to need it for an hour or two, it seemed reasonable enough. It gave her some assurance of safety in any case, for the doors have no bolts.'

John frowned. 'But you're down here. Have you seen

him? Does he seem trustworthy?'

'If you consider a tousle of hair, seeing. We looked in, saw a hump in the bed, realised he was out for the count, and decided to come down for something to eat. Griet didn't want anything bar water, which Robert took up to her. I thought we mightn't need to trouble him at all, which in our circumstances would have been all to the good, but now…'

'Young, you say? We may pray he isn't blessed with overmuch curiosity.'

Chapter 26

They looked in on Griet, and when she didn't stir, they crossed the narrow landing to the second attic room. The door was ajar, the sound of snoring coming from under the blanket on one of the two beds.

'Whoever he is, he's still out for the count,' John said. 'We'd better draw lots for the floor.'

'Whoever he is, he'd better roll over or wake up. We've paid good money to get at least a share of a mattress. I've no intention of roughing it on the floor. Besides, the best way to make sure he doesn't slip out without us knowing and spread word of our presence is to have someone in beside him.' Hugh pulled back the blanket and prepared to shift the lad. He was lying face up, his mouth open. Hugh's mouth dropped open too. He grabbed the lad's shoulders and shook him vigorously.

Robbie sat up, clearly ready to fight his corner, his eyes widening. 'Uncle Hugh! What are *you* doing here?'

'We might ask you the same thing? Why aren't you in Paris?' Hugh's eyes narrowed. 'And where's your uniform?'

'Long story, but I'm no longer in the Gardes.'

There is a story here, Hugh thought, though perhaps now isn't the time to quiz him, but equally impossible to say nothing. 'It was all you ever wanted, Robbie, right from when you were a child.'

'Yes, well, things are different now.'

'You're going home? Are you a fugitive too?'

'In a manner of speaking.' Robbie hesitated. 'I'm going to Edinburgh, with a letter from Henri to King James.'

'That'll be some story,' John echoed Hugh's thought. 'And one I'd like to hear, but first we should introduce you.' He drew Robert forward. 'Robert Montgomerie, a near kinsman of Hugh, and, until lately, in the service of Maurice of Nassau. Until four days ago, as it happens, so you have something in common. Across the landing is his betrothed. And this is Robbie Munro, a close friend of Braidstane's family.'

Robbie was half a head smaller, but of similar build. They eyed each other up, clearly wary – as if they were pups, Hugh thought, sniffing each other. He turned to John. 'I don't know about you, but I'm thoroughly awake now, and it's as good a time as any to share our experiences. I'll bring up some ale. We could be in for a long night.'

It was gone five in the morning, the candle that Hugh had brought with the ale burned down to a stump, before they were finished.

John Cunninghame and Robert Montgomerie were sitting crossways on one bed, their backs against the wall,

Robbie and Hugh facing them. In the silence that fell, John said, 'This ship of yours, when will it be ready to sail?'

'The early tide tomorrow, I think, or at the worst the next day. We should have been away early last week, but there was a delay in getting the topmast. Du Bois wasn't best pleased, though,' he grinned. 'I suspect the men were happy with the extra free time in a port.'

'Twenty-four hours,' Hugh said. 'No chance it could be sooner?'

'I don't think so.'

John was still worrying away at other practicalities. 'He will have room for us?'

'Father saved his nephew's life, and you saved Mother's. He'll squeeze you all in, whatever it takes.'

'I hope Griet...' Robert began.

The door opened, to reveal her framed in the entrance. Robert jumped up and put his arm around her shoulder.

'Whatever it takes,' she said.

It was a long day. All of them, bar Robbie, crammed into the one room, which as the hours wore on became more and more airless, despite the open window. Robert had suggested a minister might be found.

'We can't risk it.' Hugh grinned. 'Her honour will be safe on the journey, for I suspect we may all be sharing a cabin.' The sky, which had been streaked with pink when Griet arose, darkened to purple, the temperature almost unbearable.

John, taking care not to be visible from the street, was leaning against the wall beside the open window, seeking some respite from the heat. 'Just as well we didn't get away today,' he said. 'I think it's going to thunder.' As if to prove him right, there was a low rumble in the distance, gradually building in intensity, and then the rain came, huge drops that fell like arrows, hitting the cobbles and spreading out until the street was awash.

There was a clatter on the stair, all of them tensing until the door opened, Robbie shaking himself to get rid of the rain. He jerked his head towards the window. 'That's what did for us in the Channel and sent us running for shelter here.' His satisfaction was obvious. 'Maybe it'll do for William.'

'Here's hoping not,' John Cunninghame said, to the obvious surprise of everyone else. 'I'd rather keep distance between us than play cat and mouse all the way to Edinburgh. Du Bois' vessel is a brig?'

'Yes.'

'So is the ship William's on. It's likely they'd make a similar speed. If we cannot be ahead of him, I'd rather be a day or two behind.'

'What word from the ship?' Hugh asked.

'The morning tide for sure, provided the weather looks suitable. We are to be aboard by four.' He looked across at Griet. 'The captain has offered you his cabin, the rest of us will muck in with the crew. As half of them will be on duty at all times, there are enough spare hammocks to go round.'

Robert squeezed Griet's shoulder. 'It seems you are to be spared our company.'

'How long might it take us? I've never been on a ship before,' Griet said.

John did a quick mental calculation. 'With a favourable

wind we could do it in three days, if the winds are against us, five, maybe six.'

She made a face. 'Will it be rough? I'm not overly confident of my stomach.'

'That also depends on the direction and strength of the wind. We may pray for a moderate south-westerly, which will allow us to move along nicely. If we get it, you'll be in Scotland and Robert here able to make an honest woman of you before you know.'

Robbie stiffened, and despite that he'd only just come in, said, 'I have another message I must do. I'll be back later. I ordered food for us all, but don't wait for me if I'm not here when it arrives.'

'What brought that on?' Hugh said.

John turned back from the window. 'I should have thought before I spoke. I imagine it cannot be easy for him seeing Robert and Griet together and happiness within their grasp, when Eugenie is a fugitive in France and he banished.'

Griet ducked out from under Robert's arm. 'And we should be more circumspect.'

A fine lass, indeed, John thought, and a kind heart and sensitivity to boot. I trust Robert appreciates his good fortune.

Robbie was away less than an hour. He spilled into the chamber and leaned on the table, his breathing ragged, his speech disjointed. 'Maurice's men ... and others with them at the Scots houses on the quay. Enquiring after you all.'

'Thank God we didn't look for a bed there then,' Hugh said. 'I had thought on it.'

501

'You can't stay here. The St Julian will be their next port of call. It's well known to be clean and suitable for a lady.'

Robert looked apprehensive. 'Can we get from here to the ship without being seen?'

John said, 'Separately perhaps.' He became brisk. 'Robbie, ask downstairs for the loan of a cloak from one of the serving girls. And some ash…mud if you can get it, and scissors, if possible, a sharp knife if not. I'm afraid, my dear,' he took Griet's hand, 'you will need a new gown when you reach Scotland, but I'm sure Hugh will oblige.'

By the time Cunninghame had finished with her she was barely recognisable as the girl who'd left The Hague. Her face was filthy, smears of mud on her cheeks and ash rubbed into the lines on her forehead she'd made by frowning to order. The hem of her gown was ripped in several places, exposing a ragged-edged petticoat splattered with mud. He tugged at the pins holding one side of her hair and trailed it down over her ear, messing through it with his fingers. He stood back to examine her, and then, with an apology, asked for a shoe and twisted the heel until it came loose. She was reminiscent of Kate Munro, escaping from the belfry tower at Bishopton, but he thrust the memory away. This was a journey of no more than three-quarters of a mile, and surely manageable. 'It'll not be the easiest walking,' he said, 'but will give you an excuse to cling onto Robbie as you go.'

Robert protested, 'I can take her.'

'No you can't.' Hugh was abrupt. 'Your face is well enough known to put her at risk, disguised or no.'

'Give us fifteen minutes,' Robbie said, and then come

one at a time.' He gestured towards the ash and mud – a bit of dirt won't hurt any of you.'

John Cunninghame was the last to arrive. It had been a close-run thing, Maurice's men arriving at the front of the inn as he slipped out the back. He had waited with his ear to the cellar door listening to the innkeeper. He'd been more than obliging when he'd been given a florin in return for spinning a yarn to Maurice's men, should they come enquiring, but it was aye safest to make sure. He'd answered their questions with every appearance of reluctance, waiting for the clink of money on the counter before launching into Cunninghame's story. 'Tell them,' he'd said, 'if it's fugitives you're after, there *was* a group who sought passage on a Scots vessel only yesterday, and left on the early tide. They're likely halfway to the Wash by now. Tell them three men and a young lass, and emphasise that it was a Scot's ship, and the only one in port. We don't want them poking around the harbour.'

He found the others squashed into the captain's cabin, their relief when he put his head round the door palpable. He pulled off the woollen cap that Robbie had borrowed from one of the sailors and tossed it on the end of the bunk, wrinkling his nose. 'Never did like the smell of fish,' he said, 'especially stale.' He set a parcel on the table and pulled back the paper, the aroma of fresh bread filling the cabin. 'I thought we'd all benefit from the last decent food we're likely to get this side of Leith.'

'Are we safe?' Griet asked. She had clearly made an attempt to tidy herself, but her face still showed some traces of John's efforts at disguise.

'As safe as we can be anywhere in Veere. The innkeeper was well into his stride with Maurice's men when I left, and I think enjoying elaborating on the tale I'd fed him.'

'Not overdoing it, I hope,' said Hugh.

'I don't think so. They had paid him for his pains, and the last thing I heard was the leader talking of thirsty work and needing a mug of the best to quench their thirst. With luck they'll be there for the night, or until they're incapable, whichever comes first

Chapter 27

They were four days out, the wind the steady south-westerly that John had hoped for, all of them, including Griet, spending most of the daylight hours on deck. Robbie, now that they were under way, shrank into himself, remaining hunched at the stern, avoiding conversation. It wasn't that he envied Robert and Griet their good fortune, but each time he saw her smile at Robert, Eugenie's face swam before him, the smile she had for him at the first transformed into the stiff reserve of their final days, Madame Picarde's *Do not set your heart on something that may never be*, haunting him.

They had seen ships in the distance ahead of them, but none near enough to trouble them nor, according to Du Bois, any that matched the ship William sailed on.

Midway through the afternoon, Hugh and Robert sat, their backs to the breeze, playing cent with a pack of well-thumbed cards borrowed from the bo'sun. John Cunninghame was stretched out beside them, eyes half-shut, making occasional contributions to the conversation. Robbie could hear them but wasn't listening, until mention of the weather caught his attention.

Hugh was fifteen points up. 'If we were here by choice,' he said, 'we couldn't ask for better weather. Get this all the way to Leith and we'll be doing all right.'

John Cunninghame sat up. 'Don't tempt fate. We've been fortunate thus far but there is at least a day's travelling yet. Our luck may not hold. This is a treacherous coast, safe enough in moderate seas, and while the westerly holds us offshore, fraught with dangers should the wind change.'

Robbie looked towards the coastline. In the foreground, the Farne Islands, seabirds wheeling above them, dark specks in an otherwise clear sky. Far off on the horizon a single cloud the size of a man's hand.

John gestured towards the islands. 'The folk there have plenty of tales of wrecks to tell.'

'We'll not be adding to them,' Hugh said, taking another trick.

'Likely not. But there are a fair few other hazards between us and Edinburgh, and I'm not for cheering until we reach it.'

He was right. It was towards evening when the wind strengthened and veered round to the north-east. There was a flurry of activity as the sailors took their stations to prepare to tack. Du Bois ushered his passengers towards the hatch with an apology. 'One bystander on deck would be fine, five is an inconvenience, I'm afraid.'

'How much will it slow us?' Hugh asked.

'We were making almost five knots. Now we'll be lucky if we make two.'

'Some headway is better than none, I suppose. At least it isn't rough.'

Du Bois tilted his head as if sniffing the air. 'Don't tempt fate,' he said, and then, as if to reassure Griet, 'But if a storm does come in, we'll head for a harbour and

wait it out.' He nodded at Robbie. 'I've already lost one
topmast this voyage. I'd rather not make it two.'

It wasn't a storm that woke Robbie early on the fifth day,
but an eerie silence, broken only by the faint creaking
of stays and a rubbing of rope against the rigging. It
took him a few minutes to realise they had stopped, his
feeling of apprehension instant. He tumbled from the
hammock – one of these days, he thought, as his knee
cracked against a locker, I will master it. He headed up
the companionway and stuck his head out through the
hatch into a white world, the haar so thick visibility was
almost zero – no wonder they were stationary. He climbed
onto the deck and, although it was only a few feet away,
found he could barely see the base of the mainmast and
nothing at all above head height, bar the ghostly lights
posted on each mast. They were riding at anchor, the only
movement their rhythmic lift and fall on the gentle swell.
The air was damp and chill and it settled on his head and
shoulders and clung to him like a blanket. He had no way
of telling if they were in mid-channel or close inshore,
but as Du Bois materialised out of the fog, Robbie said,
'At least it's not a storm.'

Du Bois was discouraging. 'Every bit as dangerous,
in its own way. That's why we've stopped. A ship could
pass us at ten yards and we wouldn't see it. And fine if
it passed us. But we could just as easily have a collision

and not enough time to avoid it. That's why we're posting lights at the bow and the stern and on the masts. So that if there is someone foolhardy enough to try and make way in this, at least we have a chance of being seen.'

'Whereabouts are we?'

'Just north of Bamburgh. And here we stay until this lifts.'

'Are we close to shore?'

'A bit too far out for comfort. But it would be a folly to try to edge in now. I'm afraid we're stuck for the time being.'

'How long for?'

Du Bois shrugged. 'Depends on the wind. As soon as it strengthens it'll disperse the fog. While it remains light, as now, it could be hours, days even.'

'So what do we do?'

Ride it out and pray any other ship near at hand is doing the same.'

They lay at anchor for thirty-six hours, a skeleton crew on deck at all times, taking soundings every hour and keeping an eye on the candles in the lanterns, replacing them when they burned low.

'Why the soundings?' Robbie asked on one of his brief excursions on deck.

'Though the wind is light, if the anchors dragged we could drift onshore and scarcely notice the movement until we went aground. Taking soundings ensures we know if we've moved and can set additional anchors as required.'

Robbie was leaning on the rail, staring into the nothingness, unable to stop thinking of the past months and what his folly had brought him to. He heard muted footsteps on the deck, and turning saw a shadowy figure coming towards him from the companionway. For a fraction of a second it was Eugenie, and he stepped forward, then stopped.

Griet reached him. 'It is hard for you, is it not?' she said.

Cloaked in the haar, it was as if they two were alone in the world, and he found himself admitting, 'Your height, your build, you could be Eugenie, and yes, it is hard.' His voice broke. 'But perhaps I deserve nothing more.'

'If we only ever got what we deserved, it would be a miserable life,' she said.

He shivered and she placed her hand over his. 'But I have found fortune kinder than that, and perhaps one day you will too.'

They were standing side by side, the warmth of her hand on his comforting, when he felt a stir in the air, the ship beginning to swing. 'The wind is shifting.' For the first time he found himself able to smile at Griet. 'We may not be stuck here for much longer.' He put his other hand on top of hers. 'And ... thank you.'

Hugh was climbing out from the hatch as Robbie reached it. 'Has the wind veered? I thought I felt movement.'

'I think so.' The haar was thinning and lifting, the mast above their heads beginning to emerge, skeletal and insubstantial.

Du Bois was at Hugh's shoulder. 'How long more now?' Hugh asked.

'A couple of hours perhaps. And I can't say I'm sorry.

I wouldn't have said anything until it became necessary, but we're running short on supplies and fresh water. Much longer and we'd have been on short rations.' Above their heads the mast dipped and straightened. 'With a following wind we may yet reach Leith today.'

It was as Tantallon Castle came into sight that they saw the wreckage. The ship had been broken in two, one-half still upended on the rocks, a few floating spars all that remained of the rest.

'Poor devils,' Du Bois said.

John reached for the spyglass that Du Bois held out to him and focused on the wreck. He turned towards Hugh. 'William's ship,' he said. 'And likely wrecked yesterday or the day before.' Then to Du Bois, 'What are the chances of survivors?'

'It depends.'

'Whether they were below or on deck when they struck?' Robbie asked.

'That, and other factors.' He was frowning. 'It looks too violent a strike to be as a result of anchor drag, so perhaps they tried to continue through the haar, or more likely they sailed into it unexpectedly at night, the crew on watch inexperienced. If that was the case, above or below, the chances of survival are poor. If, however, they drifted on, and if they could swim, which many sailors cannot, the chances are much higher.'

510

'How close can we safely get?'

'Not close enough. But we can anchor out opposite the shore and send a couple of men in the dory. It's unlikely to be worth the effort, but we should try.'

They lined up at the rail, watching as the sailors rowed the dory in towards the wreck. Their calls went unanswered, but just as they were turning back, Robbie shouted out, 'Over there! Look.' He was gesturing towards a piece of wreckage, alternately being driven against the rocks and sucked back.

Du Bois followed his pointing finger and raised the spyglass to his eye. There *was* movement. It could just be a bundle of something stirred by the breeze, but still. He shouted to the men in the dory and waved them round to the other side of the wreck. They saw them stop a little way out, one of the men jumping into the water, a rope around his waist, then return dragging the wreckage with him. There was a figure lying on the wood, a rope looped around his chest.

Beside him, Robbie felt Griet suck in her breath as the sailor in the water cut the rope and pulled the figure to the side of the dory, willing hands hauling him in. He was too small to be William, and Robbie couldn't help his leap of relief. If William *had* drowned, there would be many who would think it justice.

The dory was bumping against the side of the ship when the boy struggled upright and leaning over the side vomited into the sea, and though he was still shivering and white-faced, he managed to climb aboard unaided.

'Let's get you dry, lad, and then you can tell us what happened.'

They were crowded into the captain's cabin, the boy perched on the edge of the bunk, wrapped in a blanket, clutching a mug with both hands, steam rising. He was looking towards the scuttle.

'It came on us so fast,' he said, 'One minute we were on a larboard leg, heading towards land, the next the haar hit and we couldn't see a thing. The bo'sun was giving orders for the tack when we struck. I heard the grinding of the hull against the rocks and thought we'd be holed for sure, but maybe not so badly that it couldn't be repaired, but then,' he shuddered, 'the ship canted and a jagged tip of rock came up through the deck. When the ship split I was thrown overboard, others too. I saw the spar and grabbed onto it, but I was being tossed about and was afraid I wouldn't be able to hold on … I can't swim, see … If there hadn't been the rope … I tied it as tight as I could one-handed and let the swell take me. I remember another piece of wreckage coming towards me, looming over me … and then nothing … until I heard the calls. My head was hurting and I couldn't make my voice work … and next thing I knew I was in the dory.' He put his hand up to his head.

Hugh nodded to him. 'You took a right knock, but you'll be fine now. How long were you in the sea?'

'What day is it?'

'Thursday.'

The boy's eyes widened. 'The storm was Tuesday night.'

'The passengers?' John Cunninghame asked.

'Most were below when we struck.' The lad shook his head. 'I don't know what happened to them.'

512

'Can we check?' Griet said.

Du Bois was dismissive. 'I'm not risking my crew on the wreck.'

'But what…?'

'If anyone was still alive, they would have answered our calls.'

They were making good time, rounding the point at North Berwick and heading into the firth, when John Cunninghame said. 'I don't relish the task of telling Lady Glencairn, for a son is a son whatever his character, but if William hadn't died in this way, it's likely he would in another, and well before his time. If I feel any guilt in this it's that I didn't see him onto a ship myself. If I had he would have been home and dry long before this.'

Their first stop was an inn on the dockside at Leith, Du Bois waving away their thanks and the offer of payment for the crossing. 'Call it quits,' he said. 'I've ever been fond of my nephew.'

Hugh was for going straight home to Braidstane. 'Not that I'm looking forward to facing Elizabeth, but it has to be done, and the sooner the better. At least Dand is alive, and now that he's no longer in Edinburgh, there is nothing to keep me here.

'Except a pardon from the King?'

'For what? For a duel I didn't fight?'

'The intention was there. And though William may not

be around to denounce you, there could be any number of folk who've carried the tale home from The Hague.' John Cunninghame's irritation showed. 'I didn't bring you back to Scotland to have you imprisoned, or worse. That would have been wasted effort. At least speak to Alexander before you leave.'

And so it was decided.

The girl that opened the door to them at Alexander's lodgings took a step back, her face blanching. 'I thought...'

Hugh said, 'Where's Alexander?'

'At Holyrood, but...'

He ushered Robert and Griet forward. 'This is a kinsman and his bride-to-be. Look after them for us. The rest of us have business at the court.'

'Shouldn't we take time to change our attire?' John Cunninghame suggested.

Hugh sniffed at his sleeve. 'I suppose ten minutes more will be of little moment. And James has a sensitive nose.' No doubt there will be something of Alexander's to fit.

Robbie saw the same shock registering in the eyes of the men outside the door of the audience chamber as they had seen in the servant girl. 'Some story has come home,' he said.

'The question is what?' John Cunninghame said, grimly. 'And from whom?' He pushed open the door and stood back for Hugh and Robbie to pass him. It was as if it was happening in slow motion: the circle of James' closest advisors clustered around the King parting to let them through, James looking up, rising to his feet. Alexander and Dand turning towards them, a smile breaking on Dand's face. On the other side of James, William Cunninghame, Master of Glencairn, also turning, his expression one of disbelief, or disappointment, or both – as mine must be, Robbie thought.

The King was the first to recover. 'Braidstane. Not detained at Maurice of Nassau's pleasure? At least you will now be able to answer in person the charges against you.'

Hugh bowed over the King's hand. 'I am at your pleasure, Sire.'

William began to bluster. 'As I said, Sire, Braidstane followed me to The Hague and attacked me in plain sight of many witnesses and left me for dead. For that he was imprisoned.'

'So you said. Yet he is here now,' James said.

'He must have escaped. And therefore is a disgrace to Scotland, and to you. He should be put to the horn, sent back to face justice.'

The reprimand was swift. 'Indeed? It may have slipped your mind, Cunninghame, no doubt because you have not been much about the court yourself in recent times, that it is my place to be the judge of that. And as you are all here now, I will hear the arguments and make judgement accordingly.' He nodded to John Cunninghame. 'I believe you were also at The Hague, or so your nephew said, and can corroborate his version.'

515

John looked past William to the King. 'I was not an eyewitness, Sire, though I gathered evidence from many who were.'

'In that case, I will hear you later, when the others have had their chance.'

He is both judge and jury, Robbie thought. But will the trial be fair?

William stepped forward again, but James waved him back, beckoned to Alexander and Dand instead. 'I think we must go back to the beginning, if we are to sift out this sorry story.' He spoke directly to Dand. 'You are the lad injured by the Master of Glencairn's man at the West Port?'

'Yes, Sire.' The boy was undersized, but his voice was surprisingly strong.

He has courage, Robbie thought. He looked at the pinned-up sleeve – and will likely need it.

'In your own words, lad,' James prompted.

He was brief and to the point, finishing by indicating his stump. 'The result, as you see.' Robbie glanced towards Alexander, saw his fractional nod – well schooled.

James' gaze switched to Hugh. 'I understand the provocation, Braidstane, but,' his voice hardened, 'did you doubt my sense of justice? Or that this was a case in which I would have authorised the duel and saved you the trouble of the journey to Holland.'

'I think, Sire...' Alexander began.

'When I want to hear from you, Montgomerie, I will ask. Well, Braidstane?'

Hugh dropped on one knee. 'I was too hasty, Sire, and for that I apologise. I have no reason to doubt your

516

justice, and have had every reason to be grateful for it in the past. If I did not, I would not be here now to face your judgement and crave your pardon. But as for Holland. That was William's idea. No doubt to avoid facing the consequences of his man's actions, coward as he is. Once freed...'

'Freed?' James beckoned John Cunninghame. 'Your version of events, if you please.'

John gestured towards Dand. 'As you say, Sire, Braidstane had good reason to be angered, but I could not commend his action in following my nephew, threatening, as it did, the peace of Ayrshire and your good work in healing the breach between our families. It was for that reason I followed them, with the intention of bringing them both back, repentant and unscathed.'

'But you did not.'

'I could not. For when I reached The Hague the fight was over, honour satisfied, and though my nephew had the merest scratch, Braidstane was in prison. I sent William home and sought a pardon for Braidstane. He was once, as you no doubt know, in the service of Maurice of Nassau.'

'I must write to thank Maurice then, for returning one of my loyal subjects.' James' expression was unreadable, but Robbie had the impression that he knew very well it was only a partial truth. He was aware of suppressed anger in William, of John Cunninghame moving to stand beside him and grasping his arm.

'I returned with Braidstane as soon as I could, helped by this young man,' John indicated Robbie, 'who also has reason to be grateful to you.'

James raised his eyebrows. 'And who is this young man?'

'Robbie Munro, Sire. Sir Adam and Lady Munro's son.'

William pushed through. 'A deserter no doubt. For he is a Scots Garde and should be in France.'

James ignored William's interruption. 'Are you a deserter?'

Robbie saw the look that Alexander directed at him and joined Hugh on the floor. He fished in his doublet and produced Henri's letter. 'No, Sire, I bring a letter from the French King. I was to place it directly in your hands.'

James broke the seal and scanned the contents, and when he looked up there was a glimmer of understanding in his eyes. What, Robbie thought, has Henri said?

'It is rather tattered.' There was a humorous twist to James' mouth. 'Could you not have taken more care?'

'The journey was arduous, Sire. The weather unkind. Twice our ship nearly foundered.'

'Fortune has shined on you then. And on me.' He tapped Robbie on the shoulder. 'You may rise. We will talk of this later.' He turned to Maitland, who hovered behind him, and handed over the letter. 'Arrange accommodation for young Munro. It seems we may have his company for some time.' He smiled. 'I will be glad to hear news of how your parents fare.' His gaze switched back to Hugh. 'Get up man. Hasty, you say? That is not a quality I value, and in this you did not act as you should. However,' he addressed William and Hugh both, 'I am heartily sick of the troubles in Ayrshire and have no wish to see your family feud rekindled. Therefore I am disposed to overlook this last confrontation, on the payment of a fine

518

of fifty pounds Scots, each, and the public affirmation that this is the end of it. But so that you will not be tempted to forget the promise, I will also impose a bond, of one hundred pounds Scots, to be forfeit in the event of any subsequent trouble between you.' He looked directly at William. 'It seems your memory in particular is short. It is not long since I last had cause to impose sanctions on you. Perhaps an ongoing penalty will have more effect.' He indicated Dand. 'This lad deserves recompense, so to him I award a pension of five pounds Scots, to be paid annually, in perpetuity, by the Master of Glencairn and any heirs he might have.'

Dand was staring at the King, his eyes wide. Alexander ushered him forward, indicating for him to kneel, but James put out his hand and, grasping Dand's good shoulder, kept him on his feet. There was a moment of silence, and when James spoke again, though he addressed Dand directly, it was clear he spoke to all. 'This is but justice, and my sovereign will.'

Epilogue

The letters took Robbie a week to write. In the one to his family he restricted himself to sending good wishes and telling them the bare bones of the story, along with a short personal message to each. He skited over the near shipwreck, Hugh's imprisonment and the confrontation with William, focusing instead on the chance meeting at Veere and finishing with his first experience of the Scottish court. *I do not know how I will do here, but I am treated well and the King has been gracious, and particularly enquires of your health. It seems I am to send letters to you regularly, and include within them private correspondence for Henri, and the same in reverse. So I will have no excuse but to write, though I will no doubt bore you to tears.*

He imagined his mother, reading at the open window of the salon, with Ellie and the Bourbon children's squeals rising up from the gardens, and thought of her promise to Madame Picarde to visit, so added, *I shall think of you when you visit Cayeux, and pray that you will find the Lavalles much improved. I long to know how they fare.* To Maggie, he said, *I trust your studies continue to excite and that Anton de Vincennes is no longer a problem...* and to Ellie, *Do not grow too fast, for I wish to recognise you when I see you again. Give Patrick John a pat on the head from me.* The greeting to his father, though only two sentences, had taken longer to phrase than any of the others, and he hoped it was adequate. *I cannot say how sorry I am for the mistakes I made, and for their consequences. I shall take care not to make the same again.*

The letter to Eugenie, however, he had written and discarded a hundred times, unsure both of what to say and of whether she would want to hear from him at all. In the end he wrote of his safe arrival, and of the market stalls on the High Street, and the nip in the air despite the season. *As it aye is in Scotland.* He enquired of Netta and of François, and finished, *I think of you daily, and of our friendship, and pray that when I see you again we will be able to renew it in happier circumstances.* It wasn't enough. He thought of their first meeting, and all the meetings since, her smile variously tentative, shy, alight. Finally, he thought of her as she had been at Cayeux: silent and withdrawn, and of Madame Picarde's advice. It was impossible. For good or ill he risked, *You are always in my heart.*

Historical Note

James VI changed the calendar to begin the year 1600 on the 1st January, rather than on the 25th March, as previously, thus bringing Scotland into line with surrounding countries.

On 1st April 1600 he issued an edict against unauthorised individual combat, though duels could still be fought if permission was granted. The unauthorized confrontation in Edinburgh between Hugh Montgomerie and William Cunninghame is documented, though the reason for it and the date is not. William did flee, first to London and then to The Hague, where they fought, and it is said that William survived because his belt buckle deflected Hugh's thrust. Whatever the truth or otherwise, Hugh was imprisoned by the marshall provost and escaped through the collusion of the marshall's daughter, wooed by a kinsman of Hugh's. She accompanied them to Scotland where Hugh received a pardon from James and was reinstated at court.

Despite the popularity of Henri IV of Navarre, there were numerous attempts made on his life, some of which are fully documented, though most are simply enumerated. The attempt at Nantes is a fictional account of one such. The Edict of Nantes, thought to have been signed in the house of André Ruiz, officially established religious tolerance, however it did not apply to Paris or to anywhere within a five-mile radius of the city, where practising the Huguenot religion remained forbidden.

Henri did intend to marry Gabrielle d'Estrées once he received an annulment of his marriage to Marguerite de Valois, and had set a date for the wedding. However Gabrielle died in childbirth before this could happen, and when rumours of her having been poisoned began to circulate, the King established a commission to investigate her death. There was no evidence of foul play, but many in France felt her death was providential, paving the way for a more appropriate marriage and thus the possibility of a legitimate heir to the throne. Apparently heartbroken, Henri gave Gabrielle a state funeral, called for three months of mourning, and, in the first documented occurrence by a French King, wore black as mourning garb. However, before the period of mourning was over, he had become infatuated with Henriette d'Entragues, to the despair of his advisors.

Despite his sexual appetite, Henri was a popular king, who achieved much that was good for France.

Although the first documented telescope is widely considered to have been made in 1609, papers on optics existed from the 13th century. John Dee, astronomer, astrologer and physician to Elizabeth I, is thought to have presented a rudimentary spyglass to Edward Kelly in 1588, so it is certainly possible that the captain of a sea-going brig in the late 1590s would have had something similar.

Glossary

awry (adj): wrong

aye (adv): always

Bachellerie (collective n): a group of young men of
    status; etymology – 'a set of young knights'

bairn (n): child

barmkin (n): enclosed area within the outer fortification
    of a castle or tower house

bastle house (n): small-scale dwelling, often associated
    with a tower house

bawbee (n): copper coin, worth six pence Scots

bide (v): to live

birl (v): to whirl around

bravely (adj): well (health)

breeks (n): trousers

butts (n): archery field, originally with mounds of earth
    for the targets.

byre (n): cowshed

canny (adj): shrewd

chirurgeon (n): surgeon

coorie in (v): to snuggle up

coup (v): to fall, tumble

cordiner (n): leather-worker

debauchle (n): debacle

dreich (adj): damp

drookit (adj): extremely wet; drenched

drouth (n): thirst

dunt (v): to knock or bump into

feart (adj): afraid

fish (v): nautical term to repair a mast or spar with a
fillet of wood

forbye (adv): besides

founder (v): to fail, collapse

Flyting (pn): a ritual, poetic exchange of insults, popular
at the Scottish court

gey (adv): very

girn (v): to whine or cry

haar (n): fog

hunker (v): to squat

juke (v): to duck or dodge

mite (adj): little

prosector (n): a preparer of corpses for dissection

racket (n): loud noise

reek (n): stench

ructions (n): vigorous argument

rummage (v): to search through

scuttle (n): porthole

siller (n): silver, coinage

skite (v): move quickly and forcefully, especially when
glancing off a surface:

sonsy (adj): having an attractive and healthy appearance

swee (n): a horizontal bar from which pots are
suspended and swung over the fire

trug (n): shallow basket, often used for gathering
vegetables

ween (n): a small amount.

The first two books in the Munro series:

Turn of the Tide

'It is a dirty business and no one the winner,
save the coffin-makers and clothiers who
aye make good money of men's folly.'

Scotland *1586*. The 150-year-old feud between the Cunninghames and the Montgomeries is at its height.

A tale of love and loss, loyalty and betrayal, amidst the turmoil of 16th century Scotland.

'The quality of the writing and research is outstanding.'
Jeffrey Archer

'Margaret Skea brings the 16th century to vivid life.'
Sharon K Penman

A House Divided

Scotland 1597. The truce between the Cunninghame and Montgomerie clans is fragile. For the Munro family, living in hiding under assumed names, these are dangerous times.

A sweeping tale of compassion and cruelty, treachery and sacrifice, set against the backdrop of a religious war, feuding clans and the Great Scottish Witch Hunt of 1597.

'Captivating and fast-paced, you'll find yourself reading far into the night.'
Ann Weisgarber, Walter Scott and Orange Prize shortlisted author of *The Promise*

The Katharina series

Katharina: Deliverance – available now
Katharina: Fortitude (Forthcoming 2019)

Germany 1505. Five-year-old Katharina is placed in the convent at Brehna. She will never see her father again.

Sixty-five miles away, at Erfurt, Martin Luder, a promising young law student, turns his back on a lucrative career to become a monk.

The consequences of their meeting in Wittenberg, on Easter Sunday 1523, will reverberate down the centuries and throughout the Christian world.

A compelling portrayal of Katharina von Bora, set against the turmoil of the Peasant's War and the German Reformation ... and the controversial priest at its heart.

'A wonderfully vivid portrait. Skea knows her history, but more importantly, she writes with imagination and humanity.'
Prof. Alec Ryrie, Durham University (Author of *Protestants*)